Honoré de Balzac

The Poor Parents and Cousin Pons

Part II.

Honoré de Balzac

The Poor Parents and Cousin Pons
Part II.

ISBN/EAN: 9783744791045

Printed in Europe, USA, Canada, Australia, Japan

Cover: Foto ©Andreas Hilbeck / pixelio.de

More available books at **www.hansebooks.com**

"THE PAIR OF NUTCRACKERS."

H. DE BALZAC

THE POOR PARENTS

PART II.

COUSIN BETTY

(CONCLUDED) and

COUSIN PONS

TRANSLATED BY

ELLEN MARRIAGE

WITH A PREFACE BY

GEORGE SAINTSBURY

PHILADELPHIA

THE GEBBIE PUBLISHING CO., Ltd.

1898

CONTENTS

	PAGE
PREFACE	ix
COUSIN BETTY—	
PART II.	I
COUSIN PONS	91

LIST OF ILLUSTRATIONS

"THE PAIR OF NUTCRACKERS" (p. 111) . . . *Frontispiece.*

PAGE

THE RUE DE NORMANDIE 135

A COLD THRILL RAN THROUGH MME. CIBOT 221

"MADAME CIBOT, I BELIEVE?" 273

FRAISIER READ THE—— CURIOUS DOCUMENT 357

Drawn by W. Boucher.

PREFACE.

ONE of the last and largest of Balzac's great works—the very last of them, if we except "La Cousine Bette," to which it is pendant and contrast—"La Cousin Pons" has always united suffrages from very different classes of admirers. In the first place, it is not "disagreeable," as the common euphemism has it, and as "La Cousine Bette" certainly is. In the second, it cannot be accused of being a *berquinade*, as those who like Balzac best when he is doing moral rag-picking are apt to describe books like "Le Médecin de Campagne" and "Le Lys dans la Vallée," if not even like "Eugénie Grandet." It has a considerable variety of interest; its central figure is curiously pathetic and attractive, even though the curse of something like folly, which so often attends Balzac's good characters, may a little weigh on him. It would be a book of exceptional charm even if it were anonymous, or if we knew no more about the author than we know about Shakespeare.

As it happens, however, "Le Cousin Pons" has other attractions than this. In the first place, Balzac is always great—perhaps he is at his greatest—in depicting a mania, a passion, whether the subject be pleasure or gold-hunger or parental affection. Pons has two manias, and the one does not interfere with, but rather helps, the other. But this would be nothing if it were not that his chief mania, his ruling passion, is one of Balzac's own. For, as we have often had occasion to notice, Balzac is not by any means one of the great impersonal artists. He can do many things; but he is never at his best in doing any unless his own personal interests, his likings and hatreds, his sufferings and enjoyments, are concerned. He was a kind of actor-manager in his Comédie Humaine; and perhaps, like other actor-managers, he took rather disproportionate care of the parts which he played himself.

Now, he was even more desperate as a collector and fancier of *bibelots* than he was as a speculator; and while the one mania was nearly as responsible for his pecuniary troubles and his need to overwork himself as the other, it certainly gave him more constant and more comparatively harmless satisfactions. His connoisseurship has, of course, been questioned—one connoisseur would be nothing if he did not question the competence of another, if not of all others. It seems certain that Balzac frequently bought things for what they were not; and probable that his own acquisitions went, in his own eyes, through that succession of stages which Charles Lamb (a sort of Cousin Pons in his way too) described inimitably. His pictures, like John Lamb's, were apt to begin as Raphaels, and end as Carlo Marattis. Balzac too, like Pons, was even more addicted to *bric-à-brac* than to art proper; and after many vicissitudes, he and Madame Hanska seem to have succeeded in getting together a very considerable, if also a very miscellaneous and unequal, collection in the house in the Rue du Paradis, the contents of which were dispersed in part (though, I believe, the Rothschild who bought it, bought most of them too) not many years ago. Pons, indeed, was too poor, and probably too queer, to indulge in one fancy which Balzac had, and which, I think, all collectors of the nobler and more poetic class have, though this number may not be large. Balzac liked to have new beautiful things as well as old—to have beautiful things made for him. He was an unwearied customer, though not an uncomplaining one, of the great jeweler Froment Meurice, whose tardiness in carrying out his behests he pathetically upbraids in more than one extant letter.

Therefore, Balzac "did more than sympathize, he felt"— as it has been well put—with Pons in the *bric-à-brac* matter; and it would appear that he did so likewise in that of music, though we have rather less direct evidence. This other sympathy has resulted in the addition to Pons himself of the figure of Schmucke, a minor and more parochial figure, but good in itself, and very much appreciated, I believe, by fellow *mélomanes.*

It is with even more than his usual art that Balzac has surrounded these two originals—these "humorists," as our own ancestors would have called them—with figures much, very much, more of the ordinary world than themselves. The grasping worldliness of the *parvenu* family of Camusot in one degree, and the greed of the portress, Madame Cibot, on the other, are admirably represented; the latter, in particular, must always hold a very high place among Balzac's greatest successes. She is, indeed, a sort of companion sketch to Cousine Bette herself in a still lower rank of life, representing the diabolical in woman; and perhaps we should not wrong the author's intentions if we suspected that Diane de Maufrigneuse has some claims to make up the trio in a sphere even more above Lisbeth's than Lisbeth's is above Madame Cibot's own.

Different opinions have been held of the actual "*bric-à-bracery*" of this piece—that is to say, not of Balzac's competence in the matter, but of the artistic value of his introduction of it. Perhaps his enthusiasm does a little run away with him; perhaps he gives us a little too much of it, and avails himself too freely of the license, at least of the temptation, to digress which the introduction of such persons as Élie Magus affords. And it is also open to any one to say that the climax, or what is in effect the climax, is introduced somewhat too soon; that the struggle, first over the body and then over the property of Patroclus-Pons, is inordinately spun out; and that, even granting the author's mania, he might have utilized it better by giving us more of the harmless and ill-treated cousin's happy hunts, and less of the disputes over his accumulated quarry. This, however, means simply the old, and generally rather impertinent, suggestion to the artist that he shall do with his art something different from that which he has himsef chosen to do. It is, or should be, sufficient that "Le Cousin Pons" is a very agreeable book, more pathetic, if less "grimy," than its companion, full of its author's idiosyncrasy, and characteristic of his genius. It may not be uninteresting to add that "Le Cousin Pons" was originally called "Les Deux Musiciens," or "Le Parasite," and that the change, which is a great improvement, was due to the instances of Madame Hanska.

(For bibliography, see the Preface to "La Cousine Bette.")

G. S.

THE POOR PARENTS

(*Les Parents Pauvres*).

COUSIN BETTY.

PART II.

THE words spoken by Lisbeth : " He begs of his former mistresses," haunted the baroness all night. Like sick men given over by the physicians, who have recourse to quacks, like men who have fallen into the lowest Dantesque circle of despair, or drowning creatures who mistake a floating stick for a hawser, she ended by believing in the baseness of which the mere idea had horrified her ; and it occurred to her that she might apply for help to one of those odious women.

Next morning, without consulting her children or saying a word to anybody, she went to see Mademoiselle Josépha Mirah, prima donna of the Royal Academy of Music, to find or to lose the hope that had gleamed before her like a will-o'-the-wisp. At midday the great singer's waiting-maid brought her in the card of the Baronne Hulot, saying that this person was waiting at the door, having asked whether mademoiselle could receive her.

"Are the rooms done ? "

" Yes, mademoiselle."

"And the flowers fresh ? "

" Yes, mademoiselle."

" Just tell Jean to look around and see that everything is as it should be before showing the lady in, and treat her with the greatest respect. Go, and come back to dress me—I must look my very best."

She went to study herself in the long glass.

" Now, to put our best foot forward ! " said she to herself.

"Vice under arms to meet virtue! Poor woman, what can she want of me? I cannot bear to see

"'The noble victim of outrageous fortune!'"

And she sang through the famous aria as the maid came in again.

"Madame," said the girl, "the lady has a nervous trembling——"

"Offer her some orange-flower water, some rum, some soup——"

"I did, mademoiselle; but she declines everything, and says it is an infirmity, a nervous complaint——"

"Where is she?"

"In the big drawing-room."

"Well, make haste, child. Give me my smartest slippers, the dressing-gown embroidered by Bijou, and no end of lace frills. Do my hair in a way to astonish a woman. This woman plays a part against mine; and tell the lady—for she is a real, great lady, my girl; nay, more, she is what you will never be, a woman whose prayers can rescue souls from your purgatory—tell her I was in bed, as I was playing last night, but that I am getting up."

The baroness, shown into Josépha's handsome drawing-room, did not note how long she was kept waiting there, though it was a long half-hour. This room, entirely redecorated even since Josépha had had the house, was hung with silk in purple and gold color. The luxury which fine gentlemen were wont to lavish on their *petites maisons* (little houses), the scenes of their profligacy, of which the remains still bear witness to the follies from which they were so aptly named, was displayed to perfection, thanks to modern inventiveness, in the four rooms opening into each other, where the warm temperature was maintained by a system of hot-air pipes with invisible openings.

The baroness, quite bewildered, examined each work of art

with the greatest amazement. Here she found the fortunes accounted for that melt in the crucible under which pleasure and vanity feed the devouring flames. This woman, who for twenty-six years had lived among the dead relics of imperial magnificence, whose eyes were accustomed to carpets patterned with faded flowers, rubbed gilding, silks as forlorn as her heart, half understood the powerful fascinations of vice as she studied its results. It was impossible not to wish to possess these beautiful things, these admirable works of art, the creation of the unknown talent which abounds in Paris in our day and produces treasures for all Europe. Each thing had the novel charm of unique perfection. The models having been destroyed, every vase, every figure, every piece of sculpture was the original. This is the crowning grace of modern luxury. To own the thing which is not vulgarized by the two thousand wealthy citizens whose notion of luxury is the lavish display of the splendors that stores can supply is the stamp of true luxury—the luxury of the fine gentlemen of the day, the shooting stars of the Paris firmament.

As she examined the flower-stands, filled with the choicest exotic plants, mounted in chased brass and inlaid in the style of Boulle, the baroness was scared by the idea of the wealth in this apartment. And this impression naturally shed a glamour over the person round whom all this profusion was heaped. Adeline imagined that Josépha Mirah—whose portrait by Joseph Bridau was the glory of the adjoining boudoir—must be a singer of genius, a Malibran, and she expected to see a real star, a true "lionne." She was sorry she had come. But she had been prompted by so strong and so natural a feeling, by such purely disinterested devotion, that she collected all her courage for the interview. Beside, she was about to satisfy her urgent curiosity, to see for herself what the charm was of this kind of women, that they could extract so much gold from the miserly ore of Paris mud.

The baroness looked at herself to see if she were not a blot

on all this splendor; but she was well dressed in her velvet
gown, with a little cape trimmed with beautiful lace, and her
velvet bonnet of the same shade was becoming. Seeing herself still as imposing as any queen, always a queen even in her
fall, she reflected that the dignity of sorrow was a match for
the dignity of talent.

At last, after much opening and shutting of doors, she saw
Josépha. The singer bore a strong resemblance to Allori's
"Judith," which dwells in the memory of all who have ever
seen it in the Pitti palace, near the door of the grand salon.
She had the same haughty mien, the same fine features, black
hair simply knotted, and a yellow wrapper with little embroidered flowers, exactly like the brocade worn by the immortal
homicide conceived of by Bronzino's nephew.

"Madame la Baronne, I am quite overwhelmed by the
honor you do me in coming here," said the singer, resolved
to play her part as a great lady with a grace.

She pushed forward an easy-chair for the baroness and seated
herself on a stool. She discerned the faded beauty of the
woman before her, and was filled with pity as she saw her
shaken by the nervous palsy that, on the least excitement,
became convulsive. She could read at a glance the saintly
life described to her of old by Hulot and Crevel; and she not
only ceased to think of a contest with her, she humiliated
herself before a superiority she appreciated. The great artist
could admire what the courtesan laughed to scorn.

"Mademoiselle, despair brought me here. It reduces us to
any means——"

A look in Josépha's face made the baroness feel that she
had wounded the woman from whom she hoped for so much,
and she looked at her. Her beseeching eyes extinguished the
flash in Josepha's; the singer smiled. It was a wordless dia-
logue of pathetic eloquence.

"It is now two years and a half since Monsieur Hulot left
his family, and I do not know where to find him, though I

know that he lives in Paris,'' said the baroness with emotion. '' A dream suggested to me the idea—an absurd one perhaps —that you may have interested yourself in Monsieur Hulot. If you could enable me to see him—oh! mademoiselle, I would pray heaven for you every day as long as I live in this world——''

Two large tears in the singer's eyes told what her reply would be.

'' Madame,'' said she, '' I have done you an injury without knowing you ; but, now that I have the happiness of seeing in you the most perfect image of virtue on earth, believe me I am sensible of the extent of my fault ; I repent sincerely, and believe me, I will do all in my power to remedy it ! ''

She took Madame Hulot's hand, and before the lady could do anything to hinder her, she kissed it respectfully, even humbling herself to bend one knee. Then she rose, as proud as when she stood on the stage in the part of Mathilde, and rang the bell.

'' Go on horseback,'' said she to the manservant, '' and kill the horse if you must, to find little Bijou, Rue Saint-Maur-du-Temple, and bring her here. Put her into a coach and pay the coachman to come at a gallop. Do not lose a moment— or you lose your place.

'' Madame,'' she went on, coming back to the baroness, and speaking to her in respectful tones, '' you must forgive me. As soon as the Duc d'Hérouville became my protector, I dismissed the baron, having heard that he was ruining his family for me. What more could I do? In an actress' career a protector is indispensable from the first day of her appearance on the boards. Our salaries do not pay half our expenses ; we must have a temporary husband. I did not value Monsieur Hulot, who took me away from a rich man, a conceited idiot. Old Crevel would undoubtedly have married me——''

'' So he told me,'' said the baroness, interrupting her.

"Well, then, you see, madame, I might at this day have been an honest woman, with only one legitimate husband!"

"You have many excuses, mademoiselle," said Adeline, "and God will take them into account. But, for my part, far from reproaching you, I came, on the contrary, to make myself your debtor in gratitude——"

"Madame, for nearly three years I have provided for Monsieur le Baron's necessities——"

"You?" interrupted the baroness, with tears in her eyes. "Oh, what can I do for you? I can only pray——"

"I and Monsieur le Duc d'Hérouville," the singer said, "a noble soul, a true gentleman——" and Josépha related the settling and "marriage" of Monsieur Thoul.

"And so, thanks to you, the baron has wanted nothing?"

"We have done our best to that end, madame."

"And where is he now?"

"About six months ago, Monsieur le Duc told me that the baron, known to the notary by the name of Thoul, had drawn all the eight thousand francs that were to have been paid to him in fixed sums once a quarter," replied Josépha. "We have heard no more of the baron, neither I nor Monsieur d'Hérouville. Our lives are so full, we artists are so busy, that I really have no time to run after old Thoul. As it happens, for the last six months, Bijou, who works for me—his—what shall I say——?"

"His mistress," said Madame Hulot.

"His mistress," repeated Josépha, "has not been here. Mademoiselle Olympe Bijou is perhaps divorced. Divorce is common in the thirteenth arrondissement."

Josépha rose, and foraging among the rare plants in her stands, made a charming bouquet for Madame Hulot, whose expectations, it may be said, were by no means fulfilled. Like those worthy people who take men of genius to be a sort of monsters, eating, drinking, walking, and speaking unlike other people, the baroness had hoped to see Josépha the opera singer, the witch, the amorous and amusing courtesan; she saw a calm and well-mannered woman, with the dignity of talent, the simplicity of an actress who knows herself to be at night a queen, and also, better than all, a woman of the town whose eyes, attitude, and demeanor paid full and ungrudging homage to the virtuous wife, the Mother of Sorrows of the sacred hymn, and who was crowning her sorrows with flowers, as the madonna is crowned in Italy.

"Madame," said the footman, reappearing at the end of half an hour, "Madame Bijou is on her way, but you are not to expect little Olympe. Your needlewoman, madame, is settled in life; she is married——"

"More or less?" said Josépha.

"No, madame, really married. She is at the head of a very fine business; she has married the owner of a large and fashionable store, on which they have spent millions of francs, on the Boulevard des Italiens; and she has left the embroidery business to her sister and mother. She is Madame Grenouville. The fat tradesman——"

"A Crevel?"

"Yes, madame," said the man. "Well, he has settled thirty thousand francs a year on Mademoiselle Bijou by the marriage articles. And her elder sister, they say, is going to be married to a rich butcher."

"Your business looks rather hopeless, I am afraid," said Josépha to the baroness. "Monsieur le Baron is no longer where I lodged him."

Ten minutes later Madame Bijou was announced. Josépha very prudently placed the baroness in the boudoir, and drew the portière over the door.

"You would scare her," said she to Madame Hulot. "She would let nothing out if she suspected that you were interested in the information. Leave me to catechise her. Hide there, and you will hear everything. It is a scene that is played quite as often in real life as on the stage——"

"Well, Mother Bijou," she said to an old woman dressed in tartan stuff, and who looked like a charwoman in her Sunday best, "so you are all very happy? Your daughter is in luck."

"Oh, happy? As for that! My daughter gives us a hundred francs a month, while she rides in a carriage and feeds off silver plate—she is a millionary, is my daughter! Olympe might have lifted me above labor. To have to work at my age? Is that being good to me?"

"She ought not to be ungrateful, for she owes her beauty to you," replied Josépha; "but why did she not come to see me? It was I who placed her in ease by settling her with my uncle."

"Yes, madame, with old Monsieur Thoul, but he is so very old and broken——"

"But what have you done with him? Is he with you? She was very foolish to leave him; he is worth millions now."

"Heaven above us!" cried the mother. "What did I tell her when she behaved so badly to him, and he as mild as milk, poor old fellow? Oh! didn't she just give it him hot? Olympe was perverted, madame!"

"But how?"

"She got to know a *claqueur*, madame, saving your presence, a man paid to clap, you know, the grand-nephew of an old mattress-picker of the Faubourg Saint-Marceau. This good-for-nought, as all your good-looking fellows are, paid to make a piece go, is the cock-of-the-walk out on the Boulevard du Temple, where he works up the new plays, and takes care that the actresses get a reception, as he calls it. First, he has a good breakfast in the morning; then, before the play, he dines, to be 'up to the mark,' as he says; in short, he is a born lover of billiards and drams. 'But that is not following a trade,' as I said to Olympe."

"It is a trade men follow, unfortunately," said Josépha.

"Well, the rascal turned Olympe's head, and he, madame, did not keep good company—when I tell you he was very near being nabbed by the police in a tavern where thieves meet. 'Wever, Monsieur Braulard, the leader of the claque, got him out of that. He wears gold earrings, and he lives by doing nothing, hanging on to women, who are fools about these good-looking scamps. He spent all the money Monsieur Thoul used to give the child.

"Then the business was going to grief; what embroidery brought in went out across the billiard table. 'Wever, the young fellow, had a pretty sister, madame, who, like her brother, lived by hook and by crook, and no better than she should be neither, over in the students' quarter."

"One of the lorettes at the Chaumière," said Josépha.

"So, madame," said the old woman. "So Idamore—his name is Idamore, leastways that is what he calls himself, for his real name is Chardin—Idamore fancied that your uncle had a deal more money than he owned to, and he managed to send his sister Élodie—and that was a stage name he gave her—to send her to be a workwoman at our place, without my daughter's knowing who she was; and, gracious goodness! but that girl turned the whole place topsy-turvy; she got all them poor girls corrupted, brutalized—impossible to whitewash 'em, saving your presence——

"And she was so sharp, she won over poor old Thoul, and took him away, and we don't know where, and left us in a pretty fix, with a lot of bills coming in. To this day as ever is we have not been able to settle up; but my daughter, who knows all about such things, keeps an eye on them as they fall due. Then, when Idamore saw he had got hold of the old man, through his sister, you understand, he threw over my daughter, and now he has got hold of a little actress at the Funambules. And that was how my daughter came to get married, as you will see——"

"But you know where the mattress-picker lives?" said Josépha.

"What! old Chardin? As if he lived anywhere at all!

He is drunk by six in the morning; he makes a mattress once a month; he hangs about the low wineshops all day; he plays at pools——''

"He plays at pools?" said Josépha.

"You do not understand, madame; pools of billiards, I mean, and he wins three or four a day, and then he drinks."

"Water out of the pools, I suppose?" said Josépha. "But if Idamore haunts the boulevard, by inquiring through my friend Braulard, we could find him."

"I don't know, madame; all this was six months ago. Idamore was one of the sort who are bound to find their way into the police court, and from that to Melun—and then—who knows——?"

"To the galleys!" said Josépha.

"Well, madame, you know everything," said the old woman, smiling. "Well, if my girl had never known that scamp, she would now be—— Still, she was in luck, all the same, you will say, for Monsieur Grenouville fell so much in love with her that he married her——"

"And what brought that about?"

"Olympe was desperate, madame. When she found herself left in the lurch for that little actress—and she took a rod out of pickle for her, I can tell you; my word, but she gave her a dressing!—and when she had lost poor old Thoul, who worshiped her, she would have nothing more to say to the men. 'Wever, Monsieur Grenouville, who had been dealing largely with us—to the tune of two hundred embroidered China-crepe shawls every quarter—he wanted to console her; but whether or no, she would not listen to anything without the mayor and the priest. 'I mean to be respectable,' said she, 'or perish!' and she stuck to it. Monsieur Grenouville consented to marry her, on condition of her giving us all up, and we agreed——"

"For a handsome consideration?" said Josépha, with her usual perspicacity.

"Yes, madame, ten thousand francs, and an allowance to my father, who is past work."

"I begged your daughter to make old Thoul happy, and she has thrown me over. That is not fair. I will take no interest in any one for the future! That is what comes of trying to do good! Benevolence certainly does not answer as a speculation! Olympe ought, at least, to have given me notice of this jobbing. Now, if you find the old man Thoul within a fortnight, I will give you a thousand francs."

"That'll be a hard task, my dear lady; still, there are a good many five-franc pieces in a thousand francs, and I will try to earn your money."

"Good-morning, then, Madame Bijou."

On going into the boudoir, the singer found that Madame Hulot had fainted; but in spite of having lost consciousness, her nervous trembling kept her still perpetually shaking, as the pieces of a snake that has been cut up still wriggle and move. Strong salts, cold water, and all the ordinary remedies were applied to recall the baroness to her senses, or rather, to the apprehension of her sorrows.

"Ah! mademoiselle, how far has he fallen!" cried she, recognizing Josépha, and finding that she was alone with her.

"Take heart, madame," replied the actress, who had seated herself on a cushion at Adeline's feet, and was kissing her hands. "We shall find him; and if he is in the mire, well, he must wash himself. Believe me, with people of good breeding it is all a matter of clothes. Allow me to make up for the harm I have done you, for I see how much you are attached to your husband, in spite of his misconduct—or you would not have come here. Well, you see, the poor man is so fond of the women. If you had had a little of our *chic,* you would have kept him from running about the world; for you would have been what we can never be—all the women in one that a man wants.

"The State ought to subsidize a school of manners for honest

women! But governments are so prudish! Still, they are
guided by the men, whom we privately guide. My word, I
pity nations!

"But the matter in question is how you can be helped, and
not to laugh at the world. Well, madame, be easy, go home
again, and do not worry. I will bring your Hector back to
you as he was as a man of thirty."

"Ah, mademoiselle, let us go to see that Madame Grenouville," said the baroness. "She surely knows something!
Perhaps I may see the baron this very day, and be able to
snatch him at once from poverty and disgrace."

"Madame, I will show you the deep gratitude I feel toward
you by not displaying the stage-singer Josépha, the Duc
d'Hérouville's mistress, in the company of the noblest, saint-
liest image of virtue. I respect you too much to be seen by
your side. This is not acted humility; it is sincere homage.
You make me sorry, madame, that I cannot tread in your
footsteps, in spite of the thorns that tear your feet and hands.
But it cannot be helped! I am one with art, as you are one
with virtue."

"Poor child!" said the baroness, moved amid her own
sorrows by a strange sense of compassionate sympathy; "I
will pray God for you; for you are the victim of society,
which must have theatres. When you are old, repent—you
will be heard if God vouchsafes to hear the prayers of a——"

"Of a martyr, madame," Josépha put in, and she respectfully kissed the baroness' skirt.

But Adeline took the actress' hand, and, drawing her toward
her, kissed her on the forehead. Coloring with pleasure,
Josépha saw the baroness into the hackney-coach with the
humblest politeness.

"It must be some visiting lady of charity," said the man-
servant to the maid, "for she does not do so much for any
one, not even for her dear friend Madame Jenny Cadine."

"Wait a few days," said she, "and you will see him,

madame, or I renounce the God of my fathers—and that from a Jewess, you know, is a promise of success."

At the very time when Madame Hulot was calling on Josépha, Victorin, in his study, was receiving an old woman of about seventy-five, who, to gain admission to the lawyer, had used the terrible name of the head of the detective force. The man in waiting announced—

"Madame de Saint-Estève."

"I have assumed one of my business names," said she, taking a seat.

Victorin felt a sort of internal chill at the sight of this dreadful old woman. Though handsomely dressed, she was terrible to look upon, for her flat, colorless, strongly-marked face, furrowed with wrinkles, expressed a sort of cold malignity. Marat, as a woman of that age, might have been like this creature, a living embodiment of the Reign of Terror.

This sinister old woman's small pale eyes twinkled with a tiger's blood-thirsty greed. Her broad, flat nose, with nostrils expanded into oval cavities, breathed the fires of hell, and resembled the beak of some evil bird of prey. The spirit of intrigue lurked behind her low cruel brow. Long hairs had grown from her wrinkled chin, betraying the masculine character of her schemes. Any one seeing that woman's face would have said that artists had failed in their conceptions of Mephistopheles.

"My dear sir," she began, with a patronizing air, "I have long since given up active business of any kind. What I have come to you to do, I have undertaken, for the sake of my dear nephew, whom I love more than I could love a son of my own. Now, the head of the police—to whom the president of the Council said two words in his ear as regards yourself, in talking to Monsieur Chapuzot—thinks as the police ought not to appear in a matter of this description, you understand. They gave my nephew a free hand, but my nephew will have nothing to say to it, except as before the Council ; he will not be seen in it."

" Then your nephew is——"

" You have hit it, and I am rather proud of him ; I am the aunt of Vautrin," said she, interrupting the lawyer, " for he is my pupil, and he soon taught his teacher. We have considered this case, and have come to our own conclusions. Will you hand over thirty thousand francs to have the whole thing taken off your hands ? I will make a clean sweep of it all, and you need not pay till the job is done."

" Do you know the persons concerned ? "

" No, my dear sir ; I look for information from you. What we are told is, that a certain old idiot has fallen into the clutches of a widow. This widow, of nine-and-twenty, has played her cards so well that she has forty thousand francs a year, of which she has robbed two fathers of families. She is now about to swallow down eighty thousand francs a year by marrying an old boy of sixty-one. She will thus ruin a respectable family, and hand over this vast fortune to the child of some lover by getting rid at once of the old husband. That is the case as stated."

" Quite correct," said Victorin. " My father-in-law, Monsieur Crevel——"

" Formerly a perfumer ; a mayor—yes, I live in his district under the name of Ma'ame Nourrisson," said the woman.

" The other person is Madame Marneffe."

"I do not know her," said Madame de Saint-Estève. " But within three days I will be in a position to count her chemises."

" Can you hinder the marriage ? " asked Victorin.

" How far have they gone ? "

" To the second time of asking."

" We must carry off the woman. To-day is Sunday—there are but three days, for they will be married on Wednesday, no doubt ; it is impossible. But she may be killed——"

Victorin Hulot started with an honest man's horror at hearing these five words uttered in cold blood.

"Murder?" said he. "And how could you do it?"

"For forty years now, monsieur, we have played the part of fate," replied she, with terrible pride, "and do just what we will in Paris. More than one family—even in the Faubourg Saint-Germain—has told me all its secrets, I can tell you! I have made and spoiled many a match, I have destroyed many a will, and saved many a man's honor. I hold penned in there," and she tapped her forehead, "a flock of secrets which are worth thirty-six thousand francs a year to me; and you—you will be one of my lambs, hoh! Could such a woman as I am be what I am if she revealed her ways and means? I act.

"Whatever I may do, sir, will be the result of an accident; you need feel no remorse. You will be like a man cured by a clairvoyant, by the end of a month; it seems all the work of Nature."

Victorin broke out in a cold sweat. The sight of an executioner would have shocked him less than this prolix and pretentious Sister of the Hulks. As he looked at her purple-red gown, she seemed to him dyed in blood.

"Madame, I do not accept the help of your experience and skill if success is to cost anybody's life, or the least criminal act is to come of it."

"You are a great baby, monsieur," replied the woman; "you wish to remain blameless in your own eyes, while you want your enemy to be overthrown."

Victorin shook his head in denial.

"Yes," she went on, "you want this Madame Marneffe to drop the prey she has between her teeth. But how do you expect to make a tiger drop his piece of beef? Can you do it by patting his back and saying: 'pussy! pussy?' You are illogical. You want a battle fought, but you object to blows. Well, I grant you the innocence you are so careful over. I have always found that there was material for hypocrisy in honesty! One day, three months hence, a poor priest will come to beg of you forty thousand francs for a pious work—a convent to be rebuilt in the Levant—in the desert. If you are satisfied with your lot, give the good man the money. You will pay more than that into the treasury. It will be a mere trifle in comparison with what you will get, I can tell you."

She rose, standing on the broad feet that seemed to overflow her satin shoes; she smiled, bowed, and vanished.

"The devil has a sister," said Victorin, rising.

He saw the hideous stranger to the door, a creature called up from the dens of the police, as on the stage a monster comes up from the third cellar at the touch of a fairy's wand in a ballet-extravaganza.

After finishing what he had to do at the Courts, Victorin went to call on Monsieur Chapuzot, the head of one of the most important branches of the central police, to make some inquiries about the stranger. Finding Monsieur Chapuzot alone in his office, Victorin thanked him for his help.

"You sent me an old woman who might stand for the incarnation of the criminal side of Paris."

Monsieur Chapuzot laid his spectacles on his papers and looked at the lawyer with astonishment.

"I should not have taken the liberty of sending anybody to see you without giving you notice beforehand, or a line of introduction," said he.

"Then it was Monsieur le Préfet——?"

"I think not," said Chapuzot. "The last time that the Prince de Wissembourg dined with the minister of the interior, he spoke to the préfet of the position in which you find yourself—a deplorable position—and asked him if you could be helped in any friendly way. The préfet, who was interested by the regrets his excellency expressed as to this family affair, did me the honor to consult me about it.

"Ever since the present préfet has held the reins of this

department—so useful and so vilified—he has made it a rule
that family matters are never to be interfered in. He is right
in principle and in morality; but in practice he is wrong. In
the forty-five years that I have served in the police, it did,
from 1799 till 1815, great service in family concerns. Since
1820 a constitutional government and the press have completely altered the conditions of existence. So my advice,
indeed, was not to intervene in such a case, and the préfet
did me the honor to agree with my remarks. The head of
the detective branch had orders, in my presence, to take no
steps; so if you have had any one sent to you by him, he
will be reprimanded. It might cost him his place. 'The
police will do this or that,' is easily said; the police, the
police! But, my dear sir, the marshal and the Ministerial
Council do not know what the police is. The police alone
knows the police. The old Kings, Napoleon and Louis
XVIII., knew their police; but as for ours, only Fouché,
Monsieur Lenoir, and Monsieur de Sartines have had any
notion of it. Everything is changed now; we are reduced
and disarmed! I have seen many private disasters develop,
which I could have checked with five grains of despotic
power. We shall be regretted by the very men who have
crippled us when they, like you, stand face to face with some
moral monstrosities, which ought to be swept away as we
sweep away mud! In public affairs the police is expected to
foresee everything, or when the safety of the public is involved
—but the family? It is sacred! I would do my utmost to
discover and hinder a plot against the King's life, I would
see through the walls of a house; but as to laying a finger on
a household, or peeping into private interests—never, so long
as I sit in this office. I should be afraid."

"Of what?"

"Of the press, Monsieur the Deputy, of the Left Centre."

"What, then, can I do?" said Hulot, after a pause.

"Well, you are the Family," said the official. "That

2

settles it; you can do what you please. But as to helping you, as to using the police as an instrument of private feelings and interests, how is it possible? There lies, you see, the secret of the persecution, necessary, but pronounced illegal by the bench, which was brought to bear against the predecessor of our present chief detective. Bibi-Lupin undertook investigations for the benefit of private persons. This might have led to great social dangers. With the means at his command, the man would have been formidable, an underlying fate——"

"But in my place?" said Hulot.

"What, you ask my advice? You who sell it!" replied Monsieur Chapuzot. "Come, come, my dear sir, you are making fun of me."

Hulot bowed to the functionary, and went away without seeing that gentleman's almost imperceptible shrug as he rose to open the door.

"And he expects to be a statesman!" said Chapuzot to himself as he returned to his reports.

Victorin went home, still full of perplexities which he could confide to no one.

At dinner the baroness joyfully announced to her children that within a month their father might be sharing their comforts, and end his days in peace among his family.

"Oh, I would gladly give my three thousand six hundred francs a year to see the baron here!" cried Lisbeth. "But, my dear Adeline, do not dream beforehand of such happiness, I entreat you!"

"Betty is right," said Célestine. "My dear mother, wait till the end."

The baroness, all feeling and all hope, related her visit to Josépha, expressed her sense of the misery of such women in the midst of good fortune, and mentioned Chardin the mattress-picker, the father of the Oran storekeeper, thus showing that her hopes were not groundless.

By seven next morning Lisbeth had driven in a hackney-coach to the Quai de la Tournelle, and stopped the vehicle at the corner of the Rue de Poissy.

"Go to the Rue des Bernardins," said she to the driver, "No. 7, a house with an entry and no porter. Go up to the fifth floor, ring at the door to the left, on which you will see ' Mademoiselle Chardin—Lace and Shawls Mended.' She will answer the door. Ask for the chevalier. She will say he is out. Say in reply, ' Yes, I know, but find him, for his maid is out on the quay in a coach, and wants to see him.' "

Twenty minutes later, an old man, who looked about eighty, with perfectly white hair, and a nose reddened by the cold, and a pale, wrinkled face like an old woman's, came shuffling slowly along in list slippers, a shiny alpaca overcoat hanging on his stooping shoulders, no ribbon at his button-hole, the sleeves of an under-vest showing below his coat-cuffs, and his shirt-front unpleasantly dingy. He approached timidly, looked at the coach, recognized Lisbeth, and came to the window.

"Why, my dear cousin, what a state you are in !"

"Élodie keeps everything for herself," said Baron Hulot. "Those Chardins are a blackguard crew."

"Will you come home to us?"

"Oh, no, no !" cried the old man. "I would rather go to America."

"Adeline is on the scent."

"Oh, if only some one would pay my debts !" said the baron, with a suspicious look, "for Samanon is after me."

"We have not paid up the arrears yet ; your son still owes a hundred thousand francs."

"Poor boy !"

"And your pension will not be free before seven or eight months. If you will wait a minute, I have two thousand francs here."

The baron held out his hand with fearful avidity.

"Give it me, Lisbeth, and may God reward you! Give it me; I know where to go."

"But you will tell me where, old wretch?"

"Yes, yes. Then I can wait eight months, for I have discovered a little angel, a good child, an innocent thing not old enough to be depraved."

"Do not forget the police court," said Lisbeth, who flattered herself that she would some day see Hulot there.

"No. It is in the Rue de Charonne," said the baron, "a part of the town where no fuss is made about anything. No one will ever find me there. I am called Père Thorec, Betty, and I shall be taken for a retired cabinetmaker; the girl is fond of me, and I will not allow my back to be shorn any more."

"No, that has been done," said Lisbeth, looking at his coat. "Supposing I take you there."

Baron Hulot got into the coach, deserting Mademoiselle Élodie without taking leave of her, as he might have tossed aside a novel he had finished.

In half an hour, during which Baron Hulot talked to Lisbeth of nothing but little Atala Judici—for he had fallen by degrees to those base passions that ruin old men—she set him down, with two thousand francs in his pocket, in the Rue de Charonne, Faubourg Saint-Antoine, at the door of a doubtful and sinister-looking house.

"Good-day, cousin; so now you are to be called Thorec, I suppose? Send none but commissionaires if you need me, and always take them from different parts."

"Trust me! Oh, I am really very lucky!" said the baron, his face beaming with the prospect of new and future happiness.

"No one can find him there," said Lisbeth; and she paid the coach at the Boulevard Beaumarchais, and returned to the Rue Louis-le-Grand in the omnibus.

On the following day Crevel was announced at the hour when all the family were together in the drawing-room, just after breakfast. Célestine flew to throw her arms round her father's neck, and behaved as if she had seen him only the day before, though in fact he had not called there for more than two years.

"Good-morning, father," said Victorin, offering him his hand.

"Good-morning, children," said the pompous Crevel. "Madame la Baronne, I throw myself at your feet! Good heavens, how the children grow! they are pushing us off the perch—'Grand-pa,' they say, 'we want our turn in the sun-shine.' Madame la Comtesse, you are as lovely as ever," he went on, addressing Hortense. "Ah, ha! and here is the best of good money: Cousin Betty, the wise virgin.

"Why, you are really very comfortable here," said he, after scattering these greetings with a cackle of loud laughter that hardly moved the rubicund muscles of his broad face.

He looked at his daughter with some contempt.

"My dear Célestine, I will make you a present of all my furniture out of the Rue des Saussayes; it will just do here. Your drawing-room wants furbishing up. Ha! there is that little monkey Wenceslas. Well, and are we very good chil-dren, I wonder? You must have pretty manners, you know."

"To make up for those who have none," said Lisbeth.

"That sarcasm, my dear Lisbeth, has lost its sting. I am going, my dear children, to put an end to the false position in which I have so long been placed; I have come, like a good father, to announce my approaching marriage without any circumlocution."

"You have a perfect right to marry," said Victorin. "And for my part, I give you back the promise you made me when you gave me the hand of my dear Célestine——"

"What promise?" said Crevel.

"Not to marry," replied the lawyer. "You will do me the justice to allow that I did not ask you to pledge yourself, that you gave your word quite voluntarily and in spite of my

desire, for I pointed out to you at the time that you were un-
wise to bind yourself."

"Yes, I do remember, my dear fellow," said Crevel,
ashamed of himself. "But, on my honor, if you will but live
with Madame Crevel, my children, you will find no reason to
repent. Your good feeling touches me, Victorin, and you
will find that generosity to me is not unrewarded. Come,
by the poker! welcome your stepmother and come to the
wedding."

"But you have not told us the lady's name, papa," said
Célestine.

"Why, it is an open secret," replied Crevel. "Do not let
us play at guess who can! Betty must have told you."

"My dear Monsieur Crevel," replied Lisbeth, "there are
certain names we never utter here——"

"Well, then, it is Madame Marneffe."

"Monsieur Crevel," said the lawyer very sternly, "neither
my wife nor I can be present at that marriage; not out of
interest, for I spoke in all sincerity just now. Yes, I am most
happy to think that you may find happiness in this union; but
I act on considerations of honor and good feeling which you
must understand, and which I cannot speak of here, as they
reopen wounds still ready to bleed——"

The baroness telegraphed a signal to Hortense, who tucked
her little one under her arm, saying, "Come, Wenceslas, and
have your bath! Good-by, Monsieur Crevel."

The baroness also bowed to Crevel without a word; and
Crevel could not help smiling at the child's astonishment
when threatened with this impromptu tubbing.

"You, monsieur," said Victorin, when he found himself
alone with Lisbeth, his wife, and his father-in-law, "are about
to marry a woman loaded with the spoils of my father; it was
she who, in cold blood, brought him down to such depths; a
woman who is the son-in-law's mistress after ruining the father-
in-law; who is the cause of constant grief to my sister! And

you fancy that I shall be seen to sanction your madness by my presence? I deeply pity you, dear Monsieur Crevel; you have no family feeling; you do not understand the unity of the honor which binds the members of it together. There is no arguing with passion—as I have too much reason to know. The slaves of their passions are as deaf as they are blind. Your daughter Célestine has too strong a sense of her duty to proffer a word of reproach."

"That would, indeed, be a pretty state of things!" cried Crevel, trying to cut short this harangue.

"Célestine would not be my wife if she made the slightest remonstrance," the lawyer went on. "But I, at least, may try to stop you before you step over the precipice, especially after giving you ample proof of my disinterestedness. It is not your fortune, it is you that I care about. Nay, to make it quite plain to you, I may add, if it were only to set your mind at ease with regard to your marriage-contract, that I am now in a position which leaves me with nothing to wish for that——"

"Thanks to me!" exclaimed Crevel, whose face had turned purple.

"Thanks to Célestine's fortune," replied Victorin. "And if you regret having given to your daughter, as a present from yourself, a sum which is not half what her mother left her, I can only say that we are prepared to give it back."

"And do you not know, my respected son-in-law," said Crevel, striking an attitude, "that under the shelter of my name Madame Marneffe is not called upon to answer for her conduct excepting as my wife—as Madame Crevel?"

"That is, no doubt, quite the correct thing," said the lawyer; "very generous so far as the affections are concerned and the vagaries of passion; but I know of no name, nor law, nor title that can shelter the theft of three hundred thousand francs so meanly wrung from my father! I tell you plainly, my dear father-in-law, your future wife is unworthy of you;

she is false to you, and is madly in love with my brother-in-law, Steinbock, whose debts she has paid.''

"It was I who paid them!"

"Very good," said Hulot; "I am glad for Count Steinbock's sake; he may some day repay the money. But he is loved, much loved, and often——''

"Loved!" cried Crevel, whose face showed his utter bewilderment. "It is cowardly, and dirty, and mean, and cheap, to calumniate a woman! When a man says such things, monsieur, he must bring proof.''

"I will bring proof.''

"I shall expect it.''

"By the day after to-morrow, my dear Monsieur Crevel, I shall be able to tell you the day, the hour, the very minute when I can expose the horrible depravity of your future wife.''

"Very well; I shall be delighted," said Crevel, who had recovered himself.

"Good-by, my children, for the present; good-by, Betty.''

"See him out, Lisbeth," said Célestine in an undertone.

"And is this the way you take yourself off?" cried Lisbeth to Crevel.

"Ah, ha!" said Crevel, "my son-in-law is too clever by half; he is getting on. The Courts and the Chamber, judicial trickery and political dodges, are making a man of him with a vengeance! So he knows I am to be married on Wednesday, and on a Sunday my gentleman proposes to fix the hour, within three days, when he can prove that my wife is unworthy of me. That is a good story! Well, I am going back to sign the contract. Come with me, Betty—yes, come. They will never know. I meant to have left Célestine forty thousand francs a year; but Hulot has just behaved in a way to alienate my affection for ever.''

"Give me ten minutes, Father Crevel; wait for me in your carriage at the gate. I will make some excuse for going out.''

" Very well—all right.''

" My dears,'' said Lisbeth, who found all the family reas-
sembled in the drawing-room, " I am going with Crevel : the
marriage-contract is to be signed this afternoon, and I shall
hear what he has settled. It will probably be my last visit
to that woman. Your father is furious; he will disinherit
you.''

" His vanity will prevent that,'' said the son-in-law. " He
was bent on owning the estate of Presles, and he will keep it;
I know him. Even if he were to have children, Célestine
would still have half of what he might leave. The law forbids
his giving away all his fortune. Still, these questions are
nothing to me ; I am thinking only of our honor. Go, then,
cousin,'' and he pressed Lisbeth's hand, " and listen carefully
to the contract.''

Twenty minutes after, Lisbeth and Crevel reached the house
in the Rue Barbet, where Madame Marneffe was awaiting, in
mild impatience, the result of a step taken by her commands.
Valérie had in the end fallen a prey to the absorbing love
which, once in her life, masters a woman's heart. Wenceslas
was its object, and, a failure as an artist, he became in Madame
Marneffe's hands a lover so perfect that he was to her what
she had been to Baron Hulot.

Valérie was holding a slipper in one hand, and Steinbock
clasped the other, while her head rested on his shoulder. The
rambling conversation in which they had been engaged ever
since Crevel went out may be ticketed, like certain lengthy
literary efforts of our day, "*All rights reserved*," for it cannot
be reproduced. This masterpiece of personal poetry naturally
brought a regret to the artist's lips, and he said, not without
some bitterness—

" What a pity it is that I married ; for if I had but waited
as Lisbeth told me, I might now have married you.''

" Who but a Pole would wish to make a wife of a devoted

mistress?" cried Valérie. "To change love into duty, and pleasure into a bore."

"I know you to be so fickle," replied Steinbock. "Did I not hear you talking to Lisbeth of that Brazilian, Baron Montèz?"

"Do you want to rid me of him?"

"It would be the only way to hinder his seeing you," said the ex-sculptor.

"Let me tell you, my darling—for I tell you everything," said Valérie—"I was saving him up for a husband. The promises I have made to that man! Oh, long before I knew you," said she, in reply to a movement from Wenceslas. "And those promises, of which he avails himself to plague me, oblige me to get married almost secretly; for if he should hear that I am marrying Crevel, he is the sort of man that—that would kill me."

"Oh, as to that!" said Steinbock, with a scornful expression, which conveyed that such a danger was small indeed for a woman beloved by a Pole.

And in the matter of valor there is no brag or bravado in a Pole, so thoroughly and seriously brave are they all.

"And that idiot Crevel," she went on, "who wants to make a great display and indulge his taste for cheap splendor in honor of the wedding, places me in difficulties from which I see no escape."

Could Valérie confess to this man, whom she adored, that, since the discomfiture of Baron Hulot, this Baron Henri Montèz had inherited the privilege of calling on her at all hours of the day or night; and that, notwithstanding her cleverness, she was still puzzled to find a cause of quarrel in which the Brazilian might seem to be solely in the wrong? She knew the baron's almost savage temper—not unlike Lisbeth's—too well not to quake as she thought of this Othello of Rio de Janeiro.

As the carriage drove up, Steinbock released Valérie, for his arm was round her waist, and took up a newspaper, in which he was found absorbed. Valérie was embroidering with elaborate care at the slippers she was working for Crevel.

"How they slander her!" whispered Lisbeth to Crevel, pointing to this picture as they opened the door. "Look at her hair—not in the least tumbled. To hear Victorin you might have expected to find two turtle-doves in a nest."

"My dear Lisbeth," replied Crevel, in his favorite position, "you see that to turn Lucretia into Aspasia, you have only to inspire a passion!"

"And have I not always told you," said Lisbeth, "that women like a burly profligate like you?"

"And she would be most ungrateful not to," said Crevel; "for as to the money I have spent here, Grindot and I alone can tell!"

And he waved a hand at the staircase.

In decorating this house, which Crevel regarded as his own, Grindot had tried to compete with Cleretti, in whose hands the Duc d'Hérouville had placed Josépha's villa. But Crevel, incapable of understanding art, had, like all sordid souls, wanted to spend a certaim sum fixed beforehand. Grindot, fettered by a contract, had found it impossible to embody his architectural dream.

The difference between Josépha's house and that in the Rue Barbet was just that between the individual stamp on things and commonness. The objects you admired at Josépha's were to be seen nowhere else; those that glittered at Crevel's were to be bought in any store. These two types of luxury are divided by the river Million. A mirror, if unique, is worth six thousand francs; a mirror designed by a manufacturer who turns them out by the dozen costs five hundred. A genuine chandelier by Boulle will sell at public auction for three thousand francs; the same thing reproduced by casting may be made for a thousand or twelve hundred; one is archæologically what a picture by Raphael is in painting, the other is a copy. At what would you value a copy of a Raphael? Thus Crevel's mansion was a splendid example of the luxury of idiots, while Josépha's was a perfect model of an artist's home.

"War is declared," said Crevel, going up to Madame Marneffe.

She rang the bell.

"Go and find Monsieur Berthier," said she to the man-servant, "and do not return without him. If you had succeeded," said she, embracing Crevel, "we would have postponed our happiness, my dear daddy, and have given a really splendid entertainment; but when a whole family is set against a match, my dear, decency requires that the wedding shall be a quiet one, especially when the lady is a widow."

"On the contrary, I intend to make a display of magnificence *à la* Louis XIV.," said Crevel, who of late had held the eighteenth century rather cheap. "I have ordered new carriages; there is one for monsieur and one for madame, two neat coupés; and a chaise, a handsome traveling carriage with a splendid hammercloth, on springs that tremble like Madame Hulot."

"Oh, ho! *You intend?* Then you have ceased to be my lamb? No, no, my friend, you will do what *I* intend. We will sign the contract quietly—just ourselves—this afternoon. Then, on Wednesday, we will be regularly married, really married, in mufti, as my poor mother would have said. We will walk to church, plainly dressed, and have only a low mass. Our witnesses are Stidmann, Steinbock, Vignon, and Massol, all wide-awake men, who will be at the mayor's office by chance, and who will so far sacrifice themselves as to attend mass.

"Your colleague will perform the civil marriage, for once in a way, as early as half-past nine. Mass is at ten; we shall be at home to breakfast by half-past eleven.

"I have promised our guests that we will sit at table till

the evening. There will be Bixiou, your old official chum du Tillet, Lousteau, Vernisset, Léon de Lora, Vernou, all the wittiest men in Paris, who will not know that we are married. We will play them a little trick, we will get just a little tipsy, and Lisbeth must join us. I want her to study matrimony; Bixiou shall make proposals to her, and—and enlighten her darkness."

For two hours Madame Marneffe went on talking nonsense, and Crevel made this judicious reflection—

"How can so light-hearted a creature be utterly depraved? Feather-brained, yes! but wicked? Nonsense!"

"Well, and what did the young people say about me?" said Valérie to Crevel at a moment when he sat down by her on the sofa. "All sorts of horrors?"

"They will have it that you have a criminal passion for Wenceslas—you, who are virtue itself."

"I love him! I should think so, my little Wenceslas!" cried Valérie, calling the artist to her, taking his face in her hands, and kissing his forehead. "A poor boy with no fortune, and no one to depend on! Cast off by a carrotty giraffe! What do you expect, Crevel? Wenceslas is my poet, and I love him as if he were my own child, and make no secret of it. Bah! your virtuous women see evil everywhere and in everything. Bless me, could they not sit by a man without doing wrong? I am a spoilt child who has had all it ever wanted, and bonbons no longer excite me. Poor things! I am sorry for them!

"And who slandered me so?"

"Victorin," said Crevel.

"Then why did you not stop his mouth, the odious legal parrot! with the story of the two hundred thousand francs and his mamma?"

"Oh, the baroness had fled," said Lisbeth.

"They had better take care, Lisbeth," said Madame Marneffe, with a frown. "Either they will receive me and do it handsomely, and come to their stepmother's house—all the party!—or I will see them in lower depths than the baron has reached, and you may tell them I said so! At last I shall turn nasty. On my honor, I believe that evil is the scythe with which to cut down the good."

At three o'clock Monsieur Berthier, Cardot's successor, read the marriage-contract, after a short conference with Crevel, for some of the articles were made conditional on the action taken by Monsieur and Madame Victorin Hulot.

Crevel settled on his wife a fortune consisting, in the first place, of forty thousand francs in dividends on specified securities; secondly, of the house and all its contents; and thirdly, of three million francs not invested. He also assigned to his wife every benefit allowed by law; he left all the property free of duty; and in the event of their dying without issue, each devised to the survivor the whole of their property and real estate.

By this arrangement the fortune left to Célestine and her husband was reduced to two millions of francs in capital. If Crevel and his second wife should have children, Célestine's share was limited to five hundred thousand francs, as the life-interest in the rest was to accrue to Valérie. This would be about the ninth part of his whole real and personal estate.

Lisbeth returned to dine in the Rue Louis-le-Grand, despair written on her face. She explained and bewailed the terms of the marriage-contract, but found Célestine and her husband insensible to the disastrous news.

"You have provoked your father, my children. Madame Marneffe swears that you shall receive Monsieur Crevel's wife and go to her house," said she.

"Never!" said Victorin.

"Never!" said Célestine.

"Never!" said Hortense.

Lisbeth was possessed by the wish to crush the haughty attitude assumed by all the Hulots.

"She seems to have arms that she can turn against you," she replied. "I do not know all about it, but I shall find out. She spoke vaguely of some history of two hundred thousand francs in which Adeline is implicated."

The baroness fell gently backward on the sofa she was sitting on in a fit of hysterical sobbing.

"Go there, go, my children!" she cried. "Receive the woman! Monsieur Crevel is an infamous wretch. He deserves the worst punishment imaginable. Do as the woman desires you! She is a monster—she knows all!"

After gasping out these words with tears and sobs, Madame Hulot collected her strength to go to her room, leaning on her daughter and Célestine.

"What is the meaning of all this?" cried Lisbeth, left alone with Victorin.

The lawyer stood rigid, in very natural dismay, and did not hear her.

"What is the matter, my dear Victorin?"

"I am horrified!" said he, and his face scowled darkly. "Woe to anybody who hurts my mother! I have no scruples then. I would crush that woman like a viper if I could! What, does she attack my mother's life, my mother's honor?"

"She said, but do not repeat it, my dear Victorin—she said you should all fall lower even than your father. And she scolded Crevel roundly for not having shut your mouths with this secret that seems to be such a terror to my dear Adeline."

A doctor was sent for, for the baroness was evidently worse. He gave her a draught containing a large dose of opium, and Adeline, having swallowed it, fell into a deep sleep; but the whole family was greatly alarmed.

Early next morning Victorin went out, and on his way to the courts called at the prefecture of the police, where he begged Vautrin, the head of the detective department, to send him Madame de Saint-Estéve.

"We are forbidden, monsieur, to meddle in your affairs; but Madame de Saint-Estève is in business, and will attend to your orders," replied this famous police-officer.

On his return home, the unhappy lawyer was told that his mother's reason was in danger. Doctor Bianchon, Doctor Larabit, and Professor Angard had met in consultation, and were prepared to apply heroic remedies to hinder the rush of blood to the head. At the moment when Victorin was listening to Doctor Bianchon, who was giving him, at some length, his reasons for hoping that the crisis might be got over, the manservant announced that a client, Madame de Saint-Estève, was waiting to see him. Victorin left Bianchon in the middle of a sentence and flew downstairs like a madman.

"Is there any hereditary lunacy in the family?" said Bianchon, addressing Larabit.

The doctors departed, leaving a hospital attendant, instructed by them, to watch Madame Hulot.

"A whole life of virtue!——" was the only sentence the sufferer had spoken since the attack.

Lisbeth never left Adeline's bedside; she sat up all night, and was much admired by the two younger women.

"Well, my dear Madame de Saint-Estève," said Victorin, showing the dreadful old woman into his study and carefully shutting the doors, "how are we getting on!"

"Ah, ha! my dear friend," said she, looking at Victorin with cold irony. "So you have thought things over?"

"Have you done anything?"

"Will you pay fifty thousand francs?".

"Yes," replied Victorin, "for we must get on. Do you know that by one single phrase that woman has endangered my mother's life and reason? So, I say, get on."

"We have got on!" replied the old woman.

"Well?" cried Victorin, with a gulp.

"Well, you do not cry off the expenses?"

"On the contrary."

" They run up to twenty-three thousand francs already."

Victorin looked helplessly at the woman.

"Well, could we hoodwink you, you, one of the shining lights of the law?" said she. "For that sum we have secured a maid's conscience and a picture by Raphael. It is not dear."

Hulot, still bewildered, sat with wide-open eyes.

"Well, then," his visitor went on, "we have purchased the honesty of Mademoiselle Reine Tousard, a damsel from whom Madame Marneffe has no secrets——"

" I understand ! "

" But if you shy, say so."

" I will pay blindfold," he replied. " My mother has told me that that couple deserve the worst torments——"

" The rack is out of date," said the old woman.

" You answer for the result ? "

" Leave it all to me," said the woman ; " your vengeance is simmering."

She looked at the clock ; it was six.

" Your avenger is dressing; the fires are lighted at the Rocher de Cancale ; the horses are pawing the ground ; my irons are getting hot. Oh, I know your Madame Marneffe by heart ! Everything is ready. And there are some boluses in the rat-trap; I will tell you to-morrow morning if the mouse is poisoned. I believe she will be ; good-evening, my son."

" Good-by, madame."

" Do you know English ? "

" Yes."

" Have you ever seen ' Macbeth ' in English ? "

" Yes."

" Well, my son: 'All hail ! Thou shalt be King hereafter.' That is to say, you shall come into your inheritance," said the dreadful old witch, foreseen by Shakespeare, and who seemed to know her author.

She left Hulot amazed at the door of his study.

3

"The consultation is for to-morrow!" said she, with the gracious air of a regular client.

She saw two persons coming, and wished to pass in their eyes as a pinchbeck countess.

"What impudence!" thought Hulot, bowing to his pretended client.

Baron Montèz de Montejanos was a lion, but a lion not accounted for. Fashionable Paris, Paris of the turf and of the town, admired the ineffable vests of this foreign gentleman, his spotless patent-leather shoes, his incomparable canes, his much-coveted horses, and the negro servants who rode the horses and who were entirely slaves and most consumedly thrashed.

His fortune was well known; he had a credit account up to seven hundred thousand francs in the great banking house of du Tillet; but he was always seen alone. When he went to "first nights," he was in a stall. He frequented no drawing-rooms. He had never given his arm to a girl on the streets. His name could not be coupled with that of any pretty woman of the world. To pass his time he played whist at the Jockey-Club. The world was reduced to calumny, or, which it thought funnier, to laughing at his peculiarities; he went by the name of Combabus.

Bixiou, Léon de Lora, Lousteau, Florine, Mademoiselle Héloïse Brisetout, and Nathan, supping one evening with the notorious Carabine, with a large party of lions and lionesses, had invented this name with an excessively burlesque explanation. Massol, as being in the Council of State, and Claud Vignon, erewhile professor of Greek, had related to the ignorant damsels the famous anecdote, preserved in Rollin's "Ancient History," concerning Combabus, that voluntary Abelard who was placed in charge of the wife of a King of Assyria, Persia, Bactria, Mesopotamia, and other geographical divisions peculiar to old Professor du Bocage, who continued the work of d'Anville, the creator of the East of antiquity. This nickname, which gave Carabine's guests laughter for a quarter of an hour, gave rise to a series of over-free jests, to which the Academy could not award the Montyon prize; but among which the name was taken up, to rest thenceforth on the curly mane of the handsome baron, called by Josépha the splendid Brazilian—as one might say a splendid *Catoxantha.*

Carabine, the loveliest of her tribe, whose delicate beauty and amusing wit had snatched the sceptre of the thirteenth arrondissement from the hands of Mademoiselle Turquet, better known by the name of Malaga—Mademoiselle Séraphine Sinet (this was her real name) was to du Tillet the banker what Josépha Mirah was to the Duc d'Hérouville.

Now, on the morning of the very day when Madame de Saint-Estève had prophesied success to Victorin, Carabine had said to du Tillet at about seven o'clock—

"If you want to be very nice, you will give me a dinner at the Rocher de Cancale and bring Combabus. We want to know, once for all, whether he has a mistress. I bet that he has, and I should like to win."

"He is still at the Hôtel des Princes; I will call," replied du Tillet. "We will have some fun. Ask all the youngsters —the youngster Bixiou, the youngster Lora, in short, all the clan."

At half-past seven that evening, in the handsomest room of the restaurant where all Europe has dined, a splendid silver service was spread, made on purpose for entertainments where vanity pays the bill in bank-notes. A flood of light fell in ripples on the chased rims; waiters, whom a provincial might have taken for diplomatists but for their age, stood solemnly, as knowing themselves to be overpaid.

Five guests had arrived, and were waiting for nine more. There were first and foremost Bixiou, still flourishing in 1843, the salt of every intellectual dish, always supplied with fresh wit—a phenomenon as rare in Paris as virtue is; Léon de

Lora, the greatest living painter of landscape and the sea, who
has this great advantage over all his rivals, that he has never
fallen below his first successes. The courtesans could never
dispense with these two kings of ready wit. No supper, no
dinner, was possible without them.

Séraphine Sinet, called Carabine, as the mistress *en titre*
(notoriously) of the amphitryon, was one of the first to arrive;
and the brilliant lighting showed off her shoulders, unrivaled
in Paris, her throat, as round as if turned in a lathe, without
a crease, her saucy face, and dress of satin brocade in two
shades of blue, trimmed with English lace, costing enough to
have fed a whole village for a month.

Pretty Jenny Cadine, not acting that evening, came in a
dress of incredible splendor; her portrait is too well known
to need any description. A party is always a Longchamps
of evening dress for these ladies, each anxious to win the prize
for her millionaire by thus announcing to her rivals—

"This is the price I am worth!"

A third woman, evidently at the initial stage of her career,
gazed, almost shamefaced, at the luxury of her two established
and wealthy companions. Simply dressed in white cashmere
trimmed with blue, her head had been dressed with real
flowers by a coiffeur of the old-fashioned school, whose awkward hands had unconsciously given the charm of ineptitude
to her fair hair. Still unaccustomed to any finery, she showed
the timidity—to use a hackneyed phrase—inseparable from a
first appearance. She had come from Valognes to find in
Paris some use for her distracting youthfulness, her innocence,
that might have stirred the senses of a dying man, and her
beauty, worthy to hold its own with any that Normandy has
ever supplied to the theatres of the capital. The lines of that
unblemished face were the ideal of angelic purity. Her milk-
white skin reflected the light like a mirror. The delicate pink
in her cheeks might have been laid on with a brush. She was
called Cydalise, and, as will be seen, she was an important

pawn in the game played by Ma'ame Nourrisson to defeat Madame Marneffe.

"Your arm is not a match for your name, my child," said Jenny Cadine, to whom Carabine had introduced this master-piece of sixteen, having brought her with her.

And, in fact, Cydalise displayed to public admiration a fine pair of arms, smooth and satiny, but red with healthy young blood.

"What do you want for her?" said Jenny Cadine, in an undertone to Carabine.

"A fortune."

"What are you going to do with her?"

"Well—Madame Combabus!"

"And what are you to get for such a job?"

"Guess."

"A service of plate?"

"I have three."

"Diamonds?"

"I am selling them."

"A green monkey?"

"No. A picture by Raphael."

"What maggot is that in your brain?"

"Josépha makes me sick with her pictures," said Carabine. "I want some better than hers."

Du Tillet came with the Brazilian, the hero of the feast; the Duc de Hérouville followed with Josépha. The singer wore a plain velvet gown, but she had on a necklace worth a hundred and twenty thousand francs, pearls hardly distinguishable from her skin like white camellia petals. She had stuck one scarlet camellia in her black hair—a patch—the effect was dazzling, and she had amused herself by putting eleven rows of pearls on each arm. As she shook hands with Jenny Cadine, the actress said: "Lend me your mittens!"

Josépha unclasped them one by one and handed them to her friend on a plate.

"There's style!" said Carabine. "Quite the duchess! You have robbed the ocean to dress the nymph, Monsieur le Duc," she added, turning to the little Duc d'Hérouville.

The actress took two of the bracelets; she clasped the other twenty on the singer's beautiful arms, which she kissed.

Lousteau, the literary cadger, la Palférine and Malaga, Massol, Vauvinet, and Theodore Gaillard, a proprietor of one of the most important political newspapers, completed the party.   The Duc d'Hérouville, polite to everybody, as a great gentleman knows how to be, greeted the Comte de la Palférine with the particular nod which, while it does not imply either esteem or intimacy, conveys to all the world: "We are of the same race, the same blood—equals!"   And this greeting, the shibboleth of the aristocracy, was invented to be the despair of the upper citizen class.

Carabine placed Combabus on her left and the Duc d'Hérouville on her right.   Cydalise was next to the Brazilian, and beyond her was Bixiou.   Malaga sat by the duke.

Oysters appeared at seven o'clock; at eight they were drinking iced punch.   Every one is familiar with the bill of fare of such a banquet.   By nine o'clock they were talking as people talk after forty-two bottles of various wines, drunk by fourteen persons.   Dessert was on the table, the odious dessert of the month of April.   Of all the party, the only one affected by the heady atmosphere was Cydalise, who was humming a tune. None of the other guests, with the exception of the poor country girl, had lost their reason; the drinkers and the women were the experienced *élite* of the society that sups.   Their wits were bright, their eyes glistened, but with no loss of intelligence, though the talk drifted into satire, anecdote, and gossip.   Conversation, hitherto confined to the inevitable circle of racing, horses, hammerings on the Bourse, the different occupations of the lions themselves, and the scandals of the town, showed a tendency to break up into intimate *têtes-à-tête*, the dialogues of two hearts.

And at this stage, at a signal from Carabine to Léon de Lora, Bixiou, la Palférine,* and du Tillet, love came under discussion.

"A doctor in good society never talks of medicine, true nobles never speak of their ancestors, men of genius do not discuss their works," said Josépha; "why should we talk business? If I got the opera put off in order to dine here, it was assuredly not to work. So let us change the subject, dear children."

"But we are speaking of *real* love, my beauty," said Malaga, "of the love that makes a man fling all to the dogs—father, mother, wife, children—and retire to Clichy."

"Talk away, then, 'don't know yer,' " said the singer.

The slang words, borrowed from the street Arab, and spoken by these women, may be a poem on their lips, helped by the expression of the eyes and face.

"What, do not I love you, Josépha?" said the duke in a low voice.

"You, perhaps, may love me truly," said she in his ear, and she smiled. "But I do not love you in the way they describe, with such love as makes the world dark in the absence of the man beloved. You are delightful to me, useful—but not indispensable; and if you were to throw me over to-morrow, I could have three dukes for one."

"Is true love to be found in Paris?" asked Léon de Lora. "Men have not even time to make a fortune; how can they give themselves over to true love, which swamps a man as water melts sugar? A man must be enormously rich to indulge in it, for love annihilates him—for instance, like our Brazilian friend over there. As I said long ago, 'Extremes defeat—themselves.' A true lover is like a eunuch; women have ceased to exist for him. He is mystical; he is like the true Christian, an anchorite of the desert! See our noble Brazilian."

* See "A Prince of Bohemia."

Every one at table looked at Henri Montèz de Montejanos, who was shy at finding every eye centred on him.

"He has been feeding there for an hour without discovering, any more than an ox at pasture, that he is sitting next to —I will not say, in such company, the loveliest—but the freshest woman in all Paris."

"Everything is fresh here, even the fish; it is what the house is famous for," said Carabine.

Baron Montèz looked good-naturedly at the painter, and said—

"Very good! I drink to your very good health," and bowing to Léon de Lora, he lifted his glass of port wine and drank it with much dignity.

"Are you then truly in love?" asked Malaga of her neighbor, thus interpreting his toast.

The Brazilian refilled his glass, bowed to Carabine, and drank again.

"To the lady's health then!" said the courtesan, in such a droll tone that Lora, du Tillet, and Bixiou burst out laughing.

The Brazilian sat like a bronze statue. This impassibility provoked Carabine. She knew perfectly well that Montèz was devoted to Madame Marneffe, but she had not expected this dogged fidelity, this obstinate silence of conviction.

A woman is as often gauged by the attitude of her lover as a man is judged from the tone of his mistress. The baron was proud of his attachment to Valérie, and of hers to him; his smile had, to these experienced connoisseurs, a touch of irony; he was really grand to look upon; wine had not flushed him; and his eyes, with their peculiar lustre as of tarnished gold, kept the secrets of his soul. Even the knowing Carabine said to herself—

"What a woman she must be! How she has sealed up that heart!"

"He is a rock!" said Bixiou in an undertone, imagining

that the whole thing was a practical joke, and never suspecting the importance to Carabine of reducing this so obdurate a fortress.

While this conversation, apparently so frivolous, was going on at Carabine's right, the discussion of love was continued on her left between the Duc d'Hérouville, Lousteau, Josépha, Jenny Cadine, and Massol. They were wondering whether such rare phenomena were the result of passion, obstinacy, or affection. Josépha, bored to death by it all, tried to change the subject.

"You are talking of what you know nothing about. Is there a man among you who ever loved a woman—a woman beneath him—enough to squander his fortune and his children's, to sacrifice his future and blight his past, to risk going to the hulks for robbing the Government, to kill an uncle and a brother, to let his eyes be so effectually blinded that he did not even perceive that it was done to hinder his seeing the abyss into which, as a crowning jest, he was being driven? Du Tillet has a cash-box under the left breast; Léon de Lora has his wit; Bixiou would laugh at himself for a fool if he loved any one but himself; Massol has a minister's portfolio in the place of a heart; Lousteau can have nothing but viscera, since he could endure to be thrown over by Madame de Baudraÿe; Monsieur le Duc is too rich to prove his love by his ruin; Vauvinet is not in it—I do not regard a bill-broker as one of the human race; and you have never loved, nor I, nor Jenny Cadine, nor Malaga. For my part, I never but once even saw the phenomenon I have described. It was," and she turned to Jenny Cadine, "that poor Baron Hulot, whom I am going to advertise for like a lost dog, for I want to find him."

"Oh, hŏ!" said Carabine to herself, and looking keenly at Josépha, "then Madame Nourrisson has two pictures by Raphael, since Josépha is playing my hand!"

"Poor fellow," said Vauvinet, "he was a great man!

Magnificent! And what a figure, what a style, the air of Francis I.! What a volcano! and how full of ingenious ways of getting money! He must be looking for it now, wherever he is, and I make no doubt he extracts it even from the walls built of bones that you may see in the suburbs of Paris near the city gates——"

"And all that," said Bixiou, "for that little Madame Marneffe! There is a precious wanton for you!"

"She is just going to marry my friend Crevel," said du Tillet.

"And she is madly in love with my friend Steinbock," Léon de Lora put in.

These three phrases were like so many pistol-shots fired point-blank at Montès. He turned white, and the shock was so painful that he rose with difficulty.

"You are a set of blackguards!" cried he. "You have no right to speak the name of an honest woman in the same breath with those of fallen creatures—above all, not to make it a mark for your slander!"

He was interrupted by unanimous bravos and applause. Bixiou, Léon de Lora, Vauvinet, du Tillet, and Massol set the example, and there was a chorus.

"Hurrah for the Emperor!" said Bixiou.

"Crown him! crown him!" cried Vauvinet.

"Three groans for such a good dog! Hurrah for Brazil!" cried Lousteau.

"So my copper-colored baron, it is our Valérie that you love; and you are not yet disgusted?" said Léon de Lora.

"His remark is not parliamentary, but it is grand!" observed Massol.

"But my most delightful customer," said du Tillet, "you were recommended to me; I am your banker; your innocence reflects on my credit."

"Yes, tell me, you who are a reasonable creature——" said the Brazilian to the banker.

"Thanks on behalf of the company," said Bixiou with a bow.

"Tell me the real facts," Montèz went on, heedless of Bixiou's interjection.

"Well, then," replied du Tillet, "I have the honor to tell you that I am asked to the Crevel wedding."

"Ah, ha! Combabus holds a brief for Madame Marneffe!" said Josépha, rising solemnly.

She went round to Montèz with a tragic look, patted him kindly on the head, looked at him for a moment with comical admiration, and nodded sagely.

"Hulot was the first instance of love through fire and water," said she; "this is the second. But it ought not to count, as it comes from the tropics."

Montèz had dropped into his chair again, when Josépha gently touched his forehead and looked at du Tillet as he said—

"If I am the victim of a Paris jest, if you only wanted to get at my secret—" and he sent a flashing look round the table, embracing all the guests in a flaming glance that blazed with the sun of Brazil—"I beg of you as a favor to tell me so," he went on, in a tone of almost childlike entreaty; "but do not vilify the woman I love."

"Nay, indeed," said Carabine in a low voice; "but if, on the contrary, you are shamefully betrayed, cheated, tricked by Valérie, if I should give you the proof in an hour, in my own house, what then?"

"I cannot tell you before all these Iagos," said the Brazilian.

Carabine understood him to say *magots* (baboons).

"Well, well, say no more!" she replied, smiling. "Do not make yourself a laughing-stock for all the wittiest men in Paris; come to my house, we will talk it over."

Montèz was crushed. "Proofs," he stammered; "consider——"

"Only too many," replied Carabine; "and if the mere suspicion hits you so hard, I fear for your reason."

"Is this creature obstinate, I ask you? He is worse than the late lamented King of Holland! I say, Lousteau, Bixiou, Massol, all the crew of you, are you not invited to breakfast with Madame Marneffe the day after to-morrow?" said Leon de Lora.

"*Ja*," said du Tillet; "I have the honor of assuring you, baron, that if you had by any chance thought of marrying Madame Marneffe, you are thrown out like a bill in Parliament, beaten by a blackball called Crevel. My friend, my old comrade Crevel, has eighty thousand francs a year; and you, I suppose, did not show such a good hand, for if you had, you, I imagine, would have been preferred."

Montèz listened with a half-absent, half-smiling expression, which struck them all with terror.

At this moment the head-waiter came to whisper to Carabine that a lady, a relation of hers, was in the drawing-room and wished to speak to her.

Carabine rose and went out to find Madame Nourrisson, decently veiled with black lace.

"Well, child, am I to go to your house? Has he taken the hook?"

"Yes, mother; and the pistol is so fully loaded that my only fear is that it will burst," said Carabine.

About an hour later, Montèz, Cydalise, and Carabine, returning from the Rocher de Cancale, entered Carabine's little sitting-room in the Rue-Saint-Georges. Madame Nourrisson was sitting in an armchair by the fire.

"Here is my worthy old aunt," said Carabine.

"Yes, child, I came in person to fetch my little allowance. You would have forgotten me, though you are kind-hearted, and I have some bills to pay to-morrow. Buying and selling clothes, I am always short of cash. Who is this at your heels? The gentleman looks very much put out about something."

The dreadful Madame Nourrisson, at this moment so completely disguised as to look like a respectable old body, rose to embrace Carabine, one of the hundred and odd courtesans she had launched on their horrible career of vice.

"He is an Othello who is not to be taken in, whom I have the honor of introducing to you—Monsieur le Baron Montèz de Montejanos."

"Oh! I have heard him talked about, and know his name. You are nicknamed Combabus, because you love but one woman; and, in Paris, that is the same as loving no one at all. And is it by chance the object of your affections who is fretting you? Madame Marneffe, Crevel's woman? I tell you what, my dear sir, you may bless your stars instead of cursing them. She is a good-for-nothing baggage, is that little woman. I know her tricks!"

"Get along," said Carabine, into whose hand Madame Nourrisson had slipped a note while embracing her, "you do not know your Brazilians. They are wrong-headed creatures that insist on being impaled through the heart. The more jealous they are, the more jealous they want to be. Môsieur talks of dealing death all round, but he will kill nobody because he is in love. However, I have brought him here to give him the proofs of his discomfiture, which I have got from that little Steinbock."

Montèz was drunk; he listened as if the women were talking about somebody else.

Carabine went to take off her velvet wrap, and read a facsimile of a note, as follows:

"DEAR PUSS:—He dines with Popinot this evening, and will come to fetch me from the opera at eleven. I shall go out at about half-past five and count on finding you at our paradise. Order dinner to be sent in from the Maison d'Or.

Dress, so as to be able to take me to the opera. We shall have four hours to ourselves. Return this note to me; not that your Valérie doubts you—I would give you my life, my fortune, and my honor, but I am afraid of the tricks of chance."

"Here, baron, this is the note sent to Count Steinbock this morning; read the address. The original document is burnt."

Montèz turned the note over and over, recognized the writing, and was struck by a rational idea, which is sufficient evidence of the disorder of his brain.

"And, pray," said he, looking at Carabine, "what object have you in torturing my heart, for you must have paid very dear for the privilege of having the note in your possession long enough to get it lithographed?"

"Foolish man!" said Carabine, at a nod from Madame Nourrisson, "don't you see that poor child Cydalise—a girl of sixteen, who has been pining for you these three months, till she has lost her appetite for food or drink, and who is heartbroken because you have never even so much as glanced at her?"

Cydalise put her handkerchief to her eyes with an appearance of emotion—"She is furious," Carabine went on, "though she looks as if butter would not melt in her mouth, furious to see the man she adores duped by a villainous hussy; she would kill Valérie——"

"Oh, as for that," said the Brazilian, "that is my business!"

"What, killing?" said old Nourrisson. "No, my son, we don't do that here nowadays."

"Oh!" said Montèz, "I am not a native of this country. I live in a parish where I can laugh at your laws; and if you give me proof——"

"Well, that note. Is that nothing?"

"No," said the Brazilian. "I do not believe in the writing. I must see for myself."

"See?" cried Carabine, taking the hint at once from a gesture of her supposed aunt. "You shall see, my dear tiger, all you can wish to see—on one condition."

"And that is?"

"Look at Cydalise."

At a wink from Madame Nourrisson, Cydalise cast a tender look at the baron.

"Will you be good to her? Will you make her a home?" asked Carabine. "A girl of such beauty is well worth a house and a carriage! It would be a monstrous shame to leave her to walk the streets. And beside—she is in debt. How much do you owe?" asked Carabine, nipping Cydalise's arm.

"She is worth all she can get," said the old woman. "The point is that she can't find a buyer."

"Listen!" cried Montèz, fully aware at last of this masterpiece of womankind, "you will show me Valérie——"

"And Count Steinbock. Certainly!" said Madame Nourrisson.

For the past ten minutes the old woman had been watching the Brazilian; she saw that he was an instrument tuned up to the murderous pitch she needed; and, above all, so effectually blinded that he would never heed who had led him on to it, and she spoke:

"Cydalise, my Brazilian jewel, is my niece, so her concerns are partly mine. All this catastrophe will be the work of a few minutes, for a friend of mine lets the furnished room to Count Steinbock where Valérie is at this moment taking coffee —a queer sort of coffee, but she calls it her coffee. So let us understand each other, Brazil! I like Brazil, it is a hot country.

"What is to become of my niece?"

"You old ostrich," said Montèz, the plumes in the woman's

bonnet catching his eye, "you interrupted me. If you show me—if I see Valérie and that artist together——"

"As you would wish to be——" said Carabine; "that is understood."

"Then I will take this girl and carry her away——"

"Where!" asked Carabine.

"To Brazil," replied the baron. "I will make her my wife. My uncle left me ten leagues square of entailed estate; that is how I still have that house and home. I have a hundred negroes—nothing but negroes and negresses and negro brats, all bought by my uncle——"

"Nephew to a nigger-driver," said Carabine, with a grimace. "That needs some consideration. Cydalise, child, are you fond of the blacks?"

"Pooh! Carabine, no nonsense," said the old woman. "The deuce is in it! Monsieur and I are doing business."

"If I take up another Frenchwoman, I mean to have her to myself," the Brazilian went on. "I warn you, mademoiselle, I am king there, and not a constitutional king. I am czar; my subjects are mine by purchase, and no one can escape from my kingdom, which is a hundred leagues from any human settlement, hemmed in by savages on the interior, and divided from the sea by a wilderness as wide as France."

"I should prefer a garret here."

"So thought I," said Montèz, "since I sold all my land and possessions at Rio de Janeiro to come back to Madame Marneffe."

"A man does not make such a voyage for nothing," remarked Madame Nourrisson. "You have a right to look for love for your own sake, particularly being so good-looking. Oh, he is very handsome!" said she to Carabine.

"Very handsome, handsomer than the Postillon de Longjumeau," replied the courtesan.

Cydalise took the Brazilian's hand, but he released it as politely as he could.

"I came back for Madame Marneffe," the man went on where he had left off, " but you do not know why I was three years thinking about it."

" No, savage," said Carabine.

"Well, she had so repeatedly told me that she longed to live with me alone in a desert——"

"Oh, ho! he is not a savage after all," cried Carabine, with a shout of laughter. " He is of the highly civilized tribe of Flats! "

" She had told me this so often," Montèz went on, regardless of the courtesan's mockery, "that I had a lovely house fitted up in the heart of that vast estate. I came back to France to fetch Valérie, and the very first evening I beheld her——"

" 'Beheld her' is very proper! " said Carabine. "I will remember it."

" She told me to wait till that wretched Marneffe was dead; and I agreed, and forgave her for having admitted the attentions of Hulot. Whether the devil had her in hand I don't know, but from that instant that woman has humored my every whim, complied with all my demands—never for one moment has she given me cause to suspect her—— ! "

" That is supremely clever ! " said Carabine to Madame Nourrisson, who nodded in sign of assent.

"My faith in that woman," said Montèz, and he shed a tear, " was a match for my love. Just now, I was ready to fight everybody at table——"

" So I saw," said Carabine.

"And if I am cheated, if she is going to be married, if she is at this moment in Steinbock's arms, she deserves a thousand deaths! I will kill her as I would smash a fly——"

"And how about the gendarmes, my son?" said Madame Nourrisson, with a smile that made your flesh creep.

"And the police agents, and the judges, and the galleys; and all the set-out?" added Carabine.

4

"You are bragging, my dear fellow," said the old woman, who wanted to know all the Brazilian's schemes of vengeance.

"I will kill her," he calmly repeated. "You called me a savage. Do you imagine that I am fool enough to go, like a Frenchman, and buy poison at the chemist's store? During the time while we were driving here, I thought out my means of revenge, if you should prove to be right as concerns Valérie. One of my negroes has the most deadly of animal poisons, that gives a disease more fatal than any vegetable poison, and incurable anywhere but in Brazil. I will administer it to Cydalise, who will give it to me; then by the time when death is a certainty to Crevel and his wife, I shall be beyond the Azores with your cousin, who will be cured, and I will marry her. We have our own little tricks, we savages! Cydalise," said he, looking at the country girl, "is the animal I need. How much does she owe?"

"A hundred thousand francs," said Cydalise.

"She says little—but to the purpose," said Carabine, in a low tone to Madame Nourrisson.

"I am going mad!" cried the Brazilian, in a husky voice, dropping on to a sofa. "I shall die of this! But I must see, for it is impossible! A lithographed note! What is to assure me that it is not a forgery? Baron Hulot was in love with Valérie?" said he, recalling Josépha's harangue. "Nay; the proof that he did not love is that she is still alive—I will not leave her living for anybody else, if she is not wholly mine."

Montèz was terrible to behold. He bellowed; he stormed; he broke everything he touched; rosewood was as brittle as glass.

"How he destroys things!" said Carabine, looking at the old woman. "My good boy," said she, giving the Brazilian a little slap, "Roland the Furious is very fine in a poem; but in a drawing-room he is prosaic and expensive."

"My son," said old Nourrisson, rising to stand in front of the crestfallen baron, "I am of your way of thinking. When you love in that way, and are joined 'till death does you part,' life must answer for love. The one who first goes, carries everything away; it is a general wreck. You command my esteem, my admiration, my consent, especially for your inoculation, which will make me a friend of the negro. But you love her! You will hark back?"

" I? If she is so infamous, I——"

" Well, come now, you are talking too much, it strikes me. A man who means to be avenged, and who says he has the ways and means of a savage, doesn't do that. If you want to see your ' object' in her paradise, you must take Cydalise and walk straight in with her on your arm, as if the servant had made a mistake. But no scandal! If you mean to be revenged, you must eat the leek, seem to be in despair, and allow her to bully you. Do you see?" said Madame Nourrisson, finding the Brazilian quite amazed by so subtle a scheme.

"All right, old ostrich," he replied. "Come along: I understand."

" Good-by, little one!" said the old woman to Carabine.

She signed to Cydalise to go on with Montèz, and remained a minute with Carabine.

" Now, child, I have but one fear, and that is that he will strangle her! I should be in a very tight place; we must do everything gently. I believe you have won your picture by Raphael; but they tell me it is only a Mignard. Never mind, it is much prettier; all the Raphaels are gone black, I am told, whereas this one is as bright as a Girodet."

" All I want is to crow over Josépha; and it is all the same to me whether I have a Mignard or a Raphael! That little thief had on such pearls this evening!—you would sell your soul for them."

Cydalise, Montèz, and Madame Nourrisson got into a hackney-coach that was waiting at the door. Madame Nourrisson whispered to the driver the address of a house in the same block as the Italian Opera-House, which they could have reached in five or six minutes from the Rue Saint-Georges; but Madame Nourrisson desired the man to drive along the Rue le Peletier, and to go very slowly, so as to be able to examine the carriages in waiting.

"Brazilian," said the old woman, "look out for your angel's carriage and servants."

The baron pointed out Valérie's carriage as they passed it.

"She has told them to come for her at ten o'clock, and she is gone in a hack to the house where she visits Count Steinbock. She has dined there, and will come to the opera in half an hour. It is well contrived!" said Madame Nourrisson. "Thus you see how she has kept you so long in the dark."

The Brazilian made no reply. He had become the tiger, and had recovered the imperturbable cool ferocity that had been so striking at dinner. He was as calm as a bankrupt the day after he has stopped payment.

At the door of the house stood a hackney-coach with two horses, of the kind known as a Compagnie-Genérale, from the company that runs them.

"Stay here in the box," said the old woman to Montèz. "This is not an open house like a tavern. I will send for you."

The paradise of Madame Marneffe and Wenceslas was not at all like that of Crevel—who, finding it useless now, had just sold his to the Comte Maxime de Trailles. This paradise, the paradise of all comers, consisted of a room on the fifth floor opening to the landing, in a house close to the Italian Opera. On each floor of this house there was a room which had originally served as the kitchen to the apartments on that floor. But the house having become a sort of inn, let out for clandestine love affairs at an exorbitant price, the owner, the real Madame Nourrisson, an old-clothes buyer in the Rue Neuve Saint-Marc, had wisely appreciated the great value of these kitchens, and had turned them into a sort of dining-rooms. Each of these rooms, built between thick party-walls and with windows to the street, was entirely shut in by very thick double doors on the landing. Thus the most important secrets could be discussed over a dinner, with no risk of being overheard. For greater security, the windows had shutters inside and out. These rooms, in consequence of this peculiarity, were let for twelve hundred francs a month. The whole house, full of such paradises and mysteries, was rented by Madame Nourrisson the First for twenty-eight thousand francs a year, and one year with another she made twenty thousand francs of clear profit, after paying her housekeeper, Madame Nourrisson the Second, for she did not manage it herself.

The paradise let to Count Steinbock had been hung with chintz; the cold, hard floor, of common tiles reddened with encaustic, was not felt through a soft, thick carpet. The furniture consisted of two pretty chairs and a bed in an alcove, just now half hidden by a table loaded with the remains of an elegant dinner, while two bottles with long necks and an empty champagne-bottle in ice strewed the field of Bacchus cultivated by Venus.

There were also—the property, no doubt, of Valérie—a low easy-chair and a man's smoking-chair, and a pretty toilet chest of drawers in rosewood, the mirror handsomely framed *à la* Pompadour. A lamp hanging from the ceiling gave a subdued light, increased by wax-candles on the table and on the mantel.

This sketch will suffice to give an idea, *urbi et orbi*, of clandestine passion in the squalid style stamped on it in Paris in 1840. How far, alas! from the adulterous love, symbolized by Vulcan's nets, three thousand years ago.

When Montèz and Cydalise came upstairs, Valérie, standing before the fire, where a log was blazing, was teaching Wenceslas to lace her corset.

This is a moment when a woman who is neither too fat nor

too thin, but, like Valérie, elegant and slender, displays divine beauty. The rosy skin, moistly soft, invites the sleepiest eye. The lines of her figure, so little hidden, are so charmingly outlined by the white pleats of the chemise and the support of the corset, that she is irresistible—like everything that must be parted from.

With a happy face smiling at the glass, a foot impatienly marking time, a hand put up to restore order among the tumbled curls, and eyes expressive of gratitude; with the glow of satisfaction which, like a sunset, warms the least details of the countenance—everything makes such a moment a mine of memories.

Any man who dares look back on the early errors of his life may, perhaps, recall some such reminiscences, and understand, though not excuse, the follies of Hulot and Crevel. Women are so well aware of their power at such a moment, that they find in it what may be called the aftermath of the meeting.

"Come, come; after two years' practice, you do not yet know how to lace a woman's stays! You are too much a Pole! There, it is ten o'clock, my Wenceslas!" said Valérie, laughing at him.

At this very moment, a mischievous waiting-woman, by inserting a knife, pushed up the hook of the double doors that formed the whole security of Adam and Eve. She hastily pulled the door open—for the servants of these dens have little time to waste—and discovered one of the bewitching *tableaux de genre* which Gavarni has so often shown at the Salon.

"In here, madame," said the girl; and Cydalise went in, followed by Montèz.

"But there is some one here. Excuse me, madame," said the country girl, in alarm.

"What? Why! it is Valérie!" cried Montèz, violently slamming the door.

Madame Marneffe, too genuinely agitated to dissemble her feelings, dropped on to the chair by the fireplace. Two tears rose to her eyes, and at once dried away. She looked at Montèz, saw the girl, and burst into a cackle of forced laughter. The dignity of the insulted woman redeemed the scantiness of her attire; she walked close up to the Brazilian, and looked at him so defiantly that her eyes glittered like knives.

"So that," said she, standing face to face with the baron, and pointing to Cydalise—"that is the other side of your fidelity? You, who have made me promises that might convert a disbeliever in love! You, for whom I have done so much—have even committed crimes! You are right, monsieur, I am not to compare with a child of her age and of such beauty!

"I know what you are going to say," she went on, looking at Wenceslas, whose undress was proof too clear to be denied. "This is my concern. If I could love you after such gross treachery—for you have spied upon me, you have paid for every step up these stairs, paid the mistress of the house, and the servant, perhaps even Reine—a noble deed! If I had any remnant of affection for such a mean wretch, I could give him reasons that would renew his passion! But I leave you, monsieur, to your doubts, which will become remorse—Wenceslas, my gown!"

She took her dress and put it on, looked at herself in the glass, and finished dressing without heeding the baron, as calmly as if she had been alone in the room.

"Wenceslas, are you ready? Go first."

She had been watching Montèz in the glass and out of the corner of her eye, and fancied she could see in his pallor an indication of the weakness which delivers a strong man over to a woman's fascinations; she now took his hand, going so close to him that he could not help inhaling the terrible perfumes which men love, and by which they intoxicate themselves; then, feeling his pulses beat high, she looked at him reproachfully.

"You have my full permission to go and tell your history to Monsieur Crevel; he will never believe you. I have a perfect right to marry him, and he becomes my husband the day after to-morrow. I shall make him very happy. Good-by; try to forget me."

"Oh! Valérie," cried Henri Montèz, clasping her in his arms, "that is impossible! Come to Brazil!"

Valérie looked in his face, and saw him her slave.

"Well, if you still love me, Henri, two years hence I will be your wife; but your expression at this moment strikes me as very suspicious."

"I swear to you that they made me drink, that false friends threw this girl on my hands, and that the whole thing is the outcome of chance!" said Montèz.

"Then I am to forgive you?" she asked, with a very fetching smile.

"But you will marry, all the same?" asked the baron, in an agony of jealousy.

"Eighty thousand francs a year!" said she, with almost comical enthusiasm. "And Crevel loves me so much that he will soon die of it!"

"Ah! I understand," said Montèz.

"Well, then, in a few days we will come to an understanding," said she.

And she departed triumphant.

"I have no scruples," thought the baron, standing transfixed for a few minutes. "What! That woman believes she can make use of his passion to be quit of that dolt, as she counted on Marneffe's decease! I shall be the instrument of divine wrath."

Two days later those of du Tillet's guests who had demolished Madame Marneffe tooth and nail were seated round her table an hour after she had shed her skin and changed her name for the illustrious name of a Paris mayor. This verbal treason is one of the commonest forms of Parisian levity.

Valérie had had the satisfaction of seeing the Brazilian in the church ; for Crevel, now so entirely the husband, had invited him out of bravado. And the baron's presence at the breakfast astonished no one. All these men of wit and of the world were familiar with the meanness of passion, the compromises of pleasure.

Steinbock's deep melancholy—for he was beginning to despise the woman whom he had adored as an angel—was considered to be in excellent taste. The Pole thus seemed to convey that all was at an end between Valérie and himself. Lisbeth came to embrace her dear Madame Crevel, and to excuse herself for not staying to the breakfast on the score of Adeline's sad state of health.

" Be quite easy," said she to Valérie, " they will call on you, and you will call on them. Simply hearing the words ' two hundred thousand francs ' has brought the baroness to death's door. Oh, you have them all hard and fast by that tale ! But you must tell it to me."

Within a month of her marriage, Valérie was at her tenth quarrel with Steinbock ; he insisted on explanations as to Henri Montès, reminding her of the words spoken in their paradise ; and, not content with speaking to her in terms of scorn, he watched her so closely that she never had a moment of liberty, so much was she fettered by his jealousy on one side and Crevel's devotion on the other.

Bereft now of Lisbeth, whose advice had always been so valuable, she flew into such a rage as to reproach Wenceslas for the money she had lent him. This so effectually roused Steinbock's pride, that he came no more to the Crevels' house. So Valérie had gained her point, which was to be rid of him for a time, and enjoy some freedom. She waited till Crevel should make a little journey into the country to see Comte Popinot, with a view to arranging for her introduction to the countess, and was then able to make an appointment to meet the baron, whom she wanted to have at her command for a whole day to give him those " reasons " which were to make him love her more than ever.

On the morning of that day, Reine, who estimated the magnitude of her crime by that of the bribe she received, tried to warn her mistress, in whom she naturally took more interest than in strangers. Still, as she had been threatened with madness, and ending her days in the Salpêtrière in case of indiscretion, she was cautious.

" Madame, you are so well off now," said she. " Why take on again with that Brazilian ? I do not trust him at all."

" You are very right, Reine, and I mean to be rid of him."

" Oh, madame, I am glad to hear it ; he frightens me, does that big Moor ! I believe him to be capable of anything."

" Silly child ! you have more reason to be afraid for him when he is with me."

At this moment Lisbeth came in.

" My dear little pet Nanny, what an age since we met ! " cried Valérie. " I am so unhappy ! Crevel bores me to death ; and Wenceslas is gone—we quarreled."

" I know," said Lisbeth, " and that is what brings me here. Victorin met him at about five in the afternoon going into an eating-house at five-and-twenty sous, and he brought him home, hungry, by working on his feelings, to the Rue Louis-le-Grand. Hortense, seeing Wenceslas lean and ill and badly dressed, held out her hand. This is how you throw me over and——"

" Monsieur Henri, madame," the manservant announced in a low voice to Valérie.

" Leave me now, Betty ; I will explain it all to-morrow." But, as will be seen, Valérie was ere long not in a state to explain anything to anybody.

Toward the end of May, Baron Hulot's pension was released by Victorin's regular payments to Baron Nucingen. As everybody knows, pensions are paid half-yearly, and only on the presentation of a certificate that the recipient is alive ; and as Hulot's residence was unknown, the arrears unpaid on Vauvinet's demand remained to his credit in the Treasury. Vauvinet now signed his renunciation of any further claims, but it was still indispensable to find the pensioner before the arrears could be drawn.

Thanks to Bianchon's care, the baroness had recovered her health ; and to this Josépha's good heart had contributed by a letter, of which the orthography betrayed the collaboration of the Duc d'Hérouville. This was what the singer wrote to the baroness, after twenty days of anxious search—

" MADAME LA BARONNE :—Monsieur Hulot was living, two months since, in the Rue des Bernardins, with Élodie Chardin, a lace-mender, for whom he had left Mademoiselle Bijou; but he went away without a word, leaving everything behind him, and no one knows where he went. I am not without hope, however, and I have put a man on his track who believes he has already seen him in the Boulevard Bourdon.

"The poor Jewess means to keep the promise she made to the Christian. Will the angel pray for the devil ? That must sometimes happen in heaven. I remain, with the deepest respect, always your humble servant, JOSÉPHA MIRAH."

The lawyer, Maître Hulot d'Ervy, hearing no more of the dreadful Madame Nourrisson, seeing his father-in-law married, having brought back his brother-in-law to the family fold, suffering from no importunity on the part of his new step-mother, and seeing his mother's health improve daily, gave himself up to his political and judicial duties, swept along by the tide of Paris life, in which the hours count for days.

One night, toward the end of the session, having occasion to write up a report to the Chamber of Deputies, he was obliged to sit at work till late at night. He had gone into his study at nine o'clock, and, while waiting till the man-servant should bring in the candles with green shades, his thoughts turned to his father. He was blaming himself for leaving the inquiry so much to the singer, and had resolved to see Monsieur Chapuzot himself on the morrow, when he saw in the twilight, outside the window, a handsome old head, bald and yellow, with a fringe of white hair.

"Would you please to give orders, sir, that a poor hermit is to be admitted, just come from the desert, and who is instructed to beg for contributions toward rebuilding a holy house."

This apparition, which suddenly reminded the lawyer of a prophecy uttered by the terrible Nourrisson, gave him a shock.

"Let in that old man," said he to the servant.

"He will poison the place, sir," replied the man. "He has on a brown gown which he has never changed since he left Syria, and he has no shirt——"

"Show him in," repeated the master.

The old man came in. Victorin's keen eye examined this so-called pilgrim hermit, and he saw a fine specimen of the Neapolitan friars, whose frocks are akin to the rags of the *lazzaroni* (beggars), whose sandals are tatters of leather, as the friars are tatters of humanity. The get-up was so perfect that the lawyer, though still on his guard, was vexed with him-self for having believed it to be one of Madame Nourrisson's tricks.

"How much do you want of me?"

"Whatever you feel that you ought to give."

Victorin took a five-franc piece from a little pile on his table, and handed it to the stranger.

"That is not much on account of fifty thousand francs," said the pilgrim of the desert.

This speech removed all Victorin's doubts.

"And has heaven kept its word?" he said, with a frown.

"The question is an offense, my son," said the hermit. "If you do not choose to pay till after the funeral, you are in your rights. I will return in a week's time."

"The funeral!" cried the lawyer, starting up.

"The world moves on," said the old man, as he withdrew, "and the dead move quickly in Paris!"

When Hulot, who stood looking down, was about to reply, the stalwart old man had vanished.

"I don't understand one word of all this," said Victorin to himself. "But at the end of the week I will ask him again about my father, if we have not yet found him. Where does Madame Nourrisson—yes, that is her real name—pick up such actors?"

On the following day, Dr. Bianchon allowed the baroness to go down into the garden, after examining Lisbeth, who had been obliged to keep to her room for a month by a slight bronchial attack. The learned doctor, who dared not pronounce a definite opinion on Lisbeth's case till he had seen some decisive symptoms, went into the garden with Adeline to observe the effect of the fresh air on her nervous trembling after two months of seclusion. He was interested and allured by the hope of curing this nervous complaint. On seeing the great physician sitting with them and sparing them a few minutes, the baroness and her family conversed with him on general subjects.

"Your life is a very full and a very sad one," said Madame Hulot. "I know what it is to spend one's days in seeing poverty and physical suffering."

"I know, madame," replied the doctor, "all the scenes of which charity compels you to be a spectator; but you will get used to it in time, as we all do. It is the law of existence. The confessor, the magistrate, the lawyer would find life unendurable if the spirit of the State did not assert itself above the feelings of the individual. Could we live at all but for that? Is not the soldier in time of war brought face to face with spectacles even more dreadful than those we see? And every soldier that has been under fire is kind-hearted. We medical men have the pleasure now and again of a successful cure, as you have that of saving a family from the horrors of hunger, depravity, or misery, and of restoring it to social respectability. But what comfort can the magistrate find, the police agent, or the attorney, who spend their lives in investigating the basest schemes of self-interest, the social monster whose only regret is when it fails, but on whom repentance never dawns?

"One-half of society spends its life in watching the other half. A very old friend of mine is an attorney, now retired, who told me that for fifteen years past notaries and lawyers have distrusted their clients quite as much as their adversaries. Your son is a pleader; has he never found himself compromised by the client for whom he held a brief?"

"Very often," said Victorin, with a smile.

"And what is the cause of this deep-seated evil?" asked the baroness.

"The decay of religion," said Bianchon, "and the preëminence of finance, which is simply solidified selfishness. Money used not to be everything; there were some kinds of superiority that ranked above it—nobility, genius, service done to the State. But nowadays the law takes wealth as the universal standard, and regards it as the measure of public capacity. Certain magistrates are ineligible to the Chamber; Jean-Jacques Rousseau would be ineligible! The perpetual subdivision of estates compels every man to take care of himself from the age of twenty.

"Well, then, between the necessity for making a fortune and the depravity of speculation there is no check or hindrance; for the religious sense is wholly lacking in France, in spite of the laudable endeavors of those who are working for a Catholic revival. And this is the opinion of every man who, like me, studies society at the core."

"And you have few pleasures?" said Hortense.

" The true physician, madame, is in love with his science," replied the doctor. " He is sustained by that passion as much as by the sense of his usefulness to society.

" At this very time you see me in a sort of scientific rapture, and many superficial judges would regard me as a man devoid of feeling. I have to announce a discovery to-morrow to the College of Medicine, for I am studying a disease that had disappeared—a mortal disease for which no cure is known in temperate climates, though it is curable in the West Indies —a malady known here in the Middle Ages. A noble fight is that of the physician against such a disease. For the last ten days I have thought of nothing but these cases—for there are two, a husband and wife. Are they not connections of yours? For you, madame, are surely Monsieur Crevel's daughter?" said he, addressing Célestine.

"What, is my father your patient?" asked Célestine. "Living in the Rue Barbet-de-Jouy?"

" Precisely so," said Bianchon.

"And the disease is inevitably fatal?" said Victorin in dismay.

" I will go to see him," said Célestine, rising.

" I positively forbid it, madame," Bianchon quietly said. " The disease is contagious."

" But you go there, monsieur," replied the young woman. " Do you think that a daughter's duty is less binding than a doctor's?"

" Madame, a physician knows how to protect himself against infection, and the rashness of your devotion proves to me that you would probably be less prudent than I."

Célestine, however, got up and went to her room, where she dressed to go out.

"Monsieur," said Victorin to Bianchon, " have you any hope of saving Monsieur and Madame Crevel?"

" I hope, but I do not believe that I can," said Bianchon.

"The case is to me quite inexplicable. The disease is peculiar to negroes and the American tribes, whose skin is differently constituted to that of the white races. Now I can trace no connection with the copper-colored tribes, with negroes or half-castes, in Monsieur or Madame Crevel.

"And though it is a very interesting disease to us, it is a terrible thing for the sufferers. The poor woman, who is said to have been very pretty, is punished for her sins, for she is now squalidly hideous if she is still anything at all. She is losing her hair and teeth, her skin is like a leper's, she is a horror to herself; her hands are horrible, covered with greenish pustules, her nails are loose, and the flesh is eaten away by the poisoned humors."

"And the cause of such a disease?" asked the lawyer.

"Oh!" said the doctor, "the cause lies in a form of rapid blood-poisoning; it generates with most terrific rapidity. I hope to act on the blood; I am having it analyzed; and I am now going home to ascertain the result of the labors of my friend Professor Duval, the famous chemist, with a view to trying one of those desperate measures by which we sometimes attempt to defeat death."

"The hand of God is there!" said Adeline, in a voice husky with emotion. "Though that woman has brought sorrows on me which have led me in moments of madness to invoke the vengeance of heaven, I hope—God knows I hope—you may succeed, doctor."

Victorin felt dizzy. He looked at his mother, his sister, and the physician by turns, quaking lest they should read his thoughts. He felt himself a murderer.

Hortense, for her part, thought God was just.

Célestine came back to beg her husband to accompany her.

"If you insist on going, madame, and you too, monsieur, keep at least a foot between you and the bed of the sufferer, that is the chief precaution. Neither you nor your wife must dream of kissing the dying man. And, indeed, you ought to go with your wife, Monsieur Hulot, to hinder her from disobeying my injunctions."

Adeline and Hortense, when they were left alone, went to sit with Lisbeth. Hortense had such a virulent hatred of Valérie that she could not contain the expression of it.

"Cousin Betty," she exclaimed, "my mother and I are avenged! That venomous snake is herself bitten—she is rotting in her bed!"

"Hortense, at this moment you are not a Christian. You ought to pray God to vouchsafe repentance to this wretched woman," said Madame Hulot.

"What are you talking about?" said Betty, rising from her couch. "Are you speaking of Valérie?"

"Yes," replied Adeline; "she is past hope—dying of some horrible disease of which the mere description makes one shudder——"

Lisbeth's teeth chattered, a cold sweat broke out all over her; the violence of the shock showed how passionate her attachment to Valérie had been.

"I must go there," said she.

"But the doctor forbids your going out."

"I do not care—I must go! Poor Crevel! what a state he must be in; for he loves that woman."

"He is dying, too," replied Countess Steinbock. "Ah! all our enemies are in the devil's clutches——"

"In God's hands, my child——"

Lisbeth dressed in the famous yellow Indian shawl and her black velvet bonnet, and put on her shoes; in spite of her relations' remonstrances, she set out as if driven by some irresistible power.

She arrived in the Rue Barbet a few minutes after Monsieur and Madame Hulot, and found seven physicians there, brought by Bianchon to study this unique case; he had just joined them. The physicians, assembled in the drawing-room, were discussing the disease; now one and now another went into

5

Valérie's room or Crevel's to take a note, and returned with an opinion based on this rapid examination.

These princes of science were divided in their opinions. One, who stood alone in his views, considered it a case of poisoning, of private revenge, and denied its identity with the disease known in the Middle Ages. Three others regarded it as a specific deterioration of the blood and the humors. The rest, agreeing with Bianchon, maintained that the blood was poisoned by some hitherto unknown morbid infection. Bianchon produced Professor Duval's analysis of the blood. The remedies to be applied, though absolutely empirical and without hope, depended on the verdict in this medical dilemma.

Lisbeth stood as if petrified three yards away from the bed where Valérie lay dying, as she saw a priest from Saint-Thomas d'Aquin standing by her friend's pillow, and a sister of charity in attendance. Religion could find a soul to save in a mass of rottenness which, of the five senses of man, had now only that of sight. The sister of charity who alone had been found to nurse Valérie stood apart. Thus the Catholic religion, that divine institution, always actuated by the spirit of self-sacrifice, under its twofold aspect of the Spirit and the flesh, was tending this horrible and atrocious creature, soothing her deathbed by its infinite benevolence and inexhaustible stores of mercy.

The servants, in horror, refused to go into the room of either their master or mistress; they thought only of themselves, and judged their betters as righteously stricken. The smell was so foul that in spite of open windows and strong perfumes, no one could remain long in Valérie's room. Religion alone kept guard there.

How could a woman so clever as Valérie fail to ask herself to what end these two representatives of the church remained with her? The dying woman had listened to the words of the priest. Repentance had risen on her darkened soul as the devouring malady had consumed her beauty. The fragile Valérie had been less able to resist the inroads of the disease than Crevel; she would be the first to succumb, and, indeed, had been the first attacked.

"If I had not been ill myself, I would have come to nurse you," said Lisbeth at last, after a glance at her friend's sunken eyes. "I have kept my room this fortnight or three weeks; but when I heard of your state from the doctor, I came at once."

"Poor Lisbeth, you at least love me still, I see!" said Valérie. "Listen. I have only a day or two left to think, for I cannot say to live. You see, there is nothing left of me —I am a heap of filth! They will not let me see myself in a glass. Well, it is no more than I deserve. Oh, if I might only win mercy, I would gladly undo all the mischief I have done."

"Oh!" said Lisbeth, "if you can talk like that, you are indeed a dead woman."

"Do not hinder this woman's repentance, leave her in her Christian mind," said the priest.

"There is nothing left!" said Lisbeth in consternation. "I cannot recognize her eyes or her mouth! Not a feature of her is there! And her wit has deserted her! Oh, it is awful!"

"You don't know," said Valérie, "what death is; what it is to be obliged to think of the morrow of your last day on earth, and of what is to be found in the grave. Worms for the body—and for the soul, what? Lisbeth, I know there is another life! And I am given over to terrors which prevent my feeling the pangs of my decomposing body. I, who could laugh at a saint, and say to Crevel that the vengeance of God took every form of disaster. Well, I was a true prophet. Do not trifle with sacred things, Lisbeth; if you love me, repent as I do."

"I!" said Lisbeth. "I see vengeance wherever I turn in

nature; insects even die to satisfy the craving for revenge when they are attacked. And do not these gentlemen tell us "—and she looked at the priest—"that God is revenged, and that His vengeance lasts through all eternity?"

The priest looked mildly at Lisbeth and said—

"You, madame, are an atheist!"

"Nothing left of her. Her mind gone too," muttered Lisbeth.

"Yes, look what I have come to," said Valérie.

"And where did you get this gangrene?" asked the old maid, unmoved from her peasant incredulity.

"I had a letter from Henri which leaves me in no doubt as to my fate. He has murdered me. And—just when I meant to live honestly—to die an object of disgust!

"Lisbeth, give up all notions of revenge. Be kind to that family to whom I have left by my will everything I can dispose of. Go, child, though you are the only creature who, at this hour, does not avoid me with horror—go, I beseech you, and leave me. I have only time to make my peace with God!"

"She is wandering in her wits," said Lisbeth to herself, as she left the room.

The strongest affection ever known, that of a woman for a woman, had not such heroic constancy as the church. Lisbeth, stifled by the miasma, went away. She found the physicians still in consultation. But Bianchon's opinion carried the day, and the only question now was how to try the remedies.

"At any rate, we shall have a splendid *post-mortem*," said one of his opponents, "and there will be two cases to enable us to make comparisons."

Lisbeth came in again with Bianchon, who went up to the sick woman without seeming aware of the maladorous atmosphere.

"Madame," said he, "we intend to try a powerful remedy which may save you——"

"And if you save my life," said she, "shall I be as good-looking as ever?"

"Possibly," said the judicious physician.

"I know your 'possibly,'" said Valérie. "I shall look like a woman who has fallen into the fire! No, leave me to the church. I can please no one now but God. I will try to be reconciled to Him, and that will be my last flirtation; yes, I must try to come round God!"

"That is my poor Valérie's last jest; that is all herself!" said Lisbeth in tears.

Lisbeth thought it her duty to go into Crevel's room, where she found Victorin and his wife sitting about a yard away from the stricken man's bed.

"Betty," said he, "they will not tell me what state my wife is in; you have just seen her—how is she?"

"She is better; she says she is saved," replied Lisbeth, allowing herself this play on the word to soothe Crevel's mind.

"That is well," said the mayor. "I feared lest I had been the cause of her illness. A man is not a traveler in perfumery for nothing; I had blamed myself. If I should lose her, what would become of me? On my honor, my children, I worship that woman."

He sat up in bed and tried to assume his favorite position.

"Oh, papa!" cried Célestine, "if only you could be well again, I would make friends with my stepmother—I make a vow!"

"Poor little Célestine!" said Crevel, "come and kiss me."

Victorin held back his wife, who was rushing forward.

"You do not know, perhaps," said the lawyer gently, "that your disease is contagious, monsieur?"

"To be sure," replied Crevel. "And the doctors are quite proud of having rediscovered in me some long-lost plague of the Middle Ages, which the Faculty has had cried like lost property—it is very funny!"

"Papa," said Célestine, "be brave, and you will get the better of this disease."

"Be quite easy, my children; Death thinks twice of it before carrying off a mayor of Paris," said he, with monstrous composure. "And if, after all, my district is so unfortunate as to lose a man it has twice honored with its suffrages—you see what a flow of words I have! Well, I shall know how to pack up and go. I have been a commercial traveler; I am experienced in such matters. Ah! my children, I am a man of strong mind."

"Papa, promise me to admit the church——"

"Never," replied Crevel. "What is to be said? I drank the milk of Revolution; I have not Baron Holbach's wit, but I have his strength of mind. I am more Regency than ever, more musketeer, Abbé Dubois, and Maréchal de Richelieu! By the Holy Poker! My wife, who is wandering in her head, has just sent a man in a cassock to me—to *me!* the admirer of Béranger, the friend of Lisette, the son of Voltaire and Jean-Jacques. The doctor, to feel my pulse, as it were, and see if sickness had subdued me—'You saw Monsieur l'Abbé,' said he. Well, I imitated the great Montesquieu. Yes, I looked at the doctor—see, like this"—and he turned to show three-quarters face, like his portrait, and extended his hand authoritatively—"and I said—

> "'The slave he came,
> And showed his order, but he left with shame.'

"'His Order' is a pretty jest, showing that even in death Monsieur le Président de Montesquieu preserved his elegant wit, for they had sent him a jesuit. I admire that passage—I cannot say of his life, but of his death—the passage—another joke! The passage from life to death—the Passage-Montesquieu!"

Victorin gazed sadly at his father-in-law, wondering whether folly and vanity were not forces on a par with true greatness of soul. The causes that act on the springs of the soul seem to be quite independent of the results. Can it be that the fortitude which upholds a great criminal is the same as that with which a Champcenetz so proudly walks to the scaffold?

By the end of the week Madame Crevel was buried, after dreadful sufferings; and Crevel followed her within two days. Thus the marriage-contract was annulled. Crevel was heir to Valérie.

On the very day after the funeral, the friar called again on the lawyer, who received him in perfect silence. The monk held out his hand without a word, and without a word Victorin Hulot gave him eighty thousand-franc notes, taken from a sum of money found in Crevel's desk.

Young Madame Hulot inherited the estate of Presles and thirty thousand francs a year.

Madame Crevel had bequeathed a sum of three hundred thousand francs to Baron Hulot. Her scrofulous boy Stanislas was to inherit, at his majority, the Hôtel Crevel and eighty thousand francs a year.

Among the many noble associations founded in Paris by Catholic charity, there is one, originated by Madame de la Chanterie, for promoting civil and religious marriages between persons who have formed a voluntary but illicit union. Legislators, who draw large revenues from the registration fees, and the Bourgeois dynasty, which benefits by the notary's profits, affect to overlook the fact that three-fourths of the poorer class cannot afford fifteen francs for the marriage-contract. In this the corporation of notaries is inferior to that of the pleaders in Paris. The pleaders, a sufficiently vilified body, gratuitously defend the cases of the indigent, while the notaries have not as yet agreed to charge nothing for the marriage-contract of the poor. As to the revenue collectors, the whole machinery of Government would have to be dislocated

to induce the authorities to relax their demands.   The registrar's office is deaf and dumb.

Then the church, too, receives a duty on marriages.   In
France the church depends largely on such revenues ; even in
the House of God it traffics in chairs and kneeling stools in a
way that offends foreigners ; though it cannot have forgotten
the anger of the Saviour who drove the money-changers out
of the Temple.   If the church is so loth to relinquish its dues,
it must be supposed that these dues, known as vestry dues, are
one of its sources of maintenance, and then the fault of the
church is the fault of the State.

The coöperation of these conditions, at a time when charity
is too greatly concerned with the woes of the negro and the
petty offenders discharged from prison to trouble itself about
honest people in difficulties, results in the existence of a number of decent couples who have never been legally married
for lack of thirty francs, the lowest figure for which the notary,
the registrar, the mayor, and the church will unite two citizens
of Paris.   Madame de la Chanterie's fund, founded to restore
poor households to their religious and legal status, hunts up
such couples, and with all the more success because it helps
them in their poverty before attacking their unlawful union.

As soon as Madame Hulot had recovered, she returned to
her occupations.   And then it was that the admirable Madame
de la Chanterie came to beg that Adeline would add the legali-
zation of these voluntary unions to the other good works of
which she was the instrument.

One of the baroness' first efforts in this cause was made in
the ominous-looking district, formerly known as la Petite
Pologne—Little Poland—bounded by the Rue du Rocher,
Rue de la Pépinière, and Rue de Miroménil.   There exists
there a sort of offshoot of the Faubourg Saint-Marceau.   To
give an idea of this part of the town, it is enough to say that
the landlords of some of the houses tenanted by workingmen
without work, by dangerous characters, and by the very poor

employed in unhealthy toil, dare not demand their rents, and can find no bailiffs bold enough to evict insolvent lodgers. At the present time speculating builders, who are fast changing the aspect of this corner of Paris, and covering the waste ground lying between the Rue d'Amsterdam and the Rue Faubourg-du-Roule, will no doubt alter the character of the inhabitants; for the trowel is a more civilizing agent than is generally supposed. By erecting substantial and handsome houses, with janitors at the doors, by bordering the streets with footwalks and stores, speculation, while raising the rents, disperses the squalid class, families bereft of furniture, and lodgers that cannot pay. And so these districts are cleared of such objectionable residents, and the dens vanish into which the police never venture unless in the pursuit of criminals.

In June, 1844, the purlieus of the Place de Laborde were still far from inviting. The genteel pedestrian, who, by chance, should turn out of the Rue de la Pépinière into one of these dreadful side-streets, would have been dismayed to see how vile a bohemia dwelt cheek by jowl with the aristocracy. In such places as these, haunted by ignorant poverty and misery driven to bay, flourish the last public letter-writers who are to be found in Paris. Wherever you see the two words "Écrivain Public" written in a fine copy hand on a sheet of letter-paper stuck to the window-pane of some low entresol or mud-splashed first-floor room, you may safely conclude that the neighborhood is the lurking place of many unlettered folk, and of much vice and crime, the outcome of misery; for ignorance is the mother of all sorts of crime. A crime is, in the first instance, a defect of reasoning power.

While the baroness had been ill, this quarter, to which she was a minor Providence, had seen the advent of a public writer who settled in the Passage du Soleil—Sun Alley—a spot of which the name is one of the antitheses dear to the Parisian, for the passage is especially dark. This writer, supposed to be a German, was named Vyder, and he lived on matrimonial terms with a young creature of whom he was so jealous that he never allowed her to go anywhere except to some honest stove and flue-fitters, in the Rue Saint-Lazare, Italians, as such fitters always are, but long since established in Paris. These people had been saved from a bankruptcy, which would have reduced them to misery, by the baroness, acting in behalf of Madame de la Chanterie. In a few months comfort had taken the place of poverty, and Religion had found a home in hearts which once had cursed heaven with the energy peculiar to Italian stove-fitters.

So one of Madame Hulot's first visits was to this family. She was pleased at the scene that presented itself to her eyes at the back of the house where this worthy family lived in the Rue Saint-Lazare, not far from the Rue du Rocher. High above the stores and workshops, now well filled, where toiled a swarm of apprentices and workmen—all Italians from the valley of Domo d'Ossola—the master's family occupied a set of rooms, which hard work had blessed with abundance. The baroness was hailed like the Virgin Mary in person.

After a quarter of an hour's questioning, Adeline, having to wait for the father to inquire how his business was prospering, pursued her saintly calling as a spy by asking whether they knew of any families living out of the pale of wedlock.

"Ah! dear lady, you who could save the damned from hell!" said the Italian wife, "there is a girl quite near here to be saved from perdition."

"A girl well known to you?" asked the baroness.

"She is the granddaughter of a master my husband formerly worked for, who came to France in 1798, after the Revolution, by name Judici. Old Judici, in Napoleon's time, was one of the principal stove-fitters in Paris; he died in 1819, leaving his son a fine fortune. But the younger Judici wasted all his money on bad women; till, at last, he married one who was sharper than the rest, and she had this poor little girl, who is just turned fifteen."

"And what is wrong with her?" asked Adeline, struck by the resemblance between this Judici and her husband.

"Well, madame, this child, named Atala, ran away from her father, and came to live close by here with an old German of eighty at least, named Vyder, who does odd jobs for people who cannot read and write. Now, if this old sinner, who bought the child of her mother, they say, for fifteen hundred francs, would but marry her, as he certainly has not long to live, and as he is said to have some few thousands of francs a year—well, the poor thing, who is a sweet little angel, would be out of mischief, and above want, which must be the ruin of her."

"Thank you very much for the information. I may do some good, but I must act with caution. Who is the old man?"

"Oh! madame, he is a good old fellow; he makes the child very happy, and he has some sense too, for he left the part of town where the Judicis live, as I believe, to snatch the child from her mother's clutches. The mother was jealous of her, and I dare say she thought she could make money out of her beauty and make a ' Mademoiselle ' of the girl.

"Atala remembered us, and advised her gentleman to settle near us; and as the goodman sees how decent we are, he allows her to come here. But get them married, madame, and you will do an action worthy of you. Once married, the child will be independent and free from her mother, who keeps an eye on her, and who, if she could make money by her, would like to see her on the stage, or successful in the wicked life she meant her to lead."

"Why doesn't the old man marry her?"

"There was no necessity for it, you see," said the Italian. "And though old Vyder is not a bad old fellow, I fancy he is sharp enough to wish to remain the master, while if he once got married—why, the poor man is afraid of the stone that hangs round every old husband's neck."

"Could you send for the girl to come here?" said Madame Hulot. "I should see her quietly, and find out what could be done——"

The stove-fitter's wife signed to her eldest girl, who ran off. Ten minutes later she returned, leading by the hand a child of fifteen and a-half, a beauty of the Italian type. Mademoiselle Judici inherited from her father that ivory skin which, rather yellow by day, is by artificial light of lily-whiteness; eyes of Oriental beauty, form, and brilliancy, close curling lashes like black feathers, hair of ebony hue, and that native dignity of the Lombard race which makes the foreigner, as he walks through Milan on a Sunday, fancy that every porter's daughter is a princess.

Atala, told by the stove-fitter's daughter that she was to meet the great lady of whom she had heard so much, had hastily dressed in a black silk gown, a smart little cape, and neat shoes. A cap with a cherry-colored bow added to the brilliant effect of her coloring. The child stood in an attitude of artless curiosity, studying the baroness out of the corner of her eye, for her palsied trembling puzzled her greatly.

Adeline sighed deeply as she saw this jewel of womanhood in the mire of prostitution, and determined to rescue her to virtue.

"What is your name, my dear?"

"Atala, madame."

"And can you read and write?"

"No, madame; but that does not matter, as monsieur can."

"Did your parents ever take you to church? Have you been to your first communion? Do you know your catechism?"

"Madame," said Atala Judici, "papa wanted to make me do something of the kind you speak of, but mamma would not have it——"

"Your mother?" exclaimed the baroness. "Is she bad to you, then?"

"She was always beating me. I don't know why, but I was always being quarreled over by my father and mother——"

"Did you never hear of God?" cried the baroness.

The girl looked up wide-eyed.

"Oh yes, papa and mamma often said 'Good God,' and 'In God's name,' and 'God's thunder,'" said she, with perfect simplicity.

"Then you never saw a church? Did you never think of going into one?"

"A church?—Notre-Dame, the Panthéon? I have seen them from a distance, when papa took me into town; but that was not very often. There are no churches like those in the Faubourg."

"Which Faubourg did you live in?"

"In the Faubourg."

"Yes, but which?"

"In the Rue de Charonne, madame."

The inhabitants of the Faubourg Saint-Antoine never call that notorious district other than *the* Faubourg. To them it is the one and only Faubourg; and manufacturers generally understand the words as meaning the Faubourg Saint-Antoine.

"Did no one ever tell you what was right or wrong?"

"Mamma used to beat me when I did not do what pleased her."

"But did you not know that it was very wicked to run away from your father and mother to go to live with an old man?" asked Madame Hulot.

Atala Judici gazed at the baroness with a haughty stare, but made no reply.

"She is a perfect little savage," murmured Adeline.

"There are a great many like her in the Faubourg, madame," said the stove-fitter's wife.

"But she knows nothing—not even what is wrong. Good

heavens! Why do you not answer me?" said Madame Hulot, putting out her hand to take Atala's.

Atala indignantly withdrew a step.

"You are an old fool!" said she. "Why, my father and mother had had nothing to eat for a week. My mother wanted to make something bad of me, I think, for my father thrashed her and called her a thief! However, Monsieur Vyder paid all their debts, and gave them some money—oh, a bagful! And he brought me away, and poor papa was crying. But we had to part! Was it wicked?" she asked.

"And are you very fond of Monsieur Vyder?"

"Fond of him?" said she. "I should think so! He tells me beautiful stories, madame, every evening; and he has given me nice gowns, and linen, and a shawl. Why, I am figged out like a princess, and I never wear sabots now. And, then, I have not known what it is to be hungry these two months past. And I don't live on potatoes now. He brings me bonbons and burnt almonds, and chocolate almonds. Aren't they good? I do anything he pleases for a bag of chocolate. Then my old daddy is very kind; he takes such care of me, and is so nice; I know now what my mother ought to have been. He is going to get an old woman to help me, for he doesn't like me to dirty my hands with cooking. For the last month, too, he has been making a little money, and he gives me three francs every evening that I put into a money-box. Only he will never let me go out except to come here—and he calls me his little kitten! Mamma never called me anything but bad names—and thief, and vermin!"

"Well, then, my child, why should not Daddy Vyder be your husband?"

"But he is, madame," said the girl, looking at Adeline with calm pride, without a blush, her brow smooth, her eyes steady. "He told me I was his little wife; but it is a horrid bore to be a man's wife—if it were not for the burnt almonds!"

"Good heavens!" said the baroness to herself, "what monster can have had the heart to betray such perfect, such holy innocence? To restore this child to the ways of virtue would surely atone for many sins. I knew what I was doing," thought she, remembering the scene with Crevel. "But she —she knows nothing."

"Do you know Monsieur Samanon?" asked Atala, with an insinuating look.

"No, my child; but why do you ask?"

"Really and truly?" said the artless girl.

"You have nothing to fear from this lady," said the Italian woman. "She is an angel."

"It is because my good old boy is afraid of being caught by Samanon. He is hiding, and I wish he could be altogether free——"

"Why?"

"Oh! then he would take me to Bobino, perhaps to the Ambigu."

"What a delightful creature!" said the baroness, kissing the girl.

"Are you rich?" asked Atala, who was fingering the baroness' lace ruffles.

"Yes, and No," replied Madame Hulot. "I am rich for dear little girls like you when they are willing to be taught their duties as Christians by a priest, and to walk in the right way."

"What way is that?" said Atala; "I walk on my two feet."

"The way of virtue."

Atala looked at the baroness with a crafty smile.

"Look at madame," said the baroness, pointing to the stove-fitter's wife, "she has been quite happy because she was received into the bosom of the church. You married like the beasts that perish."

"I?" said Atala. "Why, if you will give me as much as

Daddy Vyder gives me, I shall be quite happy unmarried again. It is a grind. Do you know what it is to——?"

"But when once you are united to a man as you are," the baroness put in, "virtue requires you to remain faithful to him."

"Till he dies," said Atala, with a knowing flash. "I shall not have to wait long. If you only knew how Daddy Vyder coughs and blows. Poof, poof," and she imitated the old man.

"Virtue and morality require that the church, representing God, and the mayor, representing the law, should consecrate your marriage," Madame Hulot went on. "Look at madame; she is legally married——"

"Will it make it more amusing?" asked the girl.

"You will be happier," said the baroness, "for no one then could blame you. You would satisfy God! Ask her if she was married without the sacrament of marriage!"

Atala looked at the Italian.

"How is she any better than I am?" she asked. "I am prettier than she is."

"Yes, but I am an honest woman," said the wife, "and you may be called by a bad name."

"How can you expect God to protect you if you trample every law, human and divine, under foot?" said the baroness. "Don't you know that God has paradise in store for those who obey the injunctions of His church?"

"What is there in paradise? Are there playhouses?"

"Paradise!" said Adeline, "is every joy you can conceive of. It is full of angels with white wings. You see God in all His glory, you share His power, you are happy for every minute of eternity!"

Atala listened to the lady as she might have listened to music; but Adeline, seeing that she was incapable of understanding her, thought she had better take another line of action and speak to the old man.

"Go home, then, my child, and I will go to see Monsieur Vyder. Is he a Frenchman?"

"He is an Alsatian, madame. But he will be quite rich soon. If you would pay what he owes to that vile Samanon, he would give you back your money, for in a few months he will be getting six thousand francs a year, he says, and we are to go to live in the country a long way off, in the Vosges."

At the word Vosges the baroness sat lost in reverie. It called up the vision of her native village. She was roused from her melancholy meditation by the entrance of the stove-fitter, who came to assure her of his prosperity.

"In a year's time, madame, I can repay the money you lent us, for it is God's money, the money of the poor and wretched. If ever I make a fortune, come to me for what you want, and I will render through you the help to others which you first brought us."

"Just now," said Madame Hulot, "I do not need your money, but I ask your assistance in a good work. I have just seen that little Judici, who is living with an old man, and I mean to see them regularly and legally married."

"Ah! old Vyder; he is a very worthy old fellow, with plenty of good sense. The poor old man has already made friends in the neighborhood, though he has been here but two months. He keeps my accounts for me. He is, I believe, a brave colonel who served the Emperor well. And how he adores Napoleon! He has some orders, but he never wears them. He is waiting till he is straight again, for he is in debt, poor old boy! In fact, I believe he is hiding, threatened by the law——"

"Tell him that I will pay his debts if he will marry the child."

"Oh, that will soon be settled. Suppose you were to see him, madame; it is not two steps away, in the Passage du Soleil."

6

So the lady and the stove-fitter went out.

"This way, madame," said the man, turning down the Rue de la Pépinière.

The alley runs, in fact, from the bottom of this street through to the Rue du Rocher. Half-way down this passage, recently opened through, where the stores let at a very low rent, the baroness saw on the window, screened up to a height with a green gauze curtain, which excluded the prying eyes of the passer-by, the words—

"ÉCRIVAIN PUBLIC;" and on the door the announcement—

BUSINESS TRANSACTED.

Petitions Drawn Up, Accounts Audited, Etc.

With Secrecy and Dispatch.

The store was like one of the little offices where travelers by omnibus await the vehicles to take them on to their destination. A private staircase led up, no doubt, to the living rooms on the entresol which were let with the store. Madame Hulot saw a dirty writing-table of some light wood, some letter-boxes, and a wretched second-hand chair. A cap with a peak and a greasy green shade for the eyes suggested either precautions for disguise or weak eyes, which was not unlikely in an old man.

"He is upstairs," said the stove-fitter. "I will go up and tell him to come down."

Adeline lowered her veil and took a seat. A heavy step made the narrow stairs creak, and Adeline could not restrain a piercing cry when she saw her husband, Baron Hulot, in a gray knitted jersey, old gray flannel trousers, and slippers.

"What is your business, madame?" said Hulot, with a flourish.

She rose, seized Hulot by the arm, and said in a voice hoarse with emotion—

"At last—I have found you!"

"Adeline!" exclaimed the baron in bewilderment, and he locked the store-door. "Joseph, go out the back way," he added to the stove-fitter.

"My dear!" she said, forgetting everything in her excessive joy, "you can come home to us all; we are rich. Your son draws a hundred and sixty thousand francs a year! Your pension is released; there are fifteen thousand francs of arrears you can get on showing that you are alive. Valérie is dead, and left you three hundred thousand francs.

"Your name is quite forgotten by this time; you may reappear in the world, and you will find a fortune awaiting you at your son's house. Come; our happiness will be complete. For nearly three years have I been seeking you, and I felt so sure of finding you that a room is ready waiting for you. Oh! come away from this, come away from the dreadful state I see you in!"

"I am very willing," said the bewildered baron, "but can I take the girl?"

"Hector, give her up! Do that much for your Adeline, who has never before asked you to make the smallest sacrifice. I promise you I will give the child a marriage portion; I will see that she marries well, and has some education. Let it be said of one of the women who have given you happiness that she, too, is happy; and did not relapse into vice, into the mire."

"So it was you," said the baron, with a smile, "who wanted to see me married? Wait a few minutes," he added, "I will go upstairs and dress; I have some decent clothes in a trunk."

Adeline, left alone, and looking round the squalid den, melted into tears.

"He has been living here, and we rolling in wealth!" said she to herself. "Poor man, he has indeed been punished— he who was elegance itself."

The stove-fitter returned to make his bow to his benefactress, and she desired him to fetch a coach. When he came back, she begged him to give little Atala Judici a home, and to take her away at once.

"And tell her that if she will place herself under the guidance of Monsieur the Curé of the Madeleine, on the day when she attends her first communion I will give her thirty thousand francs and find her a good husband, some worthy young man."

"My eldest son, then, madame! He is two-and-twenty, and he worships the child."

The baron now came down; there were tears in his eyes.

"You are forcing me to desert the only creature who has ever begun to love me at all as you do!" said he in a whisper to his wife. "She is crying bitterly, and I cannot abandon her so——"

"Be quite easy, Hector. She will find a home with honest people, and I will answer for her conduct."

"Well, then, I can go with you," said the baron, escorting his wife to the cab.

Hector, the Baron d'Ervy once more, had put on a blue coat and trousers, a white vest, a black stock, and gloves. When the baroness had taken her seat in the vehicle, Atala slipped in like an eel.

"Oh, madame," she said, "let me go with you. I will be so good, so obedient; I will do whatever you wish; but do not part me from my Daddy Vyder, my kind daddy, who gives me such nice things. I shall be beaten——"

"Come, come, Atala," said the baron, "this lady is my wife—we must part——"

"She? As old as that! and shaking like a leaf!" said the child. "Look at her head!" and she laughingly mimicked the baroness' palsy.

The stove-fitter, who had run after the girl, came to the carriage-door.

"Take her away!" said Adeline. The man put his arms round Atala and fairly carried her off.

"Thanks for such a sacrifice, my dearest," said Adeline, taking the baron's hand and clutching it with delirious joy. "How much you are altered! you must have suffered so much! What a surprise for Hortense and for your son!"

Adeline talked as lovers talk who meet after a long absence, of a hundred things at once.

In ten minutes the baron and his wife reached the Rue Louis-le-Grand, and there Adeline found this note awaiting her:

"MADAME LA BARONNE:—Monsieur le Baron Hulot d'Ervy lived for one month in the Rue de Charonne under the name of Thorec, an anagram of Hector. He now is in the Passage de Soleil by the name of Vyder. He says he is an Alsatian, and does writing, and he lives with a girl named Atala Judici. Be very cautious, madame, for search is on foot; the baron is wanted, on what score I know not.

"The actress has kept her word, and remains as ever,

"Madame le Baronne, your humble servant,

"J. M."

The baron's return was hailed with such joy as reconciled him to domestic life. He forgot little Atala Judici, for excesses of profligacy had reduced him to the volatility of feeling that is characteristic of childhood. But the happiness of the family was dashed by the change that had come over him. He had been still hale when he had gone away from his home; he had come back almost a hundred, broken, bent, and his expression even debased.

A splendid dinner, improvised by Célestine, reminded the old man of the singer's banquets; he was dazzled by the splendor of his home.

"A feast in honor of the return of the prodigal father?" said he in a murmur to Adeline.

"Hush!" said she, "all is forgotten."

"And Betty?" he asked, not seeing the old maid.

"I am sorry to say she is in bed," replied Hortense. "She can never get up, and we shall have the grief of losing her ere long.

"She hopes to see you after dinner."

At daybreak next morning Victorin Hulot was informed by the porter's wife that soldiers of the municipal guard were posted all around the premises; the police demanded Baron Hulot. The bailiff, who had followed the woman, laid a summons in due form before the lawyer, and asked him whether he meant to pay his father's debts. The claim was for ten thousand francs at the suit of a usurer named Samanon, who had probably lent the baron two or three thousand at most. Victorin desired the bailiff to dismiss his men, and paid.

"But is it the last?" he anxiously wondered.

Lisbeth, miserable already at seeing the family so prosperous, could not survive this happy event. She grew so rapidly worse that Bianchon gave her but a week to live, conquered at last in the long struggle in which she had scored so many victories.

She kept the secret of her hatred even through a painful death from pulmonary consumption. And, indeed, she had the supreme satisfaction of seeing Adeline, Hortense, Hulot, Victorin, Steinbock, Célestine, and their children standing in tears around her bed and mourning for her as the angel of the family.

Baron Hulot, enjoying a course of solid food such as he had not known for nearly three years, recovered flesh and strength, and was almost himself again. This improvement was such a joy to Adeline that her nervous trembling perceptibly diminished.

"She will be happy after all," said Lisbeth to herself on the day before she died, as she saw the veneration with which the baron regarded his wife, of whose sufferings he had heard from Hortense and Victorin.

And vindictiveness hastened Cousin Betty's end. The family followed her, weeping, to the grave.

The baron and baroness, having reached the age which looks for perfect rest, gave up the handsome rooms on the second floor to the Count and Countess Steinbock, and took those above. The baron by his son's exertions found an official position in the management of a railroad, in 1845, with a salary of six thousand francs, which, added to the six thousand of his pension and the money left to him by Madame Crevel, secured him an income of twenty-four thousand francs. Hortense having enjoyed her independent income during the three years of separation from Wenceslas, Victorin now invested the two hundred thousand francs he had in trust, in his sister's name, and he allowed her twelve thousand francs annually.

Wenceslas, as the husband of a rich woman, was not unfaithful, but he was an idler; he could not make up his mind to begin any work, however trifling. Once more he became the artist *in partibus;* he was popular in society, and consulted by amateurs; in short, he became a critic, like all the feeble folk who fall below their promise.

Thus each household, though living as one family, had its own fortune. The baroness, taught by bitter experience, left the management of matters to her son, and the baron was thus reduced to his salary, in the hope that the smallness of his income would prevent his relapsing into mischief. And by some singular good fortune, on which neither the mother nor the son had reckoned, Hulot seemed to have forsworn the fair sex. His subdued behavior, ascribed to the course of nature, so completely reassured the family, that they enjoyed to the full his recovered amiability and delightful qualities. He was unfailingly attentive to his wife and children, escorted them to the play, reappeared in society, and did the honors of his son's house with exquisite grace. In short, this reclaimed prodigal was the joy of his family.

He was a most agreeable old man, a ruin, but full of wit, having retained no more of his vice than made it an added social grace.

Of course, everybody was quite satisfied and easy. The young people and the baroness lauded the model father to the skies, forgetting the death of the two uncles. Life cannot go on without much forgetting!

Madame Victorin, who managed this enormous household with great skill, due, no doubt, to Lisbeth's training, had found it necessary to have a man-cook. This again necessitated a kitchen-maid. Kitchen-maids are in these days ambitious creatures, eager to detect the chef's secrets, and to become cooks as soon as they have learnt to stir a sauce. Consequently, the kitchen-maid is liable to frequent change.

At the beginning of 1845 Célestine engaged as kitchen-maid a sturdy Normandy peasant come from Isigny—short-waisted, with strong red arms, a common face, as dull as an "occasional piece" at the play, and hardly to be persuaded out of wearing the classical linen cap peculiar to the women of Lower Normandy. This girl, as buxom as a wet-nurse, looked as if she would burst the blue cotton check in which she clothed her person. Her florid face might have been hewn out of stone, so hard were its tawny outlines.

Of course no attention was paid to the advent in the house of this girl, whose name was Agathe—an ordinary, wide-awake specimen, such as is daily imported from the provinces. Agathe had no attractions for the cook, her tongue was too rough, for she had served in a suburban inn, waiting on carters; and instead of making a conquest of her chief and winning from him the secrets of the high art of the kitchen, she was the object of his great contempt. The chef's attentions were, in fact, devoted to Louise, the Countess Steinbock's maid. The country girl, thinking herself ill-used, complained bitterly that she was always sent out of the way on some pretext when the chef was finishing a dish or putting the crowning touch to a sauce.

"I am out of luck," said she, "and I shall go to another place."

And yet she stayed, though she had twice given notice to quit.

One night, Adeline, roused by some unusual noise, did not see Hector in the bed he occupied near hers; for they slept side by side in two beds, as beseemed an old couple. She lay awake an hour, but he did not return. Seized with a panic, fancying some tragic end had overtaken him—an apoplectic attack, perhaps—she went upstairs to the floor occupied by the servants, and there was attracted to the room where Agathe slept, partly by seeing a light below the door, and partly by the murmur of voices. She stood still in dismay on recognizing the voice of her husband, who, a victim to Agathe's charms, to vanquish this strapping wench's not disinterested resistance, went to the length of saying—

"My wife has not long to live, and if you like you may be a baroness."

Adeline gave a cry, dropped her candlestick, and fled.

Three days later the baroness, who had received the last sacraments, was dying, surrounded by her weeping family.

Just before she died, she took her husband's hand and pressed it, murmuring in his ear—

"My dear, I had nothing left to give up to you but my life. In a minute or two you will be free, and can make another Baroness Hulot."

And, rare sight, tears oozed from her dead eyes.

This desperateness of vice had vanquished the patience of the angel, who, on the brink of eternity, gave utterance to the only reproach she had ever spoken in her life.

The baron left Paris three days after his wife's funeral.

Eleven months later Victorin heard indirectly of his father's marriage to Mademoiselle Agathe Piquetard, solemnized at Isigny, on the 1st February, 1846.

"Parents may hinder their children's marriage, but children cannot interfere with the insane acts of their parents in their second childhood," said Maître Hulot to Maître Popinot, the second son of the minister of commerce, who was discussing this marriage.

THE POOR PARENTS

(*Les Parents Pauvres*).

COUSIN PONS.

TOWARD three o'clock in the afternoon of one October day in the year 1844, a man of sixty or thereabout, whom any-body might have credited with more than his actual age, was walking along the Boulevard des Italiens with his head bent down, as if he were tracking some one. There was a smug expression about the mouth—he looked like a merchant who has just done a good stroke of business, or a bachelor emerging from a boudoir in the best of humors with himself; and in Paris this is the highest degree of self-satisfaction ever registered by a human countenance.

As soon as the elderly person appeared in the distance, a smile broke out over the faces of the frequenters of the boulevard, who daily, from their chairs, watch the passers-by, and indulge in the agreeable pastime of analyzing them. That smile is peculiar to Parisians; it says so many things—ironical, quizzical, pitying; but nothing save the rarest of human curiosities can summon that look of interest to the faces of Parisians, sated as they are with every possible sight.

A saying recorded of Hyacinthe, an actor celebrated for his repartees, will explain the archæological value of the old gentleman, and the smile repeated like an echo by all eyes. Somebody once asked Hyacinthe where the hats were made that set the house in a roar as soon as he appeared. " I don't have them made," he said; " I keep them ! " So also among the million actors who make up the great troupe of Paris, there are unconscious Hyacinthes who " keep " all the absurd freaks of vanished fashions upon their backs; and the appari-

tion of some bygone decade will startle you into laughter as
you walk the streets in bitterness of soul over the treason of
one who was your friend in the past.

In some respects the passer-by adhered so faithfully to the
fashions of the year 1806 that he was not so much a burlesque
caricature as a reproduction of the Empire period.   To an
observer, accuracy of detail in a revival of this sort is extremely valuable, but accuracy of detail, to be properly appreciated, demands the critical attention of an expert *flaneur*, or
rambler; while the man in the street who raises a laugh as
soon as he comes in sight is bound to be one of those outrageous exhibitions which stare you in the face, as the saying
goes, and produce the kind of effect which an actor tries to
secure for the success of his entry.   The elderly person, a
thin, spare man, wore a nut-brown spencer over a coat of
uncertain green, with white metal buttons.   A man in a
spencer in the year eighteen hundred and forty-four ! it was
as if Napoleon himself had vouchsafed to come to life again
for a couple of hours.

The spencer, as its name indicates, was the invention of an
English lord, vain, doubtless, of his handsome shape.   Some
time before the Peace of Amiens, this nobleman solved the
problem of covering the bust without destroying the outlines
of the figure and encumbering the person with the hideous
boxcoat, now finishing its career on the backs of aged hackney-
coach drivers; but, elegant figures being in the minority, the
success of the spencer was short-lived in France, English
though it was.

At sight of the spencer, men of forty or fifty mentally invested the wearer with top-boots, pistachio-colored kerseymere
small clothes adorned with a knot of ribbon; and beheld
themselves in the costumes of their youth.   Elderly ladies
thought of former conquests; but the younger men were asking each other why the aged Alcibiades had cut off the skirts
of his overcoat.   The rest of the costume was so much in

keeping with the spencer, that you would not have hesitated to call the wearer " an Empire man," just as you call a certain kind of furniture. " Empire furniture ; " yet the new-comer only symbolized the Empire for those who had known. that great and magnificent epoch at any rate by seeing, for a certain accuracy of memory was needed for the full appreciation of the costume, and even now the Empire is so far away that not every one of us can picture it to himself in its Gallo-Grecian reality.

The stranger's hat, for instance, tipped to the back of his head so as to leave almost the whole forehead bare, recalled a certain jaunty air, with which civilians and officials attempted to swagger it with military men ; but the hat itself was a shocking specimen of the fifteen-franc variety. Constant friction with a pair of enormous ears had left marks which no brush could efface from the underside of the brim ; the silk tissue (as usual) fitted badly over the cardboard foundation, and hung in wrinkles here and there ; and some skin-disease (apparently) had attacked the nap in spite of the hand which rubbed it down of a morning.

Beneath the hat, which seemed ready to drop off at any moment, lay an expanse of countenance grotesque and droll, as the faces which the Chinese alone of all people can imagine for their quaint curiosities. The broad visage was as full of holes as a colander, honey-combed with the shadows of the dents, hollowed out like a Roman mask. It set all the laws of anatomy at defiance. Close inspection failed to detect the substructure. Where you expected to find a bone, you discovered a layer of cartilaginous tissue, and the hollows of an ordinary human face were here filled out with flabby bosses. A pair of gray eyes, red-rimmed and lashless, looked forlornly out of a countenance which was flattened something after the fashion of a pumpkin, and surmounted by a Don Quixote nose that rose out of it like a monolith above a plain. It was the kind of nose, as Cervantes must surely have explained somewhere, which denotes an inborn enthusiasm for all things great, a tendency which is apt to degenerate into credulity.

And yet, though the man's ugliness was something almost ludicrous, it aroused not the slightest inclination to laugh. The exceeding melancholy which found an outlet in the poor man's faded eyes reached the mocker himself and froze the gibes on his lips; for all at once the thought arose that this was a human creature to whom Nature had forbidden any expression of love or tenderness, since such expression could only be painful or ridiculous to the woman he loved. In the presence of such misfortune a Frenchman is silent; to him it seems the most cruel of all afflictions—to be unable to please!

The man so ill-favored was dressed after the fashion of shabby gentility, a fashion which the rich not seldom try to copy. He wore low shoes beneath gaiters of the pattern worn by the Imperial Guard, doubtless for the sake of economy, because they kept the socks clean. The rusty tinge of his black breeches, like the cut and the white or shiny line of the creases, assigned the date of the purchase some three years back. The roomy garments failed to disguise the lean proportions of the wearer, due apparently rather to constitution than to a Pythagorean regimen, for the worthy man was endowed with thick lips and a sensual mouth; and, when he smiled, displayed a set of white teeth which would have done credit to a shark.

A shawl-vest, likewise of black cloth, was supplemented by a white under-vest, and yet again beneath this gleamed the edge of a red knitted under-jacket, to put you in mind of Garat's five vests. A huge white lawn stock with a conspicuous bow, invented by some exquisite to charm "the charming sex" in 1809, projected so far above its wearer's chin that the lower part of his face was lost, as it were, in a lawn abyss. A silk watch-guard, plaited to resemble the keepsakes made of hair, meandered down his shirt-front and secured his watch from improbable theft. The greenish coat, though older by some three years than the breeches, was remarkably neat; the black velvet collar and shining metal buttons, recently renewed, told of carefulness which descended even to trifles.

The particular manner of fixing the hat on the occiput, the triple vest, the vast cravat engulfing the chin, the gaiters, the metal buttons on the greenish coat—all these reminiscences of Imperial fashions were blended with a sort of afterwaft and lingering perfume of the coquetry of the Incroyable*—with an indescribable finical something in the folds of the garments, a certain air of stiffness and correctness in the demeanor that smacked of the school of David, that recalled Jacob's spindle-legged furniture.

At first sight, moreover, you set him down either for the gentleman by birth fallen a victim to some degrading habit, or for the man of small independent means whose expenses are calculated to such a nicety that the breakage of a window-pane, a rent in a coat, or a visit from the philanthropic pest who asks you for subscriptions to a charity, absorbs the whole of a month's little surplus of pocket-money. If you had seen him that afternoon, you would have wondered how that grotesque face came to be lighted up with a smile; usually, surely, it must have worn the dispirited, passive look of the obscure toiler condemned to labor without ceasing for the barest necessaries of life. Yet when you noticed that the odd-looking old man was carrying some object (evidently precious) in his right hand with a mother's care, concealing it under the skirts of his coat to keep it from collisions in the crowd; and still more, when you remarked that important air always assumed by an idler when intrusted with a commission, you would have suspected him of recovering some piece of lost property, some modern equivalent of the marquise's poodle; you would have recognized the assiduous gallantry of the " man of the Empire" returning in triumph from his mission to some charm-

---

* A non-such.

ing woman of sixty, reluctant as yet to dispense with the daily visit of her elderly *attentif.*

In Paris only among great cities will you see such spectacles as this ; for of her boulevards Paris makes a stage where a never-ending drama is played gratuitously by the French nation in the interests of art.

In spite of the rashly assumed spencer, you would scarcely have thought, after a glance at the contours of the man's bony frame, that this was an artist—that conventional type which is privileged, in something the same way as a Paris gamin, to represent riotous living to the bourgeois and philistine mind, the most *mirific* joviality, in short (to use the old Rabelaisian word newly taken into use). Yet, this elderly person had once taken the medal and the traveling scholarship ; he had composed the first cantata crowned by the Institute at the time of the reëstablishment of the Academie de Rome ; he was M. Sylvain Pons, in fact—M. Sylvain Pons, whose name appears on the covers of well-known sentimental songs trilled by our mothers, to say nothing of a couple of operas, played in 1815 and 1816, and divers unpublished scores. The worthy soul was now ending his days as the conductor of an orchestra in a boulevard theatre, and a music master in several young ladies' boarding-schools, a post for which his face particularly recommended him. He was entirely dependent upon his earnings. Running about to give private lessons at his age ! Think of it. How many a mystery lies in that unromantic situation !

But the last man to wear the spencer carried something else about him beside his Empire associations ; a warning and a lesson was written large over that triple vest. Wherever he went, he exhibited, without fee or charge, one of the many victims of the fatal system of competition which still prevails in France in spite of a century of trial without result ; for Poisson de Marigny, brother of the Pompadour and Director of Fine Arts, somewhere about 1746, invented this method of applying pressure to the brain. That was a hundred years ago. Try if you can count upon your fingers the men of genius among the prizemen of those hundred years.

In the first place, no deliberate effort of schoolmaster or administrator can replace the miracles of chance which produce great men: of all the mysteries of generation, this most defies the ambitious modern scientific investigator. In the second—the ancient Egyptians (we are told) invented incubator-stoves for hatching eggs; what would be thought of Egyptians who should neglect to fill the beaks of the callow fledglings? Yet this is precisely what France is doing. She does her utmost to produce artists by the artificial heat of competitive examination; but, the sculptor, painter, engraver, or musician once turned out by this mechanical process, she no more troubles herself about them and their fate than the dude cares for yesterday's flower in his button-hole. And so it happens that the really great man is a Greuze, a Watteau, a Félicien David, a Pagnesi, a Géricault, a Decamps, an Auber, a David d'Angers, a Eugène Delacroix, or a Meissonier— artists who take but little heed of great prizes, and spring up in the open field under the rays of that invisible sun called Vocation.

To resume: The Government sent Sylvain Pons to Rome to make a great musician of himself; and in Rome Sylvain Pons acquired a taste for the antique and works of art. He became an admirable judge of those masterpieces of the brain and hand which are summed up by the useful neologism "bric-à-brac;" and when the child of Euterpe returned to Paris somewhere about the year 1810, it was in the character of a rabid collector, loaded with pictures, statuettes, frames, wood-carving, ivories, enamels, porcelains, and the like. He had sunk the greater part of his patrimony, not so much in the purchases themselves as on the expenses of transit; and every sou inherited from his mother had been spent in the course of a three years' travel in Italy after the residence in Rome came

7

to an end. He had seen Venice, Milan, Florence, Bologna, and Naples leisurely, as he wished to see them, as a dreamer of dreams, and a philosopher; careless of the future, for an artist looks to his talent for support as the *fille de joie* (daughter of pleasure or lorette) counts upon her beauty.

All through those splendid years of travel Pons was as happy as was possible to a man with a great soul, a sensitive nature, and a face so ugly that any "success with the fair" (to use the stereotyped formula of 1809) was out of the question; the realities of life always fell short of the ideals which Pons created for himself; the world without was not in tune with the soul within, but Pons had made up his mind to the dissonance. Doubtless the sense of beauty that he had kept pure and living in his inmost soul was the spring from which the delicate, graceful, and ingenious music flowed and won him reputation between 1810 and 1814.

Every reputation founded upon the fashion or the fancy of the hour, or upon the short-lived follies of Paris, produces its Pons. No place in the world is so inexorable in great things; no city of the globe so disdainfully indulgent in small. Pons' notes were drowned before long in floods of German harmony and the music of Rossini; and if in 1824 he was known as an agreeable musician, a composer of various drawing-room melodies, judge if he was likely to be famous in 1831! In 1844, the year in which the single drama of his obscure life began, Sylvain Pons was of no more value than an antediluvian semiquaver; dealers in music had never heard of his name though he was still composing, on scanty pay, for his own orchestra or for neighboring theatres.

And yet, the worthy man did justice to the great masters of our day; a masterpiece finely rendered brought tears to his eyes; but his religion never bordered on mania, as in the case of Hoffmann's Kreislers; he kept his enthusiasm to himself; his delight, like the paradise reached by opium or hashish, lay within his own soul.

The gift of admiration, of comprehension, the single faculty by which the ordinary man becomes the brother of the poet, is rare in this city of Paris, that inn whither all ideas, like travelers, come to stay for a while ; so rare is it, that Pons surely deserves our respectful esteem. His personal failure may seem anomalous, but he frankly admitted that he was weak in harmony. He had neglected the study of counterpoint ; there was a time when he might have begun his studies afresh and held his own among modern composers, when he might have been, not certainly a Rossini. but a Hérold. But he was alarmed by the intricacies of modern orchestration ; and at length, in the pleasures of collecting, he found such ever-renewed compensation for his failure, that if he had been made to choose between his curiosities and the fame of Rossini—will it be believed?—Pons would have pronounced for his beloved collection.

Pons was of the opinion of Chenavard, the print-collector, who laid it down as an axiom—that you only fully enjoy the pleasure of looking at your Ruysdael, Hobbema, Holbein, Raphael, Murillo, Greuze, Sebastian del Piombo, Giorgione, Albrecht Dürer, or what not, when you have paid less than sixty francs for your picture. Pons never gave more than a hundred francs for any purchase. If he laid out as much as fifty francs, he was careful to assure himself beforehand that the object was worth three thousand. The most beautiful thing in the world, if it cost three hundred francs, did not exist for Pons. Rare had been his bargains ; but he possessed the three qualifications for success—a stag's legs, an idler's disregard of time, and the patience of a Jew.

This system, carried out for forty years, in Rome or Paris alike, had borne its fruits. Since Pons returned from Italy, he had regularly spent about two thousand francs a year upon a collection of masterpieces of every sort and description, a collection hidden away from all eyes but his own ; and now his catalogue had reached the incredible number 1907.

Wandering about Paris between 1811 and 1816, he had picked up many a treasure for ten francs, which would fetch a thousand or twelve hundred to-day. Some forty-five thousand paintings change hands annually in Paris picture sales, and these Pons had sifted through year by year. Pons had Sèvres porcelain, *pâte tendre*, bought of Auvergnats, those satellites of the Black Band who sacked castles and carried off the marvels of Pompadour France in their tumbrils; he had, in fact, collected the drifted wreck of the seventeenth and eighteenth centuries; he recognized the genius of the French school, and discerned the merit of the Lepautres and Lavallée-Poussins and the rest of the great obscure creators of the Genre Louis Quinze and the Genre Louis Seize. Our modern craftsmen now draw without acknowledgment from them, pore incessantly over the treasures of the Cabinet des Estampes, borrow adroitly, and give out their *pastiches** for new inventions. Pons had obtained many a piece by exchange, and therein lies the ineffable joy of the collector. The joy of buying bric-à-brac is a secondary delight; in the give-and-take of barter lies the joy of joys. Pons had begun by collecting snuff-boxes and miniatures; his name was unknown in bric-à-bracology, for he seldom showed himself in salesrooms or in the stores of well-known dealers; Pons was not aware that his treasures had any commercial value.

The late lamented Dusommerard tried his best to gain Pons' confidence, but the prince of bric-à-brac died before he could gain an entrance to the Pons museum, the one private collection which could compare with the famous Sauvageot museum. Pons and M. Sauvageot indeed resembled each other in more ways than one. M. Sauvageot, like Pons, was a musician; he was likewise a comparatively poor man, and he had collected his bric-à-brac in much the same way, with the same love of art, the same hatred of rich capitalists with well-known names who collect for the sake of running up

* Copies.

prices as cleverly as possible.   There was yet another point of resemblance between the pair: Pons, like his rival competitor and antagonist, felt in his heart an insatiable craving after specimens of the craftsman's skill and miracles of workmanship; he loved them as a man might love a fair mistress; an auction in the salesrooms in the Rue des Jeûneurs, with its accompaniments of hammer-strokes and brokers' men, was a crime of "lèse-bric-à-brac" in Pons' eyes.   Pons' museum was for his own delight at every hour; for the soul created to know and feel all the beauty of a masterpiece has this in common with the lover—to-day's joy is as great as the joy of yesterday; possession never palls; and a masterpiece, happily, never grows old.   So the object that he held in his hand with such fatherly care could only be a "find," carried off with what affection amateurs alone know!

After the first outlines of this biographical sketch, every one will cry at once, "Why! this is the happiest man on earth, in spite of his ugliness!"   And, in truth, no spleen, no dullness can resist the counter-irritant supplied by a "craze," the intellectual moxa of a hobby.   You who can no longer drink of "the cup of pleasure," as it has been called through all ages, try to collect something, no matter what (people have been known to collect placards), so shall you receive the small change for the gold ingot of happiness. Have you a hobby?   You have transferred pleasure to the plane of ideas.   And yet, you need not envy the worthy Pons; such envy, like all kindred sentiments, would be founded upon a misapprehension.

With a nature so sensitive, with a soul that lived by tireless admiration of the magnificent achievements of art, of the high rivalry between human toil and the work of Nature—Pons was a slave to that one of the Seven Deadly Sins with which God surely will deal least hardly; Pons was a glutton.   A narrow income, combined with a passion for bric-à-brac, condemned him to a regimen so abhorrent to a discriminating palate, that, bachelor as he was, he had cut the knot of the problem by dining out every day.

Now, in the time of the Empire, celebrities were more sought after than at present, perhaps because there were so few of them, perhaps because they made little or no political pretension. In those days, beside, you could·set up for a poet, a musician, or a painter, with so little expense. Pons, being regarded as the probable rival of Nicolo, Paër, and Berton, used to receive so many invitations, that he was forced to keep a list of engagements, much as barristers note down the cases for which they are retained. And Pons behaved like an artist. He presented his amphitryons with copies of his songs, he " obliged " at the pianoforte, he brought them orders for boxes at the Feydeau, his own theatre, he organized concerts, he was not above taking the fiddle himself sometimes in a friend's house, and getting up a little impromptu dance. In those days, all the handsome men in France were away at the wars exchanging sabre-cuts with the handsome men of the Coalition. Pons was said to be, not ugly, but " peculiar-looking," after the grand rule laid down by Molière in Éliante's famous couplets ; but if he sometimes heard himself described as a " charming man " (after he had done some fair lady a service), his good fortune went no further than words.

It was between the years 1810 and 1816 that Pons contracted the unlucky habit of dining out ; he grew accustomed to see his hosts taking pains over the dinner, procuring the first and best of everything, bringing out their choicest vintages, seeing carefully to the dessert, the coffee, and liqueurs, giving him of their best, in short ; the best, moreover, of those times of the Empire when Paris was glutted with kings and queens and princes, and many a private house emulated royal splendors.

People used to play at Royalty then as they play nowadays at parliament, creating a whole host of societies with presidents, vice-presidents, secretaries and what not—agricultural societies, industrial societies, societies for the promotion of sericulture, viticulture, the growth of flax, and so forth. Some have even gone so far as to look about them for social evils in order to start a society to cure them.

But to return to Pons. A stomach thus educated is sure to react upon the owner's moral fibre; the demoralization of the man varies directly with his progress in the wisdom of cookery. Voluptuousness, lurking in every secret recess of the heart, lays down the law therein. Honor and resolution are battered in breach. The tyranny of the palate has never been described; as a necessity of life it escapes the criticism of literature; yet no one imagines how many have been ruined by the table. The luxury of the table is indeed, in this sense, the courtesan's one competitor in Paris, beside representing in a manner the credit side in another account, where she figures as the expenditure.

With Pons' decline and fall as an artist came his simultaneous transformation from invited guest to parasite and hanger-on; he could not bring himself to quit dinners so excellently served for the Spartan soup of a two-franc dinner. Alas! alas! a shudder ran through him at the mere thought of the great sacrifices which independence required him to make. He felt that he was capable of sinking to even lower depths for the sake of good living, if there was no other way of enjoying the first and best of everything, of gobbling (vulgar but expressive word) nice little dishes carefully prepared. Pons lived like a bird, pilfering his meal, flying away when he had taken his fill, singing a few notes by way of return; he took a certain pleasure in the thought that he lived at the expense of society, which asked of him—what but the trifling toll of grimaces? Like all confirmed bachelors, who hold their lodgings in horror, and live as much as possible in other people's houses, Pons was accustomed to the formulas and facial contortions which do duty for feeling in the world; he used compliments as small change; and as far as others were concerned, he was satisfied with the labels they bore, and never plunged a too curious hand into the sack.

This not intolerable phase lasted for another ten years. Such years! Pons' life was closing with a rainy autumn. All through those years he contrived to dine without expense by making himself necessary in the houses which he frequented. He took the first step in the downward path by undertaking a host of small commissions; many and many a time Pons ran on errands instead of the porter or the servant; many a purchase he made for his entertainers. He became a kind of harmless, well-meaning spy, sent by one family into another; but he gained no credit with those for whom he trudged about, and so often sacrificed self-respect.

"Pons is a bachelor," said they; "he is at a loss to know what to do with his time; he is only too glad to trot about for us. What else would he do?"

Very soon the cold which old age spreads about itself began to set in; the communicable chill which sensibly lowers the social temperature, especially if the old man is ugly and poor. Old and ugly and poor—is not this to be thrice old? Pons' winter had begun, the winter which brings the reddened nose, and frost-nipped cheeks, and the numbed fingers, numb in how many ways!

Invitations very seldom came for Pons now. So far from seeking the society of the parasite, every family accepted him much as they accepted the taxes; they valued nothing that Pons could do for them; real services from Pons counted for naught. The family circles in which the worthy artist revolved had no respect for art or letters; they went down on their knees to practical results; they valued nothing but the fortune or social position acquired since the year 1830. The bourgeoisie is afraid of intellect and genius, but Pons' spirit and manner were not haughty enough to overawe his relations, and naturally he had come at last to be accounted less than nothing with them, though he was not altogether despised.

He had suffered acutely among them, but, like all timid creatures, he kept silence as to his pain; and so by degrees schooled himself to hide his feelings, and learned to take sanctuary in his inmost self. Many superficial persons interpret this conduct by the short word "selfishness;" and, indeed, the resemblance between the egoist and the solitary human creature is strong enough to seem to justify the harsher verdict; and this is especially true in Paris, where nobody observes others closely, where all things pass swift as waves, and last as little as a ministry.

So Cousin Pons was accused of selfishness (behind his back); and, if the world accuses any one, it usually finds him guilty and condemns him into the bargain. Pons bowed to the decision. Do any of us know how such a timid nature is cast down by an unjust judgment? Who will ever paint all that the timid suffer? This state of things, now growing daily worse, explains the sad expression on the poor old musician's face; he lived by capitulations of which he was ashamed. Every time we sin against self-respect at the bidding of the ruling passion, we rivet its hold upon us; the more that passion requires of us, the stronger it grows, every sacrifice increasing, as it were, the value of a satisfaction for which so much has been given up, till the negative sum-total of renouncements looms very large in a man's imagination. Pons, for instance, after enduring the insolently patronizing looks of some bourgeois, incased in the buckram of stupidity, sipped his glass of port or finished his quail with bread-crumbs, and relished something of the savor of revenge beside. "It is not too dear at the price!" he said to himself.

After all, in the eyes of the moralist, there were extenuating circumstances in Pons' case. Man only lives, in fact, by some personal satisfaction. The passionless, perfectly righteous man is not human; he is a monster, an angel wanting wings. The angel of Christian mythology has nothing but a head. On earth, the righteous person is the sufficiently tiresome Grandison, for whom the very palpable Venus of the Cross-roads is sexless.

Setting aside one or two commonplace adventures in Italy, in which probably the climate accounted for his success, no woman had ever smiled upon Pons. Plenty of men are doomed to this fate. Pons was an abnormal birth; the child of parents well stricken in years, he bore the stigma of his untimely genesis; his cadaverous complexion might have been contracted in the flask of spirit-of-wine in which science preserves some extraordinary fœtus. Artist though he was, with his tender, dreamy, sensitive soul, he was forced to accept the character which belonged to his face; it was hopeless to think of love, and he remained a bachelor, not so much of choice as of necessity. Then Gluttony, the sin of the continent monk, beckoned to Pons; he rushed upon temptation, as he had thrown his whole soul into the adoration of art and the cult of music. Good cheer and bric-à-brac gave him the small change for the love which could spend itself in no other way. As for music, it was his profession, and where will you find the man who is in love with his means of earning a livelihood? For it is with a profession as with marriage: in the great length you are sensible of nothing but the drawbacks.

Brillat-Savarin has deliberately set himself to justify the gastronome, but perhaps even he has not dwelt sufficiently on the reality of the pleasures of the table. The demands of digestion upon the human economy produce an internal wrestling-bout of human forces which rivals the highest degree of amorous pleasure. The gastronome is conscious of an expenditure of vital power, an expenditure so vast that the brain is atrophied (as it were), that a second brain, located in the diaphragm, may come into play, and the suspension of all the faculties is in itself a kind of intoxication. A boa-constrictor gorged with an ox is so stupid with excess that the creature is easily killed. What man, on the wrong side of forty, is rash enough to work after dinner? And remark in the same connection, that all great men have been moderate eaters. The exhilarating effect of the wing of a chicken upon invalids recovering from serious illness, and long confined to a stinted and carefully chosen diet, has been frequently remarked. The sober Pons, whose whole enjoyment was concentrated in the exercise of his digestive organs, was in the position of chronic convalescence; he looked to his dinner to give him the utmost degree of pleasurable sensation, and hitherto he had procured such sensations daily. Who dares to bid farewell to old habit? Many a man on the brink of suicide has been plucked back on the threshold of death by the thought of the café where he plays his nightly game of dominoes.

In the year 1835, chance avenged Pons for the indifference of womankind by finding him a prop for his declining years, as the saying goes; and he, who had been old from his cradle, found a support in friendship. Pons took to himself the only life-partner permitted to him among his kind—an old man and a fellow-musician.

But for La Fontaine's fable, "Les Deux Amis," this sketch would have borne the title of *The Two Friends;* but to take the name of his divine story would surely be a deed of violence, a profanation from which every true man of letters would shrink. The title ought to be borne alone and for ever by the fabulist's masterpiece, the revelation of his soul and the record of his dreams; those three words were set once and for ever by the poet at the head of a page which is his by a sacred right of ownership; for it is a shrine before which all generations, all over the world, will kneel so long as the art of printing shall endure.

Pons' friend gave lessons on the pianoforte. They met and struck up an acquaintance in 1834, one prize-day at a boarding-school; and so congenial were their ways of thinking and living, that Pons used to say that he had found his friend too late for his happiness. Never, perhaps, did two souls, so much alike, find each other in the great ocean of humanity which

flowed forth, in disobedience to the will of God, from its
source in the Garden of Eden. Before very long the two
musicians could not live without each other. Confidences
were exchanged, and in a week's time they were like brothers.
Schmucke (for that was his name) had not believed that such
a man as Pons existed, nor had Pons imagined that a Schmucke
was possible. Here already you have a sufficient description
of the good couple ; but it is not every mind that takes kindly
to the concise synthetic method, and a certain amount of
demonstration is necessary if the credulous are to accept the
conclusion.

This pianist, like all other pianists, was a German. A
German, like the eminent Liszt and the great Mendelssohn,
and Steibelt, and Dussek, and Meyer, and Mozart, and
Dœlher, and Thalberg, and Dreschok, and Hiller, and Leo-
pold Mayer, and Cramer, and Zimmerman, and Kalkbrenner, .
and Hertz, Woërtz, Karr, Wolff, Pixis, and Clara Wieck—and
all Germans, generally speaking. Schmucke was a great
musical composer doomed to remain a music-master, so utterly
did his character lack the audacity which a musical genius
needs if he is to push his way to the front. A German's
naïveté does not invariably last him through his life ; in some
cases it fails after a certain age ; and even as a cultivator of
the soil brings water from afar by means of irrigation channels,
so, from the springs of his youth, does the Teuton draw the
simplicity which disarms suspicion—the perennial supplies
with which he fertilizes his labors in every field of science,
art, or commerce. A crafty Frenchman here and there will
turn a Parisian tradesman's stupidity to good account in the
same way. But Schmucke had kept his child's simplicity
much as Pons continued to wear his relics of the Empire—all
unsuspectingly. The true and noble-hearted German was at
once the theatre and the audience, making music within himself for himself alone. In this city of Paris he lived as a
nightingale lives among the thickets ; and for twenty years he

sang on, mateless, till he met with a second self in the sympathetic Pons.*

Both Pons and Schmucke were abundantly given, both by heart and disposition, to the peculiarly puky German sentimentality which shows itself in childlike ways—in a passion for flowers, in that form of nature-worship which prompts a German to plant his garden beds with big glass globes for the sake of seeing miniature pictures of a view which he can behold about him of a natural size; in the inquiring turn of mind that sets a learned Teuton trudging three hundred miles in his gaiters in search of a fact which smiles up in his face from a wayside spring, or lurks laughing under the jessamine leaves in the backyard; or (to take a final instance) in the German craving to endow every least detail in creation with a spiritual significance, a craving which produces sometimes the inexplicable work of a Jean Paul Richter, sometimes Hoffmann's tipsiness in type, sometimes the folios with which Germany hedges the simplest questions round about, lest haply any fool should fall into her intellectual excavations; and, indeed, if you fathom these abysses, you find nothing but a German at the bottom.

Both friends were Catholics. They went to mass and performed the duties of religion together; and, like children, found nothing to tell their confessors. It was their firm belief that music is to feeling and thought as thought and feeling are to speech; and of their converse on this system there was no end. Each made response to the other in orgies of sound, demonstrating their convictions, each for each, like lovers.

Schmucke was as absent-minded as Pons was wide-awake. Pons was a collector, Schmucke a dreamer of dreams; Schmucke was a student of beauty seen by the soul, Pons a preserver of material beauty. Pons would catch sight of a china cup and buy it in the time that Schmucke took to blow his nose, wondering the while within himself whether the

* See "A Daughter of Eve."

musical phrase that was ringing in his brain—the *motif* from
Rossini or Bellini or Beethoven or Mozart—had its origin or
its counterpart in the world of human thought and emotion.
Schmucke's economies were controlled by an absent mind,
Pons was a spendthrift through passion, and for both the
result was the same—they had not a penny on Saint Sylvester's
day.

Perhaps Pons would have given way under his troubles if it
had not been for this friendship; but life became bearable
when he found some one to whom he could pour out his
heart. The first time that he breathed a word of his difficulties, the good German had advised him to live as he himself did, and eat bread and cheese at home sooner than dine
abroad at such a cost. Alas! Pons did not dare to confess
that heart and stomach were at war within him, that he could
digest affronts which pained his heart, and, cost what it might,
a good dinner that satisfied his palate was a necessity to him,
even as your gay Lothario must have a mistress to tease.

In time Schmucke understood; not just at once, for he was
too much of a Teuton to possess that gift of swift perception
in which the French rejoice; Schmucke understood and
loved poor Pons the better. Nothing so fortifies a friendship
as a belief on the part of one friend that he is superior to the
other. An angel could not have found a word to say to
Schmucke rubbing his hand over the discovery of the hold
that gluttony had gained over Pons. Indeed, the good German adorned their breakfast-table next morning with delica-
cies of which he went in search himself; and every day he
was careful to provide something new for his friend, for they
always breakfasted together at home.

If any one imagines that the pair could escape ridicule in
Paris, where nothing is respected, he cannot know that city.
When Schmucke and Pons united their riches and poverty,
they hit upon the economical expedient of lodging together,
each paying half the rent of the very unequally divided

second-floor of a house in the Rue de Normandie in the Marais. And as it often happened that they left home together and walked side by side along their beat of boulevard, the idlers of the quarter dubbed them "the pair of nutcrackers," a nickname which makes any portrait of Schmucke quite superfluous, for he was to Pons as the famous statue of the Nurse of Niobe in the Vatican is to the Tribune Venus.

Mme. Cibot, portress of the house in the Rue de Normandie, was the pivot on which the domestic life of the nutcrackers turned; but Mme. Cibot plays so large a part in the drama which grew out of their double existence, that it will be more appropriate to give her portrait on her first appearance in this Scene of Parisian Life.

One thing remains to be said of the characters of the pair of friends; but this one thing is precisely the hardest to make clear to ninety-nine readers out of a hundred in this forty-seventh year of the nineteenth century, perhaps by reason of the prodigious financial development brought about by the railway system. It is a little thing, and yet it is much. It is a question, in fact, of giving an idea of the extreme sensitiveness of their natures. Let us borrow an illustration from the railways, if only by way of retaliation, as it were, for the loans which they levy upon us. The railway train of to-day, tearing over the metals, grinds away fine particles of dust, grains so minute that a traveler cannot detect them with the eye; but let a single one of those invisible motes find its way into the kidneys, it will bring about that most excruciating, and sometimes fatal, disease known as gravel. And our society, rushing like a locomotive along its metaled track, is heedless of the all but imperceptible dust made by the grinding of the wheels; but it was otherwise with the two musicians: the invisible grains of sand sank perpetually into the very fibres of their being, causing them intolerable anguish of heart. Tender exceedingly to the pain of others, they wept for their own powerlessness to help; and their own susceptibilities were almost morbidly acute. Neither age nor the continual spectacle of the drama of Paris life had hardened two souls still young and childlike and pure; the longer they lived indeed, the more keenly they felt their inward suffering; for so it is, alas! with natures unsullied by the world, with the quiet thinker, and with such poets among poets as have never fallen into any excess.

Since the old men began housekeeping together, the day's routine was very nearly the same for them both. They worked together in harness in the fraternal fashion of the Paris cab-horse; rising every morning, summer and winter, at seven o'clock, and setting out after breakfast to give music lessons in the boarding-schools, in which, upon occasion, they would take lessons for each other. Toward noon Pons repaired to his theatre, if there was a rehearsal on hand; but all his spare moments were spent in sauntering on the boulevards. Night found both of them in the orchestra at the theatre, for Pons had found a place for Schmucke, and upon this wise:

At the time of their first meeting, Pons had just received that marshal's baton of the unknown musical composer—an appointment as conductor of an orchestra. It had come to him unasked, by favor of Count Popinot, a bourgeois hero of July, at that time a member of the Government. Count Popinot had the license of a theatre in his gift, and Count Popinot had also an old acquaintance of the kind that the successful man blushes to meet. As he rolls through the streets of Paris in his carriage, it is not pleasant to see his boyhood's chum down at heel, with a coat of many improbable colors and trousers innocent of straps, and a head full of soaring speculations on too grand a scale to tempt shy, easily scared capital. Moreover, this friend of his youth, Gaudissart by name, had done not a little in the past toward founding the fortunes of the great house of Popinot. Popinot, now a count and a peer of France, after twice holding a portfolio, had no wish to shake off "the Illustrious Gaudissart." Quite otherwise. The pomps and vanities of the Court of the Citizen-King had not spoiled the sometime perfumer's kind heart; he wished to put his ex-commercial traveler in the way of renewing his wardrobe and replenishing his purse. So when Gaudissart, always an enthusiastic admirer of the fair sex, applied for the license of a bankrupt theatre, Popinot granted it on condition that Pons (a parasite of the Hôtel Popinot) should be engaged as conductor of the orchestra; and, at the same time, the count was careful to send certain elderly amateurs of beauty to the theatre, so that the new manager might be strongly supported financially by wealthy admirers of feminine charms revealed by the costume of the ballet.

Gaudissart & Company, who, be it said, made their fortune, hit upon the grand idea of operas for the people, and carried it out in a boulevard theatre in 1834. A tolerable conductor, who could adapt or even compose a little music upon occasion, was a necessity for ballets and pantomimes; but the last management had so long been bankrupt that they could not afford to keep a transposer and copyist. Pons therefore introduced Schmucke to the company as copier of music, a humble calling which requires considerable of musical knowledge; and Schmucke, acting on Pons' advice, came to an understanding with the *chef-de-service* at the opera-comique, so saving himself the clerical drudgery.

The partnership between Pons and Schmucke produced one brilliant result. Schmucke being a German, harmony was his strong point; he looked over the instrumentation of Pons' compositions, and Pons provided the airs. Here and there an amateur among the audience admired the new pieces of music which served as accompaniment to two or three great successes, but they attributed the improvement vaguely to "progress." No one cared to know the composer's name; like occupants of the *baignoires,** lost to view of the house,

* Bathing machine: a box on wheels, used at watering-places for the undressing of the bather, and then drawn into the sea.

to gain a view of the stage, Pons and Schmucke eclipsed themselves by their success.   In Paris (especially since the Revolution of July) no one can hope to succeed unless he will
push his way *quibuscumque viis* and with all his might through
a formidable host of competitors; but for this feat a man
needs thews and sinews, and our two friends, be it remembered, had that affection of the heart which cripples all ambitious effort.

Pons, as a rule, only went to his theatre toward eight
o'clock, when the piece in favor came on, and overtures and
accompaniments needed the strict ruling of the baton ; most
minor theatres are lax in such matters, and Pons felt the more
at ease because he himself had been by no means grasping in
all his dealings with the management ; and Schmucke, if need
be, could take his place.   Time went by, and Schmucke became an institution in the orchestra ; the Illustrious Gaudissart said nothing, but he was well aware of the value of Pon's
collaborator.   He was obliged to include a pianoforte in the
orchestra (following the example of the leading theatres) ; the
instrument was placed beside the conductor's chair, and
Schmucke played without increase of salary—a volunteer supernumerary.   As Schmucke's character, his utter lack of
ambition or pretense, became known, the orchestra recognized
him as one of themselves ; and, as time went on, he was intrusted with the often-needed miscellaneous musical instru-
ments which form no part of the regular band of a boulevard
theatre.   For a very small addition to his stipend, Schmucke
played the viola d'amore, hautboy, violoncello, and harp, as
well as the piano, the castanets for the *cachucha*, the bells,
saxehorn, and the like.   If the Germans cannot draw harmony
from the mighty instruments of Liberty, yet to play all instru-
ments of music comes to them by nature.

The two old artists were exceedingly popular at the theatre,
and took its ways philosophically.   They had put, as it were,
scales over their eyes, lest they should see the offenses that

needs must come when a *corps de ballet* is blended with actors
and actresses, one of the most trying combinations ever
created by the laws of supply and demand for the torment of
managers, authors, and composers alike.

Every one esteemed Pons with his kindness and his modesty,
his great self-respect and respect for others; for a pure and
limpid life wins something like admiration from the worst
nature in every social sphere, and in Paris a fair virtue meets
with something of the success of a large diamond, so great
a rarity it is. No actor, no dancer however brazen, would
have indulged in the mildest practical joke at the expense of
either Pons or Schmucke.

Pons very occasionally put in an appearance in the green-
room; but all that Schmucke knew of the theatre was the
underground passage from the street-door to the orchestra.
Sometimes, however, during an interval, the good German
would venture to make a survey of the house and ask a few
questions of the first flute, a young fellow from Strasbourg,
who came of a German family at Kehl. Gradually under the
flute's tuition Schmucke's childlike imagination acquired a
certain amount of knowledge of the world: he could believe
in the existence of that fabulous creature the *lorette*, the possibility of "marriages at the thirteenth arrondissement," the
vagaries of the leading lady, and the contraband traffic carried
on by box-openers. In his eyes the more harmless forms of
vice were the lowest depths of Babylonish iniquity; he did
not believe the stories, he smiled at them for grotesque inventions. The ingenious reader can see that Pons and Schmucke
were exploited, to use a word much in fashion; but what they
lost in money they gained in consideration and kindly treatment.

It was after the success of the ballet with which a run of
success began for the Gaudissart Company that the management presented Pons with a piece of plate—a group of figures
attributed to Benvenuto Cellini. The alarming costliness of

the gift caused talk in the green-room. It was a matter of twelve hundred francs! Pons, poor honest soul, was for returning the present, and Gaudissart had a world of trouble to persuade him to keep it.

"Ah!" said the manager afterward, when he told his partner of the interview, "if we could only find actors up to that sample!"

In their joint life, outwardly so quiet, there was the one disturbing element—the weakness to which Pons sacrificed, the insatiable craving to dine out. Whenever Schmucke happened to be at home while Pons was dressing for the evening, the good German would bewail this deplorable habit.

"Gif only he vas ony fatter vor it!" he many a time cried.

And Schmucke would dream of curing his friend of his degrading vice, for a true friend's instinct in all that belongs to the inner life is unerring as a dog's sense of smell; a friend knows by intuition the trouble in his friend's soul, and guesses at the cause and ponders it in his heart.

Pons, who always wore a diamond ring on the little finger of his right hand, an ornament permitted in the time of the Empire, but ridiculous to-day—Pons, who belonged to the "troubadour time," the sentimental period of the First Empire, was too much a child of his age, too much of a Frenchman to wear the expression of divine serenity which softened Schmucke's hideous ugliness. From Pons' melancholy looks, Schmucke knew that the profession of parasite was growing daily more difficult and painful. And, in fact, in that month of October, 1844, the number of houses at which Pons dined was naturally much restricted; reduced to move round and round the family circle, he had used the word family in far too wide a sense, as will shortly be seen.

M. Camusot, the rich silk mercer of the Rue des Bourdonnais, had married Pons' first cousin, Mlle. Pons, only child and heiress of one of the well-known firm of Pons Brothers, court embroiderers. Pons' own father and mother retired

from a firm founded before the Revolution of 1789, leaving
their capital in the business until Mlle. Pons' father sold it in
1815 to a M. Rivet. M. Camusot had since lost his wife and
married again, and retired from business some ten years, and
now in 1844 he was a member of the Board of Trade, a deputy,
and what not. But the Camusot clan were friendly; and
Pons, good man, still considered that he was some kind of
cousin to the children of the second marriage, who were not
relations, or even connected with him in any way.

The second Mme. Camusot being a Mlle. Cardot, Pons introduced himself as a relative into the tolerably numerous
Cardot family, a second bourgeois tribe which, taken with its
connections, formed quite as strong a clan as the Camusots;
for Cardot the notary (brother of the second Mme. Camusot)
had married a Mlle. Chiffreville; and the well-known family
of Chiffreville, the leading firm of manufacturing chemists,
was closely connected with the wholesale drug trade, of which
M. Anselme Popinot was for many years the undisputed head,
until the Revolution of July plunged him into the very centre
of the dynastic movement, as everybody knows. So Pons,
in the wake of the Camusots and Cardots, reached the Chif-
frevilles, and thence the Popinots, always in the character of
a cousin's cousin.

The above concise statement of Pons' relations with his
entertainers explains how it came to pass that an old musician
was received in 1844 as one of the family in the houses of
four distinguished persons—to wit, M. le Comte Popinot,
peer of France, and twice in office; M. Cardot, retired notary, mayor and deputy of an arrondissement in Paris; M.
Camusot senior, a member of the Board of Trade and the
Municipal Council of Paris, and a deputy on the high way
to the Upper Chamber and a peerage; and, lastly, M. Camusot de Marville, Camusot's son by his first marriage, and
Pons' one genuine relation, albeit even he was a first cousin
once removed.

This Camusot, president of a chamber of the Court of Appeals in Paris, had taken the name of his estate at Marville to distinguish himself from his father and a younger half-brother.

Cardot the retired notary had married his daughter to his successor, whose name was Berthier; and Pons, transferred as part of the connection, acquired a right to dine with the Berthiers "in the presence of a notary," as he put it.

This was the bourgeois empyrean which Pons called his "family," that upper world in which he so painfully reserved his right to a knife and fork.

Of all these houses, some ten in all, the one in which Pons ought to have met with the kindest reception should by rights have been his own cousin's; and, indeed, he paid most attention to President Camusot's family. But, alas! Mme. Camusot de Marville, daughter of the Sieur Thirion, usher of the cabinet to Louis XVIII. and Charles X., had never taken very kindly to her husband's first cousin, once removed. Pons had tried to soften this formidable relative; he wasted his time; for, in spite of the pianoforte lessons which he gave gratuitously to Mlle. Camusot, a young woman with hair somewhat inclined to red, it was impossible to make a musician of her.

And now, at this very moment, as he walked with that precious object in his hand, Pons was bound for the president's house, where he always felt as if he were at the Tuileries itself, so heavily did the solemn green curtains, the carmelite-brown hangings, thick piled carpets, heavy furniture, and general atmosphere of magisterial severity oppress his soul. Strange as it may seem, he felt more at home in the Hôtel Popinot, Rue Basse-du-Rempart, probably because it was full of works of art; for the master of the house, since he entered public life, had acquired a mania for collecting beautiful things, by way of contrast, no doubt, for a politician is obliged to pay for secret services of the ugliest kind.

President de Marville lived in the Rue de Hanovre, in a

house which his wife had bought ten years previously, on the death of her parents, for the Sieur and Dame Thirion left their daughter about a hundred and fifty thousand francs, the savings of a lifetime. With its northern aspect, the house looks gloomy enough seen from the street, but the back looks toward the south over the courtyard, with a rather pretty garden beyond it. As the president occupied the whole of the second floor, once the abode of a great financier of the time of Louis XIV., and the third was let to a wealthy old lady, the house wore a look of dignified repose befitting a magistrate's residence. President Camusot had invested all that he inherited from his mother, together with the savings of twenty years, in the purchase of the splendid Marville estate; a castle (as fine a relic of the past as you will find to-day in Normandy) standing in a hundred acres of park-land, and a fine dependent farm, nominally bringing in twelve thousand francs per annum, though, as it cost the president at least a thousand crowns to keep up a state almost princely in our days, his yearly revenue, "all told," as the saying is, was a bare nine thousand francs. With this and his salary, the president's income amounted to about twenty thousand francs; but though to all appearance a wealthy man, especially as one-half of his father's property would one day revert to him as the only child of the first marriage, he was obliged to live in Paris as befitted his official position, and M. and Mme. de Marville spent almost the whole of their incomes. Indeed, before the year 1834, they felt pinched.

This family schedule sufficiently explains why Mlle. de Marville, aged three-and-twenty, was still unwed, in spite of a hundred thousand francs of dowry and tempting prospects, frequently, skillfully, but so far vainly, held out. For the past five years Pons had listened to Mme. la Presidente's lamentations as she beheld one young lawyer after another led to the altar, while all the newly appointed judges at the Tribunal were fathers of families already; and she, all this time, had displayed Mlle. de Marville's brilliant expectations before the undazzled eyes of young Vicomte Popinot, eldest son of the great man of the drug trade, he of whom it was said by the envious tongues of the neighborhood of the Rue des Lombards that the Revolution of July had been brought about at least as much for his particular benefit as for the sake of the Orleans branch.

Arrived at the corner of the Rue de Choiseul and the Rue de Hanovre, Pons suffered from the inexplicable emotions which torment clear consciences; from a panic-terror such as the worst of scoundrels might feel at sight of a policeman, an agony caused solely by a doubt as to Mme. de Marville's probable reception of him. That grain of sand, grating continually on the fibres of his heart, so far from losing its angles, grew more and more jagged, and the family in the Rue de Hanovre always sharpened the edges. Indeed, their unceremonious treatment and Pons' depreciation in value among them had affected the servants; and, while they did not exactly fail in respect, they looked on the poor relation as a kind of beggar.

Pons' arch-enemy in the house was the ladies'-maid, a thin and weazened spinster, Madeleine Vivet by name. This Madeleine, in spite of, nay, perhaps on the strength of, a pimpled complexion and a viper-like length of spine, had made up her mind that some day she would be Mme. Pons. But in vain she dangled twenty-thousand francs of savings before the old bachelor's eyes; Pons had declined happiness accompanied by so many pimples. From that time forth the Dido of the antechamber, who fain would have called her master and mistress "cousin," wreaked her spite in petty ways upon the poor musician. She heard him on the stairs, and cried audibly, "Oh! here comes the sponger!" She stinted him of wine when she waited at dinner in the footman's absence; she filled the water-glass to the brim, to give him the difficult task of lifting it without spilling a drop; or she would pass the old man over altogether, till the mistress of the house would remind her (and in what a tone!—it brought the color to the poor cousin's face); or she would spill the gravy over his clothes. In short, she waged petty war after the manner of a small mind, knowing that she could annoy an unfortunate superior with impunity.

Madeleine Vivet was Mme. de Marville's maid and house-keeper. She had lived with M. and Mme. Camusot de Marville since their marriage; she had shared the early struggles in the provinces when M. Camusot was a judge at Alençon; she had helped them to exist when M. Camusot, president of the Tribunal of Mantes, came to Paris, in 1828, to be an examining magistrate. She was, therefore, too much one of the family not to wish, for reasons of her own, to revenge herself upon them. Beneath her desire to play a trick upon her haughty and ambitious mistress, and to call her master her cousin, there surely lurked a long-stifled hatred, built up like an avalanche, upon the pebble of some past grievance.

"Here comes your Monsieur Pons, madame, still wearing that spencer of his!" Madeleine came to tell Mme. the Presidente. "He really might tell me how he manages to make it look the same for five-and-twenty years together."

Mme. Camusot de Marville, hearing a man's footstep in the little drawing-room between the large drawing-room and her bedroom, looked meaningly at her daughter and shrugged her shoulders.

"You always make these announcements so cleverly that you leave me no time to think, Madeleine."

"Jean is out, madame; I was all alone; Monsieur Pons rang the bell, I opened the door; and, as he is almost one of the family, I could not prevent him from coming after me. There he is, taking off his spencer."

"Poor little puss!" said the presidente, addressing her daughter, "we are caught. We shall have to dine at home now. Let us see," she added, seeing that the "dear puss" wore a piteous face; "must we get rid of him for good?"

"Oh! poor man!" cried Mlle. Camusot, "deprive him of one of his dinners?"

Somebody coughed significantly in the next room by way of warning that he could hear.

"Very well, let him come in!" said Mme. Camusot, looking at Madeleine with another shrug.

"You are here so early, cousin, that you have come in upon us just as mother was about to dress," said Cécile Camusot in a coaxing tone. But Cousin Pons had caught sight of the presidente's shrug, and felt so cruelly hurt that he could not find a compliment, and contented himself with the profound remark, "You are always charming, my little cousin."

Then, turning to the mother, he continued, with a bow—

"You will not take it amiss, I think, if I have come a little earlier than usual, dear cousin; I have brought something for you; you once did me the pleasure of asking me for it."

Poor Pons! Every time he addressed the president, the president's wife, or Cécile as "cousin," he gave them excruciating annoyance. As he spoke, he drew a long, narrow cherry-wood box, marvelously carved, from his coat-pocket.

"Oh, did I? I had forgotten," the lady answered drily.

It was a heartless speech, was it not? Did not those few words deny all merit to the pains taken for her by the cousin whose one offense lay in the fact that he was a poor relation?

"But it is very kind of you, cousin," she added. "How much do I owe you for this little trifle?"

Pons quivered inwardly at the question. He had meant the trinket as a return for his dinners.

"I thought that you would permit me to offer it you——"

"What?" said Mme. Camusot. "Oh! but there need be no ceremony between us; we know each other well enough to wash our linen among ourselves. I know very well that you are not rich enough to give more than you get. And to go no further, it is quite enough that you should have spent a good deal of time in running about among the dealers——"

"If you were asked to pay the full price of the fan, my dear cousin, you would not care to have it," answered poor Pons, hurt and insulted; "it is one of Watteau's masterpieces, painted on both sides; but you may be quite easy, cousin, I did not give one-hundredth part of its value as a work of art."

To tell a rich man that he is poor! you might as well tell the Archbishop of Granada that his homilies show signs of senility. Mme. la Presidente, proud of her husband's position, of the estate of Marville, and her invitations to court balls, was keenly susceptible on this point; and, what was worse, the remark came from a poverty-stricken musician to whom she had been charitable.

"Then the people of whom you buy things of this kind are very stupid, are they?" she asked quickly.

"Stupid dealers are unknown in Paris," Pons answered almost drily.

"Then you must be very clever," put in Cécile by way of calming the dispute.

"Clever enough to know a Lancret, a Watteau, a Pater, or Greuze when I see it, little cousin; but anxious, most of all, to please your dear mamma."

Mme. de Marville, ignorant and vain, was unwilling to appear to receive the slightest trifle from the parasite; and here her ignorance served her admirably, she did not even know the name of Watteau. And, on the other hand, if anything can measure the extent of the collector's passion, which, in truth, is one of the most deeply seated of all passions, rivaling the very vanity of the author—if anything can give an idea of the lengths to which a collector will go, it is the audacity which Pons displayed on this occasion, as he held his own against his lady cousin for the first time in twenty years. He was amazed at his own boldness. He made Cécile see the beauties of the delicate carving on the sticks of this wonder, and as he talked to her his face grew serene and

gentle again.   But without some sketch of the presidente, it is
impossible fully to understand the perturbation of heart from
which Pons suffered.

Mme. de Marville had been short and fair, plump and
fresh ; at forty-six she was as short as ever, but she looked
dried up.   An arched forehead and thin lips, that had been
softly colored once, lent a soured look to a face naturally dis-
dainful, and now grown hard and unpleasant with a long
course of absolute domestic rule.   Time had deepened her
fair hair to a harsh chestnut hue ; the pride of office, intensi-
fied by suppressed envy, looked out of eyes that had lost none
of their brightness nor their satirical expression.   As a matter
of fact, Mme. Camusot de Marville felt almost poor in the
society of self-made wealthy bourgeois with whom Pons dined.
She could not forgive the rich retail druggist, ex-president of
the Commercial Court, for his successive elevations as deputy,
member of the Government, count and peer of France.   She
could not forgive her father-in-law for putting himself forward
instead of his eldest son as deputy of his arrondissement after
Popinot's promotion to the peerage.   After eighteen years of
services in Paris, she was still waiting for the post of Councilor of the Court of Cassation for her husband.   It was Camusot's own incompetence, well known at the Law Courts, which
excluded him from the Council.   The Home Secretary of 1844
even regretted Camusot's nomination to the presidency of the
Court of Indictments in 1834, though, thanks to his past experience as an examining magistrate, he made himself useful
in drafting decrees.

These disappointments had told upon Mme. de Marville,
who, moreover, had formed a tolerably correct estimate of her
husband.   A temper naturally shrewish was soured till she
grew positively terrible.   She was not old, but she had aged ;
she deliberately set herself to extort by fear all that the world
was inclined to refuse her, and was harsh and rasping as a file.
Caustic to excess, she had few friends among women : she sur-

rounded herself with prim, elderly matrons of her own stamp, who lent each other mutual support, and people stood in awe of her. As for poor Pons, his relations with this fiend in petticoats were very much those of a schoolboy with the master whose one means of communication is the ferule.

The presidente had no idea of the value of the gift. She was puzzled by her cousin's sudden access of audacity.

"Then, where did you find this?" inquired Cécile, as she looked closely at the trinket.

"In the Rue de Lappe. A dealer in second-hand furniture there had just brought it back with him from a castle that is being pulled down near Dreux, Aulnay. Madame de Pompadour used to spend part of her time there before she built Ménars. Some of the most splendid wood-carving ever known has been saved from destruction; Liénard (our most famous living wood-carver) has kept a couple of oval frames for models, as the *ne plus ultra* of the art, so fine it is. There were treasures in that place. My man found the fan in the drawer of an inlaid whatnot, which I should certainly have bought if I were collecting things of the kind, but it is quite out of the question—a single piece of Riesener's furniture is worth three or four thousand francs! People here in Paris are just beginning to find out that the famous French and German marquetry workers of the sixteenth, seventeenth, and eighteenth centuries composed perfect pictures in wood. It is a collector's business to be ahead of the fashion. Why, in five years' time, the Frankenthal ware, which I have been collecting these twenty years, will fetch twice the price of Sèvres *pâte tendre.*"

"What is Frankenthal ware?" asked Cècile.

"That is the name for the porcelain made by the Elector of the Palatinate; it dates further back than our manufactory at Sèvres; just as the famous gardens at Heidelberg, laid waste by Turenne, had the bad luck to exist before the gardens of Versailles. Sèvres copied Frankenthal to a large extent. In justice to the Germans, it must be said that they have done admirable work in Saxony and in the Palatinate.''

Mother and daughter looked at one another as if Pons were speaking Chinese. No one can imagine how ignorant and exclusive Parisians are; they only learn what they are taught, and that only when they choose.

"And how do you know the Frankenthal ware when you see it?"

"Eh! by the mark!" cried Pons with enthusiasm. "There is a mark on every one of those exquisite masterpieces. Frankenthal ware is marked with a C and T (for Charles Theodore) interlaced and crowned. On old Dresden china there are two crossed swords and the number of the order in gilt figures. Vincennes bears a hunting-horn; Vienna, a V closed and barred. You can tell Berlin by the two bars, Mayence by the wheel, and Sèvres by the two crossed L's. The queen's porcelain is marked A for Antoinette, with a royal crown above it. In the eighteenth century all the crowned heads of Europe had rival porcelain factories, and workmen were kidnapped. Watteau designed services for the Dresden factory; they fetch frantic prices at the present day. One has to know what one is about with them too, for they are turning out imitations now at Dresden. Wonderful things they used to make; they will never make the like again and——''

"Oh! pshaw!"

"No, cousin. Some inlaid work and some kinds of porcelain will never be made again, just as there will never be another Raphael, nor Titian, nor Rembrandt, nor Van Eyck, nor Cranach. Well, now! there are the Chinese; they are very ingenious, very clever; they make modern copies of their ' grand mandarin' porcelain, as it is called. But a pair of genuine old ' grand mandarin' vases of the largest size are worth six, eight, and ten thousand francs, while you can buy the modern replicas for a couple of hundred!''

"You are joking."

"You are astonished at the prices, but that is nothing, cousin. A dinner service of Sèvres *pâte tendre* (and *pâte tendre* is not porcelain)—a complete dinner-service of Sèvres *pâte tendre* for twelve persons is not merely worth a hundred thousand francs, but that is the price charged on the invoice. Such a dinner-service cost fifty thousand francs at Sèvres in 1750; I have seen the original invoices."

"But let us go back to this fan," said Cécile. Evidently in her opinion the trinket was an old-fashioned thing.

"You can understand that as soon as your dear mamma did me the honor of asking for a fan, I went the round of all the curiosity stores in Paris, but I found nothing fine enough. I wanted nothing less than a masterpiece for the dear presidente, and thought of giving her one that once belonged to Marie Antoinette, the most beautiful of all celebrated fans. But yesterday I was dazzled by this divine *chef-d'œuvre*, which certainly must have been ordered by Louis XV. himself. Do you ask how I came to look for fans in the Rue de Lappe, among an Auvergnat's stock of brass and iron and ormolu furniture? Well, I myself believe that there is an intelligence in works of art; they know art-lovers, they call to them— 'Cht-tt!'"

Mme. de Marville shrugged her shoulders and looked at her daughter; Pons did not notice the rapid pantomime.

"I know all those sharpers," continued Pons, "so I asked him, 'Anything fresh to-day, Daddy Monistrol?'—(for he always lets me look over his lots before the big buyers come) —and at that he began to tell me how Liénard, that did such beautiful work for the Government in the Chapelle de Dreux, had been at the Aulnay sale and rescued the carved panels out of the clutches of the Paris dealers, while their heads were running on china and inlaid furniture. 'I did not do much myself,' he went on, 'but I may make my traveling expenses out of *this*,' and he showed me a whatnot; a marvel!

Boucher's designs executed in marquetry, and with such art !
One could have gone down on one's knees before it. 'Look,
sir,' he said, 'I have just found this fan in a little drawer ; it
was locked, I had to force it open. You might tell me where
I can sell it '—and with that he brings me out this little carved
cherry-wood box. 'See,' says he, 'it is the kind of Pompadour that looks like decorated Gothic.' 'Yes,' I told him,
'the box is pretty ; the box might suit me ; but as for the fan,
Monistrol, I have no Mme. Pons to give the old trinket to,
and they make very pretty new ones nowadays ; you can buy
miracles of painting on vellum cheaply enough. There are
two thousand painters in Paris, you know.' And I opened
out the fan carelessly, keeping down my admiration, looking
indifferently at those two exquisite little pictures, touched off
with an ease fit to send you into raptures. I held Madame
de Pompadour's fan in my hand ! Watteau had done his
utmost for this. 'What do you want for the whatnot ?' 'Oh !
a thousand francs ; I have had a bid already.' I offered him
a price for the fan corresponding with the probable expenses
of the journey. We looked each other in the eyes, and I saw
that I had my man. I put the fan back into the box lest my
Auvergnat should begin to look at it, and went into ecstasies
over the box ; indeed, it is a jewel. 'If I take it,' said I, 'it
is for the sake of the box ; the box tempts me. As for the
whatnot, you will get more than a thousand francs for that.
Just see how the brass is wrought ; it is a model. There is
business in it. It has never been copied ; it is a unique specimen, made solely for Madame de Pompadour '—and so on,
till my man, all on fire for his whatnot, forgets the fan, and
lets me have it for a mere trifle, because I have pointed out
the beauties of this piece of Riesener's furniture. So here it
is ! but it needs a great deal of experience to make such a
bargain as that. It is a duel, eye to eye ; and who has such
eyes as a Jew or an Auvergnat ?''

The old artist's wonderful pantomime, his vivid, eager way

of telling the story of the triumph of his shrewdness over the dealer's ignorance, would have made a subject for a Dutch painter; but it was all thrown away upon the audience. Mother and daughter exchanged cold, contemptuous glances. "What an oddity!" they seemed to say.

"So it amuses you?" remarked Mme. de Marville. The question sent a cold chill through Pons; he felt a strong desire to slap the presidente.

"Why, my dear cousin, that is the way to hunt down a work of art. You are face to face with antagonists that dispute the game with you. It is craft against craft! A work of art in the hands of a Norman, an Auvergnat, or a Jew is like a princess guarded by magicians in a fairy tale."

"And how can you tell that this is by Wat—— what do you call him?"

"Watteau, cousin. One of the greatest eighteenth-century painters in France. Look! do you not see that it is his work?" (pointing to a pastoral scene, court-shepherd swains and shepherdesses dancing in a ring). "The movement! the life in it! the coloring! There it is—see!—painted with a stroke of the brush, as a writing-master makes a flourish with a pen. Not a trace of effort here! And, turn it over, look! —a ball in the drawing-room. Summer and Winter! And what ornaments! and how well preserved it is! The hinge-pin is gold, you see, and, on cleaning it, I found a tiny ruby at either end."

"If it is so, cousin, I could not think of accepting such a valuable present from you. It would be better to lay up the money for yourself," said Mme. de Marville; but, all the same, she asked no better than to keep the article of virtu, that splendid fan.

"It is time that it should pass from the service of Vice into the hands of Virtue," said the good soul, recovering his assurance. "It has taken a century to work the miracle. No princess at Court, you may be sure, will have anything to

9

compare with it; for, unfortunately, men will do more for a Pompadour than for a virtuous queen, such is human nature."

"Very well," Mme. de Marville said, laughing, "I will accept your present. Cécile, my angel, go to Madeleine and see that dinner is worthy of your cousin."

Mme. de Marville wished to make matters even. Her request, made aloud, in defiance of all rules of good taste, sounded so much like an attempt to repay at once the balance due to the poor cousin, that Pons flushed red, like a girl found out in fault. The grain of sand was a little too large; for some moments he could only let it work in his heart. Cécile, a red-haired young woman, with a touch of pedantic affectation, combined her father's ponderous manner with a trace of her mother's hardness. She went and left poor Pons face to face with the terrible presidente.

"How nice she is, my little Lili!" said the mother. She still called her Cécile by this baby name.

"Charming!" said Pons, twirling his thumbs.

"I *cannot* understand these times in which we live," broke out the presidente. "What is the good of having a president of the Court of Appeal in Paris and a commander of the Legion of Honor for your father, and for a grandfather the richest wholesale silk merchant in Paris, a deputy, and a millionaire that will be a peer of France some of these days?"

The president's zeal for the new Government had, in fact, recently been rewarded with a commander's ribbon—thanks to his friendship with Popinot, said the envious. Popinot himself, modest though he was, had, as has been seen, accepted the title of count, "for his son's sake," he told his numerous friends.

"Men look for nothing but money nowadays," said Cousin Pons. "No one thinks anything of you unless you are rich, and——"

"What would it have been if heaven had spared my poor little Charles!" cried the lady.

"Oh, with two children you would be poor," returned the cousin. "It practically means the division of the property. But you need not trouble yourself, cousin; Cécile is sure to marry sooner or later. She is the most accomplished girl I know."

To such depths had Pons fallen by adapting himself to the company of his entertainers! In their houses he echoed their ideas, and said the obvious thing, after the manner of a chorus in a Greek play. He did not dare to give free play to the artist's originality, which had overflowed in bright repartee when he was young; he had effaced himself, till he had almost lost his individuality; and if the real Pons appeared, as he had done a moment ago, he was immediately repressed.

"But I myself was married with only twenty thousand francs for my portion——"

"In 1819, cousin. And it was *you*, a woman with a head on your shoulders, and the royal protection of Louis XVIII."

"But still, my child is a perfect angel. She is clever, she has a warm heart, she will have a hundred thousand francs on her wedding-day, to say nothing of the most brilliant expectations; and yet she stays on our hands," and so on and so on. For twenty minutes, Mme. de Marville talked on about herself and her Cécile, pitying herself after the manner of mothers in bondage to marriageable daughters.

Pons had dined at the house every week for twenty years, and Camusot de Marville was the only cousin he had in the world; but he had yet to hear the first word spoken as to his own affairs—nobody cared to know how he lived. Here and elsewhere the poor cousin was a kind of sink down which his relatives poured domestic confidences. His discretion was well known; indeed, was he not bound over to silence when a single imprudent word would have shut the doors of ten houses upon him? And he must combine his rôle of listener with a second part: he must applaud continually, smile on every one, accuse nobody, defend nobody; from his point of

view, every one must be in the right. And so, in the house
of his kinsmen, Pons no longer counted as a man ; he was a
digestive apparatus.

In the course of a long tirade, Mme. Camusot de Marville
avowed with due circumspection that she was prepared to take
almost any son-in-law with her eyes shut. She was even dis-
posed to think that at eight-and-forty or so a man with twenty
thousand francs a year was a good match.

"Cécile is in her twenty-third year. If it should fall out
so unfortunately that she is not married before she is five or
six-and-twenty, it will be extremely hard to marry her at all.
When a girl reaches that age, people want to know why she
has been so long on hand. We are a good deal talked about
in our set. We have come to an end of all the ordinary
excuses—'She is so young. She is so fond of her father and
mother that she doesn't like to leave them. She is so happy
at home. She is hard to please, she would like a good
name——' We are beginning to look silly ; I feel that dis-
tinctly. And, beside, Cécile is tired of waiting, poor child,
she suffers——"

"In what way?" Pons was noodle enough to ask.

"Why, because it is humiliating to her to see all her girl
friends married before her," replied the mother, with a
duenna's air.

"But, cousin, has anything happened since the last time
that I had the pleasure of dining here? Why do you think
of men of eight-and-forty?" Pons inquired humbly.

"This has happened," returned the presidente. "We
were to have had an interview with a court councilor ; his son
is thirty years old and very well-to-do, and Monsieur de Marville would have obtained a post in the Audit Office for him
and paid the money. The young man is a supernumerary
there at present. And now they tell us that he has taken it
into his head to rush off to Italy in the train of a duchess from
the Bal Mabille—— It is nothing but a refusal in disguise.

The fact is, the young man's mother is dead; he has an income of thirty thousand francs, and more to come at his father's death, and they don't care about the match for him. You have just come in in the middle of all this, dear cousin, so you must excuse our bad temper."

While Pons was casting about for the complimentary answer which invariably occurred to him too late when he was afraid of his host, Madeleine came in, handed a folded note to the presidente, and waited for an answer. The note ran as follows:

"DEAR MAMMA:—If we pretend that this note comes to you from papa at the Palais, and that he wants us both to dine with his friend because proposals have been renewed—then the cousin will go, and we can carry out our own plan of going to the Popinots."

"Who brought the master's note?" the presidente asked quickly.

"A lad from the Salle du Palais,"* the withered waiting-woman unblushingly answered, and her mistress knew at once that Madeleine had woven the plot with Cécile, now at the end of her patience.

"Tell him that we will both be there at half-past five."

Madeleine had no sooner left the room than the presidente turned to Cousin Pons with that insincere friendliness which is about as grateful to a sensitive soul as a mixture of milk and vinegar to the palate of an epicure.

"Dinner is ordered, dear cousin; you must dine without us; my husband has just sent word from the Court that the question of the marriage has been reopened, and we are to dine with the councilor. We need not stand on ceremony at all. Do just as if you were at home. I have no secrets from you; I am perfectly open with you, as you see. I am sure you would not wish to break off the little darling's marriage."

* Palace Hall—High Court.

"I, cousin? On the contrary, I should like to find some one for her ; but in my circle——"

" Oh, that is not at all likely," said the presidente, cutting him short insolently. "Then you will stay, will you not ? Cécile will keep you company while I dress."

"Oh ! I can dine somewhere else, cousin."

Cruelly hurt though he was by her way of casting up his poverty to him, the prospect of being left alone with the servants was even more alarming.

" But why should you ? Dinner is ready ; you may just as well have it ; if you do not, the servants will eat it."

At that atrocious speech Pons started up as if he had received a shock from a galvanic battery, bowed stiffly to the lady, and went to find his spencer. Now, it so happened that the door of Cécile's bedroom, beyond the little drawing-room, stood open, and, looking into the mirror, he caught sight of the girl shaking with laughter as she gesticulated and made signs to her mother. The old artist understood beyond a doubt that he had been the victim of some cowardly hoax. Pons went slowly down the stairs ; he could not keep back the tears. He understood that he had been turned out of the house, but why and wherefore he did not know.

"I am growing too old," he told himself. "The world has a horror of old age and poverty—two ugly things. After this I will not go anywhere unless I am asked."

Heroic resolve !

Downstairs the great gate was shut, as it usually is in houses occupied by the proprietor ; the kitchen stood exactly opposite the porter's lodge, and the door was open. Pons was obliged to listen while Madeleine told the servants the whole story amid the laughter of the servants. She had not expected him to leave so soon. The footman loudly applauded a joke at the expense of a visitor who was always coming to the house and never gave you more than three francs at the year's end.

"Yes," put in the cook ; " but if he cuts up rough and does

not come back, there will be three francs the less for some of us on New Year's day."

"Eh! How is he to know?" retorted the footman.

"Pooh!" said Madeleine, "a little sooner or a little later—what difference does it make? The people at the other houses where he dines are so tired of him that they are going to turn him out."

"The gate if you please."

Madeleine had scarcely uttered the words when they heard the old musician's call to the porter. It sounded like a cry of pain. There was a sudden silence in the kitchen.

"He heard!" the footman said.

"Well, and if he did, so much the worser, or rather so much the better," retorted Madeleine. "He is an arrant skinflint."

Poor Pons had lost none of the talk in the kitchen; he heard it all, even to the last word. He made his way home along the boulevards, in the same state, physical and mental, as an old woman after a desperate struggle with burglars. As he went he talked to himself in quick spasmodic jerks; his honor had been wounded, and the pain of it drove him on as a gust of wind whirls away a straw. He found himself at last in the Boulevard du Temple; how he had come thither he could not tell. It was five o'clock, and, strange to say, he had completely lost his appetite.

But if the reader is to understand the revolution which Pons' unexpected return at that hour was to work in the Rue de Normandie, the promised biography of Mme. Cibot must be given in this place.

Any one passing along the Rue de Normandie might be pardoned for thinking that he was in some small provincial town. Grass runs to seed in the street, everybody knows everybody else, and the sight of a stranger is an event. The houses date back to the reign of Henry IV., when there was a scheme afoot for a quarter in which every street was to be named after a French province, and all should converge in a handsome square to which La France should stand godmother. The Quartier de l'Europe was a revival of the same idea; history repeats itself everywhere in the world, and even in the world of speculation.

The house in which the two musicians used to live is an old mansion with a courtyard in front and a garden at the back; but the front part of the house which gives upon the street is comparatively modern, built during the eighteenth century when the Marais was a fashionable quarter. The friends lived at the back, on the third floor of the old part of the house. The whole building belonged to M. Pillerault, an old man of eighty, who left matters very much in the hands of M. and Mme. Cibot, his janitors for the past twenty-six years.

Now, as a janitor cannot live by his lodge alone, the aforesaid Cibot had other means of gaining a livelihood; and supplemented his five per cent. on the rental and his faggot from every cartload of wood by his own earnings as a tailor. In time Cibot ceased to work for the master tailors; he made a connection among the little tradespeople of the quarter, and enjoyed a monopoly of the repairs, renovations, and finedrawing of all the coats and trousers in three adjacent streets. The lodge was spacious and wholesome, and boasted a second room; wherefore the Cibot couple were looked upon as among the luckiest porters in the arrondissement.

Cibot, small and stunted, with a complexion almost olivecolored by reason of sitting day in day out Turk-fashion on a table level with the barred window, made about twelve or fourteen francs a week. He worked still, though he was fiftyeight years old, but fifty-eight is the porter's golden age; he is used to his lodge, he and his room fit each other like the shell and the oyster, and "he is known in the neighborhood."

Mme. Cibot, sometime opener of oysters at the Cadran Bleu, after all the adventures which come unsought to the belle of an oyster-bar, left her post for love of Cibot at the age of twenty-eight. The beauty of a woman of the people is short-lived, especially if she is planted espalier fashion at a restaurant door. Her features are hardened by puffs of hot air from the kitchen ; the color of the heeltaps of customers' bottles, finished in the company of the waiters, gradually filters into her complexion—no beauty is full blown as soon as the beauty of an oyster-opener. Luckily for Mme. Cibot, lawful wedlock and a portress' life were offered to her just in time ; while she still preserved a comeliness of a masculine order slandered by rivals of the Rue de Normandie, who called her "a great blowsy thing," Mme. Cibot might have sat as a model to Rubens. Those flesh tints reminded you of the appetizing sheen on a pat of Isigny butter ; but plump as she was, no woman went about her work with more agility. Mme. Cibot had attained the time of life when women of her stamp are obliged to shave—which is as much as to say that she had reached the age of forty-eight. A porter's wife with a mustache is one of the best possible guarantees of respectability and security that a landlord can have. If Delacroix could have seen Mme. Cibot leaning proudly on her broom handle, he would assuredly have painted her as Bellona.

Strange as it may seem, the circumstances of the Cibots, man and wife (in the style of an indictment), were one day to affect the lives of the two friends ; wherefore the chronicler, as in duty bound, must give some particulars as to the Cibots' lodge.

The house brought in about eight thousand francs, for there were three complete sets of apartments—back and front, on the side nearest the Rue de Normandie, as well as the three floors in the older mansion between the courtyard and the garden, and a store kept by a rag, bottle, bone, and old iron dealer named Rémonencq, which fronted on the street. During the past few months this Rémonencq had begun to deal in old curiosities, and knew the value of Pons' collection so well that he took off his hat whenever the musician came in or went out.

A sou in the livre on eight thousand francs therefore brought in about four hundred francs to the Cibots. They had no rent to pay and no expenses for firing; Cibot's earnings amounted on an average to seven or eight hundred francs, add tips at the New Year, and the pair had altogether an income of sixteen hundred francs, every penny of which they spent, for the Cibots lived and fared better than working people usually do. "One can only live once," La Cibot used to say. She was born during the Revolution, you see, and had never learned her Catechism.

The husband of this portress with the unblenching tawny eyes was an object of envy to the whole fraternity, for La Cibot had not forgotten the knowledge of cookery picked up at the Cadran Bleu. So it had come to pass that the Cibots had passed the prime of life, and saw themselves on the threshold of old age without a hundred francs put by for the future. Well clad and well fed, they enjoyed among the neighbors, it is true, the respect due to twenty-six years of strict honesty; for if they had nothing of their own, they "hadn't nothing belonging to nobody else," according to La Cibot, who was prodigal of negatives. "There wasn't never such a love of a man," she would say to her husband. Do you ask why? You might as well ask the reason of her indifference in matters of religion.

Both of them were proud of a life lived in open day, of the esteem in which they were held for six or seven streets round about, and of the autocratic rule permitted to them by the proprietor ("perprietor," they called him); but in private they groaned because they had no money lying at interest. Cibot complained of pains in his hands and legs, and his wife would lament that her poor, dear Cibot should be forced to work at his age; and, indeed, the day is not far distant when a porter after thirty years of such a life will cry shame upon

the injustice of the Government and clamor for the ribbon of
the Legion of Honor. Every time that the gossip of the
quarter brought news of such and such a servant-maid, left an
annuity of three or four hundred francs after eight or ten
years of service, the porters' lodges would resound with complaints, which may give some idea of the consuming jealousies
in the lowest walks of life in Paris.

"Oh, indeed! It will never happen to the like of us to
have our names mentioned in a will! We have no luck, but
we do more than servants, for all that. We fill a place of
trust; we give receipts, we are on the lookout for squalls, and
yet we are treated like dogs, neither more nor less, and that's
the truth!"

"Some find fortune and some miss fortune," said Cibot,
coming in with a coat he had just finished.

"If I had left Cibot here in this lodge and taken a place as
cook, we should have had our thirty thousand francs out at
interest," cried Mme. Cibot, standing chatting with a neighbor, her hands on her prominent hips. "But I didn't understand how to get on in life; housed inside of a snug lodge
and firing found and want for nothing, but that is all."

In 1836 when the friends took up their abode on the third
floor, they brought about a sort of revolution in the Cibot
household. It befell on this wise. Schmucke, like his friend
Pons, usually arranged that the porter or the porter's wife
should undertake the cares of housekeeping; and being both
of one mind on this point when they came to live in the Rue
de Normandie, Mme. Cibot became their housekeeper at the
rate of twenty-five francs per month—twelve francs fifty centimes for each of them. Before the year was out, the emeritus
portress reigned in the establishment of the two old bachelors,
as she reigned everywhere in the house belonging to M.
Pillerault, great-uncle of Mme. la Comtesse Popinot. Their
business was her business; she called them "my gentlemen."
And at last, finding the pair of nutcrackers mild as lambs,

easy to live with, and by no means suspicious—perfect children, in fact—her heart, the heart of a woman of the people,
prompted her to protect, adore, and serve them with such
thorough devotion, that she read them a lecture now and
again, and saved them from the impositions which swell the
cost of living in Paris.   For twenty-five francs a month, the
two old bachelors inadvertently acquired a mother.

As they became aware of Mme. Cibot's full value, they
gave her outspoken praises, and thanks, and little presents,
which strengthened the bonds of the domestic alliance.   Mme.
Cibot a thousand times preferred appreciation to money payments; it is a well-known fact that the sense that one is appreciated makes up for a deficiency in wages.   And Cibot did
all that he could for his wife's two gentlemen, and ran errands
and did repairs at half-price for them.

The second year brought a new element into the friendship
between the lodge and the third floor, and Schmucke concluded a bargain which satisfied his indolence and desire for
a life without cares.   For thirty sous per day, or forty-five
francs per month, Mme. Cibot undertook to provide Schmucke
with breakfast and dinner; and Pons, finding his friend's
breakfast very much to his mind, concluded a separate treaty
for that meal only at the rate of eighteen francs.   This arrangement, which added nearly ninety francs every month to the
takings of the porter and his wife, made two inviolable beings
of the lodgers; they became angels, cherubs, divinities.   It is
very doubtful whether the King of the French, who is supposed to understand economy, is as well served as the pair of
nutcrackers used to be in those days.

For them the milk issued pure from the can; they enjoyed
a free perusal of all the morning papers taken by other lodgers,
later risers, who were told, if need be, that the newspaper had
not come yet.   Mme. Cibot, moreover, kept their clothes,
their rooms, and the landing as clean as a Flemish interior.
As for Schmucke, he enjoyed unhoped-for happiness; Mme.

Cibot had made life easy for him; he paid her about six francs a month, and she took charge of his linen, washing, and mending. Altogether his expenses amounted to sixty-six francs per month (for he spent fifteen francs on tobacco), and sixty-six francs multiplied by twelve produces the sum-total of seven hundred and ninety-two francs. Add two hundred and twenty francs for rent, rates, and taxes, and you have a thousand and twelve francs. Cibot was Schmucke's tailor; his clothes cost him on an average a hundred and fifty francs, which further swells the total to the sum of twelve hundred. On twelve hundred francs per annum this profound philosopher lived. How many people in Europe, whose one thought it is to come to Paris and live there, will be agreeably surprised to learn that you may exist in comfort upon an income of twelve hundred francs in the Rue de Normandie in the Marais, under the wing of a Mme. Cibot.

Mme. Cibot, to resume the story, was amazed beyond expression to see Pons, good man, return at five o'clock in the evening. Such a thing had never happened before; and not only so, but "her gentleman" had given her no greeting—had not so much as seen her!

"Well, well, Cibot," said she to her spouse, "Monsieur Pons has come in for a million, or gone out of his mind!"

"That is how it looks to me," said Cibot, dropping the coat-sleeve in which he was making a "dart," in tailor's language.

The savory odor of a stew pervaded the whole courtyard, as Pons returned mechanically home. Mme. Cibot was dishing up Schmucke's dinner, which consisted of scraps of boiled beef from a little cook-shop not above doing a little trade of this kind. These morsels were fricasseed in brown butter, with thin slices of onion, until the meat and vegetables had absorbed the gravy, and this true porter's dish was browned to the right degree. With that fricassee, prepared with loving care for Cibot and Schmucke, and accompanied by a bottle of beer and a piece of cheese, the old German music-master was quite content. Not King Solomon in all his glory, be sure, could dine better than Schmucke. A dish of boiled beef fricasseed with onions, scraps of *sauté* chicken, or beef and parsley, or venison, or fish served with a sauce of La Cibot's own invention (a sauce with which a mother might unsuspectingly eat her child)—such was Schmucke's ordinary, varying with the quantity and quality of the remnants of food supplied by boulevard restaurants to the cook-shop in the Rue Boucherat. Schmucke took everything that " goot Montame Zipod " gave him, and was content, and so from day to day "goot Montame Zipod " cut down the cost of his dinner, until it could be served for twenty sous.

" It won't be long afore I find out what is the matter with him, poor dear," said Mme. Cibot to her husband, " for here is Monsieur Schmucke's dinner all ready for him."

As she spoke, she covered the deep earthenware dish with a plate ; and, notwithstanding her age, she climbed the stair and reached the door before Schmucke opened it to Pons.

" Vat is de matter mit you, mein goot friend ? " asked the German, scared by the expression on Pons' face.

" I will tell you all about it ; but I have come home to have dinner with you——"

" Tinner ! tinner ! " cried Schmucke in ecstasy ; " but it is imbossible ! " the old German added, as he thought of his friend's gastronomical tastes ; and at that very moment he caught sight of Mme. Cibot listening to the conversation, as she had a right to do as his lawful housewife. Struck with one of those happy inspirations which only enlighten a friend's heart, he marched up to the portress and drew her out to the stairhead.

" Montame Zipod," he said, " der goot Bons is fond of goot dings ; shoost go rount to der Catran Pleu und order a dainty liddle tinner, mit anjovies und maggaroni. Ein tinner for Lugullus, in vact."   .

"What is that?" inquired La Cibot.

"Oh! ah!" returned Schmucke, "it is veal *à la pour-cheoise*" (*bourgeoise*, he meant), "a nice fisch, ein pottle off Porteaux, und nice dings, der fery best dey haf, like groquettes of rice und shmoked pacon!

"Bay for it, und say nodings; I vill gif you back de monny to-morrow morning."

Back went Schmucke, radiant and rubbing his hands; but his expression slowly changed to a look of bewildered astonishment as he heard Pons' story of the troubles that had but just now overwhelmed him in a moment. He tried to comfort Pons by giving him a sketch of the world from his own point of view. Paris, in his opinion, was a perpetual hurly-burly, the men and women in it were whirled away by a tempestuous waltz; it was no use expecting anything of the world, which only looked at the outside of things, "und not at der inderior." For the hundredth time he related how that the only three pupils for whom he had really cared, for whom he was ready to die, the three who had been fond of him, and even allowed him a little pension of nine hundred francs, each contributing three hundred to the amount—his favorite pupils had quite forgotten to come to see him; and so swift was the current of Parisian life which swept them away, that if he called at their houses he had not succeeded in seeing them once in three years—(it is a fact, however, that Schmucke had always thought fit to call on these great ladies at ten o'clock in the morning!)—still, his pension was paid quarterly through the medium of attorneys.

"Und yet, dey are hearts of gold," he concluded. "Dey are my liddle Saint Cecilias, sharming vimmen, Montame de Bordentuère, Montame te Fantanesse, und Montame tu Dilet. Gif I see dem at all, it is at die Jambs Elusées, und dey do not see me—— yet dey are ver' fond of me, und I might go to dine mit dem, und dey vould be ver' bleased to see me; und I might go to deir country-houses, but I would much rader be mit mein friend Bons, because I kan see him venefer I like, und efery tay."

Pons took Schmucke's hand and grasped it between his own. All that was passing in his inmost soul was communicated in that tight pressure. And so for a while the friends sat like two lovers, meeting at last after a long absence.

"Tine here, efery tay!" broke out Schmucke, inwardly blessing Mme. de Marville for her hardness of heart. "Look here! Ve shall go a prick-à-pracking togeders, und der teufel shall nefer show his tail here."

"Ve shall go prick-à-pracking togeders!"—for the full comprehension of those truly heroic words, it must be confessed that Schmucke's ignorance of bric-à-brac was something of the densest. It required all the strength of his friendship to keep him from doing heedless damage in the sitting-room and study which did duty as a museum for Pons. Schmucke, wholly absorbed in music, a composer for love of his art, took about as much interest in his friend's little trifles as a fish might take in a flower-show at the Luxembourg, supposing that it had received a ticket of admission. A certain awe which he certainly felt for the marvels was simply a reflection of the respect which Pons showed his treasures when he dusted them. To Pons' exclamations of admiration, he was wont to reply with a "Yes, it is ver' bretty," as a mother answers baby-gestures with meaningless baby-talk. Seven times since the friends had lived together, Pons had exchanged a good clock for a better one, till at last he possessed a timepiece in Boule's first and best manner, for Boule had two manners, as Raphael had three. In the first he combined ebony and copper; in the second—contrary to his convictions—he sacrificed to tortoise-shell, working miracles to outstrip his rivals, the inventors of tortoise-shell inlaid work. In spite of Pons' learned dissertations, Schmucke never could see the slightest difference between the magnificent clock in Boule's first manner and its six predecessors; but, for Pons' sake, Schmucke was even more careful among the "chimcracks" than Pons himself. So it should not be surprising that Schmucke's sublime words comforted Pons in his despair; for " Ve shall go prick-à-pracking togeders" meant, being interpreted, "I will put money into bric-à-brac, if you will only dine here."

"Dinner is ready," Mme. Cibot announced, with astonishing self-possession.

It is not difficult to imagine Pons' surprise when he saw and relished the dinner due to Schmucke's friendship. Sensations of this kind, that come so rarely in a lifetime, are never the outcome of the constant, close relationship by which friend daily says to friend, "You are a second self to me;" for this, too, becomes a matter of use and wont. It is only by contact with the barbarism of the world without that the happiness of that intimate life is revealed to us as a sudden glad surprise. It is the outer world which renews the bond between friend and friend, lover and lover, all their lives long, wherever two great souls are knit together by friendship or by love.

Pons brushed away two big tears, Schmucke himself wiped his eyes; and, though nothing was said, the two were closer friends than before. Little friendly nods and glances exchanged across the table were like balm to Pons, soothing the pain caused by the sand dropped in his heart by the president's wife. As for Schmucke, he rubbed his hands until they were sore; for a new idea had occurred to him, one of those great discoveries which cause a German no surprise, unless they sprout up suddenly in a Teuton brain frost-bound by the awe and reverence due to sovereign princes.

"Mine goot Bons?" began Schmucke.

"I can guess what you mean; you would like us both to dine together here, every day——"

"Gif only I vas rich enof to lif like dis efery tay——" began the good German in a melancholy voice. But here Mme. Cibot appeared upon the scene. Pons had given her

10

an order for the theatre from time to time, and stood in consequence almost as high in her esteem and affection as her boarder Schmucke.

"Lord love you," said she, "for three francs and wine extra I can give you both such a dinner every day that you will be ready to lick the plates as clean as if they were washed."

"It is a fact," Schmucke remarked, "dat die tinners dat Montame Zipod cooks for me are better as de messes dey eat at der royal dable!" In his eagerness, Schmucke, usually so full of respect for the powers that be, so far forgot himself as to imitate the irreverent newspapers which scoffed at the "fixed-price" dinners of royalty.

"Really?" said Pons. "Very well, I will try to-morrow."

And at that promise Schmucke sprang from one end of the table to the other, sweeping off tablecloth, bottles, and dishes as he went and hugged Pons to his heart. So might gas rush to combine with gas.

"Vat happiness!" cried he.

Mme. Cibot was quite touched. "Monsieur is going to dine here every day!" she cried proudly.

That excellent woman departed downstairs again in ignorance of the event which had brought about this result, entered her room like Josepha in "William Tell," set down the plates and dishes on the table with a bang, and called aloud to her husband—

"Cibot! run to the Café Turc for two small cups of coffee, and tell the man at the stove that it is for me."

Then she sat down and rested her hands on her massive knees, and gazed out of the window at the opposite wall.

"I will go to-night and see what Ma'am Fontaine says," she thought. (Madame Fontaine told fortunes on the cards for all the servants in the quarter of the Marais.) "Since these two gentlemen came here, we have put two thousand francs in the savings bank. Two thousand francs in eight years! What luck! Would it be better to make no profit out of

Monsieur Pons' dinner and keep him here at home? Ma'am Fontaine's hen will tell me that."

Three years ago Mme. Cibot had begun to cherish a hope that her name might be mentioned in "her gentlemen's" wills; she had redoubled her zeal since that covetous thought tardily sprouted up in the midst of that so honest mustache. Pons hitherto had dined abroad, eluding her desire to have both of "her gentlemen" entirely under her management; his "troubadour" collector's life had scared away certain vague ideas which hovered in La Cibot's brain; but now her shadowy projects assumed the formidable shape of a definite plan, dating from that memorable dinner. Fifteen minutes later she reappeared in the dining-room with two cups of excellent coffee, flanked by a couple of tiny glasses of *kirschwasser*.*

"Long lif Montame Zipod!" cried Schmucke; "she haf guessed right!"

The diner-out bemoaned himself a little, while Schmucke met his lamentations with coaxing fondness, like a home pigeon welcoming back a wandering bird. Then the pair set out for the theatre.

Schmucke could not leave his friend in the condition to which he had been brought by the Camusots—mistresses and servants. He knew Pons so well; he feared lest some cruel, sad thought should seize on him at his conductor's desk, and undo all the good done by his welcome home to the nest.

And Schmucke brought his friend back on his arm through the streets at midnight. A lover could not be more careful of his lady. He pointed out the edges of the curbstones, he was on the lookout whenever they stepped on or off the pavement, ready with a warning if there was a gutter to cross. Schmucke could have wished that the streets were paved with cotton-down; he would have had a blue sky overhead, and Pons should hear the music which all the angels in heaven were

* A Swiss liqueur distilled from the black cherry.

making for him. He had won the lost province in his friend's
heart !

For nearly three months Pons and Schmucke dined together
every day. Pons was obliged to retrench at once; for dinner
at forty-five francs a month and wine at thirty-five meant precisely eighty francs less to spend on bric-à-brac. And' very
soon, in spite of all that Schmucke could do, in spite of his
little German jokes, Pons fell to regretting the delicate dishes,
the liqueurs, the good coffee, the table-talk, the insincere politeness, the guests, and the gossip, and the houses where he
used to dine. On the wrong side of sixty a man cannot break
himself of a habit of thirty-six years' growth. Wine at a hundred and thirty francs per hogshead is scarcely a generous
liquid in a gourmand's glass; every time that Pons raised it
to his lips he thought, with infinite poignant regret, of the
exquisite wines in his entertainers' cellars.

In short, at the end of three months, the cruel pangs which
had gone near to break Pons' sensitive heart had died away;
he forgot everything but the charms of society; and languished
for them like some elderly slave of a petticoat compelled to
leave the mistress who too repeatedly deceives him. In vain
he tried to hide his profound and consuming melancholy; it
was too plain that he was suffering from one of the mysterious
complaints which the mind brings upon the body.

A single sympton will throw light upon this case of nostalgia
(as it were) produced by breaking away from an old habit; in
itself it is trifling, one of the myriad nothings which are as
rings in a coat of chain-mail enveloping the soul in a network
of iron. One of the keenest pleasures of Pons' old life, one of the
joys of the dinner-table parasite at all times, was the "surprise,"
the thrill produced by the extra dainty dish added triumphantly
to the bill of fare by the mistress of a bourgeois house, to give
a festal air to the dinner. Pons' stomach hankered after that
gastronomical satisfaction. Mme. Cibot, in the pride of her
heart, enumerated every dish beforehand; a salt and savor

once periodically recurrent, had vanished utterly from daily life. Dinner proceeded without *le plat couvert,* as our grand-sires called it. This lay beyond the bounds of Schmucke's powers of comprehension.

Pons had too much delicacy to grumble; but if the case of unappreciated genius is hard, it goes harder still with the stomach whose claims are ignored. Slighted affection, a sub-ject of which too much has been made, is founded upon an illusory longing; for, if the creature fails, love can turn to the Creator who has treasures to bestow. But the stomach! Nothing can be compared to its sufferings; for, in the first place, one must live.

Pons thought wistfully of certain creams—surely the poetry of cookery!—of certain white sauces, masterpieces of the art; of truffled chickens, fit to melt your heart; and above these, and more than all these, of the famous Rhine carp, only known at Paris, served with what condiments! There were days when Pons, thinking upon Count Popinot's cook, would sigh aloud, "Ah, Sophie!" Any passer-by hearing the exclama-tion might have thought that the old man referred to a lost mistress; but his fancy dwelt upon something rarer, on a fat Rhine carp with a sauce, thin in the sauce-boat, creamy upon the palate, a sauce that deserved the Montyon prize! The conductor of the orchestra, living on memories of past din-ners, grew visibly leaner; he was pining away, a victim to gastric nostalgia.

By the beginning of the fourth month (toward the end of January, 1845) Pons' condition attracted attention at the theatre. The flute, a young man named Wilhelm, like almost all Germans; and Schwab, to distinguish him from all other Wilhelms, if not from all other Schwabs, judged it expedient to open Schmucke's eyes to his friend's state of health. It was a first performance of a piece in which Schmucke's instru-ments were all required.

"The old gentleman is failing," said the flute; "there is

something wrong somewhere; his eyes are heavy, and he
doesn't beat time as he used to do," added Wilhelm Schwab,
indicating Pons as he gloomily took his place.

"Dat is alvays de vay, gif a man is sixty years old," answered Schmucke.

The Highland widow, in "The Chronicles of the Canon-
gate," sent her son to his death to have him beside her for
twenty-four hours; and Schmucke could have sacrificed
Pons for the sake of seeing his face every day across the dinner-table.

"Everybody in the theatre is anxious about him," continued
the flute; "and, as the *première danseuse*, Mlle. Brisetout,
says, 'he makes hardly any noise now when he blows his
nose.'"

And, indeed, a peal like the blast of a horn used to resound
through the old musician's bandana handkerchief whenever
he raised it to that lengthy and cavernous feature. The president's wife had more frequently found fault with him on that
score than on any other.

"I vould gif a goot teal to amuse him," said Schmucke,
"he gets so dull."

"Monsieur Pons always seems so much above the like of us
poor devils, that, upon my word, I didnt't dare to ask him to
my wedding," said Wilhelm Schwab. "I am going to be
married——"

"How?" demanded Schmucke.

"Oh! quite properly," returned Wilhelm Schwab, taking
Schmucke's quaint inquiry for a gibe, of which that perfect
Christian was quite incapable.

"Come, gentlemen, take your places!" called Pons, looking round at his little army, as the stage-manager's bell rang
for the overture.

The piece was a dramatized fairy tale, a pantomime called
"The Devil's Betrothed," which ran for two hundred nights.
In the interval, after the first act, Wilhelm Schwab and

Schmucke were left alone in the orchestra, with a house at a temperature of thirty-two degrees Réaumur.

"Tell me your hishdory," said Schmucke.

"Look there! Do you see that young man in the box yonder? Do you recognize him?"

"Nefer a pit——"

"Ah! That is because he is wearing yellow gloves and shines with all the radiance of riches, but that is my friend Fritz Brunner out of Frankfort-on-the-Main."

"Dat used to komm to see du blay und sit peside you in der orghestra?"

"The same. You would not believe he could look so different, would you?"

The hero of the promised story was a German of that particular type in which the sombre irony of Goethe's Mephistopheles is blended with a homely cheerfulness found in the romances of Auguste La Fontaine of pacific memory; but the predominating element in the compound of artlessness and guile, of storekeeper's shrewdness, and the studied carelessness of a member of the Jockey Club, was that form of disgust which set a pistol in the hands of a young Werther, bored to death less by Charlotte than by German princes. It was a thoroughly German face, full of cunning, full of simplicity, stupidity, and courage; the knowledge which brings weariness, the worldly wisdom which the veriest child's trick leaves at fault, the abuse of beer and tobacco—all these were there to be seen in it, and, to heighten the contrast of opposed qualities, there was a wild diabolical gleam in the fine blue eyes with the jaded expression.

Dressed with all the elegance of a city man, Fritz Brunner sat in full view of the house, displaying a bald crown of the tint beloved by Titian, and a few stray, fiery red hairs on either side of it; a remnant spared by debauchery and want, that the prodigal might have a right to spend money with the hairdresser when he should come into his fortune. A face, once fair and fresh as the traditional portrait of Jesus Christ, had grown harder since the advent of a red mustache; a tawny beard lent it an almost sinister look. The bright blue eyes had lost something of their clearness in the struggle with distress. The countless courses by which a man sells himself and his honor in Paris had left their traces upon his eyelids and carved lines about the eyes, into which a mother once looked with a mother's rapture to find a copy of her own fashioned by God's hand.

This precocious philosopher, this weazened youth, was the work of a stepmother.

Herewith begins the curious history of a prodigal son of Frankfort-on-the-Main—the most extraordinary and astounding portent ever beheld by that well-conducted, if central, city.

Gideon Brunner, father of the aforesaid Fritz, was one of the famous innkeepers of Frankfort, a tribe who make law-authorized incisions in travelers' purses with the connivance of the local bankers. An innkeeper and an honest Calvinist to boot, he had married a converted Jewess and laid the foundations of his prosperity with the money she brought him.

When the Jewess died, leaving a son, Fritz, twelve years of age, under the joint guardianship of his father and maternal uncle, a furrier at Leipsic, head of the firm of Virlaz & Company, Brunner senior was compelled by his brother-in-law (who was by no means as soft as his peltry) to invest little Fritz's money, a goodly quantity of current coin of the realm, with the house of Al-Sartchild. Not a penny of it was he allowed to touch. So, by way of revenge for the Israelite's pertinacity, Brunner senior married again. It was impossible, he said, to keep his huge hotel single-handed; it needed a woman's eye and hand. Gideon Brunner's second wife was an innkeeper's daughter, a very pearl, as he thought; but he had had no experience of only daughters spoiled by father and mother.

The second Mme. Brunner behaved as German girls may be expected to behave when they are frivolous and wayward.

She squandered her fortune, she avenged the first Mme. Brunner by making her husband as miserable a man as you could find in the compass of the free city of Frankfort-on-the-Main, where the millionaires, it is said, are about to pass a law compelling womenkind to cherish and obey them alone. She was partial to all the varieties of vinegar commonly called Rhine wine in Germany; she was fond of *articles Paris*, of horses and dress; indeed, the one expensive taste which she had not was a liking for women. She took a dislike to little Fritz, and would perhaps have driven him mad if that young offspring of Calvinism and Judaism had not had Frankfort for his cradle and the firm of Virlaz at Leipsic for his guardian. Uncle Virlaz, however, deep in his furs, confined his guardianship to the safe-keeping of Fritz's silver marks, and left the boy to the tender mercies of this stepmother.

That hyena in woman's form was the more exasperated against the pretty child, the lovely Jewess' son, because she herself could have no children in spite of efforts worthy of a locomotive engine. A diabolical impulse prompted her to plunge her young stepson, at twenty-one years of age, into dissipations contrary to all German habits. The wicked German hoped that English horses, Rhine vinegar, and Goethe's Marguerites would ruin the Jewess' child and shorten his days; for when Fritz came of age, Uncle Virlaz had handed over a very pretty fortune to his nephew. But while roulette at Baden and elsewhere, and boon companions (Wilhelm Schwab among them) devoured the substance accumulated by Uncle Virlaz, the prodigal son himself remained by the will of Providence to point a moral to younger brothers in the free city of Frankfort; parents held him up as a warning and an awful example to their offspring to scare them into steady attendance in their cast-iron counting-rooms, lined with silver marks.

But so far from perishing in the flower of his age, Fritz Brunner had the pleasure of laying his stepmother in one of

those charming little German cemeteries, in which the Teuton
indulges his unbridled passion for horticulture under the
specious pretext of honoring his dead. And as the second
Mme. Brunner expired while the authors of her being were
yet alive, Brunner senior was obliged to bear the loss of the
sums of which his wife had drained his coffers, to say nothing
of other ills which had told upon a Herculean constitution,
till at the age of sixty-seven the innkeeper had weazened and
dried up—shrunk as if the famous Borgia's poison had under-
mined his system. For ten whole years he had supported his
wife, and now he inherited nothing! The innkeeper was a
second ruin of Heidelberg, repaired continually, it is true, by
travelers' hotel bills, much as the remains of the castle of
Heidelberg itself are repaired to sustain the enthusiasm of the
tourists who flock to see so fine and well-preserved a relic of
antiquity.

At Frankfort the disappointment caused as much talk as a
failure. People pointed out Brunner, saying: "See what a
man may come to with a bad wife that leaves him nothing and
a son brought up in the French fashion."

In Italy and Germany the French nation is the root of all
evil, the target for all bullets. "But the god pursuing his
way——" (For the rest, see Lefranc de Pompignan's Ode.)

The wrath of the proprietor of the Grand Hotel de Hollande fell on others beside the travelers, whose bills were
swelled with his resentment. When his son was utterly ruined,
Gideon, regarding him as the indirect cause of all his misfortunes, refused him bread and salt, fire, lodging, and tobacco
—the force of the paternal malediction in a German and an'
innkeeper could no further go. Whereupon the local authorities, making no allowance for the father's misdeeds, regarded
him as one of the most ill-used persons in Frankfort-on-the-
Main, came to his assistance, fastened a quarrel on Fritz (*une
querelle d'Allemand*),* and expelled him from the territory

* Lit. : A German quarrel—meaning a groundless one.

of the free city. Justice in Frankfort is no whit wiser nor
more humane than elsewhere, albeit the city is the seat of the
German Diet. It is not often that a magistrate traces back
the stream of wrongdoing and misfortune to the holder of the
urn from which the first beginnings trickled forth. If Brunner
forgot his son, his son's friends speedily followed the old innkeeper's example.

Ah ! if the journalists, the dandies, and some few fair Parisians among the audience wondered how that German with
the tragical countenance had cropped up on a first night to
occupy a side-box all to himself when fashionable Paris filled
the house—if these could have seen the history played out
upon the stage before the prompter's box, they would have
found it far more interesting than the transformation scenes of
"The Devil's Betrothed," though indeed it was the two hundred thousandth representation of a sublime allegory performed
aforetime in Mesopotamia three thousand years before Christ
was born.

Fritz betook himself on foot to Strasbourg, and there found
what the prodigal son of the Bible failed to find—to wit, a
friend. And herein is revealed the superiority of Alsace,
where so many generous hearts beat to show Germany the
beauty of a combination of Gallic wit and Teutonic solidity.
Wilhelm Schwab, but lately left in possession of a hundred
thousand francs by the death of both parents, opened his arms,
his heart, his house, his purse to Fritz. As for describing
Fritz's feelings, when dusty, down on his luck, and almost
like a leper, he crossed the Rhine and found a real twenty-
franc piece held out by the hand of a real friend—that
moment transcends the powers of the prose-writer ; Pindar
alone could give it forth to humanity in Greek that should
rekindle the dying warmth of friendship in the world.

Put the names of Fritz and Wilhelm beside those of Damon
and Pythias, Castor and Pollux, Orestes and Pylades, Dubreuil
and Pmejah, Schmucke and Pons, and all the names that we

imagine for the two friends of Monomotapa, for La Fontaine
(man of genius though he was) has made of them two dis-
embodied spirits—they lack reality. The two new names may
join the illustrious company, and with so much the more
reason, since that Wilhelm who had helped to drink Fritz's
inheritance now proceeded, with Fritz's assistance, to devour
his own substance ; smoking, needless to say, every known
variety of tobacco.

The pair, strange to relate, squandered the property in the
dullest, stupidest, most commonplace fashion, in Strasbourg
brasseries (brew-houses), in the company of ballet-girls of the
Strasbourg theatres, and little Alsaciennes who had not a rag
of a tattered reputation left.

Every morning they would say : " We must really stop this,
and make up our minds and do something or other with the
money that is left."

" Pooh ! " Fritz would retort, " just one more day, and to-
morrow "—ah ! to-morrow.

In the lives of Prodigal Sons, To-DAY is a prodigious coxcomb, but To-MORROW is a very poltroon, taking fright at the
big words of his predecessor. To-DAY is the truculent captain
of old-world comedy. To-MORROW the clown of modern
pantomime.

When the two friends had reached their last thousand-franc
note, they took places in the mail-coach, styled Royal, and
departed for Paris, where they installed themselves in the
attics of the Hôtel du Rhin, in the Rue du Mail, the property
of one Graff, formerly Gideon Brunner's head-waiter. Fritz
found a situation as clerk in the Kellers' bank (on Graff's
recommendation), with a salary of six hundred francs. And
a place as book-keeper was likewise found for Wilhelm, in the
business of Graff the fashionable tailor, brother of Graff of
the Hôtel du Rhin, who found the scantily paid employment
for the pair of prodigals for the sake of old times and his
apprenticeship at the Hôtel de Hollande. These two inci-

dents—the recognition of a ruined man by a well-to-do friend, and a German innkeeper interesting himself in two penniless fellow-countrymen—give, no doubt, an air of improbability to the story, but truth is so much the more like fiction, since modern writers of fiction have been at such untold pains to imitate truth.

It was not long before Fritz, a clerk with six hundred francs, and Wilhelm, a book-keeper with precisely the same salary, discovered the difficulties of existence in a city so full of temptations. In 1837, the second year of their abode, Wilhelm, who possessed a pretty talent for the flute, entered Pons' orchestra, to earn a little occasional butter to put on his dry bread. As to Fritz, his only way to an increase of income lay through the display of the capacity for business inherited by a descendant of the Virlaz family. Yet, in spite of his assiduity, in spite of abilities which possibly may have stood in his way, his salary only reached the sum of two thousand francs in 1843. Penury, that divine stepmother, did for the two young men all that their mothers had not been able to do for them; Poverty taught them thrift and worldly wisdom; Poverty gave them her grand rough education, the lessons which she drives with hard knocks into the heads of great men, who seldom know a happy childhood. Fritz and Wilhelm, being but ordinary men, learned as little as they possibly could in her school; they dodged the blows, shrank from her hard breast and bony arms, and never discovered the good fairy lurking within, ready to yield to the caresses of genius. One thing, however, they learned thoroughly—they discovered the value of money, and vowed to clip the wings of riches if ever a second fortune should come to their door.

This was the history which Wilhelm Schwab related in German, at much greater length, to his friend the pianist, ending with—

"Well, Papa Schmucke, the rest is soon explained. Old Brunner is dead. He left four millions! He made an im-

mense amount of money out of Baden railways, though neither
his son nor Graff, with whom we lodge, had any idea that the
old man was one of the original shareholders. I am playing
the flute here for the last time this evening ; I would have left
some days ago, but this was a first performance, and I did not
want to spoil my part."

"Goot, mein frient," said Schmucke. "But who is die
prite ? "

"She is Mademoiselle Graff, the daughter of our host, the
landlord of the Hôtel du Rhin. I have loved Mlle.
Émilie these seven years; she has read so many immoral
novels, that she refused all offers for me, without knowing
what might come of it. She will be a very wealthy young
lady ; her uncles, the tailors in the Rue de Richelieu, will
leave her all their money. Fritz is giving me the money we
squandered at Strasbourg five times over ! He is putting a
million francs in a banking house, Monsieur Graff the tailor is
adding another five hundred thousand francs, and Mademoiselle Émilie's father not only allows me to incorporate her
portion—two hundred and fifty thousand francs—with the
capital, but he himself will be a shareholder with as much
again. So the firm of Brunner, Schwab & Company will
start with two million five hundred thousand francs. Fritz
has just bought fifteen hundred thousand francs' worth of
shares in the Bank of France to guarantee our account with
them. That is not all Fritz's fortune. He has his father's
house property, supposed to be worth another million, and he
has let the Grand Hôtel de Hollande already to a cousin of
the Graffs."

"You look sad ven you look at your frient," remarked
Schmucke, who had listened with great interest. "Kan you
pe chealous of him ? "

"I am jealous for Fritz's happiness," said Wilhelm.
"Does that face look as if it belonged to a happy man ? I
am afraid of Paris ; I should like to see him do as I am doing.

The old tempter may awake again. Of our two heads, his carries the less ballast. His dress, and the opera-glass, and the rest of it make me anxious. He keeps looking at the lorettes in the house. Oh! if you only knew how hard it is to marry Fritz. He has a horror of 'going a-courting,' as you say; you would have to give him a drop into a family, just as in England they give a man a drop into the next world when he is hung."

During the uproar that usually marks the end of a first night, the flute delivered his invitation to the conductor. Pons accepted gleefully; and, for the first time in three months, Schmucke saw a smile on his friend's face. They went back to the Rue de Normandie in perfect silence; that sudden flash of joy had thrown a light on the extent of the disease which was consuming Pons. Oh, that a man so truly noble, so disinterested, so great in feeling, should have such a weakness! This was the thought which struck the stoic Schmucke dumb with amazement. He grew wofully sad, for he began to see that there was no help for it; he must even renounce the pleasure of seeing "his goot Bons" opposite him at the dinner-table, for the sake of Pons' welfare; and he did not know whether he could give him up; the mere thought of it drove him distracted.

Meantime, Pons' proud silence and withdrawal to the Mons Aventinus of the Rue de Normandie had, as might be expected, impressed the presidente, not that she troubled herself much about her parasite, now that she was freed from him. She thought, with her charming daughter, that Cousin Pons had seen through her little "Lili's" joke. But it was otherwise with her husband the president.

Camusot de Marville, a short and stout man, grown solemn since his promotion at the Court, admired Cicero, preferred the Opera-Comique to the Italiens, compared the actors one with another, and followed the multitude step by step. He used to recite all the articles in the Ministerialist journals, as

if he were saying something original, and in giving his opinion at the Council Board he paraphrased the remarks of the
previous speaker.   His leading characteristics were sufficiently
well known ; his position compelled him to take everything
seriously ; and he was particularly tenacious of family ties.

Like most men who are ruled by their wives, the president
asserted his independence in trifles, in which his wife was very
careful not to thwart him.   For a month he was satisfied with
the presidente's commonplace explanations of Pons' disap-
pearance ; but at last it struck him as singular that the old
musician, a friend of forty years' standing, should first make
them so valuable a present as a fan that belonged to Mme. de
Pompadour, and then immediately discontinue his visits.
Count Popinot had pronounced the trinket a masterpiece ;
when its owner went to Court, the fan had been passed from
hand to hand, and her vanity was not a little gratified by the
compliments it received ; others had dwelt on the beauties of
the ten ivory sticks, each one covered with delicate carving,
the like of which had never been seen.   A Russian lady (Russian ladies are apt to forget that they are not in Russia) had
offered her six thousand francs for the marvel one day at
Count Popinot's house, and smiled to see it in such hands.
Truth to tell, it was a fan for a duchess.

"It cannot be denied that poor Cousin Pons understands
rubbish of that sort——" said Cécile, the day after the bid.

"Rubbish!" cried the parent.   "Why, Government is
just about to buy the late Monsieur le Conseiller Dusommerard's collection for three hundred thousand francs ; and
the State and the Municipality of Paris between them are
spending nearly a million francs over the purchase and repair
of the Hôtel de Cluny to house the 'rubbish,' as you call it.
Such 'rubbish,' dear child," he resumed, "is frequently all
that remains of vanished civilizations.   An Etruscan jar, and
a necklace, which sometimes fetch forty or fifty thousand
francs, is 'rubbish' which reveals the perfection of art at the

time of the siege of Troy, proving that the Etruscans were Trojan refugees in Italy."

This was the president's cumbrous way of joking; the short, fat man was heavily ironical with his wife and daughter.

"The combination of various kinds of knowledge required to understand such 'rubbish,' Cécile," he resumed, "is a science in itself, called archæology. Archæology comprehends architecture, sculpture, painting, goldsmiths' work, ceramics, cabinetmaking (a purely modern art), lace, tapestry —in short, human handiwork of every sort and description."

"Then Cousin Pons is learned?" said Cécile.

"Ah! by-the-by, why is he never to be seen nowadays?" asked the president. He spoke with the air of a man in whom thousands of forgotten and dormant impressions have suddenly begun to stir, and shaping themselves into one idea, reach consciousness with a ricochet, as sportmen say.

"He must have taken offense at nothing at all," answered his wife. "I dare say I was not as fully sensible as I might have been of the value of the fan that he gave me. I am ignorant enough, as you know, of——"

"You! One of Servin's best pupils, and you don't know Watteau?" cried the president.

"I know Gérard and David and Gros and Girodet, and Monsieur de Forbin and Monsieur Turpin de Crissé——"

"You ought——"

"Ought what, sir?" demanded the lady, gazing at her husband with the air of a Queen of Sheba.

"To know a Watteau when you see it, my dear. Watteau is very much in fashion," answered the president with meekness, that told plainly how much he owed to his wife.

This conversation took place a few days before that night of first performance of "The Devil's Betrothed," when the whole orchestra noticed how ill Pons was looking. But by that time all the circle of dinner-givers who were used to see Pons' face at their tables, and to send him on errands, had

11

begun to ask each other for news of him, and uneasiness increased when it was reported by some who had seen him that he was always in his place at the theatre. Pons had been very careful to avoid his old acquaintances whenever he met them in the streets; but one day it so fell out that he met Count Popinot, the ex-cabinet minister, face to face in a bric-à-brac dealer's store in the new Boulevard Beaumarchais. The dealer was none other than that Monistrol of whom Pons had spoken to the presidente, one of the famous and audacious vendors whose cunning enthusiasm leads them to set more and more value daily on their wares; for curiosities, they tell you, are growing so scarce that they are hardly to be found at all nowadays.

"Ah, my dear Pons, how comes it that we never see you now? We miss you very much, and Madame Popinot does not know what to think of your desertion."

"Monsieur le Comte," said the good man, "I was made to feel in the house of a relative that at my age one is not wanted in the world. I have never had much consideration shown me, but at any rate I had not been insulted. I have never asked anything of any man," he broke out with an artist's pride. "I have often made myself useful in return for hospitality. But I have made a mistake, it seems; I am infinitely beholden to those who honor me by allowing me to sit at table with them; my friends, my relatives——— Well and good; I have sent in my resignation as Smellfeast. At home I find daily something which no other house has offered me—a real friend."

The old artist's power had not failed him; with tone and gesture he put such bitterness into the words, that the peer of France was struck by them. He drew Pons aside.

"Come, now, my old friend, what is it? What has hurt you? Could you not tell me in confidence? You will permit me to say that at my house, surely, you have always met with consideration———"

"You are the one exception," said the artist. "And, beside, you are a great lord and a statesman, you have so many
things to think about. That would excuse anything, if there
were need for it."

The diplomatic skill that Popinot had acquired in the management of men and affairs was brought to bear upon Pons,
till at length the story of his misfortunes in the president's
house was drawn from him.

Popinot took up the victim's cause so warmly that he told
the story to Mme. Popinot as soon as he went home, and that
excellent and noble-natured woman spoke to the presidente
on the subject at the first opportunity. As Popinot himself
likewise said a word or two to the president, there was a
general explanation in the family of Camusot de Marville.

Camusot was not exactly master in his own house; but this
time his remonstrance was so well founded in law and in fact,
that his wife and daughter were forced to acknowledge the
truth. They both humbled themselves and threw the blame
on the servants. The servants, first bidden and then chidden,
only obtained pardon by a full confession, which made it
clear to the president's mind that Pons had done rightly to
stop away. The president displayed himself before the servants in all his masculine and magisterial dignity, after the
manner of men who are ruled by their wives. He informed
his household that they should be dismissed forthwith, and
forfeit any advantages which their long term of service in his
house might have brought them, unless from that time forward
his cousin and all those who did him the honor of coming to
his house were treated as he himself was. At which speech
Madeleine was moved to smile.

"You have only one chance of salvation as it is," continued the president. "Go to my cousin, make your excuses
to him, and tell him that you will lose your situations unless
he forgives you, for I shall turn you all away if he does not."

Next morning the president went out fairly early to pay a

call on his cousin before going down to the court. The apparition of M. le President de Marville, announced by Mme. Cibot, was an event in the house. Pons, thus honored for the first time in his life, saw reparation ahead.

"At last, my dear cousin," said the president after the ordinary greetings; "at last I have discovered the cause of your retreat. Your behavior increases, if that were possible, my esteem for you. I have but one word to say in that connection. My servants have all been dismissed. My wife and daughter are in despair; they want to see you to have an explanation. In all this, my cousin, there is one innocent person, and he is an old judge; you will not punish me, will you, for the escapade of a thoughtless child who wished to dine with the Popinots? especially when I come to beg for peace, admitting that all the wrong has been on our side? An old friendship of thirty-six years, even supposing that there had been a misunderstanding, has still some claims. Come, sign a treaty of peace by dining with us to-night——"

Pons involved himself in a diffuse reply, and ended by informing his cousin that he was to sign a marriage-contract that evening; how that one of the orchestra was not only going to be married, but also about to fling his flute to the winds to become a banker.

"Very well. To-morrow."

"Madame la Comtesse Popinot has done me the honor of asking me, cousin. She was so kind as to write——"

"The day after to-morrow then."

"Monsieur Brunner, a German, my first flute's future partner, returns the compliment paid him to-day by the young couple——"

"You are such pleasant company that it is not surprising that people dispute for the honor of seeing you. Very well, next Sunday? Within a week, as we say at the courts?"

"On Sunday we are to dine with Monsieur Graff, the flute's father-in-law."

"Very well, on Saturday! Between now and then you will have time to reassure a little girl who has shed tears already over her fault. God asks no more than repentance; you will not be more severe than the Eternal Father with poor little Cécile ?——"

Pons, thus reached on his weak side, again plunged into formulas more than polite, and went as far as the stairhead with the president.

An hour later the president's servants arrived in a troop on poor Pons' third floor. They behaved after the manner of their kind; they cringed and fawned; they wept. Madeleine took M. Pons aside and flung herself resolutely at his feet.

"It is all my fault; and monsieur knows quite well that I love him," here she burst into tears. "It was vengeance boiling in my veins; monsieur ought to throw all the blame of the unhappy affair on that. We are all to lose our pensions—— monsieur, I was mad, and I would not have the rest suffer for my fault. I can see now well enough that fate did not make me for monsieur. I have come to my senses, I aimed too high, but I love you still, monsieur. These ten years I have thought of nothing but the happiness of making you happy and looking after things here. What a lot! Oh! if monsieur but knew how much I love him! But monsieur must have seen it through all my mischief-making. If I were to die to-morrow, what would they find? A will in your favor, monsieur. Yes, monsieur, in my trunk under my best things."

Madeleine had set a responsive chord vibrating; the passion inspired in another may be unwelcome, but it will always be gratifying to self-love; this was the case with the old bachelor. After generously pardoning Madeleine, he extended his forgiveness to the other servants, promising to use his influence with his cousin the presidente on their behalf.

It was unspeakably pleasant to Pons to find all his old enjoyments restored to him without any loss of self-respect. The world had come to Pons, he had risen in the esteem of his circle; but Schmucke looked so downcast and dubious when he heard the story of the triumph, that Pons felt hurt. When, however, the kind-hearted German saw the sudden change wrought in Pons' face, he ended by rejoicing with his friend, and made a sacrifice of the happiness that he had known during those four months that he had had Pons all to himself. Mental suffering has this immense advantage over physical ills—when the cause is removed it ceases at once. Pons was not like the same man that morning. The old man, depressed and visibly failing, had given place to the serenely contented Pons, who entered the presidente's house that October afternoon with the Marquise de Pompadour's fan in his pocket. Schmucke, on the other hand, pondered deeply over this phenomenon, and could not understand it; your true stoic never can understand the courtier that dwells in a Frenchman. Pons was a born Frenchman of the Empire; a mixture of eighteenth-century gallantry and that devotion to womankind so often celebrated in songs of the type of " Partant pour la Syrie."

So Schmucke was fain to bury his chagrin beneath the flowers of his German philosophy; but a week later he grew so yellow that Mme. Cibot exerted her ingenuity to call in the parish doctor. The leech had fears of icterus, and left Mme. Cibot frightened half out of her wits by the Latin word for an attack of the jaundice.

Meantime the two friends went out to dinner together, perhaps for the first time in their lives. For Schmucke it was a return to the Fatherland; for Johann Graff of the Hôtel du Rhin and his daughter Émilie, Wolfgang Graff the tailor and his wife, Fritz Brunner and Wilhelm Schwab were Germans, and Pons and the notary were the only Frenchmen present at the banquet. The Graffs of the tailor's business owned a splendid house in the Rue de Richelieu, between the Rue Neuve-des-Petits-Champs and the Rue Villedo; they had brought up their niece, for Émilie's father, not without reason, had feared contact with the very mixed society of an inn for his daughter. The good tailor Graffs, who loved Émilie as if she had been their own daughter, were giving up the first floor of their great house to the young couple, and here the bank of Brunner, Schwab & Company was to be established. The arrangements for the marriage had been made about a month ago; some time must elapse before Fritz Brunner, author of all this felicity, could settle his deceased father's affairs, and the famous firm of tailors had taken advantage of the delay to redecorate the second floor and to furnish it very handsomely for the bride and bridegroom. The offices of the bank had been fitted into the wing which united a handsome business house with the old hôtel at the back, between courtyard and garden.

On the way from the Rue de Normandie to the Rue de Richelieu, Pons drew from the abstracted Schmucke the details of the story of the modern prodigal son, for whom Death had killed the fatted innkeeper. Pons, but newly reconciled with his nearest relatives, was immediately smitten with a desire to make a match between Fritz Brunner and Cécile de Marville. Chance ordained that the notary was none other than Berthier, old Cardot's son-in-law and successor, the sometime second clerk with whom Pons had been wont to dine.

"Ah! Monsieur Berthier, you here?" he said, holding out a hand to his host of former days.

"We have not had the pleasure of seeing you at dinner lately; how is it?" returned the notary. "My wife has been anxious about you. We saw you at the first performance of 'The Devil's Betrothed,' and our anxiety became curiosity?"

"Old people are very sensitive," replied the worthy musician; "they make the mistake of being a century behind the times, but see, now, how can it be helped? It is quite enough to represent one century—they cannot entirely belong to the century which sees them die."

"Ah!" said the notary, with a shrewd look, "one cannot run two centuries at once."

"By-the-by," continued Pons, drawing the young lawyer into a corner, "why do you not find some one for my cousin Cécile de Marville——"

"Ah! why——?" answered Berthier. "In this century, when luxury has filtered down to our very porters' lodges, a young fellow hesitates before uniting his lot with the daughter of a president of the Court of Appeals in Paris if she brings him only a hundred thousand francs. In the rank of life in which Mademoiselle de Marville's husband would take, the wife was never yet known that did not cost her husband three thousand francs a year; the interest on a hundred thousand francs would scarcely find her in pin-money. A bachelor with an income of fifteen or twenty thousand francs can live on an entresol; he is not expected to cut any figure; he need not keep more than one servant, and all his surplus income he can spend on his amusements; he puts himself in the hands of a good tailor, and need not trouble any further about keeping up appearances. Far-sighted mothers make much of him; he is one of the kings of fashion in Paris.

"But a wife changes everything. A wife means a properly furnished house," continued the lawyer; "she wants the carriage for herself; if she goes to the play, she wants a box, while the bachelor has only a stall to pay for; in short, a wife represents the whole of the income which the bachelor used to spend on himself. Suppose that husband and wife have thirty thousand francs a year between them—practically, the sometime bachelor is a poor devil who thinks twice before he drives out to Chantilly. Bring children on the scene—he is pinched for money at once.

"Now, as Monsieur and Madame de Marville are scarcely turned fifty, Cécile's expectations are bills that will not fall

due for fifteen or twenty years to come; and no young fellow
cares to keep them so long in his portfolio. The young feather-
heads who are dancing the polka with lorettes at the
Mabille Garden are so cankered with self-interest that they
don't stand in need of us to explain both sides of the problem
to them. Between ourselves, I may say that Mademoiselle de
Marville scarcely sets hearts throbbing so fast but that their
owners can perfectly keep their heads, and they are full of these
antimatrimonial reflections. If any eligible young man, in
full possession of his senses and an income of twenty thousand
francs, happens to be sketching out a programme of a marriage
that will satisfy his ambitions, Mademoiselle de Marville does
not altogether answer the description——"

"And why not?" asked the bewildered musician.

"Oh !——" said the notary, "well—— a young man
nowadays may be as ugly as you and I, my dear Pons, but he
is almost sure to have the impertinence to want six hundred
thousand francs, a girl of good family, with wit and good
looks and good breeding—flawless perfection, in short."

"Then it will not be easy to marry her?"

"She will not be married so long as Monsieur and Madame
de Marville cannot make up their minds to settle Marville on
her when she marries; if they had chosen, she might have been
the Vicomtesse Popinot by now. But here comes Monsieur
Brunner. We are about to read the deeds of partnership and
the marriage-contract."

Greetings and introductions over, the relations made Pons
promise to sign the contract. He listened to the reading of
the documents, and toward half-past five the party went into
the dining-room. The dinner was magnificent, as a city
merchant's dinner can be, when he allows himself a respite
from money-making. Graff of the Hôtel du Rhin was acquainted with the first provision dealers in Paris; never had
Pons nor Schmucke fared so sumptuously. The dishes were a
rapture to think of! Italian paste, delicate of flavor, unknown

to the public; smelts fried as never smelts were fried before; fish from Lake Leman, with a real Genevese sauce; and a cream for plum-pudding which would have astonished the London doctor who is said to have invented it. It was nearly ten o'clock before they rose from table. The amount of wine, German and French, consumed at that dinner would amaze the contemporary dandy; nobody knows the amount of liquor that a German can imbibe and yet keep calm and quiet; to have even an idea of the quantity, you must dine in Germany and watch bottle succeed to bottle, like wave rippling after wave along the sunny shores of the Mediterranean, and disappear as if the Teuton possessed the absorbing power of sponges or sea-sand. Perfect harmony prevails meanwhile; there is none of the racket that there would be over the liquor in France; the talk is as sober as a money-lender's extempore speech; countenances flush, like the faces of the brides in frescoes by Cornelius or Schnorr (imperceptibly, that is to say), and reminiscences are poured out slowly while the smoke puffs from the pipes.

About half-past ten that evening Pons and Schmucke found themselves sitting on a bench out in the garden, with the ex-flute between them; they were explaining their characters, opinions, and misfortunes, with no very clear idea as to why or how they had come to this point. In the thick of a pot-pourri of confidences, Wilhelm spoke of his strong desire to see Fritz married, expressing himself with vehement and vinous eloquence.

"What do you say to this programme for your friend Brunner?" cried Pons in confidential tones. "A charming and sensible young lady of twenty-four, belonging to a family of the highest distinction. The father holds a very high position as a judge; there will be a hundred thousand francs paid down and a million to come."

"Wait!" answered Schwab; "I will speak to Fritz this instant."

The pair watched Brunner and his friend as they walked round and round the garden; again and again they passed the bench, sometimes one spoke, sometimes the other.

Pons was not exactly intoxicated; his head was a little heavy, but his thoughts, on the contrary, seemed all the lighter; he watched Fritz Brunner's face through the rainbow mist made of fumes of wine, and tried to read auguries favorable to his family. Before very long Schwab introduced his friend and partner to M. Pons; Fritz Brunner expressed his thanks for the trouble which Pons had been so good as to take.

In the conversation which followed, the two old bachelors, Schmucke and Pons, extolled the estate of matrimony, going so far as to say, without any malicious intent, "that marriage was the end of man." Tea and ices, punch and cakes, were served in the future home of the betrothed couple. The wine had begun to tell upon the honest merchants, and the general hilarity reached its height when it was announced that Schwab's partner thought of following his example.

At two o'clock that morning, Schmucke and Pons walked home along the boulevards, philosophizing *à perte de raison** as they went on the harmony pervading the arrangements of this our world below.

On the morrow of the banquet, Cousin Pons betook himself to his fair cousin the presidente, overjoyed—poor dear noble soul !—to return good for evil. Surely he had attained to a sublime height, as every one will allow, for we live in an age when the Montyon prize is given to those who do their duty by carrying out the precepts of the Gospel.

"Ah !" said Pons to himself, as he turned the corner of the Rue de Choiseul, "they will lie under immense obligations to their parasite."

Any man less absorbed in his contentment, any man of the world, any distrustful nature, would have watched the presi-

* In rambling talk.

dent's wife and daughter very narrowly on this first return to the house. But the poor musician was a child, he had all the simplicity of an artist, believing in goodness as he believed in beauty; so he was delighted when Cécile and her mother made much of him. After all the vaudevilles, tragedies, and comedies which had been played under the worthy man's eyes for twelve long years, he could not detect the insincerity and grimaces of social comedy, no doubt because he had seen too much of it. Any one who goes into society in Paris, and knows the type of woman, dried up, body and soul, by a burning thirst for social position, and a fierce desire to be thought cunningly virtuous, any one familiar with the sham piety and the domineering character of a woman whose word is law in her own house, may imagine the lurking hatred she bore this husband's cousin whom she had wronged.

All the demonstrative friendliness of mother and daughter was lined with a formidable longing for revenge, that must evidently be postponed. For the first time in Amélie de Marville's life she had been put in the wrong, and that in the sight of the husband over whom she tyrannized; and not only so—she was obliged to be amiable to the author of her defeat! You can scarcely find a match for this position save in the hypocritical dramas which are sometimes kept up for years in the sacred college of cardinals, or in chapters of certain religious orders.

At three o'clock, when the president came back from the law-courts, Pons had scarcely made an end of the marvelous history of his acquaintance, M. Frédéric Brunner. Cécile had gone straight to the point. She wanted to know how Frédéric Brunner was dressed, how he looked, his height and figure, the color of his hair and eyes; and when she had conjectured a distinguished air for Frédéric, she admired his generosity of character.

"Think of his giving five hundred thousand francs to his companion in misfortune! Oh! mamma, I shall have a car-

riage and a box at the Italiens——'' Cécile grew almost
pretty as she thought that all her mother's ambitions for her
were about to be realized, that the hopes which had almost
left her were to come to something after all.

As for the presidente, all that she said was : '' My dear little
girl, you may perhaps be married within the fortnight.''

All mothers with daughters of three-and-twenty address them
as '' little girl.''

'' Still,'' added the president, '' in any case, we must have
time to make inquiries ; never will I give my daughter to just
anybody——''

'' As to inquiries,'' said Pons, '' Berthier is drawing up the
deeds. As to the young man himself, my dear cousin,
you remember what you told me? Well, he is quite forty
years old ; he is bald. He wishes to find in family life a
haven after storm ; I did not dissuade him ; every man has
his taste——''

'' One reason the more for a personal interview,'' returned
the president. '' I am not going to give my daughter to a
valetudinarian.''

'' Very good, cousin, you shall see my suitor in five days if
you like ; for, with your views, a single interview would be
enough ''—(Cécile and her mother signified their rapture)—
'' Frédéric is decidedly a distinguished amateur ; he begged
me to allow him to see my little collection at his leisure.
You have never seen my pictures and curiosities ; come and
see them,'' he continued, looking at his relatives. '' You can
come simply as two ladies, brought by my friend Schmucke,
and make Monsieur Brunner's acquaintance without betraying
yourselves. Frédéric need not in the least know who you are.''

'' Admirable ! '' cried the president.

The attention they paid to the once scorned parasite may
be left to the imagination ! Poor Pons that day became
the presidente's cousin. The happy mother drowned her dislike in floods of joy ; her looks, her smiles, her words sent

the old man into ecstasies over the good that he had done, over the future that he saw by glimpses. Was he not sure to find dinners such as yesterday's banquet over the signing of the contract, multiplied indefinitely by three, in the houses of Brunner, Schwab, and Graff? He saw before him a land of plenty—a *vie de cocagne*,* a miraculous succession of *plats couverts*, or delicate surprise dishes, and of exquisite wines.

"If Cousin Pons brings this through," said the president, addressing his wife after Pons had departed, "we ought to settle an income upon him equal to his salary at the theatre."

"Certainly," said the lady; and Cécile was informed that, if the proposed suitor found favor in her eyes, she must undertake to induce the old musician to accept a munificence in such bad taste.

Next day the president went to Berthier. He was anxious to make sure of M. Frédéric Brunner's financial position. Berthier, forewarned by Mme. de Marville, had asked his new client Schwab to come. Schwab the banker was dazzled by the prospect of such a match for his friend (everybody knows how deeply a German venerates social distinctions, so much so, that in Germany a wife takes her husband's (official) title, and is the Frau General, the Frau Rath, and so forth)—Schwab therefore was as accommodating as a collector who imagines that he is cheating a dealer.

"In the first place," said Cécile's father, "as I shall make over my estate of Marville to my daughter, I should wish the contract to be drawn up on the dotal system. In that case, Monsieur Brunner would invest a million francs in land to increase the estate, and by settling the land on his wife he would secure her and his children from any share in the liabilities of the bank."

Berthier stroked his chin. "He is coming on well, is Monsieur le President," thought he.

When the dotal system had been explained to Schwab, he

* A life of plenty.

seemed much inclined that way for his friend. He had heard
Fritz say that he wished to find some way of insuring himself
against another lapse into poverty.

"There is a farm and pasture-land worth twelve hundred
thousand francs in the market at this moment," remarked the
president.

"If we take up shares in the Bank of France to the amount
of a million francs, that will be quite enough to guarantee our
account," said Schwab. "Fritz does not want to invest more
than two million francs in business; he will do as you wish,
I am sure, Monsieur le President."

The president's wife and daughter were almost wild with
joy when he brought home this news. Never, surely, did so
rich a capture swim so complacently into the nets of matrimony.

"You will be Madame Brunner de Marville," said the
parent, addressing his child; "I will obtain permission for
your husband to add the name to his, and afterward he can
take out letters of naturalization. If I should be a peer of
France some day, he will succeed me!"

The five days were spent by Mme. de Marville in preparations. On the great day she dressed Cécile herself, taking as
much pains as the admiral of the British fleet takes over the
dressing of the pleasure yacht for Her Majesty of England
when she takes a trip to Germany.

Pons and Schwab, on their side, cleaned, swept, and dusted
Pons' museum rooms and furniture with the agility of sailors
cleaning down a man-of-war. There was not a speck of dust
on the carved wood; not an inch of brass but it glistened.
The glasses over the pastels obscured nothing of the work of
Latour, Greuze, and Liotard (illustrious painter of The Chocolate Girl), miracles of an art, alas! so fugitive. The inimi-
table lustre of Florentine bronze took all the varying hues of
the light; the painted glass glowed with color. Every line
shone out brilliantly, every object threw in its phrase in a

harmony of masterpieces arranged by two musicians—both of whom alike had attained to be poets.

With a tact which avoided the difficulties of a late appearance on the scene of action, the women were the first to arrive; they wished to be upon their own ground. Pons introduced his friend Schmucke, who seemed to his fair visitors to be an idiot; their heads were so full of the eligible gentleman with the four millions of francs, that they paid but little attention to the worthy Pons' dissertations upon matters of which they were completely ignorant.

They looked with indifferent eyes at Petitot's enamels, spaced over crimson velvet, set in three frames of marvelous workmanship. Flowers by Van Huysum, David, and Heim; butterflies painted by Abraham Mignon; Van Eycks, undoubted Cranachs and Albrecht Dürers; the Giorgione, the Sebastian del Piombo; Backhuijzen, Hobbema, Géricault, the rarities of painting—none of these things so much as aroused their curiosity; they were waiting for the sun to arise and shine upon these treasures. Still, they were surprised by the beauty of some of the Etruscan trinkets and the solid value of the snuff-boxes, and out of politeness they went into ecstasies over some Florentine bronzes which they held in their hands when Mme. Cibot announced M. Brunner! They did not turn; they took advantage of a superb Venetian mirror framed in huge masses of carved ebony to scan this phœnix of eligible young men.

Frédéric, forewarned by Wilhelm, had made the most of the little hair that remained to him. He wore a neat pair of trousers, a soft shade of some dark color; a silk vest of superlative elegance and the very newest cut; a shirt with openwork, its linen hand-woven by a Friesland woman; and a blue-and-white cravat. His watch-chain, like the head of his cane, came from Messrs. Florent and Chanor; and the coat, cut by old Graff himself, was of the very finest cloth. The Suède gloves proclaimed the man who had run through his mother's fortune. You could have seen the banker's neat little brougham and pair of horses mirrored in the surface of his speckless varnished boots, even if two pairs of sharp ears had not already caught the sound of the wheels outside in the Rue de Normandie.

When the prodigal of twenty years is a kind of chrysalis from which a banker emerges at the age of forty, the said banker is usually an observer of human nature; and so much the more shrewd if, as in Brunner's case, he understands how to turn his German simplicity to good account. He had assumed for the occasion the abstracted air of a man who is hesitating between family life and the dissipations of bachelorhood. This expression in a Frenchified German seemed to Cécile to be in the highest degree romantic; the descendant of the Virlaz was a second Werther in her eyes—where is the girl who will not allow herself to weave a little novel about her marriage? Cécile thought herself the happiest of women when Brunner, looking round at the magnificent works of art so patiently collected during forty years, waxed enthusiastic, and Pons, to his no small satisfaction, found an appreciative admirer of his treasures for the first time in his life.

"He is poetical," the young lady said to herself; "he sees millions in the things. A poet is a man that cannot count and leaves his wife to look after his money—an easy man to manage and amuse with trifles."

Every pane in the two windows was a square of Swiss painted glass; the least of them was worth a thousand francs; and Pons possessed sixteen of these unrivaled works of art for which amateurs seek so eagerly nowadays. In 1815 the panes could be bought for six or ten francs apiece. The value of the glorious collection of pictures, flawless great works, authentic, untouched since they left the master's hands, could only be proved in the fiery furnace of a salesroom. Not a picture but was set in a costly frame; there were frames of every kind—Venetians, carved with heavy ornaments, like

12

English plate of the present day; Romans, distinguishable among the others for a certain dash that artists call *flafla;* Spanish wreaths in bold relief; Flemings and Germans with quaint figures, tortoise-shell frames inlaid with copper and brass and mother-of-pearl and ivory; frames of ebony and boxwood in the styles of Louis Treize, Louis Quatorze, Louis Quinze, and Louis Seize—in short, it was a unique collection of the finest models. Pons, luckier than the art museums of Dresden and Vienna, possessed a frame by the famous Brustoloni—the Michael Angelo of wood-carvers.

Mlle. de Marville naturally asked for explanations of each new curiosity, and was initiated into the mysteries of art by Brunner. Her exclamations were so childish, she seemed so pleased to have the value and beauty of the paintings, carvings, or bronzes pointed out to her, that the German gradually thawed and looked quite young again, and both were led on further than they intended at this (purely accidental) first meeting.

The private view lasted for three hours. Brunner offered his arm when Cécile went downstairs. As they descended slowly and discreetly, Cécile, still talking fine art, wondered that M. Brunner should admire her cousin's gimcracks so much.

"Do you really think that these things that we have just seen are worth a great deal of money?"

"Mademoiselle, if your cousin would sell his collection, I would give eight hundred thousand francs for it this evening, and I should not make a bad bargain. The pictures alone would fetch more than that at a public sale."

"Since you say so, I believe it," returned she; "the things took up so much of your attention that it must be so."

"Oh! mademoiselle!" protested Brunner. "For all answer to your reproach, I will ask your mother's permission to call, so that I may have the pleasure of seeing you again."

"How clever she is, that 'little girl' of mine!" thought

the presidente, following closely upon her daughter's heels. Aloud she said, "With the greatest pleasure, monsieur. I hope that you will come at dinner-time with our Cousin Pons. The president will be delighted to make your acquaintance. Thank you, cousin."

The lady squeezed Pons' arm with deep meaning; she could not have said more if she had used the consecrated formula: "Let us swear an eternal friendship." The glance which accompanied that "Thank you, cousin," was a caress.

When the young lady had been put into the carriage, and the hired carriage had disappeared down the Rue Charlot, Brunner talked bric-à-brac to Pons, and Pons talked marriage.

"Then you see no obstacle?" said Pons.

"Oh!" said Brunner, "she is an insignificant little thing, and the mother is a trifle prim. We shall see."

"A handsome fortune one of these days. More than a million——"

"Good-by till Monday!" interrupted the millionaire. "If you should care to sell your collection of pictures, I would give you five or six hundred thousand francs——"

"Ah!" said Pons; he had no idea that he was so rich. "But they are my great pleasure in life, and I could not bring myself to part with them. I could only sell my collection to be delivered after my death."

"Very well. We shall see."

"Here we have two affairs afoot," said Pons; he was thinking only of the marriage.

Brunner shook hands and drove away in his splendid carriage. Pons watched it out of sight. He did not notice that Rémonencq was smoking his pipe in the doorway.

That evening Mme. de Marville went to ask advice of her father-in-law, and found the whole Popinot family at the Camusots' house. It was only natural that a mother who had failed to capture an eldest son should be tempted to take her little revenge; so Mme. de Marville threw out hints of the splendid marriage that her Cécile was about to make. "Whom can Cécile be going to marry?" was the question upon all lips. And Cécile's mother, without suspecting that she was betraying the secret, let fall words and whispered confidences, afterward supplemented by Madame Berthier, till gossip circulating in the bourgeois empyrean where Pons accomplished his gastronomical evolutions took something like the following form:

"Cécile de Marville is engaged to be married to a young German, a banker from philanthropic motives, for he has four millions; he is like a hero of a novel, a perfect Werther, charming and kind-hearted. He has sown his wild oats, and he is distractedly in love with Cécile; it is a case of love at first sight; and so much the more certain, since Cécile had all Pons' paintings of Madonnas for rivals," and so forth and so forth.

Two or three of the set came to call on the presidente, ostensibly to congratulate, but really to find out whether or not the marvelous tale were true. For their benefit Mme. de Marville executed the following admirable variations on the theme of son-in-law which mothers may consult, as people used to refer to the "Complete Letter Writer."

"A marriage is not an accomplished fact," she told Mme. Chiffreville, "until you have been to the mayor's office and the church. We have only come as far as a personal interview; so I count upon your friendship to say nothing of our hopes."

"You are very fortunate, madame; marriages are so difficult to arrange in these days."

"What can one do? It was chance; but marriages are often made in that way."

"Ah! well. So you are going to marry Cécile?" said Mme. Cardot.

"Yes," said Cécile's mother, fully understanding the meaning of the "so." "We were very particular, or Cécile would

have been established before this. But now we have found
everything that we wish: money, good temper, good character, and good looks; and my sweet little girl certainly deserves nothing less. Monsieur Brunner is a charming young
man, most distinguished; he is fond of luxury, he knows life;
he is wild about Cécile, he loves her sincerely; and, in spite
of his three or four millions, Cécile is going to accept him.
We had not looked so high for her; still, as the saying goes,
'store is no sore.'"

"It was not so much the fortune as the affection inspired
by my daughter which decided us," the presidente told Mme.
Lebas. "Monsieur Brunner is in such a hurry that he wants
the marriage to take place with the least possible delay."

"Is he a foreigner?"

"Yes, madame; but I am very fortunate, I confess. No,
I shall not have a son-in-law in him, but a son. Monsieur
Brunner's delicacy has quite won our hearts. No one would
imagine how anxious he was to marry under the dotal system.
It is a great security for families. He is going to invest twelve
hundred thousand francs in grazing land, which will be added
to Marville some day."

More variations followed on the morrow. For instance—
M. Brunner was a great lord, doing everything in lordly
fashion; he did not haggle. If M. de Marville could obtain
letters of naturalization, qualifying M. Brunner for an office
under Government (and the home secretary surely could strain
a point for M. de Marville), his son-in-law would be a peer
of France. Nobody knew how much money M. Brunner possessed; "he had the finest horses and the smartest carriages
in Paris!" and so on and so forth.

From the pleasure with which the Camusots published their
hopes, it was pretty clear that this triumph was unexpected.

Immediately after the interview in Pons' museum, M. de
Marville, at his wife's instance, begged the home secretary,
his chief, and the attorney for the crown to dine with him on

the occasion of the introduction of this phœnix of a son-in-law.

The three great personages accepted the invitation, albeit it was given on short notice ; they all saw the part that they were to play in the family politics, and readily came to the father's support.   In France we are usually pretty ready to assist the mother of marriageable daughters to hook an eligible son-in-law.   The Count and Countess Popinot likewise lent their presence to complete the splendor of the occasion, although they thought the invitation in questionable taste.

There were eleven in all.   Cécile's grandfather, old Camusot, came, of course, with his wife to a family reunion purposely arranged to elicit a proposal from M. Brunner.

The Camusot de Marvilles had given out that the guest of the evening was one of the richest capitalists in Germany, a man of taste (he was in love with " the little girl "), a future rival of the Nucingens, Kellers, du Tillets, and their like.

" It is our day," said the presidente with elaborate simplicity, when she had named her guests one by one for the German whom she already regarded as her son-in-law.   " We have only a few intimate friends—first, my husband's father, who, as you know, is sure to be raised to the peerage ; Monsieur le Comte and Madame la Comtesse Popinot, whose son was not thought rich enough for Cécile ; the home secretary ; our first president ; our attorney for the crown ; our personal friends, in short.   We shall be obliged to dine rather late to-night, because the Chamber is sitting, and people cannot get away before six."

Brunner looked significantly at Pons, and Cousin Pons rubbed his hands as who should say: " Our friends, you see ! *My* friends ! "

Mme. de Marville, as a clever tactician, had something very particular to say to her cousin, that Cécile and her Werther might be left together for a moment.   Cécile chattered away volubly, and contrived that Frédéric should catch sight of a

German dictionary, a German grammar, and a volume of Goethe hidden away in a place where he was likely to find them.

"Ah! are you learning German?" asked Brunner, flushing red.

(For laying traps of this kind the Frenchwoman has not her match!)

"Oh! how naughty you are!" she cried; "it is too bad of you, monsieur, to explore my hiding-places like this. I want to read Goethe in the original," she added; "I have been learning German for two years."

"Then the grammar must be very difficult to learn, for scarcely ten pages have been cut——" Brunner remarked with much candor.

Cécile, abashed, turned away to hide her blushes. A German cannot resist a display of this kind; Brunner caught Cécile's hand, made her turn, and watched her confusion under his gaze, after the manner of the heroes of the novels of Auguste La Fontaine of chaste memory.

"You are adorable," said he.

Cécile's petulant gestures replied: "So are you—who could help liking you?"

"It is all right, mamma," she whispered to her parent, who came up at that moment with Pons.

The sight of a family party on these occasions is not to be described. Everybody was well satisfied to see a mother put her hand on an eligible son-in-law. Compliments, double-barreled and double-charged, were paid to Brunner (who pretended to understand nothing); to Cécile, on whom nothing was lost; and to the president, who fished for them. Pons heard the blood singing in his ears, the light of all the blazing gas-jets of the theatre footlights seemed to be dazzling his eyes, when Cécile, in a low voice and with the most ingenious circumspection, spoke of her father's plan of the annuity of twelve hundred francs. The old artist positively declined the offer, bringing forward the value of his fortune in furniture, only now made known to him by Brunner.

The home secretary, the first president, the attorney for the crown, the Popinots, and those who had other engagements, all went ; and before long no one was left except M. Camusot senior, and Cardot the old notary, and his assistant and son-in-law Berthier.   Pons, worthy soul, looking around and seeing no one but the family, blundered out a speech of thanks to the president and his wife for the proposal which Cécile had just made to him.   So is it with those who are guided by their feelings ; they act upon impulse.   Brunner, hearing of an annuity offered in this way, thought that it had very much the look of commission paid to Pons ; he made an Israelite's return upon himself, his attitude told of more than cool calculation.

Meanwhile Pons was saying to his astonished relations, " My collection or its value will, in any case, go to your family, whether I come to terms with our friend Brunner or keep it."   The Camusots were amazed to hear that Pons was so rich.

Brunner, watching, saw how all these ignorant people looked favorably upon a man once believed to be poor so soon as they knew that he had great possessions.   He had seen, too, already, that Cécile was spoiled by her father and mother ; he amused himself, therefore, by astonishing the good bourgeois.

" I was telling mademoiselle," said he, " that Monsieur Pons' pictures were worth that sum to *me ;* but the prices of works of art have risen so much of late, that no one can tell how much the collection might sell for at a public auction. The sixty pictures might fetch a million francs ; several that I saw the other day were worth fifty thousand apiece."

" It is a fine thing to be your heir ! " remarked old Cardot, looking at Pons.

" My heir is my Cousin Cécile here," answered Pons, insisting on the relationship. There was a flutter of admiration at this.

"She will be a very rich heiress," laughed old Cardot as he took his departure.

Camusot senior, the president and his wife, Cécile, Brunner, Berthier, and Pons were now left together; for it was assumed that the formal demand for Cécile's hand was about to be made. No sooner was Cardot gone, indeed, than Brunner began with an inquiry which augured well.

"I think I understood," he said, turning to Mme. de Marville, "that mademoiselle is your only daughter."

"Certainly," the lady said proudly.

"Nobody will make any difficulties," Pons, good soul, put in by way of encouraging the backward Brunner to bring out his proposal.

But Brunner grew thoughtful, and an ominous silence brought on a coolness of the strangest kind. The presidente might have admitted that her "little girl" was subject to epileptic fits. The president, thinking that Cécile ought not to be present, signed to her to go. She went. Still Brunner said nothing. They all began to look at one another. The situation was growing awkward.

Camusot senior, a man of experience, took the German to Mme. de Marville's room, ostensibly to show him Pons' fan. He saw that some difficulty had arisen, and signed to the rest to leave him alone with Cécile's suitor-designate.

"Here is the masterpiece," said Camusot, opening out the fan.

Brunner took it in his hand and looked at it. "It is worth five thousand francs," he said after a moment.

"Did you not come here, sir, to ask for my granddaughter?" inquired the future peer of France.

"Yes, sir," said Brunner; "and I beg you to believe that no possible marriage could be more flattering to my vanity. I shall never find any one more charming nor more amiable nor a young lady who answers to my ideas like Mademoiselle Cécile; but——"

"Oh, no *buts!*" old Camusot broke in; "or let us have the translation of your 'buts' at once, my dear sir. It is due us."

"I am very glad, sir, that the matter has gone no further on either side," Brunner answered gravely. "I had no idea that Mademoiselle Cécile was an only daughter. Anybody else would consider this an advantage; but to me, believe me, it is an insurmountable obstacle to——"

"What, sir!" cried Camusot, amazed beyond measure. "Do you find a positive drawback in an immense advantage? Your conduct is really extraordinary; I should very much like to hear the explanation of it."

"I came here this evening, sir," returned the German phlegmatically, "intending to ask Monsieur le President for his daughter's hand. It was my desire to give Mademoiselle Cécile a brilliant future by offering her so much of my fortune as she would consent to accept. But an only daughter is a child whose will is law to indulgent parents, who has never been contradicted. I have had the opportunity of observing this in many families, where parents worship divinities of this kind. And your granddaughter is not only the idol of the house, but Madame la Presidente—— you know what I mean. I have seen my own father's house turned into a hell, sir, from this very cause. My stepmother, the source of all my misfortunes, an only daughter, idolized by her parents, the most charming betrothed imaginable, after marriage became a fiend incarnate. I do not doubt that Mademoiselle Cécile is an exception to the rule; but I am not a young man, I am forty years old, and the difference between our ages entails difficulties which would put it out of my power to make the young lady happy, when Madame la Presidente has always carried out her daughter's every wish and listened to her as if mademoiselle was an oracle. What right have I to expect Mademoiselle Cécile to change her habits and ideas? Instead of a father and mother who indulge her every whim, she would find an egoistic man of forty; if she should resist, the man of forty would have the worst of it. So, as an honest man—I withdraw. If there should be any need to explain my visit here, I desire to be entirely sacrificed——"

"If these are your motives, sir," said the future peer of France, "however singular they may be, they are plausible, they——"

"Do not call my sincerity in question, sir," Brunner interrupted quickly. "If you know of a penniless girl, one of a large family, well brought up but without fortune, as happens very often in France; and if her character offers me security, I will marry her."

A pause followed; Frédéric Brunner left Cécile's grandfather and politely took leave of his host and hostess. When he was gone, Cécile appeared, a living commentary upon her Werther's leave-taking; she was ghastly pale. She had hidden herself in her mother's wardrobe and overheard the whole conversation.

"Refused!—— " she said in a low voice for her mother's ear.

"And why?" asked the presidente, fixing her eyes upon her embarrassed father-in-law.

"Upon the fine pretext that an only daughter is a spoilt child," replied that gentleman. "And he is not altogether wrong there," he added, seizing an opportunity of putting the blame on the daughter-in-law, who had worried him not a little for twenty years.

"It will kill my child!" cried the presidente, "and it is your doing!" she exclaimed, addressing Pons, as she supported her fainting daughter, for Cécile thought well to make good her mother's words by sinking into her arms. The president and his wife carried Cécile to an easy-chair, where she swooned outright. The grandfather rang for the servants.

"It is a plot of his weaving; I see it all now," said the infuriated mother.

Pons sprang up as if the trump of doom were sounding in his ears.

"Yes!" said the lady, her eyes like two springs of green bile, "this gentleman wished to repay a harmless joke by an insult. Who will believe that that German was right in his mind? He is either an accomplice in a wicked scheme of revenge, or he is crazy. I hope, Monsieur Pons, that in future you will spare us the annoyance of seeing you in the house where you have tried to bring shame and dishonor."

Pons stood like a statue, with his eyes fixed on the pattern of the carpet.

"Well! Are you still here, monster of ingratitude?" cried she, turning round on Pons, who was twirling his thumbs. "Your master and I are never at home, remember, if this gentleman calls," she continued, turning to the servants. "Jean, go for the doctor; and bring hartshorn, Madeleine."

In the presidente's eyes, the reason given by Brunner was simply an excuse, there was something else behind; but, at the same time, the fact that the marriage was broken off was only the more certain. A woman's mind works swiftly in great crises, and Mme. de Marville had hit at once upon the one method of repairing the check. She chose to look upon it as a scheme of revenge. This notion of ascribing a fiendish scheme to Pons satisfied family honor. Faithful to her dislike of the cousin, she treated a feminine suspicion as a fact. Women, generally speaking, hold a creed peculiar to themselves, a code of their own; to them anything which serves their interests or their passions is true. So also their vain imaginings of implied insult to themselves by others, although quite unfounded, becomes to them a truth. The presidente went a good deal further. In the course of the evening she talked the president into her belief, and next morning found the magistrate convinced of his cousin's culpability.

Every one, no doubt, will condemn the lady's horrible conduct; but what mother in Mme. Camusot's position will not do the same? Put the choice between her own daughter and an alien, she will prefer to sacrifice the honor of the latter. There are many ways of doing this, but the end in view is the same.

The old musician fled down the staircase in haste; but he went slowly along the boulevards to his theatre, he turned in mechanically at the door, and mechanically hé took his place and conducted the orchestra. In the interval he gave such random answers to Schmucke's questions, that his old friend dissembled his fear that Pons' mind had given way. To so childlike a nature, the recent scene took the proportions of a catastrophe. He had meant to make every one happy, and he had aroused a terrible slumbering feeling of hate; everything had been turned topsy-turvy. He had at last seen mortal hate in the presidente's eyes, tones, and gestures.

On the morrow, Mme. Camusot de Marville made a great resolution; the president likewise sanctioned the step now forced upon them by circumstances. It was determined that the estate of Marville should be settled upon Cécile at the time of her marriage, as well as the house in the Rue de Hanovre and a hundred thousand francs. In the course of the morning, the presidente went to call upon the Comtesse Popinot; for she saw plainly that nothing but a settled marriage could enable them to recover after such a check. To the Comtesse Popinot she told the shocking story of Pons' revenge, Pons' hideous hoax. It all seemed probable enough when it came out that the marriage had been broken off simply on the pretext that Cécile was an only daughter. The presidente next dwelt artfully upon the advantage of adding " de Marville " to the name of Popinot; and the immense dowry. At the present price fetched by land in Normandy, at two per cent., the property represented nine hundred thousand francs, and the house in the Rue de Hanovre about two hundred and fifty thousand. No reasonable family could refuse such an alliance. The Comte and Comtesse Popinot accepted; and as they were now touched by the honor of the family which they were about to enter, they promised to help explain away the yesterday evening's mishap.

And now in the house of the elder Camusot, before the very persons who had heard Mme. de Marville singing Frédéric Brunner's praises but a few days ago, that lady, to whom nobody ventured to speak on the topic, plunged courageously into explanations.

"Really, nowadays" (she said), "one could not be too careful if a marriage was in question, especially if one had to do with foreigners."

"And why, madame?"

"What has happened to you?" asked Mme. Chiffreville.

"Do you not know about our adventure with that Brunner, who had the audacity to aspire to marry Cécile? His father was a German that kept a wine-tavern, and his uncle is a dealer in and dryer of rabbit-skins!"

"Is it possible? So clear-sighted as you are!" murmured a lady.

"These adventurers are so cunning. But we found out everything through Berthier. His friend is a beggar that plays the flute. He is friendly with a person who lets furnished lodgings in the Rue du Mail and some tailor or other—— We found out that he had led a most disreputable life, and no amount of fortune would be enough for a scamp that has run through his mother's property."

"Why, Mademoiselle de Marville would have been wretched!" said Mme. Berthier.

"How did he come to your house?" asked old Mme. Lebas.

"It was Monsieur Pons. Out of revenge, he introduced this fine gentleman to us, to make us ridiculous. This Brunner (it is the same name as Fontaine in French)—this Brunner, that was made out to be such a grandee, has poor enough health, he is bald, and his teeth are bad. The first sight of him was enough for me; I distrusted him from the first.''

"But how about the great fortune that you spoke of?" a young married woman asked shyly.

"The fortune was not nearly so large as they said. These tailors and the landlord and he all scraped the money together among them, and put all their savings into this bank that they are starting. What is a bank for those that begin in these days? Simply a license to ruin themselves. A banker's wife may lie down at night a millionaire and wake up in the morning with nothing but her settlement. At the first word, at the very first sight of him, we made up our minds about this gentleman—he is not one of us. You can tell by his gloves, by his vest, that he is a workingman, the son of a man that kept a pot-house somewhere in Germany; he has not the instincts of a gentleman; he drinks beer, and he smokes— smokes? ah! madame, *twenty-five pipes a day!*—— What would have become of poor Lili? It positively makes me shudder even now to think of it. God has indeed preserved us! And, beside, Cécile never liked him. Who would have expected such a trick from a relative, an old friend of the house that had dined with us twice a week for twenty years? We have loaded him with benefits, and he played his game so well that he said Cécile was his heir before the keeper of the seals and the attorney-general and the home secretary!—— That Brunner and Monsieur Pons had their story ready, and each of them said that the other was worth millions!—— No, I do assure you, all of you would have been taken in by an artist's hoax like that.''

In a few weeks' time, the united forces of the Camusot and Popinot families gained an easy victory in the world, for nobody undertook to defend the unfortunate Pons, that parasite, that curmudgeon, that skinflint, that smooth-faced humbug, on whom everybody heaped scorn; he was a viper cherished in the bosom of the family, he had not his match for spite, he was a dangerous mountebank whom nobody ought to mention.

About a month after the perfidious Werther's withdrawal, poor Pons left his bed for the first time after an attack of nervous fever, and walked along the sunny side of the street leaning on Schmucke's arm. Nobody in the Boulevard du Temple laughed at the " pair of nutcrackers," for one of the old men looked so shattered, and the other so touchingly careful of his invalid friend. By the time that they reached the Boulevard Poissonnière, a little color came back to Pons' face; he was breathing the air of the boulevards, he felt the vitalizing power of the atmosphere of the crowded street, the life-giving property of the air that is noticeable in quarters where human life abounds; in the filthy Roman Ghetto, for instance, with its swarming Jewish population, where malaria is unknown. Perhaps, too, the sight of the streets, the great spectacle of Paris, the daily pleasure of his life, did the invalid good. They walked on side by side, though Pons now and again left his friend to look in the store windows. Opposite the Theatre des Variétiés he saw Count Popinot, and went up to him very respectfully, for of all men Pons esteemed and venerated the ex-minister.

The peer of France answered him severely—

"I am at a loss to understand, sir, how you can have so little tact as to speak to a near connection of a family whom you tried to brand with shame and ridicule by a trick which no one but an artist could devise. Understand this, sir, that from to-day we must be complete strangers to each other. Madame la Comtesse Popinot, like every one else, feels indignant at your behavior to the Marvilles."

And Count Popinot passed on, leaving Pons thunderstruck. Passion, justice, policy, and great social forces never take into account the condition of the human creature whom they strike down. The statesman, driven by family considerations to crush Pons, did not so much as see the physical weakness of his redoubtable enemy.

"Vat is it, mine boor friend?" exclaimed Schmucke, seeing how white Pons had grown.

"It is a fresh stab in the heart," Pons replied, leaning heavily on Schmucke's arm. "I think that no one, save God in heaven, can have any right to do good, and that is why all those who meddle in His work are so cruelly punished."

The old artist's sarcasm was uttered with a supreme effort; he was trying, excellent creature, to quiet the dismay visible in Schmucke's face.

"So I dink," Schmucke replied simply.

Pons could not understand it. Neither the Camusots nor the Popinots had sent him notice of Cécile's wedding.

On the Boulevard des Italiens Pons saw M. Cardot coming toward them. Warned by Count Popinot's allocution, Pons was very careful not to accost the old acquaintance with whom he had dined once a fortnight for the last year; he lifted his hat, but the other, mayor and deputy of Paris, threw him an indignant glance and went by. Pons turned to Schmucke.

"Do go and ask him what it is that they all have against me," he said to the friend who knew all the details of the catastrophe that Pons could tell him.

"Mennesir," Schmucke began diplomatically, "mine friend Bons is chust recofering from an illness; you haf no doubt fail to rekognise him?"

"Not in the least."

"But mit vat kan you rebroach him?"

"You have a monster of ingratitude for a friend, sir; if he is still alive, it is because nothing kills ill-weeds, which ever flourish apace. People do well to mistrust artists; they are as mischievous and spiteful as monkeys. This friend of yours tried to dishonor his own family, and to blight a young girl's

13

character, in revenge for a harmless joke. I wish to have nothing to do with him; I shall do my best to forget that I have ever known him, or that such a man exists. All the members of his family and my own share the wish, sir, so do all the persons who once did the said Pons the great honor of receiving him.''

"Boot, mennesir, you are a reasonaple mann; gif you vill bermit me, I shall exblain die affair——"

"You are quite at liberty to remain his friend, sir, if you are minded that way," returned Cardot, "but you need go no further; for I must give you warning that in my opinion those who try to excuse or defend his conduct are just as much to blame."

"To chustify it?"

"Yes, for his conduct can neither be justified nor qualified." And with that word, the deputy for the Seine went his way; he would not hear another syllable.

"I have two powers in the State against me," smiled poor Pons, when Schmucke had repeated these savage speeches.

"Eferypody is against us," Schmucke answered dolorously. "Let us go avay pefore we shall meet oder fools."

Never before in the course of a truly simple life had Schmucke uttered such words as these. Never before had his almost divine meekness been ruffled. He had smiled child-like on all the mischances that befell him, but he could not look and see his sublime Pons maltreated; his Pons, his unknown Aristides, the genius resigned to his lot, the nature that knew no bitterness, the treasury of kindness, the heart of gold! Alceste's indignation filled Schmucke's soul—he was moved to call Pons' amphitryons "fools." For his pacific nature that impulse equaled the wrath of Roland.

With wise foresight, Schmucke turned to go home by the way of the Boulevard du Temple, Pons passively submitting like a fallen fighter, heedless of blows; but chance ordered that he should know that all his world was against him. The

House of Peers, the Chamber of Deputies, strangers, and the family, the strong, the weak, and the innocent, all combined to send down the avalanche.

In the Boulevard Poissonnière, Pons caught sight of that very M. Cardot's daughter, who, young as she was, had learned to be charitable to others through trouble of her own. Her husband knew a secret by which he kept her in bondage.* She was the only one among Pons' hostesses whom he called by her Christain name; he addressed Mme. Berthier as "Félicie," and he thought that she understood him. The gentle creature seemed to be distressed by the sight of Cousin Pons, as he was called (though he was in no way related to the family of the second wife of a cousin by marriage). There was no help for it, however; Félicie Berthier stopped to speak to the invalid.

"I did not think you were cruel cousin," she said; "but if even a quarter of all that I hear of you is true, you are very false. Oh! do not justify yourself," she added quickly, seeing Pons' significant gesture, "it is useless, for two reasons. In the first place, I have no right to accuse or judge or condemn anybody, for I myself know so well how much may be said for those who seem to be most guilty; secondly, your explanation would do no good. Monsieur Berthier drew up the marriage-contract for Mademoiselle de Marville and the Vicomte Popinot; he is so exasperated, that if he knew that I had so much as spoken one word to you, one word for the last time, he would scold me. Everybody is against you."

"So it seems indeed, madame," Pons said, his voice shaking, as he lifted his hat respectfully.

Painfully he made his way back to the Rue de Normandie. The old German knew from the heavy weight on his arm that his friend was struggling bravely against failing physical strength. That third encounter was like the verdict of the Lamb at the foot of the throne of God; and the anger of the

* See "The Unconscious Mummers."

Angel of the Poor, the symbol of the Peoples, is the last word
of Heaven. They reached home without the utterance of
another word.

There are moments in our lives when the sense that our
friend is near is all that we can bear. Our wounds smart under
the consoling words that only reveal the depths of pain. The
old pianist, you see, possessed a genius for friendship, the tact
of those who, having suffered much, know the customs of suffering.

Pons was never to take a walk again. From one illness he
fell into another. He was of a sanguine-bilious temperament,
the bile passed into the blood, and a violent liver attack was
the result. He had never known a day's illness in his life till
a month ago; he had never consulted a doctor; so La Cibot,
with almost motherly care and intentions at first of the very
best, called in "the doctor of the quarter."

In every quarter of Paris there is a doctor whose name and
address are only known to the working-classes, to the little
tradespeople and the porters, and in consequence he is called
"the doctor of the quarter." He undertakes confinement
cases, he lets blood, he is in the medical profession pretty
much what the "general servant" of the advertising column
is in the scale of domestic service. He must perforce be kind
to the poor, and tolerably expert by reason of much practice,
and he is generally popular. Dr. Poulain, called in by Mme.
Cibot, gave an inattentive ear to the old musician's complain-
ings. Pons groaned out that his skin itched; he had scratched
himself all night long, till he could scarcely feel. The look
of his eyes, with the yellow circles about them, corroborated
the symptoms.

"Had you some violent shock a couple of days ago?" the
doctor asked the patient.

"Yes, alas!"

"You have the same complaint that this gentleman was
threatened with," said Dr. Poulain, looking at Schmucke as

he spoke; "it is an attack of jaundice, but you will soon get over it," he added, as he wrote a prescription.

But in spite of that comfortable phrase, the doctor's eye had told another tale as he looked professionally at the patient; and the death-sentence, though hidden under stereotyped compassion, can always be read by those who wish to know the truth. Mme. Cibot gave a spy's glance at the doctor, and read his thought; his bedside manner did not deceive her; she followed him out of the room.

"Do you think he will get over it?" asked Mme. Cibot, at the stairhead.

"My dear Madame Cibot, your lodger is a dead man; not because of the bile in the system, but because his vitality is low. Still, with great care, your patient may pull through. Somebody ought to take him away for a change——"

"How is he to go?" asked Mme. Cibot. "He has nothing to live upon but his salary; his friend has just a little money from some great ladies, very charitable ladies, in return for his services, it seems. They are two children. I have looked after them for nine years."

"I spend my life in watching people die, not of their disease, but of another bad and incurable complaint—the want of money," said the doctor. "How often it happens that so far from taking a fee, I am obliged to leave a five-franc piece on the mantel-shelf when I go——"

"Poor, dear Monsieur Poulain!" cried Mme. Cibot. "Ah, if you hadn't only the hundred thousand livres a year, what some stingy people has in the quarter (regular devils from hell they are), you would be like providence on earth," she added, curtsying.

Dr. Poulain had made the little practice, by which he made a bare subsistence, chiefly by winning the esteem of the porters' lodges in his district. So he raised his eyes to heaven and thanked Mme. Cibot with a solemn face worthy of Tartuffe.

"Then you think that with careful nursing our dear patient will get better, my dear Monsieur Poulain?"

"Yes, if this shock has not been too much for him."

"Poor man! who can have vexed him? There isn't nobody like him on earth, except his friend Monsieur Schmucke. I will find out what is the matter, and I will undertake to give them that upset my gentleman a hauling over the coals——"

"Look here, my dear Madame Cibot," said the doctor as they stood in the gateway, "one of the principal symptoms of his complaint is great irritability; and as it is hardly to be supposed that he can afford a nurse, the task of nursing him will fall to you. So——"

"Are you talking of Mouchieu Ponsh?" asked the marine-store-dealer. He was sitting smoking on the curb-post in the gateway, and now he rose to join in the conversation.

"Yes, Daddy Rémonencq."

"All right," said Rémonencq, "ash to moneysh, he ish better off than Mouchieur Monishtrol and the big men in the curioshity line. I know enough in the art line to tell you thish—the dear man hash treasursh!" he spoke with a broad Auvergne dialect.

"Look here, I thought you were laughing at me the other day when my gentlemen were out and I showed you the old rubbish upstairs," said Mme. Cibot.

In Paris where walls have ears, where doors have tongues, and window-bars have eyes, there are few things more dangerous than the practice of standing to chat in a gateway. Partings are like postscripts to a letter—indiscreet utterances that do as much mischief to the speaker as to those who overhear them. A single instance will be sufficient as a parallel to an event in this history.

In the time of the Empire when men paid considerable attention to their hair, one of the first coiffeurs of the day came out of a house where he had just been dressing a pretty woman's head. This artist in question enjoyed the custom of all the lower floor inmates of the house ; and, among these, there flourished an elderly bachelor guarded by a housekeeper who detested her master's next-of-kin. The *ci-devant* young man, falling seriously ill, the most famous doctors of the day (they were not as yet styled the "princes of science") had been called in to consult upon his case ; and it so chanced that the learned gentlemen were taking leave of one another in the gateway just as the hairdresser came out. They were talking as doctors usually talk among themselves when the farce of a consultation is over. "He is a dead man," quoth Dr. Haudry. "He has not a month to live," added Desplein, "unless a miracle takes place." These were the words overheard by the hairdresser.

Like all hairdressers, he kept up a good understanding with his customers' servants. Prodigious greed sent the man upstairs again ; he mounted to the *ci-devant* young man's apartment, and promised the servant-mistress a tolerably handsome commission to persuade her master to sink a large proportion of his money in an annuity. The dying bachelor, fifty-six by count of years, and twice as old as his age by reason of amorous campaigns, owned, among other property, a splendid house in the Rue de Richelieu, worth at that time about two hundred and fifty thousand francs. It was this house that the hairdresser coveted ; and on agreement to pay an annuity of thirty thousand francs so long as the bachelor lived, it passed into his hands. This happened in 1806. And in this present year 1846 the hairdresser is still paying that annuity. He has retired from business, he is seventy years old ; the *ci-devant* young man is in his dotage ; and as he has married his Mme. Evrard, he may last for a long while yet. As the hairdresser gave the woman thirty thousand francs, his bit of real estate has cost him, first and last, more than a million, and the house at this day is worth eight or nine hundred thousand francs.

Like the hairdresser, Rémonencq the Auvergnat had over-heard Brunner's parting remark in the gateway on the day of Cécile's first interview with that phœnix of eligible men. Rémonencq at once longed to gain a sight of Pons' museum; and as he lived on good terms with his neighbors the Cibots, it was not very long before the opportunity came, one day when the friends were out. The sight of such treasures daz-zled him; he saw a "good haul," in dealers' phrase, which being interpreted means a chance to steal a fortune. He had been meditating this for five or six days.

"I am sho far from joking," he said, in reply to Mme. Cibot's remark, "that we will talk the thing over; and if the good shentleman will take an annuity of fifty thoushand francsh, I will shtand a hamper of wine, if——"

"Fifty thousand francs!" interrupted the doctor; "what are you thinking about? Why, if the good man is so well off as that, with me in attendance, and La Cibot to nurse him, he may get better—for liver complaint is a disease that attacks strong constitutions."

"Fifty, did I shay? Why, a shentleman here, on your very doorshtep, offered him sheven hundred thoushand francsh, shimply for the pictursh, *fouchtra!*"

While Rémonencq made this announcement, Mme. Cibot was looking at Dr. Poulain. There was a strange expression in her eyes; the devil might have kindled that sinister glitter in their tawny depths.

"Oh, come! we must not pay any attention to such idle tales," said the doctor, well pleased, however, to find that his patient could afford to pay for his visits.

"If my dear Madame Chibot, here, would let me come and bring an ekshpert (shinsh the shentleman upshtairs ish in bed), I will shertainly find the money in a couple of hoursh, even if sheven hundred thoushand francsh ish in queshtion——"

"All right, my friend," said the doctor. "Now, Madame Cibot, be careful never to contradict the invalid. You must be prepared to be very patient with him, for he will find everything irritating and wearisome, even your services; nothing will please him; you must expect grumbling——"

"He will be uncommonly hard to please," said La Cibot.

"Look here, mind what I tell you," the doctor said in a tone of authority, "Monsieur Pons' life is in the hands of those that nurse him; I shall come perhaps twice a day. I shall take him first on my round."

The doctor's profound indifference to the fate of a poor patient had suddenly given place to a most tender solicitude when he saw that the speculator was serious, and that there was a possible fortune in question.

"He will be nursed like a king," said Madame Cibot, forcing up enthusiasm. She waited till the doctor turned the corner into the Rue Charlot; then she fell to talking again with the dealer in old iron. Rémonencq had finished smoking his pipe, and stood in the doorway of his store, leaning against the frame; he had purposely taken this position; he meant the portress to come to him.

The store had once been a café. Nothing had been changed there since the Auvergnat discovered it and took over the lease; you could still read "Café de Normandie" on the strip left above the windows in all modern stores. Rémonencq had found somebody, probably a house-painter's apprentice, who did the work for nothing, to paint another inscription in the remaining space below—it ran: "RÉMONENCQ, DEALER IN MARINE STORES, FURNITURE BOUGHT"—painted in small black letters. All the mirrors, tables, seats, shelves, and fittings of the Café de Normandie had been sold, as might have been expected, before Rémonencq took possession of the store as it stood, paying a yearly rent of six hundred francs for the place, with a back store, a kitchen, and a single room above, where the head-waiter used to sleep, for the house belonging to the Café de Normandie was let separately. Of the former splendor of the café, nothing now remained save the plain light green paper on the walls, and the strong iron bolts and bars of the store-front.

When Rémonencq came hither in 1831, after the Revolution of July, he began by displaying a selection of broken door-bells, cracked plates, old iron, and the obsolete scales and weights abolished by a Government which alone fails to carry out its own regulations, for deux-sous and sous of the time of Louis XVI. are still in circulation. After a time this Auvergnat, a match for five ordinary Auvergnats, bought up old saucepans and kettles, old picture-frames, old copper, and chipped china. Gradually, as the store was emptied and filled, the quality of the stock-in-trade improved, like Nicolet's farces. Rémonencq persisted in an unfailing and prodigiously profitable martingale,* a "system" which any philosophical idler may study as he watches the increasing value of the stock kept by this intelligent class of trader. Picture-frames and copper succeed to tinware, argand lamps, and damaged crockery; china marks the next transition; and after no long tarrying in the "omnium gatherum" stage, the store becomes a museum. Some day or other the dusty windows are cleaned, the interior is restored, the Auvergnat relinquishes velveteen and jackets for a greatcoat, and there he sits like a dragon guarding his treasure, surrounded by masterpieces! He is a cunning connoisseur by this time; he has increased his capital tenfold; he is not to be cheated; he knows the tricks of the trade. The monster among his treasures looks like some old hag among a score of young girls that she offers to the public. Beauty and miracles of art are alike indifferent to him; subtle and dense as he is, he has a keen eye to profits, he talks roughly to those who know less than he does; he has learned to act a part, he pretends to love his pictures and his marquetry, or he tells you that he is short of money, or again he lets you know the price he himself gave for the things, he offers to let you see the memoranda of the sale. He is a

* *Jouer à la martingale*—playing for double or quits.

Proteus; in one hour he can be Jocrisse, Janot, *Queue-rouge*, Mondor, Harpagon, or Nicodème.

The third year found armor, and old pictures, and some tolerably fine clocks in Rémonencq's store. He sent for his sister, and La Rémonencq came on foot all the way from Auvergne to take charge of the store while her brother was away. A big and very ugly woman, dressed like a Japanese idol, a half-idiotic creature with a vague, staring gaze, she would not bate a centime of the prices fixed by her brother. In the intervals of business she did the work of the house, and solved the apparently insoluble problem—how to live on "the mists of the Seine." The Rémonencqs' diet consisted of bread and herrings, with the outside leaves of lettuce or vegetable refuse selected from the heaps deposited in the kennel before the doors of eating-houses. The two between them did not spend more than ten sous a day on food (bread included), and La Rémonencq earned the whole money by sewing or spinning.

Rémonencq came to Paris in the first instance to work as an errand-boy. Between the years 1825 and 1831 he ran errands for dealers in curiosities in the Boulevard Beaumarchais or coppersmiths in the Rue de Lappe. It is the usual start in life in his line of business. Jews, Normans, Auvergnats, and Savoyards, those four different races of men all have the same instincts, and make their fortunes in the same way; they spend nothing, make small profits, and let them accumulate at compound interest. Such is their trading charter, and *that* charter is no delusion.

Rémonencq at this moment had made it up with his old master Monistrol; he did business with wholesale dealers, he was a *chineur* (the technical word), plying his trade in the district, which, as everybody knows, extend for some forty leagues round Paris.

After fourteen years of business, he had sixty thousand francs in hand and a well-stocked store. He lived in the

Rue de Normandie because the rent was low, but casual customers were scarce, most of his goods were sold to other
dealers, and he was content with moderate gains. All his
business transactions were carried on in the Auvergne dialect
or *charabia*, as people call it.

Rémonencq cherished a dream! He wished to establish
himself on a boulevard, to be a rich dealer in curiosities,
and do a direct trade with amateurs some day. And, indeed, within him there was a formidable man of business.
His countenance was the more inscrutable because it was
glazed over by a deposit of dust and particles of metal glued
together by the sweat of his brow; for he did everything
himself, and the use and wont of bodily labor had given
him something of the stoical impassability of the old soldiers of 1799.

In personal appearance Rémonencq was short and thin;
his little eyes were set in his head in porcine fashion; a
Jew's slyness and concentrated greed looked out of those dull
blue circles, though in his case the false humility that masks
the Israelite's unfathomed contempt for the Gentile was
lacking.

The relations between the Cibots and the Rémonencqs
were those of benefactors and recipients. Mme. Cibot, convinced that the Auvergnats were wretchedly poor, used to let
them have the remainder of "her gentlemen's" dinners at
ridiculous prices. The Rémonencqs would buy a pound of
broken bread, crusts and crumbs, for a centime, a porringer
full of cold potatoes for something less, and other scraps in
proportion. Rémonencq shrewdly allowed them to believe
that he was not in business on his own account, he worked
for Monistrol, the rich storekeepers preyed upon him, he
said, and the Cibots felt sincerely sorry for Rémonencq.
The velveteen jacket, vest, and trousers, particularly affected
by Auvergnats, were covered with patches of Cibot's making,
and not a penny had the little tailor charged for repairs

which kept the three garments together after eleven years of wear.

Thus we see that all Jews are not in Israel.

"You are not laughing at me, Rémonencq, are you?" asked the portress. "Is it possible that Monsieur Pons has such a fortune, living as he does? There is not a hundred francs in the place——"

"Amateursh are all like that," Rémonencq remarked sententiously.

"Then do you think that my gentleman has the worth of seven hundred thousand francs, eh?——"

"In pictures alone," continued Rémonencq (it is needless, for the sake of clearness in the story, to give any further specimens of his frightful dialect). "If he would take fifty thousand francs for one up there that I know of, I would find the money if I had to hang myself. Do you remember those little frames full of enameled copper on crimson velvet, hanging among the portraits?—— Well, those are Petitot's enamels; and there is a cabinet minister as used to be a druggist that will give three thousand francs apiece for them."

La Cibot's eyes opened wide. "There are thirty of them in the pair of frames!" she said.

"Very well, you can judge for yourself how much he is worth."

Mme. Cibot's head was swimming; she wheeled round. In a moment came the thought that she would have a legacy, *she* would sleep sound on old Pons' will, like the other servant-mistresses whose annuities had aroused such envy in the Marais. Her thoughts flew to some commune in the neighborhood of Paris; she saw herself strutting proudly about her house in the country, looking after her garden and poultry-yard, ending her days, served like a queen, along with her poor dear Cibot, who deserved such good fortune, like all angelic creatures whom nobody but one's self knows nor appreciates.

Her abrupt, unthinking movement told Rémonencq that success was sure. In the *chineur's* way of business—the *chineur,* be it explained, goes about the country picking up bargains at the expense of the ignorant—in the *chineur's* way of business, the one real difficulty is the problem of gaining an entrance to a house. No one can imagine the Scapin's roguery, the tricks of a Sganarelle, the wiles of a Dorine by which the *chineur* contrives to make a footing for himself. These comedies are as good as a play, and founded indeed on the old stock theme of the dishonesty of servants. For thirty francs in money or goods, servants, and especially country servants, will sometimes conclude a bargain on which the *chineur* makes a profit of a thousand or two thousand francs. If we could but know the history of such and such a service of Sèvres porcelain, *pâte tendre,* we should find that all the intellect, all the diplomatic subtlety displayed at Münster, Nimeguen, Utrecht, Ryswick, and Vienna was surpassed by the *chineur.* His is the more frank comedy; his methods of action fathom depths of personal interest quite as profound as any that plenipotentiaries can explore in their difficult search for any means of breaking up the best cemented alliances.

"I have set La Cibot nicely on fire," Rémonencq told his sister when she came to take up her position again on the ramshackle chair. "And now," he continued, "I shall go to consult the only man that knows, our Jew, a good sort of Jew that did not ask more than fifteen per cent. of us for his money."

Rémonencq had read La Cibot's heart. To will is to act with women of her stamp. Let them see the end in view; they will stick at nothing to gain it, and pass from scrupulous honesty to the last degree of scoundrelism in the twinkling of an eye. Honesty, like most dispositions of mind, is divided into two classes—negative and positive. La Cibot's honesty was of the negative order; she and her like are honest until they see their way clear to gain money belonging to somebody else. Positive honesty, the honesty of the bank collector, can wade knee-deep through temptations.

A torrent of evil thoughts invaded La Cibot's heart and brain so soon as Rémonencq's diabolical suggestion opened the floodgates of self-interest. La Cibot climbed, or, to be more accurate, flew up the stairs, opened the door on the landing, and showed a face disguised in false solicitude in the doorway of the room where Pons and Schmucke were bemoaning themselves. As soon as she came in, Schmucke made her a warning sign; for, true friend and sublime German that he was, he, too, had read the doctor's eyes, and he was afraid that Mme. Cibot might repeat the verdict. Mme. Cibot answered by a shake of the head, indicative of deep woe.

"Well, my dear monsieur," asked she, "how are you feeling?" She sat down on the foot of the bed, hands on hips, and fixed her eyes lovingly upon the patient; but what a glitter of metal there was in them, a terrible, tiger-like gleam if any one had watched her.

"I feel very ill," answered poor Pons. "I have not the slightest appetite left. Oh! the world, the world!" he groaned, squeezing Schmucke's hand. Schmucke was sitting by his bedside, and doubtless the sick man was talking of the causes of his illness. "I should have done far better to follow your advice, my good Schmucke, and dined here every day, and given up going into this society, that has fallen on me with all its weight, like a tumbril crushing an egg! And why?"

"Come, come, don't complain, Monsieur Pons," said La Cibot; "the doctor told me just how it is——"

Schmucke tugged at her gown. "And you will pull through," she continued, "only we must take great care of you. Be easy, you have a good friend beside you, and, without boasting, a woman as will nurse you like a mother nurses her first child. I nursed Cibot round once when Dr. Poulain had given him over; he had the shroud up to his eyes, as the

saying is, and they gave him up for dead.   Well, well, you
have not come to that yet, God be thanked, ill though you
may be.   Count on me; I would pull you through all by myself, I would !   Keep still, don't you fidget like that."

She pulled the coverlet over the patient's hands as she
spoke.

"There, sonny !   Monsieur Schmucke and I will sit up
with you of nights.   A prince won't be no better nursed—
and, beside, you needn't refuse yourself nothing that's necessary, you can afford it.   I have just been talking things over
with Cibot, for what would he do without me, poor dear?
Well, and I talked him round; we are both so fond of you,
that he will let me stop up with you of a night.   And that is
a good deal to ask of a man like him, for he is as fond of me
as ever he was the day we was married.   I don't know how it
is.   It is the lodge, you see; we are always there together !
Don't you throw off the things like that ! " she cried, making
a dash for the bedhead to draw the coverlet over Pons' chest.
"If you are not good, and don't do just as Dr. Poulain says
—and Dr. Poulain is the image of Providence on earth—I
will have no more to do with you.   You must do as I tell
you——"

"Yes, Montame Zipod, he vill do vat you tell him," put
in Schmucke; " he vants to lif for his boor friend Schmucke's
sake, I'll pe pound."

"And of all things, don't fidget yourself," continued La
Cibot, "for your illness makes you quite bad enough without
your making it worse for want of patience.   God sends us our
troubles, my dear good gentleman ; He punishes us for our
sins.   Haven't you nothing to reproach yourself with? some
poor little bit of a fault or other ? "

The invalid shook his head.

"Oh! go on !   You were young once, you had your fling,
there is some love-child of yours somewhere—cold, and starving, and homeless.   What monsters men are !   Their love

doesn't last only for a day, and then in a jiffy they forget, they don't so much as think of the child at the breast for months. Poor women !"

"But no one has ever loved me except Schmucke and my mother," poor Pons broke in sadly.

"Oh ! come, you ain't no saint ! You were young in your time, and a fine-looking young fellow you must have been at twenty. I should have fallen in love with you myself, so nice as you are——"

"I always was as ugly as a toad," Pons put in desperately.

"You say that because you are modest ; nobody can't say that you ain't modest."

"My dear Madame Cibot, NO, I tell you. I always was ugly, and I never was loved in my life."

"You, indeed !" cried the portress. "You want to make me believe at this time of day that you are as innocent as a young maid at your time of life. Tell that to your granny ! A musician at a theatre too ! Why, if a woman told me that, I wouldn't believe her."

"Montame Zipod, you irritate him !" cried Schmucke, seeing that Pons was writhing under the bedclothes.

"You hold your tongue too ! You are a pair of old libertines. If you were ugly, it don't make no difference ; there was never so ugly a saucepan-lid but it found a pot to match, as the saying is. There is Cibot, he got one of the handsomest oyster-women in Paris to fall in love with him, and you are sómewhat better looking than him ! You are a nice pair, you are ! Come, now, you have sown your wild oats, and God will punish you for deserting your children, like Abraham and——"

Exhausted though he was, the invalid gathered up all his strength to make a vehement gesture of denial.

"Do lie quiet ; if you have, it won't prevent you from living as long as Methuselah."

14

"Then, pray let me be quiet!" groaned Pons. "I have never known what it is to be loved. I have had no child; I am alone on the earth."

"Really, eh?" returned the portress. "You are so kind, and that is what women like, you see—it draws them—and it looked to me impossible that when you were in your prime that——"

"Take her away," Pons whispered to Schmucke; "she sets my nerves on edge."

"Then there's Daddy Schmucke, he has children. You old bachelors are not all like that——"

"*I!*" cried Schmucke, springing to his feet, "vy!——"

"Come, then, you have none to come after you either, eh? You both sprung up out of the earth like mushrooms——"

"Look here, komm mit me," said Schmucke. The good German manfully took Mme. Cibot by the waist and carried her off into the next room, in spite of her exclamations.

"At your age, you would not take advantage of a defenseless woman!" cried La Cibot, struggling in his arms.

"Don't make a noise!"

"You too, the better one of the two!" returned La Cibot. "Ah! it is my fault for talking about love to two old men who have never had nothing to do with women. I have roused your passions," cried she, as Schmucke's eyes glittered with wrath. "Help! help! police!"

"You are a stoopid!" said the German. "Look here, vat tid de toctor say?"

"You are a ruffian to treat me so," wept La Cibot, now released, "me, that would go through fire and water for you both! Ah! well, well, they say that is the way with men—and true it is! There is my poor Cibot, *he* would not be rough with me like this—— And I treated you like my children, for I have none of my own; and yesterday, yes, only yesterday I said to Cibot, 'God knew well what He was doing, dear,' I said, 'when He refused us children, for I have two children there upstairs.' By the holy crucifix and the soul of my mother, that was what I said to him——''

"Eh! but vat did der doctor say?" Schmucke demanded furiously, stamping on the floor for the first time in his life.

"Well," said Mme. Cibot, drawing Schmucke into the dining-room, "he just said this—that our dear, darling love lying ill there would die if he wasn't carefully nursed; but I am here in spite of all your brutality, for brutal you were, you that I thought so gentle. And you are one of that sort! Ah, now, you would not abuse a woman at your age, great black-guard——''

"Placard? I? Vill you not oonderstand that I lof nopody but Bons?"

"Well and good, you will let me alone then, won't you?" said she, smiling at Schmucke. "You had better; for if Cibot knew that anybody had attempted his honor, he would break every bone in his skin."

"Take crate care of him, dear Montame Zipod," answered Schmucke, and he tried to take the portress' hand.

"Oh! look here now, *again.*"

"Chust listen to me. You shall haf all dot I haf, gif ve safe him."

"Very well; I will go round to the chemist's to get the things that are wanted; this illness is going to cost a lot, you see, sir, and what will you do?"

"I shall vork; Bons shall be nursed like ein brince."

"So he shall, Monsieur Schmucke; and look here, don't you trouble about nothing. Cibot and I, between us, have saved a couple of thousand francs; they are yours; I have been spending money on you this long time, I have."

"Goot voman!" cried Schmucke, brushing the tears from his eyes. "Vat ein heart!"

"Wipe your tears; they do me honor; this is my reward," said La Cibot melodramatically. "There isn't no more dis-interested creature on earth than me; but don't you go into the room with tears in your eyes, or Monsieur Pons will be thinking himself worse than he is.''

Schmucke was touched by this delicate feeling. He took La Cibot's hand and gave it a final squeeze.

"Spare me!" cried the ex-oysterseller, leering at Schmucke.

"Bons," the good German said when he returned, "Montame Zipod is an anchel; 'tis an anchel dat brattles, but an anchel all der same.''

"Do you think so! I have grown suspicious in the past month," said the invalid, shaking his head. "After all I have been through, one comes to believe in nothing but God and my friend——"

"Get bedder, and ve vill lif like kings, all tree of us," exclaimed Schmucke.

"Cibot!" panted the portress as she entered the lodge. "Oh, my dear, our fortune is made. My two gentlemen haven't nobody to come after them, no natural children, no nothing, in short! Oh, I shall go round to Dame Fontaine's to get her to tell me my fortune on the cards, then we shall know how much we are going to have——"

"Wife," said the little tailor, "it's ill counting on dead men's shoes."

"Oh, I say, are *you* going to worry me?" asked she, giving her spouse a playful tap, "I know what I know! Dr. Poulain has given up Monsieur Pons. And we are going to be rich! My name will be down in the will. I'll see to that. Draw your needle in and out, and look after the lodge; you will not do it for long now. We will retire, and go into the country, out at Batignolles. A nice house and a fine garden; you will amuse yourself with gardening, and I shall keep a servant!"

"Well, neighbor, and how are things going on upstairs?" The words were spoken with the thick Auvergnat accent, and Rémonencq put his head in at the door. "Do you know what the collection is worth?"

"No, no, not yet. One can't go at that rate, my good man. I have begun, myself, by finding out more important things——"

"More important!" exclaimed Rémonencq; "why, what things can be more important?"

"Come, let me do the steering, ragamuffin," said La Cibot authoritatively.

"But thirty per cent. on seven hundred thousand francs," persisted the dealer in old iron; "you could be your own mistress for the rest of your days on that."

"Be easy, Daddy Rémonencq; when we want to know the value of the things that the old man has got together, then we will see."

La Cibot went for the medicine ordered by Dr. Poulain, and put off her consultation with Mme. Fontaine until the morrow; the oracle's faculties would be fresher and clearer in the morning, she thought; and she would go early, before anybody else came, for there was often a crowd at Mme. Fontaine's.

Mme. Fontaine was at this time the oracle of the Marais; she had survived the rival of forty years, the celebrated Mlle. Lenormand. No one imagines the part that fortune-tellers play among Parisians of the lower classes, nor the immense influence which they exert over the uneducated; general servants, portresses, kept women, workmen, all the many in Paris who live on hope, consult the privileged beings who possess the mysterious power of reading the future.

The belief in occult science is far more widely spread than scholars, lawyers, doctors, magistrates, and philosophers imagine. The instincts of the people are ineradicable. One among those instincts, so foolishly styled "superstition," runs in the blood of the populace, and tinges no less the intellects of better educated people. More than one French statesman has been known to consult the fortune-teller's cards. For skeptical minds, astrology, in French, so oddly termed *astrol-*

ogie judiciaire, is nothing more than a cunning device for making a profit out of one of the strongest of all the instincts of human nature—to wit, curiosity. The skeptical mind consequently denies that there is any connection between human destiny and the prognostications obtained by the seven or eight principal methods known to astrology; and the occult sciences, like many natural phenomena, are passed over by the freethinker or the materialist philosopher, *id est,* by those who believe in nothing but visible and tangible facts, in the results given by the chemist's retort and the scales of modern physical science. The occult sciences still exist; they are at work, but they make no progress, for the greatest intellects of two centuries have abandoned the field.

If you only look at the practical side of divination, it seems absurd to imagine that events in a man's past life and secrets known only to himself can be represented on the spur of the moment by a pack of cards which he shuffles and cuts for the fortune-teller to lay out in piles according to certain mysterious rules; but then the steam-engine was condemned as absurd, aerial navigation is still said to be absurd, so in their time were the inventions of gunpowder, printing, spectacles, engraving, and that latest great discovery of all—the daguerreotype. If any man had come to Napoleon to tell him that a building or a figure is at all times and in all places represented by an image in the atmosphere, that every existing object has a spectral intangible double which may become visible, the Emperor would have sent his informant to Charenton for a lunatic, just as Richelieu before his day sent that Norman martyr, Salomon de Caux, to the Bicêtre for announcing his immense triumph, the idea of navigation by steam. Yet Daguerre's discovery amounts to nothing more nor less than this.

And if for some clairvoyant eyes God has written each man's destiny over his whole outward and visible form, if a man's body is the record of his fate, why should not the hand in a manner epitomize the body? Since the hand represents the deed of man, and by his deeds he is known.

Herein lies the theory of palmistry. Does not Society imitate God? At the sight of a soldier we can predict that he will fight; of a lawyer, that he will talk; of a shoemaker, that he shall make shoes or boots; of a worker of the soil, that he shall dig the ground and dung it; and is it a more wonderful thing that such a one with the " seer's " gift should foretell the events of a man's life from his hand?

To take a striking example. Genius is so visible in a man that a great artist cannot walk along the streets of Paris but the most ignorant people are conscious of his passing. He is a sun, as it were, in the mental world, shedding light that colors everything in his path. And who does not know an idiot at once by an impression the exact opposite of the sensation of the presence of genius. Most observers of human nature in general, and Parisian nature in particular, can guess the profession or calling of the man in the street.

The mysteries of the witches' Sabbath, so wonderfully painted in the sixteenth century, are no mysteries for us. The Egyptian ancestors of that mysterious people of Indian origin, the gypsies of the present day, simply used to drug their clients with hashish, a practice that fully accounts for broomstick rides and flights up the chimney, the real-seeming visions, so to speak, of old crones transformed into young damsels, the frantic dances, the exquisite music, and all the fantastic tales of devil-worship.

So many proven facts have been first discovered by occult science, that some day we shall have professors of occult science, as we already have professors of chemistry and astronomy. It is even singular that here in Paris, where we are founding chairs of Mantchu and Slav and literatures so little professable (to coin a word) as the literatures of the North (which so far from providing lessons stand very badly in need of them); when the curriculum is full of the everlasting lec-

tures on Shakespeare and the sixteenth century—it is strange
that some one has not restored the teaching of the occult
philosophies, once the glory of the University of Paris, under
the title of anthropology.   Germany, so child-like and so
great, has outstripped France in this particular ; in Germany
they have professors of a science of far more use than a knowledge of the heterogeneous philosophies, which all come to the
same thing at bottom.

Once admit that certain beings have the power of discerning
the future in its germ-form of the Cause, as the great inventor
sees a glimpse of the industry latent in his invention, or a
science in something that happens every day unnoticed by
ordinary eyes—once allow this, and there is nothing to cause
an outcry in such phenomena, no violent exception to nature's
laws, but the operation of a recognized faculty; possibly a
kind of mental somnambulism, as it were.   If, therefore, the
hypothesis upon which the various ways of divining the future
are based seems absurd, the facts remain.   Remark that it is
not really more wonderful that the seer should foretell the
chief events of the future than that he should read the past.
Past and future, on the skeptic's system, equally lie beyond
the limits of knowledge.   If the past has left traces behind it,
it is not improbable that future events have, as it were, their
roots in the present.

If a fortune-teller gives you minute details of past facts
known only to yourself, why should he not foresee the events
to be produced by existing causes?   The world of ideas is cut
out, so to speak, on the pattern of the physical world ; the
same phenomena should be discernible in both, allowing for
the difference of the medium.   As, for instance, a corporeal
thing actually projects an image upon the atmosphere—a
spectral double detected and recorded by the daguerreotype ;
so also ideas, having a real and effective existence, leave an
impression, as it were, upon the atmosphere of the spiritual
world ; they likewise produce effects, and exist spectrally (to

coin a word to express phenomena for which no words exist), and certain human beings are endowed with the faculty of discerning these "forms" or traces of ideas.

As for the material means employed to assist the seer—the objects arranged by the hands of the consultant that the accidents of his life may be revealed to him—this is the least inexplicable part of the process. Everything in the material world is part of a series of causes and effects. Nothing happens without a cause, every cause is a part of a whole, and, consequently, the whole leaves its impression on the slightest accident. Rabelais, the greatest mind among moderns, being a resumption of Pythagoras, Hippocrates, Aristophanes, and Dante, pronounced, three centuries ago, that "man is a microcosm"—a little world. Three hundred years later, the great seer Swedenborg declared that "the world was a man." The prophet and the precursor of incredulity meet thus in the greatest of all formulas.

Everything in human life is predestined, so is it also with the existence of the planet. The least event, the most futile phenomena, are all subordinate parts of a scheme. Great things, therefore, great designs, and great thoughts are of necessity reflected in the smallest actions, and that so faithfully, that should a conspirator shuffle and cut a pack of playing-cards, he will write the history of his plot for the eyes of the seer-styled gypsy, fortune-teller, charlatan, or what not. If you once admit fate, which is to say, the chain of links of cause and effect, astrology has a *locus standi*, and becomes what it was of yore, a boundless science, requiring the same faculty of deduction by which Cuvier became so great, a faculty to be exercised spontaneously, however, and not merely in nights of study in the closet.

For seven centuries astrology and divination have exercised an influence not only (as at present) over the uneducated, but over the greatest minds, over kings and queens and wealthy people. Animal magnetism, one of the great sciences of an-

tiquity, had its origin in occult philosophy; chemistry is the
outcome of alchemy; phrenology and neurology are no less
the fruit of similar studies. The first illustrious workers in
these, to all appearance, untouched fields, made one mistake,
the mistake of all inventors; that is to say, they erected an
absolute system on a basis of isolated facts for which modern
analysis as yet cannot account. The Catholic Church, the
law of the land, and modern philosophy, in agreement for
once, combined to proscribe, persecute, and ridicule the mysteries of the Cabala as well as the adepts; the result is a lament-
able interregnum of a century in occult philosophy. But the
uneducated classes, and not a few cultivated people (women
especially), continue to pay a tribute to the mysterious power
of those who can raise the veil of the future; they go to buy
hope, strength, and courage of the fortune-teller; in other
words, to ask of him all that religion alone can give. So the
art is still practiced in spite of a certain amount of risk. The
eighteenth-century encyclopædists procured tolerance for the
sorcerer, he is no longer amenable to a court of law, unless,
indeed, he lends himself to fraudulent practices, and frightens
his "clients" to extort money from them, in which case he
may be prosecuted on a charge of obtaining money under false
pretenses. Unluckily, the exercise of the sublime art is only
too often used as a method of obtaining money under false
pretenses, and for the following reasons :

The seer's wonderful gifts are usually bestowed upon those
who are described by the epithets rough and uneducated.
The rough and uneducated are the chosen vessels into which
God pours the elixirs at which we marvel. From among the
rough and uneducated, prophets arise—an Apostle Peter, or
St. Peter the Hermit. Wherever mental power is imprisoned,
and remains intact and entire for want of an outlet in conversation, in politics, in literature, in the imaginings of the
scholar, in the efforts of the statesman, in the conceptions of
the inventor, or the soldier's toils of war; the fire within is

apt to flash out in gleams of marvelously vivid light, like the sparks hidden in an unpolished diamond. Let the occasion come, and the spirit within kindles and glows, finds wings to traverse space, and the god-like power of beholding all things. The coal of yesterday, under the play of some mysterious influence, becomes a radiant diamond. Better educated people, many-sided and highly polished, continually giving out all that is in them, can never exhibit this supreme power, save by one of the miracles which God sometimes vouchsafes to work. For this reason the soothsayer is almost always a beggar, whose mind is virgin soil, a creature coarse to all appearance, a pebble borne along the torrent of misery and left in the ruts of life, where it spends nothing of itself save in mere physical suffering.

The prophet, the seer, in short, is some "Martin le Laboureur" making a Louis XVIII. tremble by telling him a secret known only to the King himself; or it is a Mlle. Lenormand, or a domestic servant like Mme. Fontaine, or, again, perhaps it is some half-idiotic negress, some herdsman living among his cattle, who receives the gift of vision; some Hindoo fakir, seated by a pagoda, mortifying the flesh till the spirit gains the mysterious power of the somnambulist.

Asia, indeed, through all time, has been the home of the heroes of occult science. Persons of this kind, recovering their normal state, are usually just as they were before. They fulfill, in some sort, the chemical and physical functions of bodies which conduct electricity; at times inert metal, at other times a channel filled with a mysterious current. In their normal condition they are given to practices which bring them before the magistrate, yea, verily, like the notorious Balthazar, even unto the criminal court, and so to the hulks. You could hardly find a better proof of the immense influence of fortune-telling upon the working-classes than the fact that poor Pons' life and death hung upon the prediction that Mme. Fontaine was to make from the cards.

Although a certain amount of repetition is inevitable in a canvas so considerable and so full of detail as a complete picture of French society in the nineteenth century, it is needless to repeat the description of Mme. Fontaine's den, already given in "Les Comédiens sans le savoir;" suffice it to say that Mme. Cibot used to go to Mme. Fontaine's house in the Rue Vieille-du-Temple as regularly as frequenters of the Café Anglais drop in at that restaurant for lunch. Mme. Cibot, being a very old customer, often introduced young persons and old gossips consumed with curiosity to the wise-woman.

The old servant who acted as provost-marshal flung open the door of the sanctuary with no further ceremony than the remark: "It's Madame Cibot. Come in, there's nobody here."

"Well, child, what can bring you here so early of a morning?" asked the sorceress, as Mme. Fontaine might well be called, for she was seventy-eight years old, and looked like one of the Parcæ.

"Something has given me a turn," said La Cibot; "I want the *grand jeu;* * it is a question of my fortune." Therewith she explained her position, and wished to know if her sordid hopes were likely to be realized.

"Do you know what the *grand jeu* means?" asked Mme. Fontaine, with much solemnity.

"No. I haven't never seen the trick, I am not rich enough. A hundred francs! It's not as if it cost so much! Where was the money to come from? But now I can't help myself, I must have it."

"I don't do it often, child," returned Mme. Fontaine; "I only do it for rich people on great occasions, and they pay me twenty-five louis for doing it; it tires me, you see, it wears me out. The 'Spirit' rives my inside, here. It is like going to the 'Sabbath,' as they used to say."

* The Great Play; *i. e.,* all that can be known.

A COLD THRILL RAN THROUGH MME. CIBOT.

"But when I tell you that it means my whole future, my dear good Ma'am Fontaine——"

"Well, as it is you that have come to consult me so often, I will submit myself to the Spirit!" replied Mme. Fontaine, with a look of genuine terror on her face.

She rose from her filthy old chair by the fireside, and went to a table covered with a green cloth so worn that you could count the threads. A huge toad sat dozing there beside a cage inhabited by a black disheveled-looking fowl.

"Astaroth! here, my son!" she said, and the creature looked up intelligently at her as she rapped him on the back with a long knitting-needle. "And you, Mademoiselle Cléopâtre!—attention!" she continued, tapping the ancient fowl on the beak.

Then Mme. Fontaine began to think; for several seconds she did not move; she looked like a corpse, her eyes rolled in their sockets and grew white; then she rose stiff and erect, and a cavernous voice cried—

"Here I am!"

Automatically she scattered millet for Cléopâtra, took up the pack of cards, shuffled them convulsively, and held them out to Mme. Cibot to cut, sighing heavily all the time. At the sight of that image of DEATH in the filthy turban and uncanny looking bed-jacket, watching the black-fowl as it pecked at the millet-grains, calling to the toad Astaroth to walk over the cards that lay out on the table, a cold thrill ran through Mme. Cibot; she shuddered. Nothing but strong belief can give strong emotions. An assured income, to be or not to be, that was the question.

The sorceress opened a magical work and muttered some unintelligible words in a sepulchral voice, looked at the remaining millet-seeds, and watched the way in which the toad retired. Then after seven or eight minutes, she turned her white eyes on the cards and expounded them.

"You will succeed, although nothing in the affair will fall

out as you expect. You will have many steps to take, but
you will reap the fruits of your labors. You will behave very
badly; it will be with you as it is with all those who sit by a
sick-bed and covet part of the inheritance. Great people will
help you in this work of wrongdoing. Afterward in the death-
agony you will repent. Two escaped convicts, a short man
with red hair and an old man with a bald head, will murder
you for the sake of the money you will be supposed to have in
the village whither you will retire with your second husband.
Now, my daughter, it is still open to you to choose your
course."

The excitement which seemed to glow within, lighting up
the bony hollows about the eyes, was suddenly extinguished.
As soon as the horoscope was pronounced, Mme. Fontaine's
face wore a dazed expression ; she looked exactly like a sleep-
walker aroused from sleep, gazed about her with an astonished
air, recognized Mme. Cibot, and seemed surprised by her
terrified face.

" Well, child," she said, in a totally different voice, " are
you satisfied ? "

Mme. Cibot stared stupidly at the sorceress, and could not
answer.

" Ah ! you would have the *grand jeu;* I have treated you
as an old acquaintance. I only want a hundred francs instead
of——"

" Cibot—going to die ? " gasped the portress.

" So I have been telling you very dreadful things, have I ? "
asked Mme. Fontaine, with an extremely ingenuous air.

" Why, yes ! " said La Cibot, taking a hundred francs from
her pocket and laying them down on the edge of the table.
" Going to be murdered, think of it——"

" Ah ! there it is ! You would have the *grand jeu;* but
don't take on so, all the people that are murdered on the
cards don't die."

" But is it possible, Ma'am Fontaine ? "

"Oh, *I* know nothing about it, my pretty dear! You would rap at the door of the future; I pull the cord, and It came."

"*It*, what?" asked Mme. Cibot.

"Well, then, the Spirit!" cried the sorceress impatiently.

"Good-by, Ma'am Fontaine," exclaimed the portress. "I did not know what the *grand jeu* was like. You have given me a good fright, that you have."

"The mistress will not put herself in that state twice in a month," said the servant, as she went with La Cibot to the landing. "She would do herself to death if she did, it tires her so. She will eat cutlets now and sleep for three hours afterward."

Out in the street, La Cibot took counsel of herself as she went along, and, after the manner of all who ask for advice of any sort or description, she took the favorable part of the prediction and rejected the rest. The next day found her confirmed in her resolutions—she would set all in train to become rich by securing a part of Pons' collection. Nor for some time had she any other thought than the combination of various plans to this end. The faculty of self-concentration seen in rough uneducated persons, explained on a previous page, the reserve power accumulated in those whose mental energies are unworn by the daily wear and tear of social life, and brought into action so soon as that terrible weapon the "fixed idea" is brought into play—all this was preëminently manifested in La Cibot. Even as the "fixed idea" works miracles of evasion, and brings forth prodigies of sentiment, so greed transformed the portress till she became as formidable as a Nucingen at bay, as subtle beneath her seeming stupidity as the irresistible La Palférine.

About seven o'clock one morning, a few days afterward, she saw Rémonencq taking down his shutters. She went across to him.

"How could one find out how much the things yonder in

my gentlemen's rooms are worth?" she asked in a wheedling tone.

"Oh! that is quite easy," replied the owner of the old curiosity shop. "If you will play fair and above-board with me, I will tell you of somebody. a very honest man, who will know the value of the pictures to a centime——"

"Who?"

"Monsieur Magus, a Jew. He only does business to amuse himself now."

Élie Magus has appeared so often in the Comédie Humaine that it is needless to say more of him here. Suffice it to add that he had retired from business, and as a dealer was following the example set by Pons the amateur. Well-known valuers like Henry, Messrs. Pigeot and Moret, Théret, Georges, and Roëhn, the experts of the Musée in fact, were but children compared with Élie Magus. He could see a masterpiece beneath the accumulated grime of a century; he knew all schools and the handwriting of all painters.

He had come to Paris from Bordeaux, and so long ago as 1835 he had retired from business without making any change for the better in his dress, so faithful is the race to old tradition. The persecutions of the Middle Ages compelled them to wear rags, to snuffle and whine and groan over their poverty in self-defense, till the habits induced by the necessities of other times have come to be, as usual, instinctive, a racial defect.

Élie Magus had amassed a vast fortune by buying and selling the diamonds, pictures, lace, enamels, delicate carvings, old jewelry, and rarities of all kinds, a kind of commerce which has developed enormously of late, so much so indeed that the number of dealers has increased tenfold during the last twenty years in this city of Paris, whither all the curiosities in the world come to rub against one another. And for pictures there are but three marts in the world—Rome, London, and Paris.

Élie Magus lived in the Chaussée des Minimes, a short, broad street leading to the Place Royale. He had bought the house, an old-fashioned mansion, for a song, as the saying is, in 1831. Yet there were sumptuous apartments within it, decorated in the time of Louis XV.; for it had once been the Hôtel Maulaincourt, built by the great president of the Cour des Aides, and its remote position had saved it at the time of the Revolution.

You may be quite sure that the old Jew had sound reasons for buying house property, contrary to the Hebrew law and custom. He had ended, as most of us end, with a hobby that bordered on a craze. He was as miserly as his friend the late lamented Gobseck; but he had been caught by the snare of the eyes, by the beauty of the pictures in which he dealt. As his taste grew more and more fastidious, it became one of the passions which princes alone can indulge when they are wealthy and art-lovers. As the second King of Prussia found nothing that so kindled enthusiasm as the spectacle of a grenadier over six feet high, and gave extravagant sums for a new specimen to add to his living museum of a regiment, so the retired picture-dealer was roused to passion-pitch only by some canvas in perfect preservation, untouched since the master laid down the brush; and what was more, it must be a picture of the painter's best time. No great sales, therefore, took place but Élie Magus was there; every mart knew him, he traveled all over Europe. The ice-cold, money-worshiping soul in him kindled at the sight of a perfect work of art, precisely as a libertine, weary of fair women, is roused from apathy by the sight of a beautiful girl, and sets out afresh upon the quest of flawless loveliness. A Don Juan among fair works of art, a worshiper of the Ideal, Élie Magus had discovered joys that transcend the pleasure of the miser gloating over his gold—he lived in a seraglio of great paintings.

His masterpieces were housed as became the children of

15

princes; the whole second floor of the great old mansion was given up to them.

The rooms had been restored under Élie Maguus' orders, and with what magnificence !

The windows were hung with the richest Venetian brocade ; the most splendid carpets from the Savonnerie covered the parquetry flooring. The frames of the pictures, nearly a hundred in number, were magnificent specimens, regilded cunningly by Servais, the one gilder in Paris whom Élie Magus thought sufficiently painstaking ; the old Jew himself had taught him to use the English leaf, which is infinitely superior to that produced by French gold-beaters. Servais is among gilders as Thouvenin among bookbinders—an artist among craftsmen, making his work a labor of love. Every window in that gallery was protected by iron-barred shutters. Élie Magus himself lived in a couple of attics on the floor above ; the furniture was wretched, the rooms were full of rags, and the whole place smacked of the Ghetto ; Élie Magus was finishing his days without any change in his life.

The whole of the first floor was given up to the picture trade (for the Jew still dealt in works of art). Here he stored his paintings, here also packing-cases were stowed on their arrival from other countries ; and still there was room for a vast studio, where Moret, most skillful of restorers of pictures, a craftsman whom the Musée ought to employ, was almost always at work for Magus. The rest of the rooms on the first floor were given up to Magus' daughter, the child of his old age, a Jewess beautiful as a Jewess can be when the Semitic type reappears in its purity and nobility in a daughter of Israel. Noémi was guarded by two servants, fanatical Jewesses, to say nothing of an advanced-guard, a Polish Jew, Abramko by name, once involved in a fabulous manner in political troubles, from which Élie Magus saved him as a business speculation. Abramko, janitor of the silent, grim, deserted mansion, divided his office and his lodge with three remarkably ferocious animals—an English bull-dog, a Newfoundland dog, and another of the Pyrenean breed.

Behold the profound observations of human nature upon which Élie Magus based his feeling of security, for secure he felt; he left home without misgivings, slept with both ears shut, and feared no attempt upon his daughter (his chief treasure), his pictures, nor his money. In the first place, Abramko's salary was increased every year by two hundred francs so long as his master should live; and Magus, moreover, was training Abramko as a money-lender in a small way. Abramko never admitted anybody until he had surveyed them through a formidable grated opening. He was a Hercules for strength, he worshiped Élie Magus, as Sancho Panza worshiped Don Quixote. All day long the dogs were shut up without food; at nightfall Abramko let them loose; and by a cunning device the old Jew kept each animal at his post in the courtyard or the garden by hanging a piece of meat just out of reach on the top of a pole. The animals guarded the house, and sheer hunger guarded the dogs. No odor that reached their nostrils could tempt them from the neighborhood of that piece of meat; they would not have left their places at the foot of the poles for the most engaging female of the canine species. If a stranger by any chance intruded, the dogs suspected him of ulterior designs upon their rations, which were only taken down in the morning by Abramko himself when he awoke. The advantages of this fiendish scheme are patent.

The animals never barked, Magus' ingenuity had made savages of them; they were treacherous as Mohicans. And now for the result.

One night burglars, emboldened by the silence, decided too hastily that it would be easy enough to " clean out " the old Jew's strong box. One of their number told off to advance to the assault scrambled up the garden-wall and prepared to descend. This the bull-dog allowed him to do. The animal, knowing perfectly well what was coming, waited for the burglar to reach the ground ; but when that gentleman directed a kick at him, the bull-dog flew at the visitor's shins, and, making but one bite of it, snapped the ankle-bone clean in two. The thief had the courage to tear himself away, and returned, walking upon the bare bone of the mutilated stump till he reached the rest of the gang, when he fell fainting, and they carried him off. The "Police News," of course, did not fail to report this delightful night incident, but no one believed in it.

Magus at this time was seventy-five years old, and there was no reason why he should not live to a hundred. Rich man though he was, he lived like the Rémonencqs. His necessary expenses, including the money he lavished on his daughter, did not exceed three thousand francs. No life could be more regular ; the old man rose as soon as it was light, breakfasted on bread rubbed with a clove of garlic, and ate no more food until dinner-time. Dinner, a meal frugal enough for a convent, he took at home. All the forenoon he spent among his treasures, walking up and down the gallery where they hung in their glory. He would dust everything himself, furniture and pictures ; he never wearied of admiring. Then he would go downstairs to his daughter, drink deep of a father's happiness, and start out upon his walk through Paris, to attend sales or visit exhibitions and the like.

If Élie Magus found a great work of art under the right conditions, the discovery put new life into the man ; here was a bit of sharp practice, a bargain to make, a battle of Marengo to win. He would pile ruse on ruse to buy the new sultana as cheaply as possible. Magus had a map of Europe on which all great pictures were marked ; his co-religionists in every city spied out business for him, and received a commission on the purchase. And then—what rewards for all his pains ! The two lost Raphaels so earnestly sought after by Raphael-lovers are both in his collection. Élie Magus owns the original portrait of Giorgione's Mistress, the woman for whom the painter died ; the so-called originals are merely copies of the famous picture, which is worth five hundred thousand francs, according to its owner's estimation.   This Jew possesses Titian's masterpiece, an Entombment painted for Charles V., sent by the great man to the great Emperor with a holograph letter, now fastened down upon the lower part of the canvas. And Magus has yet another Titian, the original sketch from which all the portraits of Philip II. were painted.   His remaining ninety-seven pictures are all of the same rank and distinction.   Wherefore Magus laughs at our national collection, raked by the sunlight which destroys the fairest paintings, pouring in through panes of glass that act as lenses.   Picture galleries can only be lighted from above ;* Magus opens and closes his shutters himself; he is as careful of his pictures as of his daughter, his second idol.   And well the old picture-fancier knows the laws of the lives of pictures.   To hear him talk, a great picture has a life of its own ; it is changeable, it takes its beauty from the color of the light.   Magus talks of his paintings as Dutch fanciers used to talk of their tulips ; he will come home on purpose to see some one picture in the hour of its glory, when the light is bright and clean.

And Magus himself was a living picture among the motionless figures on the wall—a little old man, dressed in a shabby overcoat, a silk vest, renewed twice in a score of years, and a very dirty pair of trousers; with a bald head, a face full of deep hollows, a wrinkled callous skin, a beard that had a trick of twitching its long white bristles, a menacing pointed chin, a toothless mouth, eyes bright as the eyes of his dogs in the yard, a nose like an obelisk—there he stood in his gallery smiling at the beauty called into being by genius.   A Jew surrounded by his millions will always be one of the finest spectacles which humanity can give.   Robert Medal, our great actor, cannot rise to this height of poetry, sublime though he is.

* All Parisian Fine Art Museums, etc., are so lighted now.

Paris of all the cities of the world holds most of such men as Magus, strange beings with a strange religion in their heart of hearts. The London "eccentric" always finds that worship, like life, brings weariness and satiety in the end; the Parisian monomaniac lives cheerfully in concubinage with his crotchet to the last.

Often shall you meet in Paris some Pons, some Élie Magus, dressed badly enough, with his face turned from the rising sun (like the countenance of the perpetual secretary of the Academy), apparently heeding nothing, conscious of nothing, paying no attention to store-windows, nor to fair passers-by, walking at random, so to speak, with nothing in his pockets, and to all appearance an equally empty head. Do you ask to what Parisian tribe this manner of man belongs? He is a collector, a millionaire, one of the most impassioned souls on earth; he and his like are capable of treading the miry ways that lead to the police court if so they may gain possession of a cup, a picture, or some such rare unpublished piece as Élie Magus once picked up one memorable day in Germany.

This was the expert to whom Rémonencq with much mystery conducted La Cibot. Rémonencq always asked advice of Élie Magus when he met him in the streets; and more than once Magus had lent him money through Abramko, knowing Rémonencq's honesty. The Chaussée des Minimes is close to the Rue de Normandie, and the two fellow-conspirators reached the house in ten minutes.

"You will see the richest dealer in curiosities, the greatest connoisseur in Paris," Rémonencq had said. And Mme. Cibot, therefore, was struck dumb with amazement to be confronted with a little old man in a greatcoat too shabby for Cibot to mend, standing watching a painter at work upon an old picture in the chilly room on the vast first floor. The old man's eyes, full of cold feline malignance, were turned upon her, and La Cibot shivered.

"What do you want, Rémonencq?" asked this person.

"It is a question of valuing some pictures; there is nobody but you in Paris who can tell a poor tinker-fellow like me how much he may give when he has not thousands to spend, like you."

"Where is it?"

"Here is the portress of the house where the gentleman lives; she does for him, and I have arranged with her——"

"Who is the owner?"

"Monsieur Pons!" put in La Cibot.

"Don't know the name," said Magus, with an innocent air, bringing down his foot very gently upon his artist's toes.

Moret the painter, knowing the value of Pons' collection, had looked up suddenly at the name. It was a move too hazardous to try with any one but Rémonencq and La Cibot, but the Jew had taken the woman's measure at sight, and his eye was as accurate as a jeweler's scales. It was impossible that either of the couple should know how often Magus and old Pons had matched their claws. And, in truth, both rabid amateurs were jealous of each other. The old Jew had never hoped for a sight of a seraglio so carefully guarded; it seemed to him that his head was swimming. Pons' collection was the one private collection in Paris which could vie with his own. Pons' idea had occurred to Magus twenty years later; but as a dealer-amateur the door of Pons' museum had been closed for him, as for Dusommerard. Pons and Magus had at heart the same jealousy. Neither of them cared about the kind of celebrity dear to the ordinary collector. And now for Élie Magus came his chance to see the poor musician's treasures! An amateur of beauty hiding in a boudoir for a stolen glance at a mistress concealed from him by his friend might feel as Élie Magus felt at that moment.

La Cibot was impressed by Rémonencq's respect for this singular person; real power, moreover, even when it cannot be explained, is always felt; the portress was supple and obedient, she dropped the autocratic tone which she was wont to use in her lodge and with the tenants, accepted Magus' conditions, and agreed to admit him into Pons' museum that very day.

So the enemy was to be brought into the citadel, and a stab dealt to Pons' very heart. For ten years Pons had carried his keys about with him; he had forbidden La Cibot to allow any one, no matter whom, to cross his threshold; and La Cibot had so far shared Schmucke's opinions of *bric-à-brac*, that she had obeyed him. The good Schmucke, by speaking of the splendors as "chimcracks," and deploring his friend's mania, had taught La Cibot to despise the old rubbish, and so secured Pons' museum from invasion for many a long year.

When Pons took to his bed, Schmucke filled his place at the theatre and gave lessons for him at his boarding-schools. He did his utmost to do the work of two; but with Pons' sorrows weighing heavily upon his mind, the task took all his strength. He only saw his friend in the morning, and again at dinner-time. His pupils and the people at the theatre, seeing the poor German look so unhappy, used to ask for news of Pons; and so great was his grief, that the indifferent would make the grimaces of sensibility which Parisians are wont to reserve for the greatest calamities. The very springs of life had been attacked, the good German was suffering from Pons' pain as well as from his own. When he gave a music-lesson, he spent half the time in talking of Pons, interrupting himself to wonder whether his friend felt better to-day, and the little school-girls listening heard lengthy explanations of Pons' symptoms. He would rush over to the Rue de Normandie in the interval between two lessons for the sake of a quarter of an hour with Pons.

When at last he saw that their common stock was almost exhausted, when Mme. Cibot (who had done her best to swell the expenses of the illness) came to him and frightened him; then the old music-master felt that he had courage of which he never thought himself capable—courage that rose above his anguish. For the first time in his life he set himself to earn money; money was needed at home. One of the school-girl pupils, really touched by their troubles, asked Schmucke how he could leave his friend alone. "Montemoiselle," he answered, with the sublime smile of those who think no evil, "ve haf Montame Zipod, ein dreasure, montemoiselle, ein bearl! Bons is nursed like ein brince."

So while Schmucke trotted about the streets, La Cibot was mistress of the house and ruled the invalid. How should Pons superintend his self-appointed guardian angel, when he had taken no solid food for a fortnight, and lay there so weak and helpless that La Cibot was obliged to lift him up and carry him to the sofa while she made the bed?

La Cibot's visit to Élie Magus was paid (as might be expected) while Schmucke breakfasted. She came in again just as the German was bidding his friend good-by; for since she learned that Pons possessed a fortune, she never left the old bachelor; she brooded over him and his treasures like a hen. From the depths of a comfortable easy-chair at the foot of the bed she poured forth for Pons' delectation the gossip in which women of her class excel. With Machiavellian skill, she had contrived to make Pons think that she was indispensable to him; she coaxed and she wheedled, always uneasy, always on the alert. Mme. Fontaine's prophecy had frightened La Cibot; she vowed to herself that she would gain her ends by kindness. She would sleep secure on M. Pons' legacy, but her rascality should keep within the limits of the law. For ten years she had not suspected the value of Pons' collection; she had a clear record behind her of ten years of devotion, honesty, and disinterestedness; it was a magnificent investment, and now she proposed to realize. In one day, Rémonencq's hint of money had hatched the serpent's egg, the craving for riches that had lain dormant within her for twenty years. Since she had cherished that craving, it had grown in

force with the ferment of all the evil that lurks in the corners
of the heart.   How she acted upon the counsels whispered
by the serpent will presently be seen.

"Well?" she asked of Schmucke, "has this cherub of ours
had plenty to drink?   Is he better?"

"He is not doing fery vell, tear Montame Zipod, not fery
vell," said poor Schmucke, brushing away the tears from his
eyes.

"Pooh! you make too much of it, my dear Monsieur
Schmucke; we must take things as we find them; Cibot
might be at death's door, and I should not take it to heart as
you do.   Come! the cherub has a good constitution.   And
he has been steady, it seems, you see; you have no idea to
what an age sober people live.   He is very ill, it is true, but
with all the care I take of him, I shall bring him round.   Be
easy, look after your affairs, I will keep him company and see
that he drinks his pints of barley-water."

"Gif you vere not here, I should die of anxiety——" said
Schmucke, squeezing his kind housekeeper's hand in both his
own to express his confidence in her.

La Cibot wiped her eyes as she went back to the invalid's
room.

"What is the matter, Madame Cibot?" asked Pons, seeing
the tears.

"It is Monsieur Schmucke that has upset me; he is crying
as if you were dead," said she.   "If you are not well, you
are not so bad yet that nobody need cry over you; but it has
given me such a turn!   Oh dear! oh dear! how silly it is of
me to get so fond of people, and to think more of you than
of Cibot!   For, after all, you ain't nothing to me, you are
only my brother by Adam's side; and yet, whenever you are
in the question, it puts me in such a taking, upon my word it
does!   I would cut off my hand—my left hand, of course—
to see you coming and going, eating your meals, and screwing
bargains out of dealers as usual.   If I had had a child of my

own, I think I should have loved it as I love you, eh! There, take a drink, dearie; come now, empty the glass. Drink it off, monsieur, I tell you! The first thing Dr. Poulain said was, 'If Monsieur Pons has no mind to go to Père Lachaise, he ought to drink as many buckets full of water in a day as an Auvergnat will sell.' So, come now, drink——"

"But I do drink, Cibot, my good woman; I drink and drink till I am deluged——"

"That is right," said the portress, as she took away the empty glass. "That is the way to get better. Dr. Poulain had another patient, ill of your complaint; but he had nobody to look after him; his children left him to himself, and he died because he didn't drink enough—so you must drink, honey, you see—he died, and they buried him two months ago. And if you were to die, you know, you would drag down old Monsieur Schmucke with you, sir. He is like a child. Ah! he loves you, he does, the dear lamb of a man; no woman never loved a man like that! He doesn't care for meat nor drink; he has grown as thin as you are in the last fortnight, and you are nothing but skin and bones. It makes me jealous to see it, for I am very fond of you; but not to that degree; I haven't lost my appetite, quite the other way; always going up and down stairs, till my legs are so tired that I drop down of an evening like a lump of lead. Here am I neglecting my poor Cibot for you; Mademoiselle Rémonencq cooks his victuals for him, and he goes on about it and says that nothing is right! At that I tell him that one ought to put up with something for the sake of other people, and that you are so ill that I cannot leave you. In the first place, you can't afford a nurse. And before I would have a nurse here!—I that have done for you these ten years. And those nurses are such eaters, they eat enough for ten; they want wine, and sugar, and foot-warmers, and all sorts of comforts. And they rob their patients unless the patients leave them something in their wills. Have a nurse in here to-day, and to-morrow we should find a picture or something or other gone——.''

"Oh! Madame Cibot!" cried Pons, quite beside himself, "do not leave me! No one must touch anything——"

"I am here," said La Cibot; "so long as I have the strength I shall be here. Be easy. There was Dr. Poulain wanting to get a nurse for you; perhaps he has his eye on your treasures. I just snubbed him, I did. 'The gentleman won't have nobody but me,' I told him. 'He is used to me, and I am used to him.' So he said no more. A nurse, indeed! They are all thieves; I hate that sort of woman, I do. Here is a tale that will show you how sly they are. There was once an old gentleman—it was Dr. Poulain himself, mind you, who told me this—well, a Madame Sabatier, a woman of thirty-six that used to sell slippers at the Palais Royal—you remember the Galerie at the Palais that they pulled down?"

Pons nodded.

"Well, at that time she had not done very well; her husband used to drink, and died of spontaneous imbustion; but she had been a fine woman in her time, truth to tell, not that it did her any good, though she had friends among the lawyer-folks. So, being hard up, she became a monthly nurse, and lived in the Rue Barre-du-Bec. Well, she went out to nurse an old gentleman that had a disease of the lurinary guts (saving your presence); they used to tap him like an artesian well, and he needed such care that she used to sleep on a truckle-bed in the same room with him. You would hardly believe such a thing! 'Men respect nothing,' you'll tell me, 'so selfish as they are.' Well, she used to talk with him, you understand; she never left him, she amused him, she told him stories, she drew him on to talk (just as we are chatting away together now, you and I, eh?), and she found out that his nephews— the old gentleman had nephews—that his nephews were wretches; they had worried him, and, final end of it, they had brought on this illness. Well, my dear sir, she saved his life,

he married her, and they have a fine child ; Ma'am Bordevin,
the butcher's wife in the Rue Charlot, a relative of hers, stood
godmother. There is luck for you!

"As for me, I am married ; and if I have no children, I
don't mind saying that it is Cibot's fault ; he is too fond of
me, but if I cared—never mind. What would have become
of me and my Cibot if we had had a family, when we have
not a sou to bless ourselves with after thirty years of faithful
service ? I have not a centime belonging to nobody else,
that is what comforts me. I have never wronged nobody.
Look here, suppose now (there is no harm in supposing when
you will be out and about again in six weeks' time, and sauntering along the boulevard) ; well, suppose that you had put
me down in your will ; very good, I shouldn't never rest till
I had found your heirs and given the money back. Such is
my horror of anything that is not earned by the sweat of my
brow.

"You will say to me, 'Why, Madame Cibot, why should
you worry yourself like that? You have fairly earned the
money ; you looked after your two gentlemen as if they had
been your children ; you saved them a thousand francs a
year—' (for there are plenty, sir, you know, that would have
had their ten thousand francs put out to interest by now if
they had been in my place)—'so if the worthy gentleman
leaves you a trifle of an annuity, it is only right.' Suppose
they told me that. Well, no ; I am not thinking of myself.
I cannot think how some women can do a kindness thinking
of themselves all the time. It ain't doing good, sir, is it? I
do not go to church myself, I haven't the time ; but my conscience tells me what is right—— Don't you fidget like that,
my lamb! Don't scratch yourself! Dear me, how yellow
you have growed! So yellow you are—quite brown. How
funny it is that one can come to look like a lemon in three
weeks!—— Honesty is all that poor people has, and one
must surely have something! Suppose that you were just at

death's door, I should be the first to tell you that you ought
to leave all that you have to Monsieur Schmucke. It is your
duty, for he is all the family you have. He loves you, he
does, as a dog loves his master."

"Ah! yes," said Pons; "nobody else has ever loved me
all my life long——"

"Ah! that is not kind of you, sir," said Mme. Cibot;
"then I do not love you, I suppose?"

"I do not say so, my dear Madame Cibot."

"Good. You take me for a servant, do you, a common
servant, as if I hadn't got no heart! Goodness me! for
eleven years you do for two old bachelors, you think of nothing but their comfort. I have turned half a score of green-
grocers' stalls upside down for you, I have talked people
round to get you good Brie cheese; I have gone down as far
as the market for fresh butter for you; I have taken such
care of things that nothing of yours hasn't been chipped nor
broken in all these ten years; I have just treated you like my
own children; and then to hear a ' My dear Madame Cibot,'
that shows that there is not a bit of feeling for you in the
heart of an old gentleman that you have cared for like a
king's son! for the little King of Rome was not so well cared
for as you have been. You may bet that he was not as well
looked after. He died in his prime; there is proof for you.
Come, sir, you are unjust! You are ungrateful! It is because I am only a poor portress. Goodness me! are *you* one
of those that think we are dogs?——"

"But, my dear Madame Cibot——"

"Indeed, you that know so much, tell me why we porters
are treated like this, and ain't supposed to have no feelings;
people look down on us in these days when they talks of
Equality! As for me, am I not as good as another woman, I
that was one of the finest women in Paris, and was called
*La belle Écailière,** and received declarations seven or eight

* The handsome oyster-opener.

times a day? And even now if I liked—— Look here, sir, you know that little scrubby marine-store-dealer downstairs? Very well, he would marry me any day, if I were a widow, that is, with his eyes shut; he has had them looking wide open in my direction so often; he is always saying, 'Oh! what fine arms you have, Ma'am Cibot! I dreamed last night that it was bread and I was butter, and I was spread on the top of you.' Look, sir, there is an arm!"

She rolled up her sleeve and displayed the shapeliest arm imaginable, as white and fresh as her hand was red and rough; a plump, round, dimpled arm, drawn from its merino sheath like a blade from the scabbard to dazzle Pons, who looked away.

"For every oyster the knife opened, that arm has opened a heart! Well, it belongs to Cibot, and I did wrong when I neglected him, poor dear; HE would throw himself over a precipice at a word from me; while you, sir, that call me 'My dear Madame Cibot,' when I do impossible things for you——"

"Do just listen to me," broke in the patient; "I cannot call you my mother, nor my wife——"

"No, never in all my born days will I take again to anybody——"

"Do let me speak!" continued Pons. "Let us see; I put Monsieur Schmucke first——"

"Monsieur Schmucke! there is a heart for you!" cried La Cibot. "Ah! he loves me, but then he is poor. It is money that deadens the heart; and you are rich! Oh, well take a nurse, you will see what a life she will lead you; she will torment you, you will be like a cockchafer on a string. The doctor will say that you must have plenty to drink, and she will do nothing but feed you. She will bring you to your grave and rob you. You do not deserve to have a Madame Cibot! there! When Dr. Poulain comes, ask him for a nurse."

"Oh fiddlestick, stop!" the patient cried angrily. "*Will* you listen to me? When I spoke of my friend Schmucke, I was not thinking of women. I know quite well that no one cares for me so sincerely as you do, you and Schmucke——"

"Have the goodness not to irritate yourself in this way!" exclaimed La Cibet, plunging down upon Pons and covering him by force with the bedclothes.

"How should I not love you?" said poor Pons.

"You love me, really? There, there, forgive me, sir!" she said, crying and wiping her eyes. "Ah, yes, of course, you love me, as you love a servant, that is the way!—a servant to whom you throw an annuity of six hundred francs like a crust you fling into a dog's kennel——"

"Oh! Madame Cibot," cried Pons, "for what do you take me? You do not know me."

"Ah! you will care even more than that for me," she said, meeting Pons' eyes. "You will love your kind old Cibot like a mother, will you not? A mother, that is it! I am your mother; you are both of you my children—— Ah, if I only knew them that caused you this sorrow, I would do that which would bring me into the police courts, and even to prison; I would scratch their eyes out! Such people deserve to die at the Barrière Saint-Jacques, and that is too good for such scoundrels. So kind, so good as you are (for you have a heart of gold), you were sent into the world to make some woman happy! Yes, you would have her happy, as anybody can see; you were cut out for that. In the very beginning, when I saw how you were with Monsieur Schmucke, I said to myself, 'Monsieur Pons has missed the life he was meant for; he was made to be a good husband.' Come, now, you like women."

"Ah, yes," said Pons, "and no woman has been mine."

"Really?" exclaimed La Cibot, with a provocative air as she came nearer and took Pons' hand in hers. "Do you not know what it is to love a woman that will do anything for her lover? Is it possible? If I were in your place, I should not

wish to leave this world for another until I had known the
greatest happiness on earth! Poor dear! If I was now what I
was once, I would leave Cibot for you! upon my word, I would!
Why, with a nose shaped like that—for you have a fine nose
—how did you manage it, poor cherub? You will tell me
that 'not every woman knows a man when she sees him;' and
a pity it is that they marry so at random as they do, it makes
you sorry to see it. Now, for my own part, I should have
thought that you had had mistresses by the dozen—dancers,
actresses, and duchesses, for you went out so much. When
you went out, I used to say to Cibot, 'Look! there is Monsieur Pons going a-gallivanting;' on my word, I did, I was so
sure that women ran after you. Heaven made you for love.
Why, my dear sir, I found that out the first day that you
dined at home, and you were so touched with Monsieur
Schmucke's pleasure. And next day Monsieur Schmucke
kept saying to me, 'Montame Zipod, he haf tined hier,' with
the tears in his eyes, till I cried along with him like a fool, as I
am. And how sad he looked when you took to gadding abroad
again and dining out! Poor man, you never saw any one
so disconsolate! Ah! you are quite right to leave everything
to him. Dear, worthy man, why, he is as good as a family to
you, he is! Do not forget him; for if you do, God will not
receive you into His paradise, for those that have been ungrateful to their friends and left them no *rentes* will not go to
heaven."

In vain Pons tried to put in a word; La Cibot talked as the
wind blows. Means of arresting steam-engines have been
invented, but it would tax a mechanician's genius to discover
any plan for stopping a portress' tongue.

"I know what you mean," continued she. "But it does
not kill you, my dear gentleman, to make a will when you are
out of health; and in your place I would not leave that poor
dear alone, for fear that something might happen; he is like
God Almighty's lamb, he knows nothing about nothing, and I

16

should not like him to be at the mercy of those sharks of lawyers and a wretched pack of relations. Let us see now, has one of them come here to see you in twenty years? And would you leave your property to *them?* Do you know, they say that all these things here are worth something."

"Why, yes," said Pons.

"Rémonencq, who deals in pictures, and knows that you are an amateur, says that he would be quite ready to pay you an annuity of thirty thousand francs so long as you live, to have the pictures afterward. There is a chance! If I were you, I should take it. Why, I thought he said it for a joke when he told me that. You ought to let Monsieur Schmucke know the value of all those things, for he is a man that could be cheated like a child. He has not the slightest idea of the value of these fine things that you have! He so little suspects it, that he would give them away for a morsel of bread if he did not keep them all his life for love of you; always supposing that he lives after you, for he will die of your death. But *I* am here; I will take his part against anybody and everybody! I and Cibot will defend him."

"Dear Madame Cibot!" said Pons, "what would have become of me if it had not been for you and Schmucke?" He felt touched by this horrible prattle; the feeling in it seemed to be ingenuous, as it usually is in the speech of the people.

"Ah! we really are your only friends on earth, that is very true, that is. But two good hearts are worth all the families in the world. Don't talk of families to me! A family, as the old actor said of the tongue, is the best and the worst of all things. Where are those relations of yours now? Have you any? I have never seen them——"

"They have brought me to lie here," said Pons, with intense bitterness.

"So you have relations!——" cried La Cibot, springing up as if her easy-chair had been heated red-hot. "Oh, well,

they are a nice lot, are your relations! What! these three
weeks—for this is the twentieth day, to-day, that you have
been ill and like to die—in these three weeks they have not
come once to ask for news of you? That's a trifle too strong,
that is! Why, in your place, I would leave all I had to the
Foundling Hospital sooner than give them one centime!"

"Well, my dear Madame Cibot, I meant to leave all that
I had to a first cousin once removed, the daughter of my first
cousin, President Camusot, you know, who came here one
morning nearly two months ago."

"Oh! a little stout man who sent his servants to beg your
pardon—for his wife's blunder? The housemaid came asking
me questions about you, an affected old creature she is, my
fingers itched to give her velvet tippet a dusting with my
broom handle! A servant wearing a velvet tippet! did anybody ever see the like? No, upon my word, the world is
turned upside down; what is the use of making a Revolution?
Dine twice a day if you can afford it, you scamps of rich folk!
But laws are no good, I tell you, and nothing will be safe if
Louis-Philippe does not keep people in their places; for, after
all, if we are all equal, eh, sir? a housemaid didn't ought to
have a velvet tippet, while I, Madame Cibot, haven't one,
after thirty years of honest work. There is a pretty thing for
you! People ought to be able to tell who you are. A housemaid is a housemaid, just as I myself am a portress. Why do
they have silk epaulettes in the army? Let everybody keep
their place. Look here, do you want me to tell you what all
this cómes to? Very well, France is going to the dogs. If
the Emperor had been here, things would have been very
different, wouldn't they, sir? So I said to Cibot, I said,
'See here, Cibot, a house where the servants wear velvet tip-
pets belongs to people that have no heart in them——'"

"No heart in them, that is just it," repeated Pons. And
with that he began to tell Mme. Cibot about his troubles and
mortifications, she pouring out abuse of the relations the while

and showing exceeding tenderness on every fresh sentence in the sad history.

She fairly wept at last.

To understand the sudden intimacy between the old musician and Mme. Cibot, you have only to imagine the position of an old bachelor lying on his bed of pain, seriously ill for the first time in his life. Pons felt that he was alone in the world; the days that he spent by himself were all the longer because he was struggling with the indefinable nausea of a liver complaint which blackens the brightest life. Cut off from all his many interests, the sufferer falls a victim to a kind of nostalgia; he regrets the sparkling boulevards, the many sights to be seen for nothing in Paris. The isolation, the darkened days, the suffering that affects the mind and spirits even more than the body, the emptiness of the life—all these things tend to induce him to cling to the human being who waits on him as a drowned man clings to a plank; and this especially if the bachelor patient's character is as weak as his nature is sensitive and credulous.

Pons was charmed to hear La Cibot's tittle-tattle. Schmucke, Mme. Cibot, and Dr. Poulain meant all humanity to him now, when his sickroom became the universe. If invalids' thoughts, as a rule, never travel beyond in the little space over which their eyes can wander; if their selfishness, in its narrow sphere, subordinates all creatures and all things to itself, you can imagine the lengths to which an old bachelor may go. Before three weeks were out he had even gone so far as to regret, once and again, that he had not married Madeleine Vivet ! Mme. Cibot, too, had made immense progress in his esteem in those three weeks; without her he felt that he should have been utterly lost; for as for Schmucke, the poor invalid looked upon him as a second Pons. La Cibot's prodigious art consisted in expressing Pons' own ideas, and this she did quite unconsciously.

"Ah ! here comes the doctor ! " she exclaimed, as the bell

rang, and away she went, knowing very well that Rémonencq
had come with the Jew.

"Make no noise, gentlemen," said she, "he must not
know anything. He is all on the fidget when his precious
treasures are concerned."

"A walk round will be enough," said the Hebrew, armed
with a magnifying-glass and a lorgnette.

The greater part of Pons' collection was installed in a great
old-fashioned salon such as French architects used to build for
the old *noblesse;* a room twenty-five feet broad, some thirty
feet in length, and thirteen in height. Pons' pictures to the
number of sixty-seven hung upon the white-and-gold paneled
walls; time, however, had reddened the gold and softened
the white to an ivory tint, so that the whole was toned down,
and the general effect subordinated to the effect of the pictures. Fourteen statues stood on pedestals set in the corners
of the room, or among the pictures, or on brackets inlaid by
Boule; sideboards of carved ebony, royally rich, surrounded
the walls to elbow height, all the shelves filled with curiosities; in the middle of the room stood a row of carved credence-tables, covered with rare miracles of handicraft—with
ivories and bronzes, wood-carvings and enamels, jewelry and
porcelain.

As soon as Élie Magus entered the sanctuary, he went
straight to the four masterpieces; he saw at a glance that these
were the gems of Pons' collection, and masters lacking in his
own. For Élie Magus these were the naturalist's *desiderata*
for which men undertake long voyages from east to west,
through deserts and tropical countries, across southern savan-
nas, through virgin forests.

The first was a painting by Sebastian del Piombo, the second a Fra Bartolommeo della Porta, the third a Hobbema
landscape, and the fourth and last a Dürer—a portrait of a
woman. Four diamonds indeed! In the history of art,
Sebastian del Piombo is like a shining point in which three

schools meet, each bringing its preëminent qualities. A Venetian painter, he went to Rome to learn the manner of Raphael under the direction of Michael Angelo, who would fain oppose Raphael on his own ground by pitting one of his own lieutenants againt the reigning king of art. And so it came to pass that in del Piombo's indolent genius Venetian color was blended with Florentine composition and a something of Raphael's manner in the few pictures which he deigned to paint, and the sketches were made for him, it is said, by Michael Angelo himself.

If you would see the perfection to which the painter attained (armed as he was with triple power), go to the Louvre and look at the Baccio Bandinelli portrait; you might place it beside Titian's Man with a Glove, or by that other Portrait of an Old Man in which Raphael's consummate skill blends with Coreggio's art; or, again, compare it with Lionardo da Vinci's Charles VIII., and the picture would scarcely lose. The four pearls are equal; there is the same lustre and sheen, the same rounded completeness, the same brilliancy. Art can go no further than this. Art has risen above Nature, since Nature only gives her creatures a few brief years of life.

Pons possessed one example of this immortal, great genius and incurably indolent painter; it was a Knight of Malta, a Templar kneeling in prayer. The picture was painted on slate, and in its unfaded color and its finish was immeasurably finer than the Baccio Bandinelli.

Fra Bartolommeo was represented by a Holy Family, which many connoisseurs might have taken for a Raphael. The Hobbema would have fetched sixty thousand francs at a public sale; and as for the Dürer, it was equal to the famous Holzschuer portrait at Nuremberg for which the Kings of Bavaria, Holland, and Prussia have vainly offered two hundred thousand francs again and again. Was it the portrait of the wife or the daughter of Holzschuer, Albrecht Dürer's personal friend? The hypothesis seems to be a certainty, for the attitude of the figure in Pons' picture suggests that it is meant for a pendant, the position of the coat-of-arms is the same as in the Nuremberg portrait; and, finally, the *ætatis suæ* XLI. accords perfectly with the age inscribed on the picture religiously kept by the Holzschuers of Nuremberg, and but recently engraved.

The tears stood in Élie Magus' eyes as he looked from one masterpiece to another. He turned round to La Cibot: "I will give you a commission of two thousand francs on each of the pictures if you can arrange that I shall have them for forty thousand francs," he said. La Cibot was amazed at this good fortune dropped from the sky. Admiration, or, to be more accurate, delirious joy, had wrought such havoc in the Jew's brain, that it had actually unsettled his habitual greed, and he fell headlong into enthusiasm, as you see.

"And I?——" put in Rémonencq, who knew nothing about pictures.

"Everything here is equally good," the Jew said cunningly, lowering his voice for Rémonencq's ear; "take ten pictures just as they come and on the same conditions. Your fortune will be made."

Again the three thieves looked each other in the face, each one of them overcome with the keenest of all joys—sated greed. All of a sudden the sick man's voice rang through the room; the tones vibrated like the strokes of a bell—

"Who is there?" called Pons.

"Monsieur! just go back to bed!" exclaimed La Cibot, springing upon Pons and dragging him by main force. "What next! Have you a mind to kill yourself? Very well, then, it is not Dr. Poulain, it is Rémonencq, good soul, so anxious that he has come to ask after you! Everybody is so fond of you that the whole house is in a flutter. So what is there to fear?"

"It seems to me that there are several of you," said Pons.

"Several? that is good! What next! Are you dreaming?

You will go off your head before you have done, upon my word! Here, look!"—and La Cibot flung open the door, signed to Magus to go, and beckoned to Rémonencq.

"Well, my dear sir," said the Auvergnat, now supplied with something to say, "I just came to ask after you, for the whole house is alarmed about you. Nobody likes death to set foot in a house! And lastly, Daddy Monistrol, whom you know very well, told me to tell you that if you wanted money he was at your service——"

"He sent you here to take a look round at my knick-knacks!" returned the old collector from his bed; and the sour tones of his voice were full of suspicion.

A sufferer from liver complaint nearly always takes momentary and special dislikes to some person or thing, and concentrates all his ill-humor upon the object. Pons imagined that some one had designs upon his precious collection; the thought of guarding it became a fixed idea with him; Schmucke was continually sent to see if any one had stolen into the sanctuary.

"Your collection is fine enough to attract the attention of *chineurs*," Rémonencq answered astutely. "I am not much in the art line myself; but you are supposed to be such a great connoisseur, sir, that, little as I know, I would willingly buy your collection, sir, with my eyes shut—supposing, for instance, that you should need money some time or other, for nothing costs so much as these confounded illnesses; there was my sister now, when she had a bad turn, she spent thirty sous on medicine in ten days, when she would have got better again just as well without. Doctors are rascals that take advantage of your condition to——"

"Thank you, good-day, good-day," broke in Pons, eying the marine-store-dealer uneasily.

"I will go to the door with him, for fear he should touch something," La Cibot whispered to her patient.

"Yes, yes," answered the invalid, thanking her by a glance,

La Cibot shut the bedroom door behind her, and Pons' suspicions awoke again at once.

She found Magus standing motionless before the four pictures. His immobility, his admiration, can only be understood by other souls open to ideal beauty, to the ineffable joy of beholding art made perfect: such as these can stand for whole hours before the Antiope—Correggio's masterpieces—before Lionardo's Gioconda, Titian's Mistress, Andrea del Sarto's Holy Family, Domenichino's Children among the Flowers, Raphael's little cameo, or his Portrait of an Old Man—Art's greatest masterpieces.

"Be quick and go, and make no noise," said La Cibot.

The Jew walked slowly backward, giving the pictures such a farewell gaze as a lover gives his love. Outside, on the landing, La Cibot tapped his bony arm. His rapt contemplation had put an idea into her head.

"Make it *four* thousand francs for each picture," said she, "or I do nothing——"

"I am so poor!——" began Magus. "I want the pictures simply for their own sake, simply and solely for the love of art, my dear lady."

"I can understand that love, sonny, you are so dried up. But if you do not promise me sixteen thousand francs now, before Rémonencq here, I shall want twenty to-morrow."

"Sixteen; I promise," returned the Jew, frightened by the woman's rapacity.

La Cibot turned to Rémonencq.

"What oath can a Jew swear?" she inquired.

"You may trust him," replied the marine-store-dealer. "He is as honest as I am."

"Very well; and you?" asked she, "if I get him to sell them to you, what will you give me?"

"Half-share of profits," Rémonencq answered briskly.

"I would rather have a lump sum," returned La Cibot; "I am not in business myself."

"You understand business uncommonly well!" put in Élie Magus, smiling; "a famous saleswoman you would make!"

"I want her to take me into partnership, me and my goods," said the Auvergnat, as he took La Cibot's plump arm and gave it playful taps like hammer-strokes. "I don't ask her to bring anything into the firm but her good looks! You are making a mistake when you stick to your Turk of a Cibot and his needle. Is a little bit of a porter the man to make a woman rich—a fine woman like you? Ah, what a figure you would make in a store on the boulevard, all among the curiosities, gossiping with amateurs and twisting them round your fingers! Just you leave your lodge as soon as you have lined your purse here, and you shall see what will become of us both."

"Lined my purse!" cried the Cibot. "I am incapable of taking the worth of a single pin; mind you that now, Rémonencq! I am known in the neighborhood for an honest woman, I am."

La Cibot's eyes flashed fire.

"There, never mind," said Élie Magus; "this Auvergnat seems to be too fond of you to mean to insult you."

"How she would draw on the customers!" cried the Auvergnat.

Mme. Cibot softened at this.

"Be fair, sonnies," quoth she, "and judge for yourselves how I am placed. These ten years past I have been wearing my life out for those two old bachelors, yonder, and neither of them has given me anything but words. Rémonencq will tell you that I feed them by contract, and lose twenty or thirty sous a day; all my savings have gone that way, by the soul of my mother (the only author of my days that I ever knew), this is as true as that I live, and that this is the light of day, and may my coffee poison me if I lie about a centime. Well, there is one up there that will die soon, eh? and he the

richer of the two that I have treated like my own children.
Would you believe it, my dear sir, I have told him over and
over again for days past that he is at death's door (for Dr.
Poulain has given him up), and yet, if the old hunks had
never heard of me, he could not say less about putting my
name down in his will. We shall only get our due by taking
it, upon my word, as an honest woman, for as for trusting to
the next-of-kin !—No fear ! There ! look you here, words
don't stink ; it is a bad world ! "

"That is true," Élie Magus answered cunningly, "that is
true ; and it is just the like of us that are among the best," he
added, looking at Rémonencq.

"Just let me be," returned La Cibot ; "I am not speaking
of you. 'Pressing company is always accepted,' as the old
actor said. I swear to you that the two gentlemen already
owe me nearly three thousand francs ; the little I have is gone
by now in medicine and things on their account ; and now
suppose they refuse to recognize my advances? I am so
stupidly honest that I did not dare to say nothing to them
about it. Now, you that are in business, my dear sir, do you
advise me to go to a lawyer?"

"A lawyer?" cried Rémonencq ; "you know more about
it than all the lawyers put together——"

Just at that moment a sound echoed in the great staircase, a
thumping sound as if some heavy body had fallen in the dining-room.

"Oh, goodness me ! " exclaimed La Cibot ; "it seems to
me that monsieur has just taken a ticket for the ground floor."

She pushed her fellow-conspirators out at the door, and
while the pair descended the stairs with remarkable agility,
she ran to the dining-room, and there beheld Pons, in his
shirt, stretched out upon the tiles. He had fainted. She
lifted him as if he had been a feather, carried him back to his
room, laid him in bed, burned feathers under his nose, bathed
his temples with eau-de-Cologne, and at last brought him to

consciousness. When she saw his eyes unclose and life return, she stood over him, hands on hips.

"No slippers! In your shirt! That is the way to kill yourself! Why do you suspect me? If this is to be the way of it, I wish you good-day, sir. Here have I served you these ten years, I have spent money on you till my savings are all gone, to spare trouble to that poor Monsieur Schmucke, crying like a child on the stairs—and *this* is my reward! You have been spying on me. God has punished you! It serves you right! Here I am straining myself to carry you, running the risk of doing myself a mischief that I shall feel all my days. Oh dear, oh dear! and the door left open too——"

"You were talking with some one. Who was it?"

"Here are notions!" cried La Cibot. "What next! Am I your bond-slave? Am I to give account of myself to you? Do you know that if you bother me like this, I shall clear out! You shall take a nurse."

Frightened by this threat, Pons unwittingly allowed La Cibot to see the extent of the power of her sword of Damocles.

"It is my illness!" he pleaded piteously.

"It is as you please," La Cibot answered roughly.

She went. Pons, confused, remorseful, admiring his nurse's scolding devotion, reproached himself for his behavior. The fall on the paved floor of the dining-room had shaken and bruised him, and aggravated his illness, but Pons was scarcely conscious of his physical sufferings.

La Cibot met Schmucke on the staircase.

"Come here, sir," she said. "There is bad news, there is. Monsieur Pons is going off his head! Just think of it! he got up with nothing on, he came after me—and down he came full-length. Ask him why—he knows nothing about it. He is in a bad way. I did nothing to provoke such violence, unless, perhaps, I waked up ideas by talking to him of his early loves. Who knows men? Old libertines that they all

are. I ought not to have shown him my arms when his eyes
were glittering like *carbuckles.*"

Schmucke listened. Mme. Cibot might have been talking
Hebrew for anything that he understood.

"I have given myself a wrench that I shall feel all my
days," added she, making as though she were in great pain.
(Her arms did, as a matter of fact, ache a little, and the
muscular fatigue suggested an idea, which she proceeded to
turn to profit.) "So stupid I am. When I saw him lying
there on the floor, I just took him up in my arms as if he had
been a child, and carried him back to bed, I did. And I
strained myself, I can feel it now. Ah! how it hurts! I
am going downstairs. Look after our patient. I will send
Cibot for Dr. Poulain. I had rather die outright than be
crippled."

La Cibot crawled downstairs, clinging to the bannisters,
and writhing and groaning so piteously that the tenants, in
alarm, came out upon their landings. Schmucke supported
the suffering creature, and told the story of La Cibot's devotion, the tears running down his cheeks as he spoke. Before
very long the whole house, the whole neighborhood indeed,
had heard of Mme. Cibot's heroism; she had given herself a
dangerous strain, it was said, with lifting one of the "nutcrackers."

Schmucke meanwhile went to Pons' bedside with the tale.
Their factotum was in a frightful state. "What shall we do
without her?" they said, as they looked at each other; but
Pons was so plainly the worse for his escapade that Schmucke
did not dare to scold him.

"Gonfounded pric-à-prac! I would sooner purn dem dan
loose mein friend!" he cried, when Pons told him of the
cause of the accident. "To susbect Montame Zipod, dot lend
us her safings! It is not goot; it is fery bad; but it is der
illness——"

"Ah! what an illness! I am not the same man, I can feel

it," said Pons. "My dear Schmucke, if only you did not suffer through me."

"Scold me," Schmucke answered, "und leaf Montame Zipod in beace."

As for Mme. Cibot, she soon recovered in Dr. Poulain's hands; and her restoration, bordering on the miraculous, shed additional lustre on her name and fame in the Marais. Pons attributed the success to the excellent constitution of the patient, who resumed her ministrations seven days later, to the great satisfaction of her two gentlemen. Her influence in their household and her tyranny were increased a hundred-fold by the accident. In the course of a week, the two nut-crackers ran into debt; Mme. Cibot paid the outstanding amounts, and took the opportunity to obtain from Schmucke (how easily!) a receipt for two thousand francs, which she had lent, she said, to the friends.

"Oh, what a doctor Monsieur Poulain is!" cried La Cibot, for Pons' benefit. "He will bring you through, my dear sir, for he pulled me out of my coffin! Cibot, poor man, thought I was dead. Well, Dr. Poulain will have told you that while I was in bed I thought of nothing but you. 'God above,' said I, 'take me, and let my dear Monsieur Pons live——'"

"Poor dear Madame Cibot, you all but crippled yourself for me."

"Ah! but for Dr. Poulain I should have been put to bed with a shovel by now, as we shall all be one day. Well, what must be must, as the old actor said. One must take things philosophically. How did you get on without me?"

"Schmucke nursed me," said the invalid, "but our poor money-box and our lessons have suffered. I do not know how he managed."

"Calm yourself, Bons," exclaimed Schmucke; "ve haf in Zipod ein panker——"

"Do not speak of it, my lamb. You are our children, both of you," cried La Cibot. "Our savings will be well invested;

you are safer than the bank. So long as we ve a morsel of bread, half of it is yours. It is not worth mentioning——"

"Boor Montame Zipod!" said Schmucke, and he went.

Pons said nothing.

"Would you believe it, my cherub?" said La Cibot, as the sick man tossed uneasily, "in my agony—for it was a near squeak for me—the thing that worried me most was the thought that I must leave you alone, with no one to look after you, and my poor Cibot without a single sou. My savings are such a trifle that I only mention them in connection with my death and Cibot, an angel that he is! No. He nursed me as if I had been a queen, he did, and cried like a calf over me! But I counted on you, upon my word. I said to him: 'There, Cibot! my gentlemen will not let you starve——'"

Pons made no reply to this thrust *ad testamentum;* but as the portress waited for him to say something—"I shall recommend you to Monsieur Schmucke," he said at last.

"Ah!" cried La Cibot, "whatever you do will be right; I trust in you and your heart. Let us never talk of this again. You make me feel ashamed, my cherub. Think of getting better; you will outlive us all yet."

Profound uneasiness filled Mme. Cibot's mind. She cast about for some way of making the sick man understand that she expected a legacy. That evening, when Schmucke was eating his dinner as usual by Pons' bedside, she went out, hoping to find Dr. Poulain at home.

Dr. Poulain lived in the Rue d'Orleans in a small first-floor establishment, consisting of a lobby, a sitting-room, and two bedrooms. A closet, opening into the lobby and the bedroom, had been turned into a study for the doctor. The kitchen, the servant's bedroom, and a small cellar were situated in a wing of the house, a huge pile built in the time of the Empire on the site of an old mansion of which the garden still remained, though it had been divided among the three first-floor tenants.

Nothing had been changed in the doctor's house since it was built. Paint and paper and ceilings were all redolent of the Empire. The grimy deposits of forty years lay thick on walls and ceilings, on paper and paint and mirrors and gilding. And yet, this little establishment, in the depths of the Marais, paid a rent of a thousand francs.

Mme. Poulain, the doctor's mother, aged sixty-seven, was ending her days in the second bedroom. She worked for a breeches-maker, stitching men's leggings, breeches, belts, and suspenders, anything, in fact, that is made in a way of business which has somewhat fallen off of late years. Her whole time was spent in keeping her son's house and superintending the one servant; she never went abroad, and took the air in the little garden entered through the glass door of the sitting-room. Twenty years previously, when her husband died, she had sold his business to his best workman, who gave his master's widow work enough to earn a daily wage of thirty sous. She had made every sacrifice to educate her only son. At all costs, he should occupy a higher station than his father before him; and now she was proud of her Æsculapius, she believed in him, and sacrificed everything to him as before. She was happy to take care of him, to work and put by a little money, and dream of nothing but his welfare, and love him with an intelligent love of which every mother is not capable. For instance, Mme. Poulain remembered that she had been a working-girl. She would not injure her son's prospects; he should not be shamed by his mother (for the good woman's grammar was something of the same kind as Mme. Cibot's); and for this reason she kept in the background, and went to her room of her own accord if any distinguished patient came to consult the doctor, or if some old schoolfellow or fellow-student chanced to call. Dr. Poulain had never had occasion to blush for the mother whom he revered; and this sublime love of hers more than atoned for a defective education.

The breeches-maker's business sold for about twenty thousand francs, and the widow invested the money in the Funds in 1820. The income of eleven hundred francs per annum derived from this source was, at one time, her whole fortune. For many a year the neighbors used to see the doctor's linen hanging out to dry upon a clothes-line in the garden, and the servant and Mme. Poulain thriftily washed everything at home; a piece of domestic economy which did not a little to injure the doctor's practice, for it was thought that if he was so poor, it must be through his own fault. Her eleven hundred francs scarcely did more than pay the rent. During those early days, Mme. Poulain, good, stout, little old woman, was the breadwinner, and the poor household lived upon her earnings. After twelve years of perseverance upon a rough and stony road, Dr. Poulain at last was making an income of three thousand francs, and Mme. Poulain had an income of about five thousand francs at her disposal. Five thousand francs for those who know Paris means a bare subsistence.

The sitting-room, where patients waited for an interview, was shabbily furnished. There was the inevitable mahogany sofa covered with yellow-flowered Utrecht velvet, four easy-chairs, a tea-table, a console, and half-a-dozen chairs, all the property of the deceased breeches-maker, and chosen by him. A lyre-shaped clock between two Egyptian candlesticks still preserved its glass shade intact. You asked yourself how the yellow chintz window-curtains, covered with red flowers, had contrived to hang together for so long; for evidently they had come from the Jouy factory, and Oberkampf received the Emperor's congratulations upon similar hideous productions of the cotton industry in 1809.

The doctor's consulting-room was fitted up in the same style, with household stuff from the paternal chamber. It looked stiff, poverty-stricken, and bare. What patient could put faith in the skill of an unknown doctor who could not even furnish his house? And this in a time when advertising is all powerful; when we gild the gas lamps in the Place de

17

la Concorde to console the poor man for his poverty by reminding him that he is rich as a citizen.

The antechamber did duty as a dining-room.   The servant
sat at her sewing there whenever she was not busy in the
kitchen or keeping the doctor's mother company.   From the
dingy, short curtains in the windows you could have guessed
at the shabby thrift behind them without setting foot in the
dreary place.   What could those wall-cupboards contain but
stale scraps of food, chipped earthenware, corks used over and .
over again indefinitely, soiled table-linen, odds and ends that
could descend but one step lower into the dust-heap, and all
the squalid necessities of a pinched household in Paris ?

In these days, when the five-franc piece is always lurking
in our thoughts and intruding itself into our speech, Dr. Poulain, aged thirty-three, was still a bachelor.   Heaven had bestowed on him a mother with no connections.   In ten years
he had not met with the faintest pretext for a romance in his
professional career ; his practice lay among clerks and small
manufacturers, people in his own sphere of life, with homes
very much like his own.   His richer patients were butchers,
bakers, and the more substantial tradespeople of the neighborhood.   These, for the most part, attributed their recovery to
Nature, as an excuse for paying for the services of a medical
man, who came on foot at the rate of two francs per visit.
In his profession, a carriage is more necessary than medical
skill.

A humdrum monotonous life tells in the end upon the most
adventurous spirit.   A man fashions himself to his lot, he
accepts a commonplace existence ; and Dr. Poulain, after ten
years of his practice, continued his labors of Sisyphus without
the despair that made early days so bitter.   And yet—like
every soul in Paris—he cherished a dream.   Rémonencq was
happy in his dream ; La Cibot had a dream of her own ; and
Dr. Poulain too dreamed.   Some day he would be called in
to attend a rich and influential patient, would effect a positive

cure, and the patient would procure a post for him ; he would be head-surgeon to a hospital, medical officer of a prison or police court, or doctor to the boulevard theatres. He had come by his present appointment as doctor to the mairie in this very way. La Cibot had called him in when the landlord of the house in the Rue de Normandie fell ill ; he had treated the case with complete success ; M. Pillerault, the patient, took an interest in the young doctor, called to thank him, and saw his carefully hidden poverty. Count Popinot, the cabinet minister, had married M. Pillerault's grand-niece, and greatly respected her uncle ; of him, therefore, M. Pillerault had asked for the post, which Poulain had now held for two years. That appointment and its meagre salary came just in time to prevent a desperate step ; Poulain was thinking of emigration ; and for a Frenchman, it is a kind of death to leave France.

Dr. Poulain went, you may be sure, to thank Count Popinot ; but as Count Popinot's family physician was the celebrated Horace Bianchon, it was pretty clear that his chances of gaining a footing in that house were something of the slenderest. The poor doctor had fondly hoped for the patronage of a powerful cabinet minister, one of the twelve or fifteen cards which a cunning hand has been shuffling for sixteen years on the green baize of the council table, and now he dropped back again into his Marais, his old groping life among the poor and the small tradespeople, with the privilege of issuing certificates of death for a yearly stipend of twelve hundred francs.

Dr. Poulain had distinguished himself to some extent as a house-student ; he was a prudent practitioner, and not without experience. His deaths caused no scandal ; he had plenty of opportunities of studying all kinds of complaints *in anima vili.* Judge, therefore, of the spleen that he nourished ! The expression of his countenance, lengthy and not too cheerful to begin with, at times was positively appalling. Set a Tartuffe's

all-devouring eyes and the sour humor of an Alceste in a
sallow parchment visage, and try to imagine for yourself the
gait, bearing, and expression of a man who thought himself as
good a doctor as the illustrious Bianchon, and felt that he was
held down in his narrow lot by an iron hand. He could not
help comparing his receipts (ten francs a day if he was fortunate) with Bianchon's five or six hundred.

Are the hatreds and jealousies of democracy incomprehen-
sible after this? Ambitious and continually thwarted, he
could not reproach himself. He had once already tried his
fortune by inventing a purgative pill, something like Morri-
son's, and intrusted the business operations to an old hospital
chum, a house-student who afterward took a retail drug business; but, unluckily, the druggist, smitten with the charms of a
ballet-dancer of the Ambigu-Comique, found himself at length
in the bankruptcy court; and as the patent had been taken
out in his name, his partner was literally without a remedy,
and the important discovery enriched the purchaser of the
business. The sometime house-student set sail for Mexico,
that land of gold, taking poor Poulain's little savings with
him; and, to add insult to injury, the opera-dancer treated
him as an extortioner when he applied to her for his stolen
money.

Not a single rich patient had come to him since he had the
luck to cure old M. Pillerault. Poulain made his rounds on
foot, scouring the Marais like a lean cat, and obtained from
two to forty sous out of a score of visits. The paying patient
was a phenomenon about as rare as that anomalous fowl known
as a "white blackbird" in all sublunary regions.

The briefless barrister, the doctor without a patient, are
preëminently the two types of a decorous despair peculiar to
this city of Paris; it is mute, dull despair in human form,
dressed in a black coat and trousers with shining seams that
recall the zinc on an attic roof, a glistening satin vest, a hat
preserved like a relic, a pair of old gloves, and a cotton shirt.

The man is the incarnation of a melancholy poem, sombre as the secrets of the Conciergerie. Other kinds of poverty, the poverty of the artist—actor, painter, musician, or poet—are relieved and lightened by the artist's joviality, the reckless gayety of the Bohemian border country—the first stage of the journey to the Thebaïd of genius. But these two black-coated professions that go afoot through the street are brought continually in contact with disease and dishonor; they see nothing of human nature but its sores; in the forlorn first stages and beginnings of their career they eye competitors suspiciously and defiantly; concentrated dislike and ambition flashes out in glances like the breaking forth of hidden flames. Let two schoolfellows meet after twenty years, the rich man will avoid the poor; he does not recognize him, he is afraid even to glance into the gulf which Fate has set between him and the friend of other years. The one has been borne through life on the mettlesome steed called Fortune, or wafted on the golden clouds of success; the other has been making his way in underground Paris through the sewers, and bears the marks of his career upon him. How many a chum of old days turned aside at the sight of the doctor's greatcoat and vest !

With this explanation, it should be easy to understand how Dr. Poulain came to lend himself so readily to the farce of La Cibot's illness and recovery. Greed of every kind, ambition of every nature, is not easy to hide. The doctor examined his patient, found that every organ was sound and healthy, admired the regularity of her pulse and the perfect ease of her movements; and as she continued to moan aloud, he saw that for some reason she found it convenient to lie at death's door. The speedy cure of a serious imaginary disease was sure to cause a sensation in the neighborhood; the doctor would be talked about. He made up his mind at once. He talked of rupture and of taking it in time, and thought even worse of the case than La Cibot herself. The portress was plied with various remedies, and finally underwent a sham operation, crowned with complete success. Poulain repaired to the Arsenal Library, looked out a grotesque case in some of Desplein's records of extraordinary cures, and fitted the details to Mme. Cibot, modestly attributing the success of the treatment to the great surgeon, in whose steps (he said) he walked. Such is the impudence of beginners in Paris. Everything is made to serve as a ladder by which to climb upon the scene; and as everything, even the rungs of a ladder, will wear out in time, the new members of every profession are at a loss to find the right sort of wood of which to make steps for themselves.

There are moments when the Parisian is not propitious. He grows tired of raising pedestals, pouts like a spoiled child, and will have no more idols; or, to state it more accurately: Paris cannot always find a proper object for infatuation. Now and then the vein of genius gives out, and at such times the Parisian may turn supercilious; he is not always willing to bow down and gild mediocrity.

Mme. Cibot, entering in her usual unceremonious fashion, found the doctor and his mother at table, before a bowl of lamb's lettuce, the cheapest of all salad-stuffs. The dessert consisted of a thin wedge of Brie cheese flanked by a plate of specked apples and a dish of foreign mixed dried fruits, known as *quatre-mendiants*, in which the raisin-stalks were abundantly conspicuous.

"You may stay, mother," said the doctor, laying a hand on Mme. Poulain's arm; "this is Madame Cibot, of whom I have told you."

"My respects to you, madame, and my duty to you, sir," said La Cibot, taking the chair which the doctor offered. "Ah! is this your mother, sir? She is very happy to have a son who has such talent; he saved my life, madame, brought me back from the depths."

The widow, hearing Mme. Cibot praise her son in this way, thought her a delightful woman.

"I have just come to tell you that, between ourselves, poor Monsieur Pons is doing very badly, sir, and I have something to say to you about him——"

"Let us go into the sitting-room," interrupted the doctor, and with a significant gesture he indicated the servant.

In the sitting-room La Cibot explained her position with regard to the pair of nutcrackers at very considerable length. She repeated the history of her loan with added embellishments, and gave a full account of the immense services rendered during the past ten years to Messrs. Pons and Schmucke. The two old men, to all appearance, could not exist without her motherly care. She posed as an angel; she told so many lies, one after another, watering them with her tears, that old Mme. Poulain was quite touched.

"You understand, my dear sir," she concluded, "that I really ought to know how far I can depend on Monsieur Pons' intentions, supposing that he should die; not that I want him to die, for looking after those two innocents is my life, madame, you see; still, when one of them is gone I shall look after the other. For my own part, I was built by Nature to rival mothers. Without nobody to care for, nobody to take for a child, I don't know what I should do. So if Monsieur Poulain only would, he might do me a service for which I should be very grateful; and that is, to say a word to Monsieur Pons for me. Goodness me! an annuity of a thousand francs, is that too much, I ask you? To M. Schmucke it will be so much gained. Our dear patient said that he should recommend me to the German, poor man; it is his idea, no doubt, that Monsieur Schmucke should be his heir. But what is a man that cannot put two ideas together in French? And, beside, he would be quite capable of going back to Germany, he will be in such despair over his friend's death——"

The doctor grew grave. "My dear Madame Cibot," he said, "this sort of thing does not in the least concern a doctor. I should not be allowed to exercise my profession if it was known that I interfered in the matter of my patients' testamentary dispositions. The law forbids a doctor to receive a legacy from a patient——"

"A stupid law! What is to hinder me from dividing my legacy with you?" La Cibot said immediately.

"I will go further," said the doctor; "my professional conscience will not permit me to speak to Monsieur Pons of his death. In the first place, he is not so dangerously ill that there is any need to speak of it; and, in the second, such talk coming from me might give a shock to the system that would do him real harm, and then his illness might terminate fatally and——"

"*I* don't put on gloves to tell him to get his affairs in order," cried Mme. Cibot, "and he is none the worse for that. He is used to it. There is nothing to fear."

"Not a word about it, my dear Madame Cibot! These things are not within a doctor's province; it is a notary's business——"

"But, my dear Monsieur Poulain, suppose that Monsieur Pons of his own accord should ask you how he is, and whether he had better make his arrangements; then, would you refuse to tell him that if you want to get better it is an excellent plan to set everything in order? Then you might just slip in a little word for me——"

"Oh, if *he* talks of making his will, I certainly shall not dissuade him," said the doctor.

"Very well, that is settled. I came to thank you for your care of me," she added, as she slipped a folded paper containing three gold-coins into the doctor's hands. "It is all I can do at the moment. Ah! my dear Monsieur Poulain, if I were rich, you should be rich, you that are the image of Providence on earth. Madame, you have an angel for a son."

La Cibot rose to her feet, Mme. Poulain bowed amiably, and the doctor went to the door with the visitor. Just then a sudden, lurid gleam of light flashed across the mind of this Lady Macbeth of the streets. She saw clearly that the doctor was surely her accomplice—he had taken the fee for a sham illness.

"Monsieur Poulain," she began, "how can you refuse to say a word or two to save me from want, when you helped me in the affair of my accident?"

The doctor felt that the devil had him by the hair, as the saying is; he felt, too, that the hair was being twisted round the pitiless red claw. Startled and afraid lest he should sell his honesty for such a trifle, he answered the diabolical suggestion by another no less diabolical.

"Listen, my dear Madame Cibot," he said, as he drew her into his consulting-room. "I will now pay a debt of gratitude that I owe you for my appointment to the mairie——"

"We go shares?" she asked briskly.

"In what?"

"In the legacy."

"You do not know me," replied Dr. Poulain, drawing himself up like Valerius Publicola. "Let us have no more of that. I have a friend, an old schoolfellow of mine, a very intelligent young fellow; and we are so much the more intimate because our lives have fallen out very much in the same way. He was studing law while I was studying medicine; and when I was a house-student, he was engrossing deeds in Maître Couture's office. His father was a shoemaker, and mine was a breeches-maker; he has not found any one to take much interest in his career, nor has he any capital; for, after all, capital is only to be had from sympathizers. He could only afford to buy a provincial connection—at Mantes—and so little do provincials understand the Parisian intellect that they set all sorts of intrigues on foot against him."

"The wretches!" cried La Cibot.

" Yes," said the doctor. " They combined against him to such purpose that they forced him to sell his connection by misrepresenting something that he had done ; the attorney for the crown interfered, he belonged to the place, and sided with his fellow-townsmen. My friend's name is Fraisier. He is lodged as I am, and he is even leaner and more threadbare. He took refuge in our arrondissement, and is reduced to appear for clients in the police court or before the magistrate. He lives in the Rue de la Perle close by. Go to number 9, third floor, and you will see his name on the door on the landing, painted in gilt letters on a small square of red leather. Fraisier makes a special point of disputes among the porters, workmen, and poor folk in the arrondissement, and his charges are low. He is an honest man ; for I need not tell you that if he had been a scamp, he would be keeping his carriage by now. I will call and see my friend Fraisier this evening. Go to him early to-morrow ; he knows Monsieur Louchard, the bailiff : Monsieur Tabareau, the clerk of the court ; and the justice of the peace, Monsieur Vitel ; and Monsieur Trognon, the notary. He is even now looked upon as one of the best men of business in the Quarter. If he takes charge of your interests, if you can secure him as Monsieur Pons' adviser, you will have a second self in him, you see. But do not make dishonorable proposals to him, as you did just now to me ; he has a head on his shoulders, you will understand each other. And as for acknowledging his services, I will be your intermediary——"

Mme. Cibot looked askance at the doctor.

" Is that the lawyer who helped Madame Florimond the haberdasher in the Rue Vieille-du-Temple out of a fix in that matter of her friend's legacy ? "

" The very same."

" Wasn't it a shame that she did not marry him after he had gained two thousand francs a year for her ? " exclaimed La Cibot. "And she thought to clear off scores by making him a present of a dozen shirts and a couple of dozen pocket-handkerchiefs; an outfit, in short."

"My dear Madame Cibot, that outfit cost a thousand francs, and Fraisier was just setting up for himself in the Quarter, and wanted the things very badly. And what was more, she paid the bill without asking any questions. That affair brought him clients, and now he is very busy; but in my line a practice brings——"

"It is only the righteous that suffer here below," said La Cibot. "Well, Monsieur Poulain, good-day and thank you."

And herewith begins the tragedy, or, if you like to have it so, a terrible comedy—the death of an old bachelor delivered over by circumstances too strong for him to the rapacity and greed that gathered about his bed. And other forces came to the support of rapacity and greed; there was the picture-collector's mania, that most intense of all passions; there was the cupidity of the Sieur Fraisier, whom you shall presently behold in his den, a sight to make you shudder; and, lastly, there was the Auvergnat thirsting for money, ready for any-thing—even for a crime—that should bring him the capital he wanted. The first part of the story serves in some sort as a prelude to this comedy in which all the actors who have hith-erto occupied the stage will reappear.

The degradation of a word is one of those curious freaks of manners upon which whole volumes of explanation might be written. Write to an attorney and address him as "Lawyer So-and-so," and you insult him as surely as you would insult a wholesale colonial produce merchant by addressing your letter to "Mr. So-and-so, Grocer." There are plenty of men of the world who ought to be aware, since the knowledge of such subtle distinctions is their province, that you cannot in-sult a French writer more cruelly than by caling him *un homme de lettres*—a literary man. The word *monsieur* is a capital · example of the life and death of words. Abbreviated from

monseigneur, once so considerable a title, and even now, in
the form of *sire*, reserved for emperors and kings, it is bestowed indifferently upon all and sundry ; while the twin word
messire, which is nothing but its double and equivalent, if by
any chance it slips into a certificate of burial, produces an
outcry in the Republican papers.

Magistrates, councilors, jurisconsults, judges, barristers,
officers for the crown, bailiffs, attorneys, clerks of the court,
procurators, solicitors, and agents of various kinds represent
or misrepresent Justice.　The "lawyer" and the bailiff's
men (commonly called "the brokers")* are the two lowest
rungs of the ladder.　Now, the bailiff's man is an outsider,
an adventitious minister of justice, appearing to see that judgment is executed ; he is, in fact, a kind of inferior executioner
employed by the county court.　But the word "lawyer"
(*homme de loi*, man of law) is a depreciatory term applied to
the legal profession.　Consuming professional jealousy finds
similar disparaging epithets for fellow-travelers in every walk
of life, and every calling has its special insult.　The scorn
flung into the words *homme de loi, homme de lettres*, is wanting
in the plural form, which may be used without offense ; but
in Paris every profession, learned or unlearned, has its *omega*,
the individual who brings it down to the level of the lowest
class ; and the written law has its connecting link with the
custom right of the streets.　There are districts where the
pettifogging man of business, known as Lawyer So-and-so, is
still to be found.　M. Fraisier was to the member of the
Incorporated Law Society as the money-lender of the Halles,
offering small loans for a short period at an exorbitant interest,
is to the great capitalist.

Working people, strange to say, are as shy of officials as of
fashionable restaurants, they take advice from irregular sources
as they turn into a little wineshop to drink.　Each rank in
life finds its own level, and there abides.　None but a chosen

* Constables.

few care to climb the heights, few can feel at ease in the presence of their betters, or take their place among them, like a Beaumarchais letting fall the watch of the great lord who tried to humiliate him. And if there are few who can even rise to a higher social level, those among them who can throw off their swaddling-clothes are rare and great exceptions.

At six o'clock the next morning Mme. Cibot stood in the Rue de la Perle; she was making a survey of the abode of her future adviser, Lawyer Fraisier. The house was one of the old-fashioned kind formerly inhabited by small tradespeople and citizens with small means. A cabinetmaker's store occupied almost the whole of the first floor, as well as the little yard behind, which was covered with his workshops and warehouses; the small remaining space being taken up by the porter's lodge and the passage entry in the middle. The staircase walls were half rotten with damp and covered with nitre to such a degree that the house seemed to be stricken with leprosy.

Mme. Cibot went straight to the porter's lodge, and there encountered one of her own fraternity, a shoemaker, his wife, and two small children, all housed in a room ten feet square, lighted from the yard at the back. La Cibot mentioned her profession, named herself, and spoke of her house in the Rue de Normandie, and the two women were on cordial terms at once. After a quarter of an hour spent in gossip while the shoemaker's wife made breakfast ready for her husband and the children, Mme. Cibot turned the conversation to the subject of the lodgers, and spoke of the lawyer.

"I have come to see him on business," she said. "One of his friends, Dr. Poulain, recommended me to him. Do you know Dr. Poulain?"

"I should think I do," said the lady of the Rue de la Perle. "He saved my little girl's life when she had the croup."

"He saved my life too, madame. What sort of man is this Monsieur Fraisier?"

"He is the sort of man, my dear lady, out of whom it is very difficult to get the postage-money at the end of the month."

To a person of La Cibot's intelligence this was enough.

"One may be poor and honest," observed she.

"I am sure I hope so," returned Fraisier's portress. "We are not rolling in coppers, let alone gold or silver; but we have not a centime belonging to anybody else."

This sort of talk sounded familiar to La Cibot.

"In short, one can trust him, child, eh?"

"Lord! when Monsieur Fraisier means well by any one, there is not his like, so I have heard Madame Florimond say."

"And why didn't she marry him when she owed her fortune to him?" La Cibot asked quickly. "It is something for a little haberdasher, kept by an old man, to be a barrister's wife——"

"Why?——" asked the portress, bringing Mme. Cibot out into the passage. "Why?—— You are going up to see him, are you not, madame? Very well, when you are in his office you will know why."

From the state of the staircase, lighted by sash-windows on the side of the yard, it was pretty evident that the inmates of the house, with the exception of the landlord and M. Fraisier himself, were all workmen. There were traces of various crafts in the deposit of mud upon the steps—brass-filings, broken buttons, scraps of gauze, and esparto grass lay scattered about. The walls of the upper stories were covered with apprentices' ribald scrawls and caricatures. The portress' last remark had roused La Cibot's curiosity; she decided, not unnaturally, that she would consult Dr. Poulain's friend; but as for employing him, that must depend upon her impressions.

"I sometimes wonder how Madame Sauvage can stop in his service," said the portress, by way of comment; she was following in Mme. Cibot's wake. "I will come up with you, madame," she added; "I am taking the milk and the newspaper up to my landlord."

Arrived on the third floor, above the entresol, La Cibot beheld a door of the most villainous description. The doubtful red paint was coated for seven or eight inches round the keyhole with a filthy glaze, a grimy deposit from which the modern house-decorator endeavors to protect the doors of more elegant apartments by glass "finger-plates." A grating, almost stopped up with some compound similar to the deposit with which a restaurant-keeper gives an air of cellar-bound antiquity to a merely middle-aged bottle, only served to heighten the general resemblance to a prison door; a resemblance further heightened by the trefoil-shaped iron-work, the formidable hinges, the clumsy nail-heads. A miser, or a pamphleteer at strife with the world at large, must surely have invented these fortifications. A leaden sink, which received the waste water of the household, contributed its quota to the fetid atmosphere of the staircase, and the ceiling was covered with fantastic arabesques traced by candle-smoke—such arabesques! On pulling a greasy acorn tassel attached to the bell-rope, a little bell jangled feebly somewhere within, complaining of the fissure in its metal sides.

Every detail was in keeping with the general dismal effect. La Cibot heard a heavy footstep, and the asthmatic wheezing of a virago within, and Mme. Sauvage presently showed herself. Adrien Brauwer might have painted just such a hag for his picture of Witches starting for the Sabbath; a stout, unwholesome slattern, five feet six inches in height, with a grenadier countenance and a beard which far surpassed La Cibot's own; she wore a cheap, hideous, ugly cotton gown, a red bandana handkerchief knotted over hair which she still continued to put in curl-papers (using for that purpose the printed circulars which her master received), and a huge pair of gold earrings like cart-wheels in her ears. This female Cerberus carried a battered skillet in one hand, and, opening the door, set free an imprisoned odor of scorched milk—a nauseous and penetrating smell, that lost itself at once, however, among the fumes outside.

"What can I do for you, missus?" demanded Mme. Sauvage, and with a truculent air she looked La Cibot over; evidently she was of the opinion that the visitor was too well dressed, and her eyes looked the more murderous because they were naturally bloodshot.

"I have come to see Monsieur Fraisier; his friend, Dr. Poulain, sent me."

"Oh! come in, missus," said La Sauvage, grown very amiable all of a sudden, which proves that she was prepared for this morning visit.

With a sweeping curtsey, the stalwart woman flung open the door of a private office, which looked upon the street, and discovered the ex-attorney of Mantes.

The room was a complete picture of a third-rate attorney's office; with the stained wooden cases, the letter-files so old that they had grown beards (in ecclesiastical language), th red tape dangling limp and dejected, the pasteboard box covered with traces of the gambols of mice, the dirty floo the ceiling tawny with smoke. A frugal allowance of woo was smouldering on a couple of fire-dogs on the hearth. And on the chimney-piece above stood a foggy mirror and a modern clock with an inlaid wooden case: Fraisier had picked it up at an execution sale, together with the tawdry imitation rococo candlesticks, with the zinc beneath showing through the lacquer in several places.

M. Fraisier was small, thin, and unwholesome looking; his red face, covered with an eruption, told of tainted blood; and he had, moreover, a trick of continually scratching his right arm. A wig pushed to the back of his head displayed

"MADAME CIBOT, I BELIEVE?"

a brick-colored cranium of ominous conformation. This person rose from a cane-seated armchair, in which he sat on a green leather cushion, assumed an agreeble expression, and brought forward a chair.

"Madame Cibot, I believe?" queried he, in dulcet tones.

"Yes, sir," answered the portress. She had lost her habitual assurance.

Something in the tones of a voice which strongly resembled the sounds of the little door-bell, something in a glance even sharper than the green eyes of her future legal adviser, scared Mme. Cibot. Fraisier's presence so pervaded the room that any one might have thought there was pestilence in the air; and in a flash Mme. Cibot understood why Mme. Florimond had not become Mme. Fraisier.

"Poulain told me about you, my dear madame," said the lawyer, in the unnatural fashion commonly described by the words "mincing tones;" tones sharp, thin, and grating as verjuice, in spite of all his efforts.

Arrived at this point, he tried to draw the skirts of his dressing-gown over a pair of angular knees encased in threadbare felt. The robe was an ancient painted cotton garment, lined with wadding which took the liberty of protruding itself through various slits in it here and there; the weight of this lining had pulled the skirts aside, disclosing a dingy hued flannel vest beneath. With something of a coxcomb's manner, Fraisier fastened this refractory article of dress, tightening the girdle to define his reedy figure; then with a blow of the tongs he effected a reconciliation between two burning brands that had long avoided one another, like brothers after a family quarrel. A sudden bright idea struck him, and he rose from his chair.

"Madame Sauvage!" called he.

"Well?"

"I am not at home to anybody!"

"Eh! bless your life, there's no need to say that!"

18

"She is my old nurse," the lawyer made remark, in some confusion.

"And she has not recovered her figure yet," remarked the heroine of the Halles.

Fraisier laughed, and drew the bolt lest his housekeeper should interrupt Mme. Cibot's confidences.

"Well, madame, explain your business," said he, making another effort to drape himself in the dressing-gown. "Any one recommended to me by the only friend I have in the world may count upon me—I may say—absolutely."

For half an hour Mme. Cibot talked, and the man of law made no interruption of any sort ; his face wore the expression of curious interest with which a young soldier listens to a pensioner of the Old Guard. Fraisier's silence and acquiescence, the rapt attention with which he appeared to listen to a torrent of gossip similar to the samples previously given, dispelled some of the prejudices inspired in La Cibot's mind by his squalid surroundings. The little lawyer with the black-speckled green eyes was in reality making a study of his client. When at length she came to a stand and looked to him to speak, he was seized with a fit of the complaint known as a "churchyard cough," and had recourse to an earthenware basin half full of herb tea, which he drained.

"But for Poulain, my dear madame, I should have been dead before this," said Fraisier, by way of answer to the portress' looks of motherly compassion ; "but he will bring me round, he says——"

As all the client's confidences appeared to have slipped from the memory of her legal adviser, she began to cast about for a way of taking leave of a man so apparently near death.

"In an affair of this kind, madame," continued the attorney from Mantes, suddenly returning to business, "there are two things which it is most important to know. In the first place, whether the property is sufficient to be worth troubling about ; and, in the second, whom the next-of-kin may be; for if the property is the booty, the next-of-kin is the enemy."

La Cibot immediately began to talk of Rémonencq and Élie Magus, and said that the shrewd couple valued the pictures at six hundred thousand francs.

"Would they take them themselves at that price?" inquired the lawyer. "You see, madame, that men of business are shy of pictures. A picture may mean a piece of canvas worth a couple of francs or a painting worth two hundred thousand. Now paintings worth two hundred thousand francs are usually well known; and what errors in judgment people make in estimating even the most famous pictures of all! There was once a great capitalist whose collection was admired, visited, and engraved—actually engraved! He was supposed to have spent millions of francs on it. He died, as men must; and—well, his *genuine* pictures did not fetch more than two hundred thousand francs! You must let me see these gentlemen. Now, for the next-of-kin," and Fraisier again relapsed into his attitude of listener.

When President Camusot's name came up, he nodded with a grimace which riveted Mme. Cibot's attention. She tried to read the forehead and the villainous face, and found what is called in business a " wooden head."

"Yes, my dear sir," repeated La Cibot. "Yes, my Monsieur Pons is own cousin to President Camusot de Marville; he tells me that ten times a day. Monsieur Camusot the silk mercer was married twice——"

"He that has just been nominated for a peer of France? who——"

"—And his first wife was a Mademoiselle Pons, Monsieur Pons' first cousin."

"Then they are first cousins once removed——"

"They are not ' cousins.' They have quarreled."

It may be remembered that before M. Camusot de Marville came to Paris, he was president of the Tribunal of Mantes for five years; and not only was his name still remembered there, but he had kept up a correspondence with Mantes. Camusot's immediate successor, the judge with whom he had been most intimate during his term of office, was still president of the Tribunal, and consequently knew all about Fraisier.

"Do you know, madame," Fraisier said, when at last the red sluices of La Cibot's torrent tongue were closed, "do you know that your principal enemy will be a man who can send you to the scaffold?"

The portress started on her chair, making a sudden spring like a jack-in-the-box.

"Calm yourself, dear madame," continued Fraisier. "You may not have known the name of the president of the Chamber of Indictments at the Court of Appeal in Paris; but you ought to have known that Monsieur Pons must have an heir-at-law. Monsieur le President de Marville is your invalid's sole heir; but as he is a collateral in the third degree, Monsieur Pons is entitled by law to leave his fortune as he pleases. You are not aware either that, six weeks ago at least, Monsieur le President's daughter married the eldest son of the Comte Popinot, peer of France, once minister of agriculture, and president of the Board of Trade, one of the most influential politicians of the day. President de Marville is even more formidable through this marriage than in his own quality of head of the Court of Assize."

At that word La Cibot shuddered.

"Yes, and it is he who sends you there," continued Fraisier. "Ah! my dear madame, you little know what a red robe means! It is bad enough to have a plain black gown against you! You see me here, ruined, bald, broken in health—all because, unwittingly, I crossed a mere attorney for the crown in the provinces. I was forced to sell my connection at a loss, and very lucky I was to come off with the loss of my money. If I had tried to stand out, my professional position would have gone as well.

"One thing more you do not know," he continued, "and this it is: If you had only to do with President Camusot himself, it would be nothing; but he has a wife, mind you!—and if you ever find yourself face to face with that wife, you will shake in your shoes as if you were on the first step of the scaffold, your hair will stand on end. The presidente is so vindictive that she would spend ten years over setting a trap to kill you. She sets that husband of hers spinning like a top. Through her a charming young fellow committed suicide at the Conciergerie. A count was accused of forgery—she made his character as white as snow. She all but drove a person of the highest quality from the Court of Charles X. Finally, she displaced the Attorney-General, Monsieur de Granville from——"

"That lived in the Rue Vieille-du-Temple, at the corner of the Rue Saint-François!"

"The very same. They say that she means to make her husband home secretary, and I do not know that she will not gain her end. If she were to take it into her head to send us both to the Criminal Court first and the hulks afterward—I should apply for a passport and set sail for America, though I am as innocent as a new-born babe. So well do I know what justice means. Now, see here, my dear Madame Cibot; to marry her only daughter to young Vicomte Popinot (heir to Monsieur Pillerault your landlord, it is said)—to make that match, she stripped herself of her whole fortune, so much so that the president and his wife have nothing at this moment except his official salary. Can you suppose, my dear madame, that under the circumstances Madame la Presidente will let Monsieur Pons' property go out of the family without a word! Why, I would sooner face guns loaded with grape-shot than have such a woman for my enemy——"

"But they have quarreled," put in La Cibot.

"What has that to do with it?" asked Fraisier. "It is one reason the more for fearing her. To kill a relative of whom you are tired is something ; but to inherit his property afterward—that is a real pleasure ! "

" But the old gentleman has a horror of his relatives.   He says over and over again that these people—Messrs. Cardot, Berthier, and the rest of them (I can't remember their names) —have crushed him as a tumbril cart crushes an egg——"

" Have you a mind to be crushed too ? "

" Oh, dear ! oh, dear ! " cried La Cibot.   " Ah ! Ma'am Fontaine was right when she said that I should meet with difficulties : still, she said that I should succeed——"

" Listen, my dear Madame Cibot.   As for making some thirty thousand francs out of this business—that is possible ; but for the whole of the property, it is useless to think of it.   We talked over your case yesterday evening, Dr. Poulain and I——"

La Cibot started again.

" Well, what is the matter ? "

" But if you knew about the affair, why did you let me chatter away like a magpie ? "

" Madame Cibot, I knew all about your business, but I knew nothing of Madame Cibot.   So many clients, so many characters——"

Mme. Cibot gave her legal adviser a queer look at this ; all her suspicions gleamed in her eyes.   Fraisier saw this.

" I resume," he continued.   " So, our friend Poulain was once called in by you to attend old Monsieur Pillerault, the Countess Popinot's great-uncle ; that is one of your claims to my devotion.   Poulain goes to see your landlord (mark this!) once a fortnight ; he learned all these particulars from him. Monsieur Pillerault was present at his grand-nephew's wedding—for he is an uncle with money to leave ; he has an income of fifteen thousand francs, though he has lived like a hermit for the last five-and-twenty years, and scarcely spends a thousand crowns—well, *he* told Poulain all about this marriage.   It seems that your old musician was precisely the cause of the row; he tried to disgrace his own family by way of revenge. If you only hear one bell, you only hear one sound. Your invalid says that he meant no harm, but everybody thinks him a monster of——"

"And it would not astonish me if he was!" cried La Cibot. "Just imagine it! For these ten years past I have been money out of pocket for him, spending my savings on him, and he knows it, and yet he will not let me lie down to sleep on a legacy! No, sir! he will *not*. He is obstinate, a regular mule he is. I have talked to him these ten days, and the cross-grained cur won't stir no more than a sign-post. He shuts his teeth and looks at me like—— The most that he would say was that he would recommend me to Monsieur Schmucke."

"Then he means to make his will in favor of this Schmucke?"

"Everything will go to him——"

"Listen, my dear Madame Cibot, if I am to arrive at any definite conclusions and think of a plan, I must know Monsieur Schmucke. I must see the property and have some talk with this Jew of whom you speak; and then let me direct you——"

"We shall see, Monsieur Fraisier."

"What is this? 'We shall see?'" repeated Fraisier, speaking in the voice natural to him, as he gave La Cibot a viperous glance. "Am I your legal adviser or am I not, I ask? Let us know exactly where we stand."

La-Cibot felt that he read her thoughts. A cold chill ran down her back.

"I have told you all I know," she said. She saw that she was at the tiger's mercy.

"We attorneys are accustomed to treachery. Just think carefully over your position; it is superb. If you follow my advice point by point, you will have thirty or forty thousand francs. But there is a reverse side to this beautiful medal.

How if the presidente comes to hear that Monsieur Pons'
property is worth a million of francs, and that you mean to
have a bite out of it? for there is always somebody ready to
take that kind of errand——" he added parenthetically.

This remark, and the little pause that came before and
after it, sent another shudder through La Cibot. She thought
at once that Fraisier himself would probably undertake that
office.

"And then, my dear client, in ten minutes old Pillerault
is asked to dismiss you, and then on a couple of hours'
notice——"

"What does that matter to me?" said La Cibot, rising to
her feet like a Bellona; "I shall stay with the gentlemen as
their housekeeper."

"And then a trap will be set for you, and some fine morning you and your husband will wake up in a prison cell, to be
tried for your lives——"

"*I?*" cried La Cibot; "I that have not a sou that doesn't
belong to me—— *I!*—— *I!*"

For five minutes she held forth, and Fraisier watched the
great artist before him as she executed a concerto of self-
praise. He was quite untouched, and even amused by the performance. His keen glances pricked La Cibot like stilettos;
he chuckled inwardly, till his shrunken wig was shaking with
laughter. He was a Robespierre at an age when the Sylla of
France was still making couplets.

"And how? And why? And on what pretext?" demanded she, when she came to an end.

"You wish to know how you may come to the guillotine?"

La Cibot turned pale as death at the words; the words
fell like the knife upon her neck. She stared wildly at
Fraisier.

"Listen to me, my dear child," began Fraisier, suppressing
his inward satisfaction at his client's discomfiture.

"I would sooner leave things as they are——" murmured La Cibot, and she rose to go.

"Stay," Fraisier said imperiously. "You ought to know the risks that you are running; I am bound to give you the benefit of my lights. You are dismissed by Monsieur Pillerault, we will say; there is no doubt about that, is there? You enter the service of these two gentlemen. Very good! That is a declaration of war against the presidente. You mean to do everything you can to gain possession of the property, and to get a slice out of it at any rate——

"Oh, I am not blaming you," Fraisier continued, in answer to a gesture from his client. "It is not my place to do so. This is a battle, and you will be led on further than you think for. One grows full of one's idea, one hits hard——"

Another gesture of denial. This time La Cibot tossed her head.

"There, there, old lady," said Fraisier, with odious familiarity, "you will go a very long way!——"

"You take me for a thief, I suppose?"

"Come, now, mamma, you hold a receipt in Monsieur Schmucke's hand which did not cost you much. Ah! you are in the confessional, my lady. Don't deceive your confessor, especially when the confessor has the power of reading your thoughts."

La Cibot was dismayed by the man's perspicacity; now she knew why he had listened to her so intently.

"Very good," continued he, "you can admit at once that the presidente will not allow you to pass her in the race for the property. You will be watched and spied upon. You get your name into Monsieur Pons' will; nothing could be better. But some fine day the law steps in, arsenic is found in a glass, and you and your husband are arrested, tried, and condemned for attempting the life of the Sieur Pons, so as to come by your legacy. I once defended a poor woman at Ver-

sailles ; she was in reality as innocent as you would be in such
a case.   Things were as I have told you, and all that I could
do was to save her life.   The unhappy creature was sentenced
to twenty years' penal servitude.   She is working out her time
now at St. Lazare."

Mme. Cibot's terror grew to the highest pitch.   She grew
paler and paler, staring at the little, thin man with the green
eyes, as some wretched Moor, accused of adhering to her own
religion, might gaze at the inquisitor who doomed her to the
stake.

"Then do you tell me that, if I leave you to act and put
my interests in your hands, I shall get something without
fear ?"

"I guarantee you thirty thousand francs," said Fraisier,
speaking like a man sure of the fact.

"After all, you know how fond I am of dear Dr. Poulain,"
she began again in her most coaxing tones ; "he told me to
come to you, worthy man, and he did not send me here to be
told that I shall be guillotined for poisoning some one."

The thought of the guillotine so moved her that she burst
into tears, her nerves were shaken, terror clutched at her
heart, she lost her head.   Fraisier gloated over his triumph.
When he saw his client hesitate, he thought that he had lost his
chance ; he had set himself to frighten and quell La Cibot
till she was completely in his power, bound hand and foot.
She had walked into his study as a fly walks into a spider's
web ; there she was doomed to remain, entangled in the toils
of the little lawyer who meant to feed upon her.   Out of this
bit of business, indeed, Fraisier meant to gain the living of old
days : comfort, competence, and consideration.   He and his
friend, Dr. Poulain, had spent the whole previous evening in
a microscopic examination of the case ; they had made mature
deliberations.   The doctor described Schmucke for his friend's
benefit, and the alert pair had plumbed all hypotheses and
scrutinized all risks and resources, till Fraisier, exultant, cried

aloud: "Both our fortunes lie in this!" He had gone so far
as to promise Poulain a hospital, and, as for himself, he meant
to be justice of the peace of an arrondissement.

To be a justice of the peace! For this man with his abun-
dant capacity, for this doctor of law without a pair of socks to
his name, the dream was a hippogriff so restive, that he thought
of it as a deputy-advocate thinks of the silk gown, as an Italian
priest thinks of the tiara. It was, indeed, a wild dream!

M. Vitel, the justice of the peace before whom Fraisier
pleaded, was a man of sixty-nine, in failing health; he talked
of retiring on a pension; and Fraisier used to talk with Poulain
of succeeding him, much as Poulain talked of saving the life of
some rich heiress and marrying her afterward. No one knows
how greedily every post in the gift of authority is sought
after in Paris. Every one wants to live in Paris. If a
stamp or tobacco license falls in, a hundred women rise up
as one and stir all their friends to obtain it. Any vacancy
in the ranks of the twenty-four collectors of taxes sends
a flood of ambitious folk surging in upon the Chamber
of Deputies. Decisions are made in committee, all appointments are made by the Government. Now the salary of a
·justice of the peace, the lowest stipendiary magistrate in Paris,
is about six thousand francs. The post of registrar to the
court is worth a hundred thousand francs. Few places are
more coveted in the administration. Fraisier, as a justice of
the peace, with the head-physician of a hospital for his friend,
would make a rich marriage himself and a good match for Dr.
Poulain. Each would lend a hand to each.

Night set its leaden seal upon the plans made by the sometime attorney of Mantes, and a formidable scheme sprouted
up, a flourishing scheme, fertile in harvests of gain and intrigue. La Cibot was the hinge upon which the whole matter
turned; and for this reason, any rebellion on the part of the
instrument must be at once put down; such action on her
part was quite unexpected; but Fraisier had put forth all the

strength of his rancorous nature, and the audacious portress lay trampled under his feet.

"Come, reassure yourself, my dear madame," he remarked, holding out his hand. The touch of the cold, serpent-like skin made a terrible impression upon the portress. It brought about something like a physical reaction, which checked her emotion; Mme. Fontaine's toad, Astaroth, seemed to her to be less deadly than this poison-sac that wore a sandy wig and spoke in tones like the creaking of a hinge.

"Do not imagine that I am frightening you to no purpose," Fraisier continued. (La Cibot's feeling of repulsion had not escaped him.) "The affairs which made Madame la Presidente's dreadful reputation are so well known at the law-courts, that you can make inquiries there if you like. The great person who was all but sent into a lunatic asylum was the Marquis d'Espard. The Marquis d'Escrignon was saved from the hulks. The handsome young man with wealth and a great future before him, who was to have married a daughter of one of the first families of France, and hanged himself in a cell of the Conciergerie, was the celebrated Lucien de Rubempré;* the affair made a great deal of noise in Paris at the time. That was the question of a will. His mistress, the notorious Esther, died and left him several millions, and they accused the young fellow of poisoning her. He was not even in Paris at the time of her death, nor did he so much as know that the woman had left the money to him! One cannot well be more innocent than that! Well, after Monsieur Camusot examined him, he hanged himself in his cell. Law, like medicine, has its victims. In the first case, one man suffers for the many, and, in the second, he dies for science," he added, and an ugly smile stole over his lips. "Well, I know the risks myself, you see; poor and obscure little attorney as I am, the law has been the ruin of me. My experience was dearly bought—it is all at your service."

* See "The Harlot's Progress."

"Thank you, no," said La Cibot; "I won't have nothing to do with it, upon my word! I shall have nourished ingratitude, that is all! I don't want nothing but my due; I have thirty years of honesty behind me, sir. Monsieur Pons says that he will recommend me to his friend Schmucke; well and good, I shall end my days in peace with the German, good man."

Fraisier had overshot his mark. He had discouraged La Cibot. Now he was obliged to remove these unpleasant impressions.

"Do not let us give up," he said; "just go away quietly home. Come, now, we will steer the affair to a good end."

"But what about my *rentes*, what am I to do to get them, and——"

"And feel no remorse?" he interrupted quickly. "Eh! it is precisely for that that men of business were invented; unless you keep within the law, you get nothing. You know nothing of law; I know a good deal. I will see that you keep on the right side of it, and you can hold your own in all men's sight. As for your conscience, that is your own affair."

"Very well, tell me how to do it," returned La Cibot, curious and delighted.

"I do not know how yet. I have not looked at the strong points of the case yet; I have been busy with the obstacles. But the first thing to be done is to urge him to make a will; you cannot go wrong over that; and find out, first of all, how Pons means to leave his fortune; for if you were his heir——"

"No, no; he does not like me. Ah! if I had but known the value of his gimcracks, and if I had known what I know now about his amours, I should be easy in my mind this day and——"

"Keep on, in fact," broke in Fraisier. "Dying folk have queer fancies, my dear madame; they disappoint hopes many a time. Let him make his will and then we shall see. And of all things, the property must be valued. So I must see this Rémonencq and the Jew; they will be very useful to us. Put entire confidence in me, I am at your disposal. When a client is a friend to me, I am his friend through thick and thin. Friend or enemy, that is my character."

"Very well," said La Cibot, "I am yours entirely; and as for fees, Monsieur Poulain——"

"Let us say nothing about that," said Fraisier. "Think how you can keep Poulain at the bedside; he is one of the most upright and conscientious men I know; and, you see, we want some one there whom we can trust. Poulain would do better than I; I have lost my character."

"You look as if you had," said La Cibot; "but, for my own part, I should trust you."

"And you would do well. Come to see me whenever anything happens—and—there !—you are an intelligent woman; all will go well."

"Good-day, Monsieur Fraisier. I hope you will recover your health. Your servant, sir."

Fraisier went to the door with his client. But this time it was he, and not La Cibot, who was struck with an idea on the threshold.

"If you could persuade Monsieur Pons to call me in, it would be a great step."

"I will try," said La Cibot.

Fraisier drew her back into his sanctum. "Look here, old lady, I know Monsieur Trognon, the notary of the quarter, very well. If Monsieur Pons has not a notary, mention Monsieur Trognon to him. Make him take this Monsieur Trognon——"

"Right," returned La Cibot.

And as she came out again she heard the rustle of a dress and the sound of a stealthy, heavy footstep.

Out in the street and by herself, Mme. Cibot to some extent recovered her liberty of mind as she walked. Though the influence of the conversation was still upon her, and she had always stood in dread of scaffolds, justice, and judges, she took a very natural resolution which was to bring about a conflict of strategy between her and her formidable legal adviser.

"What do I want with other people?" said she to herself. "Let us make a round sum, and afterward I will take all that they offer me to push their interests;" and this thought, as will shortly be seen, hastened the poor old musician's end.

"Well, dear Monsieur Schmucke, and how is our dear, adored patient?" asked La Cibot, as she came into the room.

"Fery bad; Bons haf been vandering all der night."

"Then, what did he say?"

"Chust nonsense. He vould dot I haf all his fortune, on kondition dot I sell nodings. Den he cried! Boor man! It made me ver' sad."

"Never mind, honey," returned the portress. "I have kept you waiting for your breakfast; it is nine o'clock and past; but don't scold me. I have business on hand, you see, business of yours. Here are we, without any money, and I have been out to get some."

"Vere?" asked Schmucke.

"Of my uncle."

"Onkel?"

"Up the spout."

"Shpout?"

"Oh, the dear man! how simple he is! No, you are a saint, a love, an archbishop of innocence, a man that ought to be stuffed, as the old actor said. What! you have lived in Paris for twenty-nine years; you saw the Revolution of July, you did, and you haven't never so much as heard tell of a pawn-broker—a man that lends you money on your things? I have been pawning our silver spoons and forks, eight of them, thread pattern. Pooh, Cibot can eat his victuals with horrid German silver; it is quite the fashion now, they say. It is not worth while to say anything to our angel there; it would upset him and make him yellower than before, and he is quite cross enough as it is. Let us get round him again first, and afterward we shall see. What must be must; and we must take things as we find them, eh?"

"Goot voman! nople heart!" cried poor Schmucke, with a great tenderness in his face. He took La Cibot's hand and clasped it to his breast. When he looked up, there were tears in his eyes.

"There, that will do, Papa Schmucke; how funny you are! This is too bad. I'm an old daughter of the people—my heart is in my hand. I have something *here*, you see, like you have, hearts of gold that you are," she added, slapping her chest.

"Baba Schmucke!" continued the musician. "No. To know de tepths of sorrow, to cry mit tears of blood, to mount up in der hefn—dat is mein lot! I shall not lif after Pons——"

"Gracious! I am sure you won't, you are killing yourself. Listen, pet!"

"Bet?"

"Very well, my sonny——"

"Zonny?"

"My lamb, then, if you like it better."

"It is not more clear."

"Oh, well, let *me* take care of you and tell you what to do; for if you go on like this, I shall have both of you laid up on my hands, you see. To my little way of thinking, we must do the work between us. You cannot go about Paris to give lessons, for it tires you, and then you are not fit to do anything afterward, and somebody must sit up of a night with Monsieur Pons, now that he is getting worse and worse. I will run round to-day to all your pupils and tell them that you are ill; is it not so? And then you can spend the nights with our lamb, and sleep of a morning from five o'clock till, let us say, two in the afternoon. I myself will take the day, the most tiring part, for there is your breakfast and dinner to get ready, and the bed to make, and the things to change, and the doses of medicine to give. I could not hold out for another ten days at this rate. It is a month and more already since I have been like this. What would become of you if I were to fall ill? And you yourself, it makes one shudder to see you; just look at yourself, after sitting up with him last night!"

She drew Schmucke to the glass, and Schmucke thought that there was a great change.

"So, if you are of my mind, I'll have your breakfast ready in a jiffy. Then you will look after our poor dear again till two o'clock. Let me have a list of your people, and I will soon arrange it. You will be free for a fortnight. You can go to bed when I come in, and sleep till night."

So prudent did the proposition seem, that Schmucke then and there agreed to it.

"Not a word to Monsieur Pons; he would think it was all over with him, you know, if we were to tell him in this way that his engagement at the theatre and his lessons are put off. He would be thinking that he should not find his pupils again, poor gentleman—stuff and nonsense! Monsieur Poulain says that we shall save our Benjamin if we keep him as quiet as possible."

"Ach! fery goot! Pring up der preakfast; I shall make der bett, and gif you die attresses! You are right; it vould pe too much for me."

An hour later La Cibot, in her Sunday clothes, departed in great state, to the no small astonishment of the Rémonencqs; she promised herself that she would support the character of confidential servant of the pair of nutcrackers, in the boarding-schools and private families in which they gave music-lessons.

It is needless to repeat all the gossip in which La Cibot indulged on her round. The members of every family, the head-mistress of every boarding-school, were treated to a vari-

19

ation upon the theme of Pons' illness.   A single scene, which
took place in the Illustrious Gaudissart's private room, will
give a sufficient idea of the rest.   La Cibot met with unheard-
of difficulties, but she succeeded in penetrating at last to the
presence.   Kings and cabinet ministers are less difficult of
access than the manager of a theatre in Paris ; nor is it hard
to understand why such prodigious barriers are raised between
them and ordinary mortals: a king has only to defend himself from ambition ; the manager of a theatre has reason to
dread the wounded vanity of actors and authors.

La Cibot, however, struck up an acquaintance with the
portress, and traversed all distances in a brief space.   There
is a sort of freemasonry among the janitor tribe, and, indeed,
among the members of every profession ; for each calling has
its shibboleth, as well as its insulting epithet and the mark
with which it brands its followers.

"Ah ! madame, you are the portress here," began La
Cibot.   " I myself am a janitor, in a small way, in a house
in the Rue de Normandie.   Monsieur Pons, your conductor,
lodges with us.   Oh, how glad I should be to have your
place, and see the actors and dancers and authors go past.
It is the marshal's bâton in our profession, as the old actor
said."

"And how is Monsieur Pons going on, the good man ?"
inquired the portress.

" He is not going on at all ; he has not left his bed these
two months.   He will only leave the house feet foremost, that
is certain."

" He will be missed."

" Yes.   I have come with a message to the manager from
him.   Just try to get me a word with him, dear."

" A lady from Monsieur Pons to see you, sir ! "   After this
fashion did the youth attached to the service of the manager's
office announce Mme. Cibot, whom the portress below had
particularly recommended to his care.

Gaudissart had just come in for a rehearsal. Chance so ordered it that no one wished to speak with him ; actors and authors were alike late. Delighted to have news of his conductor, he made a Napoleonic gesture, and La Cibot was admitted.

The sometime commercial traveler, now the head of a popular theatre, regarded his sleeping partners in the light of a legitimate wife ; they were not informed of all his doings. The flourishing state of his finances had reacted upon his person. Grown big and stout and high-colored with good cheer and prosperity, Gaudissart made no disguise of his transformation into a Mondor.

"We are turning into a city-father," he once said, trying to be the first to laugh.

"You are only in the Turcaret stage yet, though," repeated Bixiou, who often replaced Gaudissart in the company of the leading lady of the ballet, the celebrated Héloïse Brisetout.

The former Illustrious Gaudissart, in fact, was exploiting the theatre simply and solely for his own particular benefit, and with brutal disregard of other interests. He first insinuated himself as collaborator in various ballets, plays, and vaudevilles ; then he waited till the author wanted money and bought up the other half of the copyright. These afterpieces and vaudevilles, always added to successful plays, brought him in a daily harvest of gold coins. He trafficked by proxy in tickets, allotting a certain number to himself, as the manager's share, till he took in this way a tithe of the receipts. And Gaudissart had other methods of making money beside these official contributions. He sold boxes, he took presents from indifferent actresses burning to go upon the stage to fill small speaking parts, or simply to appear as queens, or pages, and the like ; he swelled his nominal third share of the profits to such purpose that the sleeping partners scarcely received one-tenth instead of the remaining two-thirds of the net receipts. Even so, however, the tenth paid

them a dividend of fifteen per cent. on their capital.   On the
strength of that fifteen per cent. Gaudissart talked of his intelligence, honesty, and zeal, and the good fortune of his
partners.   When Count Popinot, showing an interest in the
concern, asked Matifat, or General Gouraud (Matifat's son-
in-law), or Crevel, whether they were satisfied with Gaudissart, Gouraud, now a peer of France, answered: "They say
he robs us; but he is such a clever, good-natured fellow, that
we are quite satisfied."

"This is like La Fontaine's fable," smiled the ex-cabinet
minister.

Gaudissart found investments for his capital in other ven-
tures.   He thought well of Schwab, Brunner, and the Graffs;
that firm was promoting railways, he became a shareholder in
the lines.   His shrewdness was carefully hidden beneath the
frank carelessness of a man of pleasure; he seemed to be interested in nothing but amusements and dress, yet he thought
everything over, and his wide experience of business gained
as a commercial traveler stood him in good stead.

A self-made man, he did not take himself seriously.   He
gave suppers and banquets to celebrities in rooms sumptuously
furnished by the house decorator.   Showy by nature, with a
taste for doing things handsomely, he affected an easy-going
air, and seemed so much the less formidable because he had
kept the slang of "the road" (to use his own expression),
with a few green-room phrases superadded.   Now, artists in
the theatrical profession are wont to express themselves with
some vigor; Gaudissart borrowed sufficient racy green-room
talk to blend with his commercial traveler's lively jocularity,
and passed for a wit.   He was thinking at that moment of
selling his license and "going into another line," as he said.
He thought of being president of a railroad company, of becoming a responsible person and an administrator, and finally
of marrying Mlle. Minard, daughter of the richest mayor in
Paris.   He might hope to get into the Chamber through "his

line," and, with Popinot's influence, to take office under the Government.

"Whom have I the honor of addressing?" inquired Gaudissart, looking magisterially at La Cibot.

"I am Monsieur Pons' confidential servant, sir," answered Mme. Cibot.

"Well, and how is the dear fellow?"

"Ill, sir—very ill."

"The devil he is! I am sorry to hear it—I must come and see him; he is such a man as you don't often find."

"Ah yes! sir, he is a cherub, he is. I have always wondered how he came to be in a theatre."

"Why, madame, the theatre is a house of correction for morals," said Gaudissart. "Poor Pons! Upon my word, one ought to cultivate the species to keep up the stock. 'Tis a pattern man, and has talent too. When will he be able to take his orchestra again, do you think? A theatre, unfortunately, is like a stage-coach: empty or full, it starts at the same time. Here, at six o'clock every evening, up goes the curtain; and if we are never so sorry for ourselves, it won't make good music. Let us see now—how is he?"

La Cibot pulled out her pocket-handkerchief and held it to her eyes.

"It is a terrible thing to say, my dear sir," said she; "but I am afraid we shall lose him, though we are as careful of him as of the apple of our eyes. And, at the same time, I came to say that you must not count on Monsieur Schmucke, worthy man, for he is going to sit up with him at night. One cannot help doing as if there was hope still left, and trying one's best to snatch the dear, good soul from death. But the doctor has given him up——"

"What is the matter with him?"

"He is dying of grief, jaundice, and liver complaint, with a lot of family affairs to complicate matters."

"And a doctor as well," said Gaudissart. "He ought to

have had Lebrun, our doctor; it would have cost him nothing.''

"Monsieur Pons' doctor is a Providence on earth. But what can a doctor do, no matter how clever he is, with such complications !''

"I wanted the good pair of nutcrackers badly for the accompaniment of my new fairy piece.''

"Is it anything that I can do for them?'' asked La Cibot, and her expression would have done credit to a Jocrisse.

Gaudissart burst out laughing.

"I am their housekeeper, sir, and do many things my gentlemen——'' She did not finish her speech, for in the middle of Gaudissart's roar of laughter a woman's voice exclaimed, "If you are laughing, old man, one may come in," and the leading lady of the ballet rushed into the room and flung herself upon the only sofa. The new-comer was Héloïse Brisetout, with a splendid *algérienne,* as such scarfs used to be called, about her shoulders.

"Who is amusing you? Is it this lady? What post does she want ?'' asked this nymph, giving the manager such a glance as artist gives artist, a glance that would make a subject for a picture.

Héloïse, a young woman of exceedingly literary tastes, was on intimate terms with great and famous artists in bohemia. Elegant, accomplished, and graceful, she was more intelligent than dancers usually are. As she put her question, she sniffed at a scent-bottle full of some aromatic perfume.

"One fine woman is as good as another, madame; and if I don't sniff the pestilence out of a scent-bottle, nor daub brick-dust on my cheeks——''

"That would be a sinful waste, child, when Nature put it on for you to begin with,'' said Héloïse, with a side-glance at her manager.

"I am an honest woman——''

"So much the worse for you. It is not every one by a

long chalk that can find some one to keep them, and kept I
am, and in slap-up style, madame."

"So much the worse! What do you mean? Oh, you may
toss your head and go about in scarfs, you will never have
as many declarations as *I* have had, missus. You will never
match the *Belle Écaillère* of the Cadran Bleu."

Héloïse Brisetout rose at once to her feet, stood at attention,
and made a military salute, like a soldier who meets his
general.

"What?" asked Gaudissart, "are you really *La Belle
Écaillère* of whom my father used to talk?"

"In that case the cachucha and the polka were after your
time; and madame has passed her fiftieth year," remarked
Héloïse, and, striking an attitude, she declaimed, "'Cinna,
let us be friends.'"

"Come, Héloïse, come, the lady is not up to this; let her
alone."

"Madame is perhaps the New Héloïse," suggested La Cibot,
with sly innocence.

"Not bad, old lady!" cried Gaudissart.

"It is a venerable joke," said the dancer, "a grizzled pun;
find us another old lady—or take a cigarette."

"I beg your pardon, madame, I feel too unhappy to answer
you; my two gentlemen are very ill; and, to buy nourishment
for them and to spare them trouble, I have pawned everything
down to my husband's clothes that I pledged this morning.
Here is the ticket!"

"Oh! here, the affair is becoming tragic," cried the fair
Héloïse. "What is it all about?"

"Madame drops down upon us like——"

"Like a dancer," said Héloïse; "let me prompt you,
missus!"

"Come, I am busy," said Gaudissart. "The joke has
gone far enough. Héloïse, this is Monsieur Pons' confidential
servant; she has come to tell me that I must not count upon

him; our poor conductor is not expected to live. I don't know what to do.''

"Oh! poor man; why, he must have a benefit.''

"It would ruin him,'' said Gaudissart. "He might find next day that he owed five hundred francs to charitable institutions, and they refuse to admit that there are any sufferers in Paris except their own. No, look here, my good woman, since you are going in for the Montyon prize——''

He broke off, rang the bell, and the youth before mentioned suddenly appeared.

"Tell the cashier to send me up a thousand-franc bill. Sit down, madame.''

"Ah! poor woman, look, she is crying!'' exclaimed Héloïse. "How stupid! There, there, mother, we will go to see him; don't cry. I say, now,'' she continued, taking the manager into a corner, "you want to make me take the leading part in the ballet in 'Ariane,' you Turk. You are going to be married, and you know how I can make you miserable——''

"Héloïse, my heart is copper-bottomed like a man-of-war.''

"I shall bring your children on the scene! I will borrow some somewhere.''

"I have owned up about the attachment.''

"Do be nice, and give Pons' post to Garangeot; he has talent, poor fellow, and he has not a penny; and I promise peace.''

"But wait till Pons is dead, in case the good man may come back again.''

"Oh, as to that, no, sir,'' said La Cibot. "He began to wander in his mind last night, and now he is delirious. It will soon be over, unfortunately.''

"At any rate, take Garangeot as a stop-gap!'' pleaded Héloïse. "He has the whole press on his side——''

Just at that moment the cashier came in with a bill for a thousand francs in his hand.

"Give it to madame here," said Gaudissart. "Good-day, my good woman; take good care of the dear man, and tell him that I am coming to see him to-morrow, or some time— as soon as I can, in short."

"A drowning man," said Héloïse.*

"Ah, sir, hearts like yours are only found in a theatre. May God bless you!"

"To what account shall I post this item?" asked the cashier.

"I will countersign the order. Post it to the bonus account."

Before La Cibot went out, she made Mlle. Brisetout a fine curtsey, and heard Gaudissart remark to his mistress—

"Can Garangeot do the dance-music for the 'Mohicans' in twelve days? If he helps me out of my predicament he shall have Pons' place."

La Cibot had cut off the incomes of the two friends, she had left them without means of subsistence if Pons should chance to recover, and was better rewarded for all this mischief than for any good that she had done. In a few days' time her treacherous trick would bring about the desired result —Élie Magus would have his coveted pictures. But if this first spoliation was to be effected, La Cibot must throw dust in Fraisier's eyes, and lull the suspicions of that terrible fellow-conspirator of her own seeking; and Élie Magus and Rémonencq must be bound over to secrecy.

As for Rémonencq, he had gradually come to feel such a passion as uneducated people can conceive when they come to Paris from the depths of the country, bringing with them all the fixed ideas bred of the solitary country life; all the ignorance of a primitive nature, all the brute appetites that become so many fixed ideas. Mme. Cibot's masculine beauty, her vivacity, her market-woman's wit, had all been remarked by the marine-store-dealer. He thought at first of taking La

* A former mistress of Celestin Crevel. See "Cousin Betty."

Cibot from her husband, bigamy among the lower classes in Paris being much more common than is generally supposed ; but greed was like a slip-knot drawn more and more tightly about his heart, till reason at length was stifled. When Rémonencq computed that the commission paid by himself and Élie Magus amounted to about forty thousand francs, he determined to have La Cibot for his legitimate spouse, and his thoughts turned from a misdemeanor to a crime. A romantic purely speculative dream, persistently followed through a tobacco-smoker's long musings as he lounged in the doorway, had brought him to the point of wishing that the little tailor were dead. At a stroke he beheld his capital trebled ; and then he thought of La Cibot. What a good saleswoman she would be ! What a handsome figure she would make in a magnificent store on the boulevards ! The twofold covetousness turned Rémonencq's head. In fancy he took a store that he knew of on the Boulevard de la Madeleine, he stocked it with Pons' treasures, and then—after dreaming his dream in sheets of gold, after seeing millions in the blue spiral wreaths that rose from his pipe, he awoke to find himself face to face with the little tailor. Cibot was sweeping the yard, the doorstep, and the pavement just as his neighbor was taking down the shutters and displaying his wares ; for since Pons fell ill, La Cibot's work had fallen to her husband.

The Auvergnat began to look upon the little, swarthy, stunted, copper-colored tailor as the one obstacle in his way, and pondered how to be rid of him. Meanwhile, this growing passion made La Cibot very proud, for she had reached an age when a woman begins to understand that she may grow old.

So early one morning, she meditatively watched Rémonencq as he arranged his odds and ends for sale. She wondered how far his love could go. He came across to her.

" Well," he said, " are things going as you wish ? "

" It is you who make me uneasy," said La Cibot. " I

shall be talked about; the neighbors will see you making sheep's eyes at me."

She left the doorway and dived into the Auvergnat's back store.

"What a notion!" said Rémonencq.

"Come here, I have something to say to you," said La Cibot. "Monsieur Pons' heirs are about to make a stir; they are capable of giving us a lot of trouble. God knows what might come of it if they send the lawyers here to poke their noses into the affair like hunting-dogs. I cannot get Monsieur Schmucke to sell a few pictures unless you like me well enough to keep the secret—such a secret! With your head on the block, you must not say where the pictures come from, nor who it was that sold them. When Monsieur Pons is once dead and buried, you understand, nobody will know how many pictures there ought to be; if there are fifty-three pictures instead of sixty-seven, nobody will be any the wiser. Beside, if Monsieur Pons sold them himself while he was alive, nobody can find fault."

"No," agreed Rémonencq, "it is all one to me, but Monsieur Élie Magus will want receipts in due form."

"And you shall have your receipt too, bless your life! Do you suppose that *I* should write them? No, Monsieur Schmucke will do that.

"But tell your Jew that he must keep the secret as closely as you do," she continued.

"We will be as mute as fishes. That is our business. I myself can read, but I cannot write, and that is why I want a capable wife that has had education like you. I have thought of nothing but earning my bread all my days, and now I wish I had some little Rémonencqs. Do leave that Cibot of yours."

"Why, here comes your Jew," said the portress; "we can arrange the whole business."

Élie Magus came every third day very early in the morning to know when he could buy his pictures. "Well, my dear lady," said he, "how are we getting on?"

"Has nobody been to speak to you about Monsieur Pons and his gimcracks?" asked La Cibot.

"I received a letter from a lawyer," said Élie Magus, "a rascal that seems to me to be trying to make work for himself; I don't like people of that sort, so I took no notice of his letter. Three days afterward he came to see me, and left his card. I told my porter that I am never at home when he calls."

"You are a love of a Jew," said La Cibot. Little did she know Élie Magus' prudence. "Well, sonnies, in a few days' time I will bring Monsieur Schmucke to the point of selling you seven or eight pictures, ten at most. But on two conditions. Absolute secrecy in the first place. Monsieur Schmucke will send for you, sir, is not that so? And Monsieur Rémonencq suggested that you might be a purchaser, eh? And, come what may, I will not meddle in it for nothing. You are giving forty-six thousand francs for four pictures, are you not?"

"So be it," groaned the Jew.

"Very good. This is the second condition. You will give me *forty-three* thousand francs, and pay three thousand only to Monsieur Schmucke; Rémonencq will buy four for two thousand francs, and hand over the surplus to me. But, at the same time, you see, my dear Monsieur Magus, I am going to help you and Rémonencq to a splendid bit of business—on condition that the profits are shared among the three of us. I will introduce you to that lawyer, as he, no doubt, will come here. You shall make a valuation of Monsieur Pons' things at the prices which you can give for them, so that Monsieur Fraisier may know how much the property is worth. But—not until after our sale, you understand!"

"I understand," said the Jew, "but it takes time to look at the things and value them."

"You shall have half a day. But, there, that is my affair. Talk it over between yourselves, my boys, and for that matter the business will be settled by the day after to-morrow. I will go round to speak to this Fraisier; for Dr. Poulain tells tells him everything that goes on in the house, and it is a great bother to keep that scarecrow quiet."

La Cibot met Fraisier halfway between the Rue de la Perle and the Rue de Normandie; so impatient was he to know the "elements of the case" (to use his own expression), that he was coming to see her.

"I say! I was going to you," said she.

Fraisier grumbled because Élie Magus had refused to see him. But La Cibot extinguished the spark of distrust that gleamed in the lawyer's eyes by informing him that Élie Magus had returned from a journey, and that she would arrange for an interview in Pons' rooms and for the valuation of the property; for the day after to-morrow at latest.

"Deal frankly with me," returned Fraisier. "It is more than probable that I shall act for Monsieur Pons' next-of-kin. In that case, I shall be even better able to serve you."

The words were spoken so drily that La Cibot quaked. This starving limb of the law was sure to manœuvre on his side as she herself was doing. She resolved forthwith to hurry on the sale of the pictures.

La Cibot was right. The doctor and lawyer had clubbed together to buy a new suit of clothes in which Fraisier could decently present himself before Mme. la Presidente Camusot de Marville. Indeed, if the clothes had been ready, the interview would have taken place sooner, for the fate of the couple hung upon its issues. Fraisier left Mme. Cibot and went to try on his new clothes. He found them waiting for him, went home, adjusted his new wig, and toward ten o'clock that morning set out in a carriage from a livery stable for the Rue de Hanovre, hoping for an audience. In his white tie, yellow gloves, and new wig, redolent of Portugal water, he looked something like a poisonous essence kept in a cut-glass bottle, seeming but the more deadly because everything about it is daintily neat, from the stopper covered with white kid to the label and the thread. His peremptory manner, the eruption on his blotched countenance, the green eyes, and a malignant something about him—all these things struck the beholder with the same sense of surprise as storm-clouds in a blue sky. If in his private office, as he showed himself to La Cibot, he was the common knife that a murderer catches up for his crime—now, at the presidente's door, he was the daintily wrought dagger which a woman sets among the ornaments of her whatnot.

A great change had taken place in the Rue de Hanovre. The Count and Countess Popinot and the young people would not allow the president and his wife to leave the house that they had settled upon their daughter to pay rent elsewhere. M. and Mme. la Presidente, therefore, were installed on the third floor, now left at liberty, for the elderly lady had made up her mind to end her days in the country.

Mme. Camusot took Madeleine Vivet, with her cook and her manservant, to the third floor, and would have been as much pinched for money as in the early days, if the house had not been rent-free, and the president's salary increased to ten thousand francs. This *aurea mediocritas* was but little satisfactory to Mme. de Marville. Even now she wished for means more in accordance with her ambitions; for when she handed over their fortune to their daughter, she spoiled her husband's prospects. Now Amélie had set her heart upon seeing her husband in the Chamber of Deputies; she was not one of those women who find it easy to give up their way; and she by no means despaired of returning her husband for the arrondissement in which Marville is situated. So for the past two months she had teased her father-in-law, M. le Baron Camusot (for the new peer of France had been advanced to that rank), and done her utmost to extort an advance of a hundred thousand francs of the inheritance which one day would be theirs. She wanted, she said, to buy a small estate worth about two thousand francs per annum set like a wedge within the Marville lands. There she and her husband would be near their children and in their own house, while the addition would round out the Marville property. With that the presidente laid stress upon the recent sacrifices which she and her husband had been compelled to make in order to marry Cécile to Viscount Popinot, and asked the old man how he could bar his eldest son's way to the highest honors of the magistracy, when such honors were only to be had by those who made themselves a strong position in parliament. Her husband would know how to take up such a position, he would make himself feared by those in office, and so on and so on. "They do nothing for you unless you tighten a halter round their necks to loosen their tongues," said she. "They are ungrateful. What do they not owe to Camusot! Camusot brought the House of Orleans to the throne by enforcing the ordinances of July."

M. Camusot senior answered that he had gone out of his depth in railway speculations. He quite admitted that it was necessary to come to the rescue, but put off the day until shares should rise, as they were expected to do.

This half-promise, extracted some few days before Fraisier's visit, had plunged the presidente into depths of affliction. It was doubtful whether the ex-proprietor of Marville was eligible for reëlection without the land qualification.

Fraisier found no difficulty in obtaining speech of Madeleine Vivet ; such viper natures own their kinship at once.

"I should like to see Madame la Presidente for a few moments, mademoiselle," Fraisier said in bland accents; "I have come on a matter of business which touches her fortune ; it is a question of a legacy, be sure you mention that. I have not the honor of being known to Madame la Presidente, so my name is of no consequence. I am not in the habit of leaving my chambers, but I know the respect that is due to a president's wife, and I took the trouble of coming myself to save all possible delay."

The matter thus broached, when repeated and amplified by the waiting-maid, naturally brought a favorable answer. It was a decisive moment for the double ambition hidden in Fraisier's mind. Bold as a petty provincial attorney, sharp, rough-spoken, and curt as he was, he felt as captains feel before the decisive battle of a campaign. As he went into the little drawing-room where Amélie was waiting for him, he felt a slight perspiration breaking out upon his forehead and down his back. Every sudorific hitherto employed had failed to produce this result upon a skin which horrible diseases had left impervious. "Even if I fail to make my fortune," said he to himself, "I shall recover. Poulain said that if I could only perspire I should recover."

The presidente came forward in her morning gown.

"Madame——" said Fraisier, stopping short to bow with the humility by which officials recognize the superior rank of the person whom they address.

"Take a seat, monsieur," said the presidente. She saw at a glance that this was a man of law.

"Madame la Presidente, if I take the liberty of calling your attention to a matter which concerns Monsieur le President, it is because I am sure that Monsieur de Marville, occupying, as he does, a high position, would leave matters to take their natural course, and so lose seven or eight hundred thousand francs, a sum which ladies (who, in my opinion, have a far better understanding of private business than the best of magistrates)—a sum which ladies, I repeat, would by no means despise——"

"You spoke of a legacy," interrupted the lady, dazzled by the wealth and anxious to hide her surprise. Amélie de Marville, like an impatient novel-reader, wanted the end of the story.

"Yes, madame, a legacy that you are like to lose; yes,

to lose altogether; but I can, that is, I *could* recover it for you, if——"

"Speak out, monsieur." Mme. de Marville spoke frigidly, scanning Fraisier as she spoke with a sagacious eye.

"Madame, your eminent capacity is known to me; I was once at Mantes. Monsieur Lebœuf, president of the Tribunal, is acquainted with Monsieur de Marville, and can answer inquiries about me——"

The presidente's shrug was so ruthlessly significant that Fraisier was compelled to make short work of his parenthetic discourse.

"So distinguished a woman will at once understand why I speak of myself in the first place. It is the shortest way to the property."

To this acute observation the lady replied by a gesture. Fraisier took the sign for a permission to continue.

"I was an attorney, madame, at Mantes. My connection was all the fortune that I was likely to have. I took over Monsieur Levroux's practice. You knew him, no doubt?"

The presidente inclined her head.

"With borrowed capital and some ten thousand francs of my own, I went to Mantes. I had been with Desroches, one of the cleverest attorneys in Paris; I had been his head-clerk for six years. I was so unlucky as to make an enemy of the attorney for the crown at Mantes, Monsieur——"

"Olivier Vinet."

"Son of the attorney-general, yes, madame. He was paying his court to a little person——"

"Whom?"

"Madame Vatinelle."

"Oh! Madame Vatinelle. She was very pretty and very —er—when I was there——"

"She was not unkind to me: *inde iræ*," Fraisier continued. "I was industrious; I wanted to repay my friends and to marry; I wanted work; I went in search of it; and before

20

long I had more on my hands than anybody else.   Bah ! I
had every soul in Mantes against me—attorneys, notaries, and
even the bailiffs.   They tried to fasten a quarrel on me.   In
our ruthless profession, as you know, madame, if you wish to
ruin a man, it is soon done.   I was concerned for both parties
in a case, and they found it out.   It was a trifle irregular ; but
it is sometimes done in Paris, attorneys in certain cases hand
the rhubarb and take the senna.   They do things differently
at Mantes.   I had done Monsieur Bouyonnet this little service
before ; but, egged on by his colleagues and the attorneys for
the crown, he betrayed me.   I am keeping back nothing, you
see.   There was a great hue and cry about it.   I was a scoundrel ; they made me out blacker than Marat ; forced me to
sell out ; ruined me.   And I am in Paris now.   I have tried
to get together a practice ; but my health is so bad that I
have only two quiet hours out of the twenty-four.

"At this moment I have but one ambition, and a very
small one.   Some day," he continued, " you will be the wife
of the keeper of the seals, or of the home secretary, it may
be ; but I, poor and sickly as I am, desire nothing but a post
in which I can live in peace for the rest of my life, a place
without any opening in which to vegetate.   I should like to
be a justice of the peace in Paris.   It would be a mere trifle
to you and Monsieur le President to gain the appointment for
me ; for the present keeper of the seals must be anxious to
keep on good terms with you——

"And that is not all, madame," added Fraisier.   Seeing
that Mme. de Marville was about to speak, he cut her short
with a gesture.   " I have a friend, the doctor in attendance
on the old man who ought to leave his property to Monsieur
le President.   (We are coming to the point, you see.)   The
doctor's coöperation is indispensable, and the doctor is precisely in my position : he has abilities, he is unlucky.   I
learned through him how far your interests were imperiled ;
for, even as I speak, all may be over, and the will disinheriting

Monsieur le President may have been made. The doctor wishes to be head-surgeon of a hospital or of a Government school. He must have a position in Paris equal to mine—— Pardon me if I have enlarged on a matter so delicate ; but we must have no misunderstandings in this business. The doctor is, beside, much respected and learned ; he saved the life of the Comtesse Popinot's great-uncle, Monsieur Pillerault.

"Now, if you are so good as to promise these two posts— the appointment of justice of the peace and the sinecure for my friend—I will undertake to bring you the property, *almost* intact. Almost intact, I say, for the coöperation of the legatee and of several other persons is absolutely indispensable, and some obligations will be incurred. You will not redeem your promises until I have fulfilled mine."

The presidente had folded her arms, and for the last minute or two sat like a person compelled to listen to a sermon. Now she unfolded her arms, and looked at Fraisier as she said : "Monsieur, all that you say concerning your interests has the merit of clearness ; but my own interests in the matter are by no means so clear——"

"A word or two will explain everything, madame. Monsieur le President is Monsieur Pons' first cousin once removed, and his sole heir. Monsieur Pons is very ill ; he is about to make his will, if it is not made already, in favor of a German, a friend of his named Schmucke ; and he has more than seven hundred thousand francs to leave. I hope to have an accurate valuation made in two or three days——"

"If this is so," said the presidente, "I made a great mistake in quarreling with him and throwing the blame——" she thought aloud, amazed by the possibility of such a sum.

"No, madame. If there had been no rupture, he would be as blithe as a lark at this moment, and might outlive you and Monsieur le President and me. The ways of Providence are mysterious, let us not seek to fathom them," he added, to palliate to some extent the hideous idea. "It cannot be helped. We men of business look at the practical aspects of things. Now you see clearly, madame, that Monsieur de Marville in his public position would do nothing, and could do nothing, as things are. He has broken off all relations with his cousin. You see nothing now of Pons; you have forbidden him the house; you had excellent reasons, no doubt, for doing as you did, but the old man is ill, and he is leaving his property to the only friend left to him. A president of the Court of Appeals in Paris could say nothing under such circumstances if the will was made out in due form. But between ourselves, madame, when one has a right to expect seven or eight hundred thousand francs—or a million, it may be (how should I know?)—it is very unpleasant to have it slip through one's fingers, especially if one happens to be the heir-at-law. But, on the other hand, to prevent this, one is obliged to stoop to dirty work; work so difficult, so ticklish, bringing you cheek by jowl with such low people, servants and subordinates; and into such close contact with them, too, that no barrister, no attorney in Paris could take up such a case.

"What you want is a briefless barrister like me," said he, "a man who should have real and solid ability, who has learned to be devoted, and yet, being in a precarious position, is brought temporarily to a level with such people. In my arrondissement I undertake business for small tradespeople and working folk. Yes, madame, you see the straits to which I have been brought by the enmity of an attorney for the crown, now a deputy public prosecutor in Paris, who could not forgive me my superiority. I know you, madame, I know that your influence means a solid certainty; and in such a service rendered to you, I saw the end of my troubles and success for my friend Dr. Poulain."

The lady sat pensive during a moment of unspeakable torture for Fraisier. Vinet, an orator of the Centre, attorney-general (*procureur-général*) for the past sixteen years, nominated half-a-score of times for the chancellorship, the father, moreover, of the attorney for the crown at Mantes who had been appointed to a post in Paris within the last year—Vinet was an enemy and a rival for the malignant presidente. The haughty attorney-general did not hide his contempt for President Camusot. This fact Fraisier did not know, and could not know.

"Have you nothing on your conscience but the fact that you were concerned for both parties?" asked she, looking steadfastly at Fraisier.

"Madame la Presidente can see Monsieur Lebœuf; he was favorable to me."

"Do you feel sure that Monsieur Lebœuf will give Monsieur de Marville and Monsieur le Comte Popinot' a good account of you?"

"I will answer for it, especially now that Monsieur Oliver Vinet has left Mantes; for between ourselves, good Monsieur Lebœuf was afraid of that crabbed little official. If you will permit me, Madame la Presidente, I will go to Mantes and see Monsieur Lebœuf. No time will be lost, for I cannot be certain of the precise value of the property for two or three days. I do not wish that you should know all the ins and outs of this affair; you ought not to know them, Madame la Presidente, but is not the reward that I expect for my complete devotion a pledge of my success?"

"Very well. If Monsieur Lebœuf will speak in your favor, and if the property is worth as much as you think (I doubt it myself), you shall have both appointments, *if* you succeed, mind you——"

"I will answer for it, madame. Only, you must be so good as to have your notary and your attorney here when I shall need them; you must give me a power of attorney to act for Monsieur le President, and tell those gentlemen to follow my instructions, and to do nothing on their own responsibility."

"The responsibility rests with you," the presidente answered solemnly, "so you ought to have full powers. But is Monsieur Pons very ill?" she asked, smiling.

"Upon my word, madame, he might pull through, especially with so conscientious a doctor as Poulain in attendance; for this friend of mine, madame, is simply an unconscious spy directed by me in your interests. Left to himself, he would save the old man's life; but there is some one else by the sick-bed, a portress, who would push him into his grave for thirty thousand francs. Not that she would kill him outright; she will not give him arsenic, she is not so merciful; she will do worse, she will kill him by inches, she will worry him to death day by day. If the poor old man were kept quiet and left in peace; if he were taken into the country and cared for and made much of by friends, he would get well again; but he is harassed by a sort of Madame Évrard. When the woman was young she was one of thirty *Belles Écaillères*, famous in Paris; she is a rough, greedy, gossiping woman; she torments him to make a will and to leave her something handsome, and the end of it will be induration of the liver; calculi are possibly forming at this moment, and he has not strength to bear an operation. The doctor, noble soul, is in a horrible predicament. He really ought to send the woman away——"

"Why, then, this vixen is a monster!" cried the lady in thin flute-like tones.

Fraisier smiled inwardly at the likeness between himself and the terrible presidente; he knew all about those suave modulations of a naturally sharp voice. He thought of another president, the hero of an anecdote related by Louis XI., stamped by that monarch's final phrase. Blessed with a wife after the pattern of Socrates' spouse, and ungifted with the sage's philosophy, he mingled salt with the corn in the mangers and forbade the grooms to give water to the horses. As his wife rode out along the Seine toward their country-house, the animals bolted into the river with the lady, and the magistrate returned thanks to Providence for ridding him of his wife " in so natural a manner." At this present moment Mme. de Marville thanked heaven for placing at Pons' bedside a woman so likely to get him " decently " out of the way.

Aloud she said, " I would not take a million at the price of a single scruple. Your friend ought to speak to Monsieur Pons and have the woman sent away."

" In the first place, madame, Messrs. Schmucke and Pons think the woman an angel; they would send my friend away. And, secondly, the doctor lies under an obligation to this horrid oyster-woman; she called him in to attend Monsieur Pillerault. When he tells her to be as gentle as possible with the patient, he simply shows the creature how to make matters worse."

" What does your friend think of *my* cousin's condition?"

This man's clear, business-like way of putting the facts of the case frightened Mme. de Marville; she felt that his keen gaze read the thoughts of a heart as greedy as La Cibot's own.

" In six weeks the property will change hands."

The presidente dropped her eyes.

" Poor man ! " she sighed, vainly striving after a dolorous expression.

" Have you any message, madame, for Monsieur Lebœuf? I am taking the train to Mantes."

" Yes. Wait a moment, and I will write asking him to dine with us to-morrow. I want to see him, so that we may act in concert to repair the injustice to which you have fallen a victim."

The presidente left the room. Fraisier saw himself a justice of the peace. He felt transformed at the thought ; he grew stouter ; his lungs were filled with the breath of success, the breeze of prosperity. He dipped into the mysterious reservoirs

of volition for fresh and strong doses of the divine essence.
To reach success, he felt, as Rémonencq had felt, that he was
ready for anything, for crime itself, provided that no proofs
of it remained. He had faced the presidente boldly ; he had
transmuted conjecture into reality ; he had made assertions
right and left, all to the end that she might authorize him to
protect her interests and win her influence. As he stood
there, he represented the infinite misery of two lives, and the
no less boundless desires of two men. He spurned the squalid
horrors of the Rue de la Perle. He saw the glitter of a thousand crowns in fees from La Cibot, and five thousand francs
from the presidente. This meant an abode such as befitted
his future prospects. Finally, he was repaying Dr. Poulain.

There are hard, ill-natured beings, goaded by distress or
disease into active malignity, that yet entertain diametrically
opposed sentiments with a like degree of vehemence. If Richelieu was a good hater, he was no less a good friend. Fraisier,
in his gratitude, would have let himself be cut in two for
Poulain.

So absorbed was he in these visions of a comfortable and
prosperous life that he did not see the presidente come in with
the letter in her hand, and she, looking at him, thought him
less ugly now than at first. He was about to be useful to her,
and as soon as a tool belongs to us we look upon it with other
eyes.

" Monsieur Fraisier," said she, " you have convinced me
of your intelligence, and I think that you can speak
frankly."

Fraisier replied by an eloquent gesture.

" Very well," continued the lady, " I must ask you to give
a candid reply to this question : Are we, either of us, Monsieur de Marville or I, likely to be compromised, directly or
indirectly, by your action in this matter ? "

" I would not have come to you, madame if I thought that
some day I should have to reproach myself for bringing so

much as a splash of mud upon you, for in your position a speck the size of a pin's head is seen by all the world. You forget, madame, that I must satisfy you if I am to be a justice of the peace in Paris. I have received one lesson at the outset of my life; it was so sharp that I do not care to lay myself open to a second thrashing. To sum it up in a last word, madame, I will not take a step in which you are directly involved without previously consulting you——''

'' Very good. Here is the letter. And now I shall expect to be informed of the exact value of the estate.''

'' There is the whole matter,'' said Fraisier shrewdly, making his bow to the presidente with as much graciousness as his countenance could exhibit.

'' What a providence!'' thought Mme. Camusot de Marville. '' So I am to be rich! Camusot will be sure of his election if we let loose this Fraisier upon the Bolbec constituency. What a tool!''

'' What a providence!'' Fraisier said to himself as he descended the staircase; '' and what a sharp woman Madame Camusot is! I should want a woman in these circumstances. Now to work!''

And he departed for Mantes to gain the good graces of a man he scarcely knew; but he counted upon Mme. Vatinelle, to whom, unfortunately, he owed all his troubles—and some troubles are of a kind that resemble a protested bill while the defaulter is yet solvent, in that they bear interest.

Three days afterward, while Schmucke slept (for in accordance with the compact he now sat up at night with the patient), La Cibot had a '' tiff,'' as she was pleased to call it, with Pons. It will not be out of place to call attention to one particularly distressing symptom of liver complaint. The sufferer is always more or less inclined to impatience and fits of anger; an outburst of this kind seems to give relief at the time, much as a patient while the fever fit is upon him feels that he has boundless strength; but collapse sets in so soon as the excitement passes off, and the full extent of mischief sustained by the system is discernible. This is especially the case when the disease has been induced by some great shock; and the prostration is so much the more dangerous because the patient is kept upon a restricted diet. It is a kind of fever affecting neither the blood nor the brain, but the humoristic mechanism, fretting the whole system, producing melancholy, in which the patient hates himself; in such a crisis anything may cause dangerous irritation.

In spite of all that the doctor could say, La Cibot had no belief in this wear and tear of the nervous system by the humoristic. She was a woman of the people, without experience or education; Dr. Poulain's explanations for her were simply "doctors' notions." Like most of her class, she thought that sick people must be fed, and nothing short of Dr. Poulain's direct order prevented her from administering ham, a nice omelette, or vanilla chocolate upon the sly.

"Give Monsieur Pons one single mouthful of any solid food whatsoever, and you will kill him as surely as if you put a bullet through him," he said.

The infatuation of the working-classes on this point is very strong. The reason of their reluctance to enter a hospital is the idea that they will be starved there. The mortality caused by the food smuggled in by the wives of patients on visiting-days was at one time so great that the doctors were obliged to institute a very strict search for contraband provisions.

If La Cibot was to realize her profits at once, a momentary quarrel must be worked up in some way. She began by telling Pons about her visit to the theatre, not omitting her passage of arms with Mlle. Héloïse the dancer.

"But why did you go?" the invalid asked for the third time. La Cibot once launched on a stream of words, he was powerless to stop her.

"So, then, when I had given her a piece of my mind, Mademoiselle Héloïse saw who I was and knuckled under, and we were the best of friends. And now do you ask me why I went?" she added, repeating Pons' question.

There are certain babblers, babblers of genius are they, who sweep up interruptions, objections, and observations in this way as they go along, by way of provision to swell the matter of their conversation, as if that source were ever in any danger of running dry.

"Why I went?" repeated she. "I went to get your Monsieur Gaudissart out of a fix. He wants some music for a ballet, and you are hardly fit to scribble on sheets of paper and do your work, dearie. So I understood, things being so, that à Monsieur Garangeot was to be asked to set the 'Mohicans' to music——"

"Garangeot!" roared Pons in fury. "*Garangeot!* a man with no talent; I would not have him for first violin! He is very clever, he is very good at musical criticism, but as to composing—I doubt it! And what the devil put the notion of going to the theatre into your head?"

"How confoundedly contrairy the man is! Look here, dearie, we mustn't boil over like milk on the fire! How are you to write music in the state that you are in? Why, you can't have looked at yourself in the glass! Will you have the glass and see? You are nothing but skin and bone—you are as weak as a sparrow, and do you think that you are fit to make your notes? why, you would not so much as make out mine. And that reminds me that I ought to go up to the fourth-floor lodger's that owes us seventeen francs; it is worth going to fetch is seventeen francs, for when the chemist has been paid we shall not have twenty left. So I had to tell le Gaudissart (I like that name), a good sort he seems to be—a regular Roger Bontemps that would just suit me. *He* will never have liver complaint! Well, so I had to tell him how you were. Lord! you are not well, and he has put some one else in your place for a bit——"

"Some one else in my place!" cried Pons in a terrible

voice, as he sat upright in bed.   Sick people, generally speaking, and those more particularly who lie within the sweep of the scythe of Death, cling to their places with the same passionate energy that the beginner displays to gain a start in life.   To hear that some one had taken his place was like a foretaste of death to the dying man.

"Why, the doctor told me that I was going on as well as possible," continued he; "he said that I should soon be about again as usual.   You have killed me, ruined me, murdered me!"

"Tut, tut, tut!" cried La Cibot, "there you go!   I am killing you, am I?   Mercy on us! these are the pretty things that you are always telling Monsieur Schmucke when my back is turned.   I hear all that you say, that I do! You are a monster of ingratitude."

" But you do not know that if I am only away for another fortnight they will tell me that I have had my day, that I am old-fashioned, out of date, Empire, rococo, when I go back. Garangeot will have made friends all over the theatre, high and low.   He will lower the pitch to suit some actress that cannot sing, he will lick Monsieur Gaudissart's boots!" cried the sick man, who clung to life.   "He has friends that will praise him in all the newspapers; and when things are like that in such a shop, Madame Cibot, they can find holes in anybody's coat.   What fiend drove you to do it?"

"Why! plague take it, Monsieur Schmucke talked it over with me for a week.   What would you have?   You see nothing but yourself!   You are so selfish that other people may die if you can only get better.   Why, poor Monsieur Schmucke has been tired out this month past! he is tied by the leg, he can go nowhere, he cannot give lessons nor take his place at the theatre.   Do you really see nothing?   He sits up with you at night, and I take the nursing in the day. If I were to sit up at night with you, as I tried to do at first when I thought you were so poor, I should have to sleep all day. And who would see to the house and look out for squalls! Illness is illness, it cannot be helped, and here are you——"

"This was not Schmucke's idea, it is quite impossible——"

"That means that it was *I* who took it into my head to do it, does it? Do you think that we are made of iron? Why, if Monsieur Schmucke had given seven or eight lessons every day and conducted the orchestra every evening at the theatre from six o'clock till half-past eleven at night, he would have died in ten days' time. Poor man, he would give his life for you, and do you want to be the death of him? By the authors of my days, I have never seen a sick man to match you! Where are your senses? have you put them in pawn? We are all slaving our lives out for you; we do all for the best, and you are not satisfied! Do you want to drive us raging mad? I myself, to begin with, am tired out as it is——"

La Cibot rattled on at her ease; Pons was too angry to say a word. He writhed on his bed, painfully uttering inarticulate sounds; the blow was killing him. And at this point, as usual, the scolding turned suddenly to tenderness. The nurse dashed at her patient, grasped him by the head, made him lie down by main force, and dragged the blankets over him.

"How any one can get into such a state!" exclaimed she. "After all, it is your illness, dearie. That is what good Monsieur Poulain says. See now, keep quiet and be good, my dear little sonny. Everybody that comes near you worships you, and the doctor himself comes to see you twice a day. What would he say if he found you in such a way? You put me out of all patience; you ought not to behave like this. If you have Ma'am Cibot to nurse you, you should treat her better. You shout and you talk!—you ought not to do it, you know that. Talking irritates you. And why do you fly into a passion? The wrong is all on your side; you are always bothering me. Look here, let us have it out! If Monsieur Schmucke and I, who love you like our life, thought that we were doing right—well, my cherub, it was right, you may be sure."

"Schmucke never could have told you to go to the theatre without speaking to me about it——"

"And must I wake him, poor dear, when he is sleeping like one of the blest, and call him in as witness?"

"No, no!" cried Pons. "If my kind and loving Schmucke made the resolution, perhaps I am worse than I thought." His eyes wandered round the room, dwelling on the beautiful things in it with a melancholy look painful to see.

"So I must say good-by to my dear pictures, to all the things that have come to be like so many friends to me—and to my divine friend Schmucke? Oh! can it be true?"

La Cibot, acting her heartless comedy, held her handkerchief to her eyes; and at that mute response the sufferer fell to dark musings—so sorely stricken was he by the double stab dealt to health and his interests by the loss of his post and the near prospect of death that he had no strength left for anger. He lay, ghastly and wan, like a consumptive patient after a wrestling bout with the Destroyer.

"In Monsieur Schmucke's interests, you see, you would do well to send for Monsieur Trognon; he is the notary of the quarter and a very good man," said La Cibot, seeing that her victim was completely exhausted.

"You are always talking about this Trognon——"

"Oh! he or another, it is all one to me, for anything you will leave me."

She tossed her head to signify that she despised riches. There was silence in the room.

A moment later Schmucke came in. He had slept for six hours, hunger awakened him, and now he stood at Pons' bedside watching his friend without saying a word, for Mme. Cibot had laid a finger on her lips.

"Hush!" she whispered. Then she rose and went up to add under her breath: "He is going off to sleep at last, thank heaven ! He is as cross as a red donkey ! What can you expect, he is struggling with his illness——"

"No, on the contrary, I am very patient," said the victim in a weary voice that told of a dreadful exhaustion ; " but, oh ! Schmucke, my dear friend, she has been to the theatre to turn me out of my place."

There was a pause. Pons was too weak to say more. La Cibot took the opportunity and tapped her head significantly. " Do not contradict him," she said to Schmucke ; "it would kill him."

Pons gazed into Schmucke's honest face. " And she says that you sent her——" he continued.

" Yes," Schmucke affirmed heroically. " It had to pe. Hush !—let us safe your life. It is absurd to vork and train your sdrength gif you haf a dreasure. Get better ; we vill sell some pric-à-prac und end our tays kvietly in a corner som-veres, mit kind Montame Zipod."

"She has perverted you," moaned Pons.

Mme. Cibot had taken up her station behind the bed to make signals unobserved. Pons thought that she had left the room. " She is murdering me," he added.

" What is that ? I am murdering you, am I ?" cried La Cibot, suddenly appearing, hand on hips and eyes aflame. "I am as faithful as a dog, and this is all I get ! God Almighty !——"

She burst into tears and dropped down into the great chair, a tragical movement which wrought a most disastrous revulsion in Pons.

" Very good," she said, rising to her feet. The woman's malignant eyes looked poison and bullets at the two friends. " Very good. Nothing that I can do is right here, and I am tired of slaving my life out. You shall take a nurse."

Pons and Schmucke exchanged glances in dismay.

" Oh ! you may look at each other like actors. I mean it. I shall ask Dr. Poulain to find a nurse for you. And now we will settle accounts.　You shall pay me back the money that I have spent on you, and that I would never have asked you for, I that have gone to Monsieur Pillerault to borrow another five hundred francs of him——"

"It ees his illness!" cried Schmucke—he sprang to Mme. Cibot and put an arm round her waist—"haf batience."

"As for you, you are an angel, I could kiss the ground you tread upon," said she.　"But Monsieur Pons never liked me, he always hated me.　Beside, he thinks perhaps that I want to be mentioned in his will——"

"Hush! you vill kill him!" cried Schmucke.

"Good-by, sir," said La Cibot, with a withering look at Pons.　"You may keep well for all the harm I wish you. When you can speak to me pleasantly, when you can believe that what I do is done for the best, I will come back again. Till then I shall stay in my own room.　You were like my own child to me; did anybody ever see a child revolt against its mother?　No, no, Monsieur Schmucke, I do not want to hear more.　I will bring you *your* dinner and wait upon *you*, but you must take a nurse.　Ask Monsieur Poulain about it."

And out she went, slamming the door after her so violently that the precious fragile objects in the room trembled.　To Pons in his torture, the rattle of china was like the final blow dealt by the executioner to a victim broken on the wheel.

An hour later La Cibot called to Schmucke through the door, telling him that his dinner was waiting for him in the dining-room.　She would not cross the threshold.　Poor Schmucke went out to her with a haggard, tear-stained face.

"Mein boor Bons is vandering," said he; "he says dat you are ein pad voman.　It ees his illness," he added hastily, to soften La Cibot and excuse his friend.

"Oh, I have had enough of his illness!　Look here, he is neither father, nor husband, nor brother, nor child of mine. He has taken a dislike to me; well and good, that is enough! As for you, you see, I would follow *you* to the end of the world; but when a woman gives her life, her heart, and all her savings, and neglects her husband (for here has Cibot fallen ill), and then hears that she is a bad woman—it is coming it rather too strong, it is.''

"Too sthrong?"

"Too strong, yes. Never mind idle words. Let us come to the facts. As to that, you owe me for three months at a hundred and ninety francs—that is five hundred and seventy francs; then there is the rent that I have paid twice (here are the receipts), six hundred more, including rates and the sou in the franc for the porter—something under twelve hundred francs altogether, and with the two thousand francs beside—without interest, mind you—the total amounts to three thousand one hundred and ninety-two francs. And remember that you will want at least two thousand francs before long for the doctor, and the nurse, and the medicine, and the nurse's board. That was why I borrowed a thousand francs of Monsieur Pillerault,'' and with that she held up Gaudissart's bill.

It may readily be conceived that Schmucke listened to this reckoning with amazement, for he knew about as much of business as a cat knows of music.

"Montame Zipod," he expostulated, "Bons haf lost his head. Bardon him, und nurse him as pefore, und pe our profidence; I peg it of you on mine knees,'' and he knelt before La Cibot and kissed the tormentor's hands.

La Cibot raised Schmucke and kissed him on the forehead. "Listen, my lamb," said she, "here is Cibot ill in bed; I have just sent for Dr. Poulain. So I ought to set my affairs in order. And what is more, Cibot saw me crying, and flew into such a passion that he will not have me set foot in here again. It is *he* who wants the money; it is his, you see. We women can do nothing when it comes to that. But if you let him have his money back again—the three thousand two hundred francs—he will be quiet perhaps. Poor man, it is

21

his all, earned by the sweat of his brow, the savings of twenty-six years of life together.   He must have his money to-morrow; there is no getting round him.   You do not know Cibot; when he is angry he would kill a man.   Well, I might perhaps get leave of him to look after you both as before.   Be easy. I will just let him say anything that comes into his head.   I will bear it all for love of you, an angel as you are.''

"No, I am ein boor man, dot lof his friend and vould gif his life to save him——''

"But the money?'' broke in La Cibot.   "My good Monsieur Schmucke, let us suppose that you pay me nothing; you will want three thousand francs, and where are they to come from? Upon my word, do you know what I should do in your place? I should not think twice, I should just sell seven or eight good-for-nothing pictures and put up some of those instead that are standing in your closet with their faces to the wall for want of room.   One picture or another, what difference does it make?''

"Und vy?''

"He is so cunning.   It is his illness, for he is a lamb when he is well.   He is capable of getting up and prying about; and if by any chance he went into the salon, he is so weak that he could not go beyond the door; he would see that they were all still there.''

"Drue!''

"And when he is quite well, we will tell him about the sale.   And if you wish to confess, throw it all upon me, say that you were obliged to pay me.   Come!   I have a broad back——''

"I cannot tispose of dings dot are not mine,'' the good German answered simply.

"Very well.   I will summons you, yes, you and your Monsieur Pons.''

"It vould kill him——''

"Take your choice!   Dear me, sell the pictures and

tell him about it afterward—— you can show him the summons——"

"Ver' goot. Summons us. Dot shall pe mine egscuse. I shall show him der chudgment."

Mme. Cibot went down to the court, and that very day at seven o'clock she called to Schmucke. Schmucke found himself confronted with M. Tabareau the bailiff, who called upon him to pay. Schmucke made answer, trembling from head to foot, and was forthwith summoned, together with Pons, to appear in the county court to hear judgment against him. The sight of the bailiff and a bit of stamped paper covered with scrawls produced such an effect upon Schmucke that he held out no longer.

"Sell die bictures," he said, with the tears in his eyes.

Next morning, at six o'clock, Élie Magus and Rémonencq took down the paintings of their choice. Two receipts for two thousand five hundred francs were made out in correct form :

"I, the undersigned, representing M. Pons, acknowledge the receipt of two thousand five hundred francs from M. Élie Magus for the four pictures sold to him, the said sum being appropriated to the use of M. Pons. The first picture, attributed to Dürer, is a portrait of a woman ; the second, likewise a portrait, is of the Italian School ; the third, a Dutch landscape by Breughel ; and the fourth, a Holy Family, by an unknown master of the Florentine School."

Rémonencq's receipt was worded in precisely the same way ; a Greuze, a Claude Lorraine, a Rubens, and a Van Dyck being disguised as pictures of the French and Flemish schools.

" Der monny makes me beleef dot the chimcracks haf some value," said Schmucke when the five thousand francs were paid over.

"They are certainly worth something," said Rémonencq. "I would willingly give a hundred thousand francs for the lot," he added.

Rémonencq, asked to do a trifling service, hung eight pictures of the proper size in the same frames, taking them from among the less valuable pictures in Schmucke's bedroom.

No sooner was Élie Magus in possession of the four great pictures than he went, taking La Cibot with him, under pretense of settling accounts. But he pleaded poverty, he found fault with the pictures, they needed rebacking, he offered La Cibot thirty thousand francs by way of commission, and finally dazzled her with the sheets of paper on which the Bank of France engraves the words "One thousand francs" in capital letters. Magus thereupon condemned Rémonencq to pay the like sum to La Cibot, by lending him the money on the security of his four pictures, which he took with him as a guarantee. So glorious were they that Magus could not bring himself to part with them, and next day he bought them of Rémonencq for six thousand francs over and above the original price, and an invoice was duly made out for the four. Mme. Cibot, the richer by sixty-eight thousand francs, once more swore her two accomplices to absolute secrecy. Then she asked the Jew's advice. She wanted to invest the money in such a way that no one should know of it.

"Buy shares in the Orleans Railway," said he; "they are thirty francs below par, you will double your capital in three years. They will give you scraps of paper, which you can keep safe in a portfolio."

"Stay here, Monsieur Magus. I will go and fetch the man of business who acts for Monsieur Pons' family. He wants to know how much you will give for the whole bag of tricks upstairs. I will go for him now."

"If only she were a widow!" said Rémonencq when she

was gone. "She would just suit me ; she will have plenty of money now——"

"Especially if she puts her money into the Orléans Railway ; she will double her capital in two years' time. I have put all my poor little savings into it," added the Jew, "for my daughter's portion. Come, let us take a turn on the boulevard until this lawyer arrives."

"Cibot is very bad as it is," continued Rémonencq ; "if it should please God to take him to Himself, I should have a famous wife to keep a store ; I could set up on a large scale——"

"Good-day, Monsieur Fraisier," La Cibot began in an ingratiating tone as she entered her legal adviser's office. "Why, what is this that your porter has been telling me? are you going to move?"

"Yes, my dear Madame Cibot. I am taking the second floor above Dr. Poulain, and trying to borrow two or three thousand francs so as to furnish the place properly ; it is very nice, upon my word, the landlord has just papered and painted it ; I am acting, as I told you, in President de Marville's interests and in yours. I am not an attorney now ; I mean to have my name entered on the roll of barristers, and I must be well lodged. A barrister in Paris cannot have his name on the rolls unless he has decent furniture and books and the like. I am a doctor of law, I have kept my terms, and have powerful interest already. Well, how are we getting on ?"

"Perhaps you would accept my savings," said La Cibot. "I have put them in the savings bank. I have not much, only three thousand francs, the fruits of twenty-five years of stinting and scraping. You might give me a bill of exchange, as Rémonencq says ; for I am ignorant myself, I only know what they tell me."

"No. It is against the rules of the guild for a barrister (*avocat*) to put his name to a bill. I will give you a receipt, bearing interest at five per cent. per annum, on the understanding that if I make an income of twelve hundred francs for you out of old Pons' estate you will cancel it."

La Cibot, caught in the trap, uttered not a word.

"Silence gives consent," Fraisier continued. "Let me have it to-morrow morning."

"Oh, I am quite willing to pay fees in advance," said La Cibot ; "it is one way of making sure of my money."

Fraisier nodded. "How are we getting on?" he repeated. "I saw Poulain yesterday; you are hurrying your invalid along, it seems. One more scene such as yesterday's, and gall-stones will form. Be gentle with him, my dear Madame Cibot, do not lay up remorse for yourself. Life is not too long."

"Just let me alone with your remorse! Are you going to talk about the guillotine again? Monsieur Pons is a contrairy old thing. You don't know him. It is him that bothers me. There is not a more cross-grained man alive ; his relations are in the right of it, he is sly, revengeful, and contrairy. Old Magus has come, as I told you, and is waiting to see you."

"Right! I will be there as soon as you. Your income depends upon the price the collection will fetch. If it brings in eight hundred thousand francs, you shall have fifteen hundred francs a year. It is a fortune."

"Very well. I will tell them to value the things on their consciences."

An hour later Pons was fast asleep. The doctor had ordered a soothing draught, which Schmucke administered, all unconscious that La Cibot had doubled the dose. Fraisier, Rémonencq, and Magus, three gallows-birds, were examining the seventeen hundred different objects which formed the old musician's collection, one by one.

Schmucke had gone to bed. The three kites, drawn by the scent of a corpse, were masters of the field.

"Make no noise," said La Cibot whenever Magus went into ecstasies or explained the value of some work of art to Rémonencq. The dying man slept on in the neighboring room, while greed in four different forms appraised the treasures that he must leave behind, and waited impatiently for him to die—a sight to wring the heart.

Three hours went by before they had finished the salon.

"On an average," said the grimy old Jew, "everything here is worth a thousand francs."

"Seventeen hundred thousand francs!" exclaimed Fraisier in bewilderment.

"Not to me," Magus answered promptly, and his eyes grew dull. "I would not give more than a hundred thousand francs myself for the collection. You cannot tell how long you may keep a thing on hand. There are masterpieces that wait ten years for a buyer, and meanwhile the purchase-money is doubled by compound interest. Still, I should pay cash."

"There is stained glass in the other room, as well as enamels and miniatures and gold and silver snuff-boxes," put in Rémonencq.

"Can they be seen?" inquired Fraisier.

"I'll see if he is sound asleep," replied La Cibot. She made a sign, and the three birds of prey came in.

"There are masterpieces yonder!" said Magus, indicating the salon, every bristle of his white beard twitching as he spoke. "But the riches are here! And what riches! Kings have nothing more glorious in royal treasuries."

Rémonencq's eyes lighted up till they glowed like carbuncles at the sight of the gold snuff-boxes. Fraisier, cool and calm as a serpent, or some snake-creature with the power of rising erect, stood with his viper's head stretched out, in such an attitude as a painter would choose for Mephistopheles. The three covetous beings, thirsting for gold as devils thirst for the dew of heaven, looked simultaneously, as it chanced,

at the owner of all this wealth. Some nightmare troubled
Pons ; he stirred, and suddenly, under the influence of those
diabolical glances, he opened his eyes with a shrill cry.

"Thieves !——   There they are !——   Help !   Murder !
Help ! "

The nightmare was evidently still upon him, for he sat up
in bed, staring before him with blank, wide-open eyes, and
had not power to move.

Élie Magus and Rémonencq made for the door, but a word
glued them to the spot.

"*Magus* here !——   I am betrayed ! "

Instinctively the sick man had known that his beloved pictures were in danger, a thought that touched him at least as
closely as any dread for himself, and he awoke. Fraisier
meanwhile did not stir.

"Madame Cibot ! who is that gentleman ? " cried Pons,
shivering at the sight.

"Goodness me ! how could I put him out of the door ? "
she inquired, with a wink and gesture for Fraisier's benefit.
"This gentleman came just a minute ago, from your family."

Fraisier could not conceal his admiration for La Cibot.

"Yes, sir," he said, "I have come on behalf of Madame
la Presidente de Marville, her husband, and her daughter to
express their regret. They learned quite by accident that you
are ill, and they would like to nurse you themselves. They
want you to go to Marville and get well there. Madame la
Vicomtesse Popinot, the little Cécile that you love so much,
will be your nurse. She took your part with her mother.
She convinced Madame de Marville that she had made a
mistake."

"So my next-of-kin have sent you to me, have they ? "
Pons exclaimed indignantly, "and sent the best judge and
expert in all Paris with you to show you the way? Oh! a.
nice commission ! " he cried, bursting into wild laughter.
"You have come to value my pictures and curiosities, my

snuff-boxes and miniatures! Make your valuation. You have a man there who understands everything, and more—he can buy everything, for he is a millionaire ten times over. My dear relatives will not have long to wait," he added with bitter irony, "they have choked the last breath out of me. Ah! Madame Cibot, you said you were a mother to me, and you bring dealers into the house, and my competitor and the Camusots, while I am asleep! Get out, all of you!——"

The unhappy man was beside himself with anger and fear; he rose from the bed and stood upright, a gaunt, wasted figure.

"Take my arm, sir," said La Cibot, rushing to the rescue, lest Pons should fall. "Pray calm yourself, the gentlemen are gone."

"I want to see the salon——" said the death-stricken man. La Cibot made a sign to the three ravens to take flight. Then she caught up Pons as if he had been a feather, and put him in bed again, in spite of his cries. When she saw that he was quite helpless and exhausted, she went to shut the door on the staircase. The three who had done Pons to death were still on the landing; La Cibot told them to wait. She heard Fraisier say to Magus—

"Let me have it in writing, and sign it, both of you. Undertake to pay nine hundred thousand francs in cash for Monsieur Pons' collection, and we will see about putting you in the way of making a handsome profit."

With that he said something to La Cibot in a voice so low that the others could not catch it, and went down after the two dealers to the porter's room.

"Have they gone, Madame Cibot?" asked the unhappy Pons, when she came back again.

"Gone?—— who?" asked she.

"Those men."

"What men? There, now! you have seen men," said she. "You have just had a raving fit; if it hadn't been for me you would have gone out of the window, and now you are still talking of men in the room. Is it always a-going to be like this?"

"What! was there not a gentleman here just now, saying that my relatives had sent him?"

"Will you still stand me out?" said she. "Upon my word, do you know where you ought to be sent? To the asylum at Charenton. You see men——"

"Élie Magus, Rémonencq, and——"

"Oh! as for Rémonencq, you may have seen *him*, for he came up to tell me that my poor Cibot is so bad that I must clear out of this and come down. My Cibot comes first, you see. When my husband is ill, I can think of nobody else. Try to keep quiet and sleep for a couple of hours; I have sent for Dr. Poulain, and I will come up with him. Take a drink and be good——"

"Then was there no one in the room just now, when I waked?——"

"No one," said she. "You must have seen Monsieur Rémonencq in one of your looking-glasses."

"You are right, Madame Cibot," said Pons, meek as a lamb.

"Well, now you are sensible again. Good-by, my cherub; keep quiet, I shall be back again in a minute."

When Pons heard the outer door close upon her, he summoned up all his remaining strength to rise.

"They are cheating me," he muttered to himself, "they are robbing me! Schmucke is a child that would let them tie him up in a sack."

The terrible scene had seemed so real, it could not be a dream, he thought; a desire to throw light upon the puzzle excited him; he managed to reach the door, opened it after many efforts, and stood on the threshold of his salon. There they were—his dear pictures, his statues, his Florentine bronzes, his porcelain; the sight of them revived him. The old collector walked in his dressing-gown along the narrow spaces between the credence-tables and the sideboards that lined the wall; his feet bare, his head on fire. His first glance of ownership told him that everything was there; he turned to go back to bed again, when he noticed that a Greuze portrait looked out of the frame that had held Sebastian del Piombo's Templar. Suspicion flashed across his brain, making his dark thoughts apparent to him, as a flash of lightning marks the outlines of the cloud-bars on a stormy sky. He looked round for the eight capital pictures of the collection; each one of them was replaced by another. A dark film suddenly overspread his eyes; his strength failed him; he fell fainting upon the polished floor.

So heavy was the swoon that for two hours he lay as he fell, till Schmucke awoke and went to see his friend, and found him laying unconscious in the salon. With endless pains Schmucke raised the half-dead body and laid it on the bed; but when he came to question the death-stricken man, and saw the look in the dull eyes and heard the vague, inarticulate words, the good German, so far from losing his head, rose to the very heroism of friendship. Man and child as he was, with the pressure of despair came the inspiration of a mother's tenderness, a woman's love. He warmed towels (he found towels!), he wrapped them about Pons' hands, he laid them over the pit of the stomach; he took the cold, moist forehead in his hands, he summoned back life with a might of will worthy of Apollonius of Tyana; laying kisses on his friend's eyelids like some Mary bending over the dead Christ, in a *pietà* carved in bas-relief by some great Italian sculptor. The divine effort, the outpouring of one life into another, the work of mother and of lover, was crowned with success. In half an hour the warmth revived Pons; he became himself again, the hues of life returned to his eyes, suspended faculties gradually resumed their play under the influence of artificial heat. Schmucke gave him balm-water with a little wine in it; the spirit of life spread through the body; intelligence lighted up the forehead so short a while ago insensible as a stone; and Pons knew that he had been brought back to life, by what sacred devotion, what might of friendship!

"But for you, I should die," he said, and as he spoke he felt the good German's tears falling on his face. Schmucke was laughing and crying at once.

Poor Schmucke! he had waited for those words with a frenzy of hope as costly as the frenzy of despair; and now his strength utterly failed him, he collapsed like a rent balloon. It was his turn to fall; he sank into the easy-chair, clasped his hands, and thanked God in fervent prayer. For him a miracle had just been wrought. He put no belief in the efficacy of the prayer of his deeds; the miracle had been wrought by God in direct answer to his cry. And yet that miracle was a natural effect, such as medical science often records.

A sick man, surrounded by those who love him, nursed by those who wish earnestly that he should live, will recover (other things being equal), when another patient tended by hirelings will die. Doctors decline to see unconscious magnetism in this phenomenon; for them it is the result of intelligent nursing, of exact obedience to their orders; but many a mother knows the virtue of such ardent projection of strong, unceasing prayer.

"My good Schmucke——"

"Say nodings; I shall hear you mit mein heart—— rest, rest!" said Schmucke, smiling at him.

"Poor friend, noble creature, child of God living in God!—— The one being that has loved me——" The words came out with pauses between them; there was a new note, a something never heard before, in Pons' voice. All the soul, so soon to take flight, found utterance in the words that filled Schmucke with happiness almost like a lover's rapture.

"Yes, yes. I shall be shtrong as a lion. I shall vork for two!"

"Listen, my good, my faithful, adorable friend. Let me speak, I have not much time left. I am a dead man. I cannot recover from these repeated shocks."

Schmucke was crying like a child.

"Just listen," continued Pons, "and cry afterward. As a Christian, you must submit. I have been robbed. It is La Cibot's doing. I ought to open your eyes before I go; you know nothing of life. Somebody has taken away eight of the pictures, and they were worth a great deal of money."

"Vorgif me—I sold dem."

"*You* sold them?"

"Yes, I," said poor Schmucke. "Dey summoned us to der court——"

"*Summoned?* Who summoned us?"

"Wait," said Schmucke. He went for the bit of stamped paper left by the bailiff, and gave it to Pons. Pons read the scrawl through with close attention, then he let the paper drop and lay quite silent for awhile. A close observer of the work of men's hands, unheedful so far of the workings of the brain, Pons finally counted out the threads of the plot woven about him by La Cibot. The artist's fire, the intellect that won the Roman scholarship—all his youth—came back to him for a little.

"My good Schmucke," he said at last, "you must do as I tell you, and obey like a soldier. Listen! go downstairs into the lodge and tell that abominable woman that I should like to see the person sent to me by my cousin the president; and that unless he comes, I shall leave my collection to the Musée. Say that a will is in question."

Schmucke went on his errand; but at the first word, La Cibot answered by a smile.

"My good Monsieur Schmucke, our dear invalid has had a delirious fit; he thought that there were men in the room.

On my word as an honest woman, no one has come from the family."

Schmucke went back with this answer, which he repeated word for word.

"She is cleverer, more astute and cunning and wily, than I thought," said Pons with a smile. "She lies even in her room. Imagine it! This morning she brought a Jew here, Élie Magus by name, and Rémonencq, and a third whom I do not know, more terrific than the other two put together. She meant to make a valuation while I was asleep; I happened to wake, and saw them all three, estimating the worth of my snuff-boxes. The stranger said, indeed, that the Camusots had sent him here; I spoke to him. That shameless woman stood me out that I was dreaming! My good Schmucke, it was not a dream. I heard the man perfectly plain; he spoke to me. The two dealers took fright and made for the door. I thought that La Cibot would contradict herself—the experiment failed. I will lay another snare, and trap the wretched woman. Poor Schmucke, you think that La Cibot is an angel; and for this month past she has been killing me by inches to gain her covetous ends. I would not believe that a woman who served us faithfully for years could be so wicked. That doubt has been my ruin. How much did the eight pictures fetch?"

"Vife tausend vrancs.'

"Good heavens! they were worth twenty times as much!" cried Pons; "the gems of the collection! I have not time now to institute proceedings; and if I did, you would figure in court as the dupe of those rascals. A lawsuit would be the death of you. You do not know what justice means—a court of justice is a sink of iniquity. At the sight of such horrors, a soul like yours would give way. And, beside, you will have enough. The pictures cost me forty thousand francs. I have had them for thirty-six years. Oh, we have been robbed with surprising dexterity. I am on the brink of the grave, I care for nothing now but thee—for thee, the best soul under the sun.

"I will not have you plundered; all that I have is yours. So you must trust nobody, Schmucke, you that have never suspected any one in your life. I know God watches over you, but He may forget for one moment, and you will be seized like a vessel among pirates. La Cibot is a monster! She is killing me; and you think her an angel! You shall see what she is. Go and ask her to give you the name of a notary, and I will show you her with her hand in the bag."

Schmucke listened as if Pons proclaimed an apocalypse. Could so depraved a creature as La Cibot exist? If Pons was right, it seemed to imply that there was no God in the world. He went down again to Mme. Cibot.

"Mein boor vriend Bons feel so ill," he said, "dat he vish to make his vill. Go und pring ein nodary."

This was said in the hearing of several persons, for Cibot's life was despaired of. Rémonencq and his sister, two women from neighboring porters' lodges, two or three servants, and the lodger from the second floor on the side next the street were all standing outside in the gateway.

"Oh! you can just fetch a notary yourself, and have your will made as you please," cried La Cibot, with tears in her eyes. "My poor Cibot is dying, and it is no time to leave him. I would give all the Ponses in the world to save Cibot, that has never given me an ounce of unhappiness in these thirty years since we were married."

And in she went, leaving Schmucke in confusion.

"Is Monsieur Pons really seriously ill, sir?" asked the second-floor lodger, one Jolivard, a clerk in the registrar's office at the Palais de Justice.

"He nearly died chust now," said Schmucke, with deep sorrow in his voice.

"Monsieur Trognon lives near by in the Rue Saint-Louis," said Monsieur Jolivard, "he is the notary of the quarter."

" Would you like me to go for him ? " asked Rémonencq.

" I should pe fery glad," said Schmucke ; " for gif Montame Zipod cannot pe mit mein vriend, I shall not vish to leaf him in der shtate he is in——"

"Madame Cibot told us that he was going out of his mind," resumed Jolivard.

" Bons ! out off his mind ! " cried Schmucke, terror-stricken by the idea. " Nefer vas he so clear in der head—dat is chust der reason vy I am anxious for him."

The little group of persons listened to the conversation with a very natural curiosity, which stamped the scene upon their memories. Schmucke did not know Fraisier, and could not note his satanic countenance and glittering eyes. But two words whispered by Fraisier in La Cibot's ear had prompted a daring piece of acting, somewhat beyond La Cibot's range, it may be, though she played her part throughout in a masterly style. To make others believe that the dying man was out of his mind—it was the very corner-stone of the edifice reared by the petty lawyer. The morning's incident had done Fraisier good service ; but for him, La Cibot in her trouble might have fallen into the snare innocently spread by Schmucke, when he asked her to send back the person sent by the family.

Rémonencq saw Dr. Poulain coming toward them, and asked no better than to vanish. The fact was that for the last ten days the Auvergnat had been playing Providence in a manner singularly displeasing to Justice, which claims the monopoly of that part. He had made up his mind to rid himself at all costs of the one obstacle in his way to happiness, and happiness for him meant capital trebled and marriage with the irresistibly charming portress. He had watched the little tailor drinking his herb-tea, and a thought struck him. He would convert the ailment into mortal sickness ; his stock of old metals supplied him with the means.

One morning as he leaned against the door-post, smoking

his pipe and dreaming of that fine store on the Boulevard de la Madeleine where Mme. Cibot, gorgeously arrayed, should some day sit enthroned, his eyes fell upon a copper disc, about the size of a five-franc piece, covered thickly with verdigris. The economical idea of using Cibot's medicine to clean the disc immediately occurred to him. He fastened the thing to a bit of twine, and came over every morning to inquire for tidings of his friend the tailor, timing his visit during La Cibot's visit to her gentlemen upstairs. He dropped the disc into the tumbler, allowed it to steep there while he talked, and drew it out again by the string when he went away.

The trace of tarnished copper, commonly called verdigris, poisoned the wholesome draught ; a minute dose administered by stealth did incalculable mischief. Behold the results of this criminal homœopathy ! On the third day poor Cibot's hair came out, his teeth were loosened in their sockets, his whole system was deranged by a scarcely perceptible trace of poison. Dr. Poulain racked his brains. He was enough of a man of science to see that some destructive agent was at work. He privately carried off the decoction, analyzed it himself, but found nothing. It so chanced that Rémonencq had taken fright and omitted to dip the disc in the tumbler that day.

Then Dr. Poulain fell back on himself and science and got out of the difficulty with a theory. A sedentary life in a damp room ; a cramped position before the barred window— these conditions had vitiated the blood in the absence of proper exercise, especially as the patient continually breathed an atmosphere saturated with the fetid exhalations of the gutter. The Rue de Normandie is one of the old-fashioned streets that slope toward the middle ; the municipal authorities of Paris as yet have laid on no water-supply to flush the central kennel which drains the houses on either side, and as a result a stream of filthy ooze meanders among the cobble-stones, filters into the soil, and produces the mud peculiar to the city. La Cibot

22

came and went; but her husband, a hard-working man, sat day in day out like a fakir on the table in the window, till his knee-joints were stiffened, the blood stagnated in his body, and his legs grew so thin and crooked that he almost lost the use of them. The deep copper tint of the man's complexion naturally suggested that he had been out of health for a very long time. The wife's good health and the husband's illness seemed to the doctor to be satisfactorily accounted for by this theory.

"Then what is the matter with my poor Cibot?" asked the portress.

"My dear Madame Cibot, he is dying of the porter's disease," said the doctor. "Incurable vitiation of the blood is evident from the general anæmic condition."

No one had anything to gain by a crime so objectless. Dr. Poulain's first suspicions were effaced by this thought. Who could have any possible interest in Cibot's death? His wife? the doctor saw her taste the herb-tea as she sweetened it. Crimes which escape social vengeance are many enough, and as a rule they are of this order—to wit, murders committed without any startling sign of violence, without bloodshed, bruises, marks of strangling, without any bungling of the business, in short; if there seems to be no motive for the crime, it most likely goes unpunished, especially if the death occurs among the poorer classes. Murder is almost always announced by its advanced guards, by hatred or greed well known to those under whose eyes the whole matter has passed. But in the case of the Cibots no one save the doctor had any interest in discovering the actual cause of death. The little copper-faced tailor's wife adored her husband; he had no money and no enemies; La Cibot's fortune and the marine-store-dealer's motives were alike hidden in the shade. Poulain knew the portress and her way of thinking perfectly well; he thought her capable of tormenting Pons, but he saw that she had neither motive enough nor wit enough for murder;

and beside—every time the doctor came and she gave her husband a draught, she took a spoonful herself. Poulain himself, the only person who might have thrown light on the matter, inclined to believe that this was one of the unaccountable freaks of disease, one of the astonishing exceptions which make medicine so perilous a profession. And in truth, the little tailor's unwholesome life and insanitary surroundings had unfortunately brought him to such a pass that the trace of copper-poisoning was like the last straw. Gossips and neighbors took it upon themselves to explain the sudden death, and no suspicion of blame lighted upon Rémonencq.

"Oh, this long time past I have said that Monsieur Cibot was not well," cried one.

"He worked too hard, he did," said another; "he heated his blood."

"He would not listen to me," put in a neighbor; "I advised him to walk out of a Sunday and keep Saint Monday; two days in the week is not too much for amusement."

In short, the gossip of the quarter, the tell-tale voice to which Justice, in the person of the commissary of police, the king of the poorer classes, lends an attentive ear—gossip explained the little tailor's demise in a perfectly satisfactory manner. Yet M. Poulain's pensive air and uneasy eyes embarrassed Rémonencq not a little, and at sight of the doctor he offered eagerly to go in search of M. Trognon, Fraisier's acquaintance. Fraisier turned to La Cibot to say in a low voice, "I shall come back again as soon as the will is made. In spite of your sorrow, you must look out for squalls." Then he slipped away like a shadow and met his friend the doctor.

"Ah, Poulain!" he exclaimed, "it is all right. We are safe! I will tell you about it to-night. Look out a post that will suit you, you shall have it! For my own part, I am a justice of the peace. Tabareau will not refuse me now for a son-in-law. And as for you, I will undertake that you shall marry Mademoiselle Vitel, granddaughter of our justice of the peace."

Fraisier left Poulain reduced to dumb bewilderment by these wild words; bounced like a ball into the boulevard, hailed an omnibus, and was set down ten minutes later by the modern coach at the corner of the Rue de Choiseul. By this time it was nearly four o'clock. Fraisier felt quite sure of a word in private with the presidente, for officials seldom leave the Palais de Justice before five o'clock.

Mme. de Marville's reception of him assured Fraisier that M. Lebœuf had kept the promise made to Mme. Vatinelle and spoken favorably of the sometime attorney of Mantes. Amélie's manner was almost caressing. So might the Duchesse de Montpensier have treated Jacques Clément. The petty attorney was a knife to her hand. But, when Fraisier produced the joint-letter signed by Élie Magus and Rémonencq offering the sum of nine hundred thousand francs in cash for Pons' collection, then the presidente looked at her man of business and the gleam of the money flashed from her eyes. That ripple of greed reached the attorney.

"Monsieur le President left a message with me," she said; "he hopes that you will dine with us to-morrow. It will be a family party. Monsieur Godeschal, Desroche's successor and my attorney, will come to meet you, and Berthier, our notary, and my daughter and son-in-law. After dinner, you and I and the notary and attorney will have the little consultation for which you ask, and I will give you full powers. The two gentlemen will do as you require and act upon your inspiration; and see that *everything* goes well. You shall have a power of attorney from Monsieur de Marville as soon as you want it."

"I shall want it on the day of the decease."

"It shall be in readiness."

"Madame le Presidente, if I ask for a power of attorney, and would prefer that your attorney's name should not appear,

I wish it less in my own interest than in yours. When I give myself, it is without reserve. And in return, madame, I ask the same fidelity ; I ask my patrons (I do not venture to call you my clients) to put the same confidence in me. You may think that in acting thus I am trying to fasten upon this affair —no, no, madame ; there may be reprehensible things done ; with an inheritance in view one is dragged on—— especially with nine hundred thousand francs in the balance. Well, now, you could not disavow a man like Maître Godeschal, honesty itself, but you can throw all the blame on the back of a miserable pettifogging lawyer——"

Mme. Camusot de Marville looked admiringly at Fraisier.

"You ought to go very high," said she, " or sink very low. In your place, instead of asking to hide myself away as a justice of the peace, I would aim at a crown attorney's appointment—at, say, Mantes !—and make a great career for myself."

"Let me have my way, madame. The post of justice of the peace is an ambling pad for Monsieur Vitel ; for me it shall be a war-horse."

And in this way the presidente proceeded to a final confidence.

"You seem to be so completely devoted to our interests," she began, "that I will tell you about the difficulties of our position and our hopes. The president's great desire, ever since a match was projected between his daughter and an adventurer who recently started a bank—the president's wish, I say, has been to round out the Marville estate with some grazing land, at that time in the market. We dispossessed ourselves of fine property, as you know, to settle it upon our daughter ; but I wish very much, my daughter being an only child, to buy all that remains of the grass land. Part has been sold already. The estate belongs to an Englishman who is returning to England after a twenty years' residence in France. He built the most charming cottage in a delightful situation, between Marville Park and the meadows which once were part of the Marville lands; he bought up covers, copse, and gardens at fancy prices to make the grounds about the cottage. The house and its surroundings make a feature of the landscape, and it lies close to my daughter's park palings. The whole, land and house, should be bought for seven hundred thousand francs, for the net revenue is about twenty thousand francs. But if Mr. Wadman finds out that *we* think of buying it, he is sure to add another two or three hundred thousand francs to the price; for he will lose money if the house counts for nothing, as it usually does when you buy land in the country."

"Why, madame," Fraisier broke in, "my opinion is you can be so sure that the inheritance is yours that I will offer to act the part of purchaser for you. I will undertake that you shall have the land at the best possible price, and have a written engagement made out under private seal, like a contract to deliver goods. I will go to the Englishman in the character of buyer. I well understand that sort of thing; it was my specialty at Mantes. Vatinelle doubled the value of his practice, while I worked in his name."

"Hence your connection with little Madame Vatinelle. He must be very well off——"

"But Madame Vatinelle has expensive tastes. So be easy, madame—I will serve you up the Englishman done to a turn——"

"If you can manage that you will have eternal claims to my gratitude. Good-day, my dear Monsieur Fraisier. Till to-morrow——"

Fraisier went. His parting bow was a degree less cringing than on the first occasion.

"I am to dine to-morrow with President de Marville!" he said to himself. "Come, now, I have these people in my power. Only, to be absolute master, I ought to be the German's legal adviser in the person of Tabareau, the justice's clerk. Tabareau will not have me now for his daughter, his only daughter, but he will give her to me when I am a justice of the peace. I shall be eligible. Mademoiselle Tabareau, that tall consumptive girl with the red hair, has a house in the Place Royale in right of her mother. At her father's death she is sure to come in for six thousand livres per annum as well. She is not handsome; but, good Lord, if you step from nothing at all to an income of eighteen thousand francs, you must not look too hard at the plank."

As he went back to the Rue de Normandie by way of the boulevards, he dreamed out his golden dream; he gave himself up to the happiness of the thought that he should never know want again. He would marry his friend Poulain to Mlle. Vitel, the daughter of the justice of the peace; together, he and his friend the doctor would reign like kings in the quarter; he would carry all the elections—municipal, military, or political. The boulevards seem short if, while you pace afoot, you mount your ambition on the steed of fancy in this way.

Schmucke meanwhile went back to his friend Pons with the news that Cibot was dying, and Rémonencq gone in search of M. Trognon the notary. Pons was struck by the name. It had come up again and again in La Cibot's interminable talk, and La Cibot always recommended him as honesty incarnate. And with that a luminous idea occurred to Pons, in whom mistrust had grown paramount since the morning, an idea which completed his plan for outwitting La Cibot and unmasking her completely for the too-credulous Schmucke.

So many unexpected things had happened that day that poor Schmucke was quite bewildered. Pons took his friend's hand.

"There must be a good deal of confusion in the house, Schmucke; if the porter is at death's door, we are almost free for a minute or two; that is to say, there will be no spies—for we are watched, you may be sure of that. Go out, take a cab, go the theatre, and tell Mlle. Héloïse Brisetout that I

should like to see her before I die.   Ask her to come here to-
night when she leaves the theatre.   Then go to your friends
Brunner and Schwab and beg them to come to-morrow morning at nine o'clock to inquire after me ; let them come up as
if they were just passing by and called in to see me."

The old artist felt that he was dying, and this was the
scheme that he forged.   He meant Schmucke to be his universal legatee.   To protect Schmucke from any possible legal
quibbles he proposed to dictate his will to a notary in the
presence of witnesses, lest his sanity should be called in question and the Camusots should attempt upon that pretext to
dispute the will.   At the name of Trognon he caught a glimpse
of machinations of some kind ; perhaps a flaw purposely in-
serted, or premeditated treachery on La Cibot's part.   He
would prevent this.   Trognon should dictate a holograph will
which should be signed and deposited in a sealed envelope in
a drawer.   Then Schmucke, hidden in one of the cabinets in
his alcove, should see La Cibot search for the will, find it,
open the envelope, read it through, and seal it again.   Next
morning, at nine o'clock, he would cancel the will and make
a new one in the presence of two notaries, everything in due
form and order.   La Cibot had treated him as a madman and
a visionary ; he saw what this meant—he saw the presidente's
hate and greed, her revenge in La Cibot's behavior.   In the
sleepless hours and lonely days of the last two months, the
poor man had sifted the events of his past life.

It has been the wont of sculptors, ancient and modern, to
set a tutelary genius with a lighted torch upon either side of a
tomb.   Those torches that light up the paths of death throw
light for dying eyes upon the spectacle of a life's mistakes and
sins ; the carved stone figures express great ideas, they are
symbols of a fact in human experience.   The agony of death
has its own wisdom.   Not seldom a simple girl, scarcely more
than a child, will grow wise with the experience of a hundred
years, will gain prophetic vision, judge her family, and see

clearly through all pretenses, at the near approach of death. Herein lies Death's poetry. But, strange and worthy of remark it is, there are two manners of death.

The poetry of prophecy, the gift of seeing clearly into the future or the past, only belongs to those whose bodies are stricken, to those who die by the destruction of the organs of physical life. Consumptive patients, for instance, or those who die of gangrene like Louis XIV., of fever like Pons, of a stomach complaint like Mme. de Mortsauf, or of wounds received in the full tide of life like soldiers on the battle-field —all these may possess this supreme lucidity to the full ; their deaths fill us with surprise and wonder. But many, on the other hand, die of *intelligential* diseases, as they may be called ; of maladies seated in the brain or in that nervous system which acts as a kind of purveyor of thought fuel—and these die wholly, body and spirit are darkened together. The former are spirits deserted by the body, realizing for us our ideas of the spirits of scripture ; the latter are bodies untenanted by a spirit.

Too late the virgin nature, the epicure-Cato, the righteous man almost without sin, was discovering the presidente's real character—the sac of gall that did duty for her heart. He knew the world now that he was about to leave it, and for the past few hours he had risen gayly to his part, like a joyous artist finding a pretext for caricature and laughter in everything. The last links that bound him to life, the chains of admiration, the strong ties that bind the art lover to Art's masterpieces, had been snapped that morning. When Pons knew that La Cibot had robbed him, he bade farewell, like a Christian, to the pomps and vanities of Art, to his collection, to all his old friendships with the makers of so many fair things. Our forefathers counted the day of death as a Christian festival, and in something of the same spirit Pons' thoughts turned to the coming end. In his tender love he tried to protect Schmucke when he should be low in the grave.

It was this father-thought that led him to fix his choice upon
the leading lady of the ballet. Mlle. Brisetout should help
him to baffle surrounding treachery, and those who in all
probability would never forgive his innocent universal legatee.

Héloïse Brisetout was one of the few natures that remain
true in a false position. She was an opera-girl of the school
of Josépha and Jenny Cadine, capable of playing any trick on
a paying adorer; yet she was a good comrade, dreading no
power on earth, accustomed as she was to see the weak side
of the strong, and to hold her own with the police at the
scarcely idyllic Bal de Mabille and the carnival.

"If she asked for my place for Garangeot, she will think
that she owes me a good turn by so much the more," said
Pons to himself.

Thanks to the prevailing confusion in the porter's lodge,
Schmucke succeeded in getting out of the house. He returned with the utmost speed, fearing to leave Pons too long
alone. M. Trognon reached the house just as Schmucke came
in. Albeit Cibot was dying, his wife came upstairs with the
notary, brought him into the bedroom, and withdrew, leaving
Schmucke and Pons with M. Trognon; but she left the door
ajar, and went no farther than the next room. Providing
herself with a little hand-glass of curious workmanship, she
took up her station in the doorway, so that she could not only
hear but see all that passed at the supreme moment.

"Sir," said Pons, "I am in the full possession of my faculties, unfortunately for me, for I feel that I am about to die;
and, doubtless, by the will of God, I shall be spared nothing
of the agony of death. This is Monsieur Schmucke"—(the
notary bowed to M. Schmucke)—"my one friend on earth,"
continued Pons. "I wish to make him my universal legatee.
Now, tell me how to word the will, so that my friend, who is a
German and knows nothing of French law, may succeed to
my possessions without any dispute."

"Anything is liable to be disputed, sir," said the notary;

" that is the drawback of human justice. But in the matter of wills, there are wills so drafted that they cannot be up-set——"

" In what way?" queried Pons.

"If a will is made in the presence of a notary, and before witnesses who can swear that the testator was in the full posses-sion of his faculties; and if the testator has neither wife nor children, nor father nor mother——"

" I have none of these ; all my affection is centred upon my dear friend Schmucke here."

The tears overflowed Schmucke's eyes.

" Then, if you have none but distant relatives, the law leaves you free to dispose of both personalty and real estate as you please, so long as you bequeath them for no unlawful purpose ; for you must have come across cases of wills disputed on ac-count of the testator's eccentricities. A will made in the presence of a notary is considered to be authentic ; for the person's identity is established, the notary certifies that the testator was sane at the time, and there can be no possible dispute over the signature. Still, a holograph will, properly and clearly worded, is quite as safe."

" I have decided, for reasons of my own, to make a holo-graph will at your dictation, and to deposit it with my friend here. Is this possible?"

" Quite possible," said the notary. " Will you write? I will begin to dictate."

" Schmucke, bring me my little Boule writing-desk. Speak low, sir," he added ; " we may be overheard."

" Just tell me, first of all, what you intend," demanded the notary.

Ten minutes later La Cibot saw the notary look over the will, while Schmucke lighted a taper (Pons watching her reflec-tion all the while in a mirror). She saw the envelope sealed, saw Pons give it to Schmucke, and heard him say that it must be put away in a secret drawer in his bureau. Then the testator asked for the key, tied it to the corner of his handkerchief, and slipped it under his pillow.

The notary himself, by courtesy, was appointed executor. To him Pons left a picture of price, such a thing as the law permits a notary to receive. Trognon went out and came upon Mme. Cibot in the salon.

"Well, sir, did Monsieur Pons remember me?"

"You do not expect a notary to betray secrets confided to him, my dear," returned M. Trognon. "I can only tell you this—there will be many disappointments, and some that are anxious after the money will be foiled. Monsieur Pons has made a good and very sensible will, a patriotic will, which I highly approve."

La Cibot's curiosity, kindled by such words, reached an unimaginable pitch. She went downstairs and spent the night at Cibot's bedside, inwardly resolving that Mlle. Rémonencq should take her place toward two or three in the morning, when she would go up and have a look at the document.

Mille. Brisetout's visit toward half-past ten that night seemed natural enough to La Cibot; but in her terror lest the ballet-girl should mention Gaudissart's gift of a thousand francs, she went upstairs with her, lavishing polite speeches and flattery as if Mlle. Héloïse had been a queen.

"Ah! my dear, you are much nicer here on your own ground than at the theatre," Héloïse remarked. "I advise you to keep to your employment."

Héloïse was splendidly dressed. Bixiou, her lover, had brought her in his carriage on the way to an evening party at Mariette's. It so fell out that the second-floor lodger, M. Chapoulot, a retired braid manufacturer from the Rue Saint-Denis, returning from the Ambigu-Comique with his wife and daughter, was dazzled by a vision of such a costume and such a charming woman upon their staircase.

"Who is that, Madame Cibot?" asked Mme. Chapoulot.

"A no-better-than-she-should-be, a light-skirts that you

may see half-naked any evening for a couple of francs," La Cibot answered in an undertone for Mme. Chapoulot's ear.

"Victorine!" called the braid manufacturer's wife, "let the lady pass, child."

The matron's alarm-signal was not lost upon Héloïse.

"Your daughter must be more inflammable than tinder, madame, if you are afraid that she will catch fire by touching me," she said.

M. Chapoulot waited on the landing. "She is uncommonly handsome off the stage," he remarked. Whereupon Mme. Chapoulot pinched him sharply and drove him indoors.

"Here is a third-floor lodger that has a mind to set up for being on the fourth floor," said Héloïse, as she continued to climb.

"But mademoiselle is accustomed to going higher and higher."

"Well, old boy," said Héloïse, entering the bedroom and catching sight of the old musician's white, wasted face. "Well, old boy, so we are not very well? Everybody at the theatre is asking after you; but though one's heart may be in the right place, every one has his own affairs, you know, and cannot find time to go to see friends. Gaudissart talks of coming round every day, and every morning the tiresome management gets hold of him. Still, we are all of us fond of you——"

"Madame Cibot," said the patient, "be so kind as to leave us; we want to talk about the theatre and my post as conductor, with this lady. Schmucke, will you go to the door with Madame Cibot?"

At a sign from Pons, Schmucke saw Mme. Cibot out at the door, and drew the bolts.

"Ah, that blackguard of a German! Is he spoiled too?" La Cibot said to herself as she heard the significant sounds. "That is Monsieur Pons' doing; he taught him these disgusting tricks. But you shall pay for this, my dears," she thought, as she went down the stairs. " Pooh ! if that tight-rope dancer tells him about the thousand francs, I shall say that it is a farce."

She seated herself by Cibot's pillow. Cibot complained of a burning sensation in the stomach. Rémonencq had called in and given him a draught while his wife was upstairs.

As soon as Schmucke had dismissed La Cibot, Pons turned to the ballet-girl.

" Dear child, I can trust no one else to find me a notary, an honest man, and send him here to make my will to-morrow morning at half-past nine precisely. I want to leave all that I have to Schmucke. If he is persecuted, poor German that he is, I shall reckon upon the notary; the notary must defend him. And for that reason I must have a very wealthy notary, highly thought of, a man above the temptations to which pettifogging lawyers yield. He must succor my poor friend. I cannot trust Berthier, Cardot's successor. And you know so many people——"

"Oh! I have the very man for you," Héloïse broke in ; "there is the notary that acts for Florine and the Comtesse du Bruel, Léopold Hannequin, a virtuous man that does not know what a lorette is ! He is a sort of chance-come father—a good soul that will not let you play ducks and drakes with your earnings ; I call him *Le Père aux Rats,** because he in-stills economical notions into the minds of all my friends. In the first place, my dear fellow, he has a private income of sixty thousand francs ; and he is a notary of the real old sort, a notary while he walks or sleeps ; his children must be little notaries and notariesses. He is a heavy, pedantic creature, and that's the truth ; but on his own ground, he is not the man to flinch before any power in creation. No woman ever got money out of him ; he is a fossil paterfamilias, his wife worships him and does not deceive him, although she is a notary's wife. What more do you want? as a notary he has

* Father to the rats.

not his match in Paris. He is in the patriarchal style; not queer and amusing, as Cardot used to be with Malaga; but he will never decamp like little What's-his-name that lived with Antonio. So I will send round my man to-morrow morning at eight o'clock. You may sleep in peace. And I hope, in the first place, that you will get better, and make charming music for us again; and yet, after all, you see, life is very dreary—managers chisel you, and kings mizzle and ministers fizzle and rich folk economizzle. Artists have nothing left *here*" (tapping her breast)—"it is a time to die in. Good-by, old boy."

"Héloïse, of all things, I ask you to keep my counsel."

"It is not a theatre affair," she said; "it is sacred for an artist."

"Who is your gentleman, child?"

"Monsieur Baudoyer, the mayor of your arrondissement, a man as stupid as the late Crevel; Crevel once financed Gaudissart, you know, and a few days ago he died and left me nothing, not so much as a pot of pomatum. That made me say just now that this age of ours is something sickening."

"What did he die of?"

"Of his wife. If he had stayed with me, he would be living now. Good-by, dear old boy. I am talking of going off, because I can see that you will be walking about the boulevards in a week or two, hunting up pretty little curiosities again. You are not ill; I never saw your eyes look so bright." And she went, fully convinced that her protege Garangeot would conduct the orchestra for good.

Every door stood ajar as she went downstairs. Every lodger, on tiptoe, watched the lady of the ballet pass on her way out. It was quite an event in the house.

Fraisier, like the bull-dog that sets his teeth and never lets go, was on the spot. He stood beside La Cibot when Mlle. Brisetout passed under the gateway and asked for the door to be opened. Knowing that a will had been made, he had come to see how the land lay, for Maître Trognon, notary, had refused to say a syllable—Fraisier's questions were as fruitless as Mme. Cibot's. Naturally the ballet-girl's visit *in extremis* was not lost upon Fraisier; he vowed to himself that he would turn it to good account.

"My dear Madame Cibot," he began, "now is the critical moment for you."

"Ah, yes—my poor Cibot!" said she. "When I think that he will not live to enjoy anything I may get——"

"It is a question of finding out whether Monsieur Pons has left you anything at all; whether your name is mentioned or left out, in fact," he interrupted. "I represent the next-of-kin, and to them you must look in any case. It is a holograph will, and consequently very easy to upset. Do you know where our man has put it?"

"In a secret drawer in his bureau, and he has the key of it. He tied it to a corner of his handkerchief, and put it under his pillow. I saw it all."

"Is the will sealed?"

"Yes, alas!"

"It is a criminal offense if you carry off a will and suppress it, but it is only a misdemeanor to look at it; and anyhow, what does it amount to? A peccadillo, and nobody will see you. Is your man a heavy sleeper?"

"Yes. But when you tried to see all the things and value them, he ought to have slept like a top, and yet he woke up. Still, I will see about it. I will take Monsieur Schmucke's place about four o'clock this morning; and if you care to come, you shall have the will in your hands for ten minutes."

"Good. I will come up about four o'clock, and I will knock very softly——"

"Mademoiselle Rémonencq will take my place with Cibot. She will know, and open the door; but tap on the window, so as to rouse nobody in the house."

"Right," said Fraisier. "You will have a light, will you not? A candle will do."

At midnight poor Schmucke sat in his easy-chair, watching with a breaking heart that shrinking of the features that comes with death; Pons looked so worn out with the day's exertions that death seemed very near.

Presently Pons spoke. "I have just enough strength, I think, to last till to-morrow night," he said philosophically. "Yes, to-morrow night the death-agony will begin; poor Schmucke! As soon as the notary and your two friends are gone, go for our good Abbé Duplanty, the curate of Saint-François. Good man, he does not know that I am ill, and I wish to take the holy sacrament to-morrow at noon."

There was a long pause.

"God so willed it that life has not been as I dreamed," Pons resumed. "I should so have loved wife and children and home. To be loved by a very few in some corner—that was my whole ambition! Life is hard for every one; I have seen people who had all that I wanted so much and could not have, and yet they were not happy. Then at the end of my life, God put untold comfort in my way, when He gave me such a friend. And one thing I have not to reproach myself with—that I have not known your worth nor appreciated you, my good Schmucke. I have loved you with my whole heart, with all the strength of love that is in me. Do not cry, Schmucke; I shall say no more if you cry, and it is so sweet to me to talk of ourselves to you. If I had listened to you, I should not be dying. I should have left the world and broken off my habits, and then I should not have been wounded to death. And now, I want to think of no one but you at the last——"

"You are missdaken——"

"Do not contradict me—listen, dear friend. You are as guileless and simple as a six-year-old child that has never left

23

its mother; one honors you for it—it seems to me that God Himself must watch over such as you. But men are so wicked, that I ought to warn you beforehand—and then you will lose your generous trust, your saint-like belief in others, the bloom of a purity of soul that only belongs to genius or to hearts like yours. In a little while you will see Madame Cibot, who left the door ajar and watched us closely while Monsieur Trognon was here—in a little while you will see her come for the will, as she believes it to be. I expect the worthless creature will do her business this morning when she thinks you are asleep. Now, mind what I say, and carry out my instructions to the letter. Are you listening?" asked the dying man.

But Schmucke was overcome with grief, his heart was throbbing painfully, his head fell back on the chair, he seemed to have lost consciousness.

"Yes," he answered, "I can hear, but it is as if you vere doo huntert baces afay from me. It seem to me dat I am going town into der grafe mit you," said Schmucke, crushed with pain.

He went over to the bed, took one of Pons' hands in both his own, and within himself put up a fervent prayer.

"What is that that you are mumbling in German?" asked the sick man.

"I asked of Gott dat He vould take us poth togedders to Himself!" Schmucke answered simply when he had finished his prayer.

Pons bent over—it was a great effort, for he was suffering intolerable pain; but he managed to reach Schmucke, and kissed him on the forehead, pouring out his soul, as it were, in benediction upon a nature that recalled the lamb that lies at the foot of the Throne of God.

"See here, listen, my good Schmucke, you must do as dying people tell you——"

"I am lisdening."

"The little door in the recess in your bedroom opens into that closet."

"Yes, but it is blocked up mit bictures."

"Clear them away at once, without making too much noise."

"Yes."

"Clear a passage on both sides, so that you can pass from your room into mine. Now, leave the door ajar. When La Cibot comes to take your place (and she is capable of coming an hour earlier than usual), you can go away to bed as if nothing had happened, and look very tired. Try to look sleepy. As soon as she settles down into the armchair, go into the closet, draw aside the muslin curtains over the glass door, and watch her. Do you understand?"

"I oondershtand; you belief dat die pad voman is going to purn der vill."

"I do not know what she will do; but I am sure of this— that you will not take her for an angel afterward. And now play for me; improvise and make me happy. It will divert your thoughts; your gloomy ideas will vanish, and for me the dark hours will be filled with your dreams——"

Schmucke sat down to the piano. Here he was in his element; and in a few moments musical inspiration, quickened by the pain with which he was quivering and the consequent irritation that followed, came upon the kindly German, and, after his wont, he was caught up and borne above the world. On one sublime theme after another he executed variations, putting into them sometimes Chopin's sorrow, Chopin's Raphael-like perfection; sometimes the stormy Dante's grandeur of Liszt—the two musicians who most nearly approach Paganini's temperament. When execution reaches this supreme degree, the executant stands beside the poet, as it were; he is to the composer as the actor is to the writer of plays, a divinely inspired interpreter of things divine. But that night, when Schmucke gave Pons an earnest of diviner symphonies, of that heavenly music for which Saint Cecilia let fall her instruments, he was at once Beethoven and Paganini, creator and interpreter. It was an outpouring of music inexhaustible as the nightingale's song—varied and full of delicate undergrowth as the forest flooded with her trills; sublime as the sky overhead. Schmucke played as he had never played before, and the soul of the old musician listening to him rose to ecstasy such as Raphael once painted in a picture which you may see at Bologna.

A terrific ring at the door-bell put an end to these visions. The second-floor lodgers sent up the servant with a message. Would Schmucke please to stop the racket overhead. Madame, Monsieur, and Mademoiselle Chapoulot had been wakened, and could not sleep for the noise; they called his attention to the fact that the day was quite long enough for rehearsals of theatrical music, and added that people ought not to "strum" all night in a house in the Marais. It was then three o'clock in the morning. At half-past three, La Cibot appeared, just as Pons had predicted. He might have actually heard the conference between Fraisier and the portress; "Did I not guess exactly how it would be?" his eyes seemed to say as he glanced at Schmucke, and, turning a little, he seemed to be fast asleep.

Schmucke's guileless simplicity was an article of belief with La Cibot (and be it noted that this faith in simplicity is the great source and secret of the success of all infantine strategy); La Cibot, therefore, could not suspect Schmucke of deceit when he came to say to her, with a face half of distress, half of glad relief—

"I haf had a derrible night! a derrible dime of it! I vas opliged to blay to keep him kviet, and the secont-floor lodgers vas kom up to tell *me* to be' kviet! It was frightful, fer der life of mein friend vas at shtake. I am so tired mit der blaying all night, dat dis morning I am all knocked up."

"My poor Cibot is very bad, too; one more day like yes-

FRAISIER READ THE——CURIOUS DOCUMENT.

terday, and he will have no strength left. One can't help it;
it is God's will."

"You haf a heart so honest, a soul so peautiful, dot gif der
Zipod die, ve shall lif togedder," said the simple but cunning
Schmucke.

The craft of simple, straightforward people is formidable
indeed; they are exactly like children, setting their unsus-
pected snares with the perfect craft of the savage.

"Oh, well, go and sleep, sonny!" returned La Cibot.
"Your eyes look tired, they are as big as my fist. But there!
if anything could comfort me for losing Cibot, it would be the
thought of ending my days with a good man like you. Be
easy. I will give Madame Chapoulot a dressing down. To
think of a retired haberdasher's wife giving herself such airs!"

Schmucke went to his room and took up his post in the
closet.

La Cibot had left the door ajar on the landing; Fraisier
came in and closed it noiselessly as soon as he heard Schmucke
shut his bedroom door. He had brought with him a lighted
taper and a bit of very fine wire to open the seal of the will.
La Cibot, meanwhile, looking under the pillow, found the
handkerchief with the key of the bureau knotted to one corner; and this so much the more easily because Pons purposely
left the end hanging out over the bolster, and lay with his face
to the wall.

La Cibot went straight to the bureau, opened it cautiously
so as to make as little noise as possible, found the spring of
the secret drawer, and hurried into the salon with the will in
her hand. Her flight roused Pons' curiosity to the highest
pitch; and as for Schmucke, he trembled as if he were the
guilty person.

"Go back," said Fraisier, when she handed over the will.
"He may wake, and he must find you there."

Fraisier opened the seal with a dexterity which proved that
his was no 'prentice hand, and read the following curious

document, headed "My Will," with ever-deepening astonishment :

"On this fifteenth day of April, eighteen hundred and forty-
five, I, being in my sound mind (as this my Will, drawn up
in concert with M. Trognon, will testify) and feeling that I
must shortly die of the malady from which I have suffered
since the beginning of February last, am anxious to dispose
of my property, and have herein recorded my last wishes :

"I have always been impressed by the untoward circumstances that injure great pictures, and not infrequently bring
about total destruction. I have felt sorry for the beautiful
paintings condemned to travel from land to land, never finding some fixed abode whither admirers of great masterpieces
may travel to see them. And I have always thought that the
truly deathless work of a great master ought to be national
property; put where every one of every nation may see it,
even as the Light, God's masterpiece, shines for all His children.

"And as I have spent my life in collecting together and
choosing a few pictures, some of the greatest masters' most
glorious work, and as these pictures are as the master left
them—genuine examples, neither repainted nor retouched—
it has been a painful thought to me that the paintings which
have been the joy of my life, may be sold by public auction,
and go, some to England, some to Russia, till they are all
scattered abroad again as if they had never been gathered
together. From this wretched fate I have determined to save
both them and the frames in which they are set, all of them
the work of skilled craftsmen.

"On these grounds, therefore, I give and bequeath the
pictures which compose my collection to the King, for the
gallery in the Louvre, subject to the charge (if the legacy is
accepted) of a life-annuity of two thousand four hundred francs
to my friend Wilhelm Schmucke.

"If the King, as usufructuary of the Louvre collection, should refuse the legacy with the charge upon it, the said pictures shall form a part of the estate which I leave to my friend Schmucke, on condition that he shall deliver the Monkey's Head, by Goya, to my cousin, President Camusot; a Flower-piece, the tulips, by Abraham Mignon, to M. Trognon, notary (whom I appoint as my executor); and allow Madame Cibot, who has acted as my housekeeper for ten years, the sum of two hundred francs per annum.

"Finally, my friend Schmucke is to give the Descent from the Cross, Rubens' sketch for his great picture at Antwerp, to adorn a chapel in the parish church, in grateful acknowledgment of M. Duplanty's kindness to me ; for to him I owe it that I can die as a Christian and a Catholic." So ran the will.

"This is ruin !" mused Fraisier, " the ruin of all my hopes. Ha! I begin to believe all that the presidente told me about this old artist and his cunning."

"Well?" La Cibot came back to say.

"Your gentleman is a monster. He is leaving everything to the Crown. Now, you cannot plead against the Crown—— The will cannot be disputed—— We are robbed, ruined, spoiled, and murdered ! "

"What has he left to me ?"

"Two hundred francs a year."

"A pretty come-down ! Why, he is a finished scoundrel !"

"Go and see," said Fraisier, "and I will put your scoundrel's will back again in the envelope."

While Mme. Cibot's back was turned, Fraisier nimbly slipped a sheet of blank paper into the envelope ; the will he put in his pocket. He next proceeded to seal the envelope again so cleverly that he showed the seal to Mme. Cibot when she returned, and asked her if she could see the slightest trace of the operation. La Cibot took up the envelope, felt it over,

assured herself that it was not empty, and heaved a deep sigh.
She had entertained hopes that Fraisier himself would have
burned the unlucky document while she was out of the room.

"Well, my dear Monsieur Fraisier, what is to be done?"

"Oh! that is your affair! I am not one of the next-of-
kin, myself; but if I had the slightest claim to any of *that*"
(indicating the collection), "I know very well what I should
do."

"That is just what I want to know," La Cibot answered,
with sufficient simplicity.

"There is a fire in the grate——" he said. Then he rose
to go.

"After all, no one will know about it but you and me——"
began La Cibot.

"It can never be proved that a will existed," asserted the
man of law.

"And you?"

"I? If Monsieur Pons dies intestate, you shall have a
hundred thousand francs."

"Oh yes, no doubt," returned she. "People promise you
heaps of money, and when they come by their own, and
there is talk of paying, they swindle you like——" Like
Élie Magus, she was going to say, but she stopped herself
just in time.

"I am going," said Fraisier; "it is not to your interest
that I should be found here: but I shall see you again downstairs."

La Cibot shut the door and returned with the sealed packet
in her hand. She had quite made up her mind to burn it;
but as she went toward the bedroom fireplace, she felt the
grasp of a hand on each arm, and saw—Schmucke on one
hand and Pons himself on the other, leaning against the par-
tition wall on either side of the door.

La Cibot cried out, and fell face downward in a fit; real or
feigned, no one ever knew the truth. The sight produced

such an impression on Pons that a deadly faintness came upon him, and Schmucke left the woman on the floor to help Pons back to bed. The friends trembled in every limb; they had set themselves a hard task, it was done, but it had been too much for their strength. When Pons lay in bed again, and Schmucke had regained strength to some extent, he heard a sound of sobbing. La Cibot, on her knees, bursting into tears, held out supplicating hands to them in very expressive pantomime.

"It was pure curiosity?" she sobbed, when she saw that Pons and Schmucke were paying any attention to her proceedings. "Pure curiosity; a woman's fault, you know. But I did not know how else to get a sight of your will, and I brought it back again——"

"Go!" said Schmucke, standing erect, his tall figure gaining in height by the full extent of his indignation. "You are a monster! You dried to kill mein goot Bons! He is right. You are worse than a monster, you are a lost soul!"

La Cibot saw the look of abhorrence in the frank German's face; she rose, proud as Tartuffe, gave Schmucke a glance which made him quake, and went out, carrying off under her dress an exquisite little picture of Metzu's pointed out by Élie Magus. "A diamond," he had called it. Fraisier downstairs in the porter's lodge was waiting to hear that La Cibot had burned the envelope and the sheet of blank paper inside it. Great was his astonishment when he beheld his fair client's agitation and dismay.

"What has happened?"

"*This* has happened, dear Maître Fraisier. Under pretense of giving me good advice and telling me what to do, you have lost me my annuity and the gentlemen's confidence."

One of the word-tornadoes in which she excelled was in full progress, but Fraisier cut her short.

"This is idle talk. The facts, the facts! and be quick about it."

" Well ; it came about in this way : "—and she told him of
the scene which she had just come through.

"You have lost nothing through me," was Fraisier's comment. "The gentlemen had their doubts, or they would not
have set this trap for you. They were lying in wait and spying upon you. You have not told me everything," he added,
with a tiger's glance at the woman before him.

"*I* hide anything from you!" cried she—"after all that
we have done together!" she added with a shudder.

"My dear madame, *I* have done nothing blameworthy,"
returned Fraisier. Evidently he meant to deny his nocturnal
visit to Pons' rooms.

Every hair on La Cibot's head seemed to scorch her, while
a sense of icy coldness swept over her from head to foot.

"*What?*" she faltered in bewilderment.

"Here is a criminal charge on the face of it. You may be
accused of suppressing the will," Fraisier made answer drily.

La Cibot started.

"Don't be alarmed ; I am your legal adviser. I only
wished to show you how easy it is, in one way or another, to
do as I once explained to you. Let us see, now ; what have
you done that this simple German should be hiding in the
room ? "

"Nothing at all, unless it was that scene the other day
when I stood Monsieur Pons out that his eyes dazzled. And
ever since, the two gentlemen have been as different as can be.
So you have brought all my troubles upon me ; I might have
lost my influence with Monsieur Pons, but I was sure of the
German ; just now he was talking of marrying me or of taking
me with him—it is all one."

The excuse was so plausible that Fraisier was fain to be
satisfied with it. "You need fear nothing," he resumed.
"I gave you my word that you shall have your money, and I
shall keep my word. The whole matter, so far, was up in
the air, but now it is as good as bank-bills. You shall have

at least twelve hundred francs per annum. But, my good lady, you must act intelligently under my orders."

"Yes, my dear Monsieur Fraisier," said La Cibot with cringing servility. She was completely subdued.

"Very good. Good-by," and Fraisier went, taking the dangerous document with him. He reached home in great spirits. The will was a terrible weapon.

"Now," thought he, "I have a hold on Madame la Presidente de Marville; she must keep her word with me. If she did not, she would lose the property."

At daybreak, when Rémonencq had taken down his shutters and left his sister in charge of the store, he came, after his wont of late, to inquire for his good friend Cibot. The portress was contemplating the Metzu,* privately wondering how a little bit of painted wood could be worth such a lot of money.

"Aha!" said he, looking over her shoulder, "that is the one picture which Monsieur Élie Magus regretted; with that little bit of a thing, he says, his happiness would be complete."

"What would he give for it?" asked La Cibot.

"Why, if you will promise to marry me within a year of widowhood, I will undertake to get twenty thousand francs for it from Élie Magus; and unless you marry me you will never get a thousand francs for the picture."

"Why not?"

"Because you would be obliged to give a receipt for the money, and then you might have a lawsuit with the heirs-at-law. If you were my wife, I myself should sell the thing to Monsieur Magus, and in the way of business it is enough to make an entry in the day-book, and I should note that Monsieur Schmucke sold it to me. There, leave the panel with me. If your husband were to die you might have a lot of bother over it, but no one would think it odd that I should

---

* A noted Dutch painter of genre. Died 1630.

have a picture in the store. You know me quite well. Beside, I will give you a receipt if you like."

The covetous portress felt that she had been caught; she agreed to a proposal which was to bind her for the rest of her life to the marine-store-dealer.

"You are right," said she, as she locked the picture away in a chest; "bring me the bit of writing."

Rémonencq beckoned her to the door.

"I can see, neighbor, that we shall not save our poor dear Cibot," he said, lowering his voice. "Dr. Poulain gave him up yesterday evening, and said that he could not last out the day. It is a great misfortune. But after all, this was not the place for you. You ought to be in a fine curiosity store on the Boulevard des Capucines. Do you know that I have made nearly a hundred thousand francs in ten years? and if you will have as much some day, I will undertake to make a handsome fortune for you—as my wife. You would be the mistress—my sister should wait on you and do the work of the house, and——"

A heart-rending moan from the little tailor cut the tempter short; the death-agony had begun.

"Go away," said La Cibot. "You are a monster to talk of such things and my poor man dying like this——"

"Ah! it is because I love you," said Rémonencq; "I could let everything else go to have you——"

"If you loved me, you would say nothing to me just now," returned she. And Rémonencq departed to his store, sure of marrying La Cibot.

Toward ten o'clock there was a sort of commotion in the street; M. Cibot was taking the sacrament. All the friends of the pair, all the porters and porters' wives in the Rue de Normandie and neighboring streets, had crowded into the lodge, under the archway, and stood on the pavement outside. Nobody so much as noticed the arrival of M. Léopold Hannequin and a brother lawyer. Schwab and Brunner reached

Pons' rooms unseen by Mme. Cibot. The notary, inquiring for Pons, was shown upstairs by the portress of a neighboring house. Brunner remembered his previous visit to the museum, and went straight in with his friend Schwab.

Pons formally revoked his previous will and constituted Schmucke his universal legatee. This accomplished, he thanked Schwab and Brunner, and earnestly begged M. Léopold Hannequin to protect Schmucke's interests. The demands made upon him by last night's scene with La Cibot, and this final settlement of his worldly affairs, left him so faint and exhausted that Schmucke begged Schwab to go for the Abbé Duplanty; it was Pons' great desire to take the sacrament, and Schmucke could not bring himself to leave his friend.

La Cibot, sitting at the foot of her husband's bed, gave not so much as a thought to Schmucke's breakfast—for that matter had been forbidden to return; but the morning's events, the sight of Pons' heroic resignation in the death-agony, so oppressed Schmucke's heart that he was not conscious of hunger. Toward two o'clock, however, as nothing had been seen of the old German, La Cibot sent Rémonencq's sister to see whether Schmucke wanted anything; prompted not so much by interest as by curiosity. The Abbé Duplanty had just heard the old musician's dying confession, and the administration of the sacrament of extreme unction was disturbed by repeated ringing of the door-bell. Pons, in his terror of robbery, had made Schmucke promise solemnly to admit no one into the house; so Schmucke did not stir. Again and again Mlle. Rémonencq pulled the cord, and finally went downstairs in alarm to tell La Cibot that Schmucke would not open the door; Fraisier made a note of this. Schmucke had never seen any one die in his life; before long he would be perplexed by the many difficulties which beset those who are left with a dead body in Paris, this more especially if they are lonely and helpless and have no one to act for them.

Fraisier knew, moreover, that in real affliction people lose their heads, and therefore immediately after breakfast he took up his position in the porter's lodge, and, sitting there in perpetual committee with Dr. Poulain, conceived the idea of directing all Schmucke's actions himself.

To obtain the important result, the doctor and the lawyer took their measures on this wise :

The beadle of Saint-François, Cantinet by name, at one time a retail dealer in glassware, lived in the Rue d'Orléans, next door to Dr. Poulain and under the same roof. Mme. Cantinet, who saw to the letting of the chairs at Saint-François, once had fallen ill and Dr. Poulain had attended her gratuitously ; she was, as might be expected, grateful, and often confided her troubles to him. The " nutcrackers," punctual in their attendance at Saint-François on Sundays and saints'-days, were on friendly terms with the beadle and the lowest ecclesiastical rank and file, commonly called in Paris *le bas clergé*, to whom the devout usually gave little presents from time to time. Mme. Cantinet, therefore, knew Schmucke almost as well as Schmucke knew her. And Mme. Cantinet was afflicted with two sore troubles which enabled the lawyer to use her as a blind and involuntary agent. Cantinet junior, a stage-struck youth, had deserted the paths of the church and turned his back on the prospect of one day becoming a beadle, to make his debut among the supernumeraries of the Cirque-Olympique ; he was leading a wild life, breaking his mother's heart and draining her purse by frequent forced loans. Cantinet senior, much addicted to spirituous liquors and idleness, had, in fact, been driven to retire from business by those two failings. So far from reforming, the incorrigible offender had found scope in his new occupation for the indulgence of both cravings ; he did nothing, and he drank with drivers of wedding-coaches, with the undertaker's men at funerals, with poor folk relieved by the vicar, till his morning's occupation was set forth in rubric on his countenance by noon.

Mme. Cantinet saw no prospect but want in her old age, and yet she had brought her husband twelve thousand francs, she said. The tale of her woes, related for the hundredth time, suggested an idea to Dr. Poulain. Once introduce her into the old bachelors' quarters, and it would be easy by her means to establish Mme. Sauvage there as working housekeeper. It was quite impossible to present Mme. Sauvage herself, for the "nutcrackers" had grown suspicious of every one. Schmucke's refusal to admit Mlle. Rémonencq had sufficiently opened Fraisier's eyes. Still, it seemed evident that Pons and Schmucke, being pious souls, would take any one recommended by the abbé, with blind confidence. Mme. Cantinet should bring Mme. Sauvage with her, and to put in Fraisier's servant was almost tantamount to installing Fraisier himself.

The Abbé Duplanty, coming downstairs, found the gateway blocked by the Cibots' friends, all of them bent upon showing their interest in one of the oldest and most respectable porters in the Marais.

Dr. Poulain raised his hat, and took the abbé aside.

"I am just about to go to poor Monsieur Pons," he said. "There is still a chance of recovery; but it is a question of inducing him to undergo an operation. The calculi are perceptible to the touch, they are setting up an inflammatory condition which will end fatally, but perhaps it is not too late to remove them. You should really use your influence to persuade the patient to submit to surgical treatment; I will answer for his life, provided that no untoward circumstance occurs during the operation."

"I will return as soon as I have taken the sacred ciborium back to the church," said the Abbé Duplanty, "for Monsieur Schmucke's condition claims the support of religion."

"I have just heard that he is alone," said Dr. Poulain. "The German, good soul, had a little altercation this morning with Madame Cibot, who has acted as housekeeper to them both for the past ten years. They have quarreled (for the moment only, no doubt), but under the circumstances they must have some one in to help upstairs. It would be a charity to look after him. I say, Cantinet," continued the doctor, beckoning to the beadle, "just go and ask your wife if she will nurse Monsieur Pons, and look after Monsieur Schmucke, and take Madame Cibot's place for a day or two. Even without the quarrel, Madame Cibot would still require a substitute. Madame Cantinet is honest?" added the doctor, turning to M. Duplanty.

"You could not make a better choice," said the good priest; "she is intrusted with the letting of chairs in the church."

A few minutes later, Dr. Poulain stood by Pons' pillow watching the progress made by death, and Schmucke's vain efforts to persuade his friend to consent to the operation. To all the poor German's despairing entreaties Pons only replied by a shake of the head and occasional impatient movements; till, after a while, he summoned up all his fast-failing strength to say, with a heart-rending look:

"Do let me die in peace!"

Schmucke almost died of sorrow, but he took Pons' hand and softly kissed it, and held it between his own, as if trying a second time to give his own vitality to his friend.

Just at this moment the bell rang, and Dr. Poulain, going to the door, admitted the Abbé Duplanty.

"Our poor patient is struggling in the grasp of death," he said. "All will be over in a few hours. You will send a priest, no doubt, to watch to-night. But it is time that Madame Cantinet came, as well as a woman to do the work, for Monsieur Schmucke is quite unfit to think of anything: I am afraid for his reason; and there are valuables here which ought to be in the custody of honest persons."

The Abbé Duplanty, a kindly, upright priest, guileless and unsuspicious, was struck with the truth of Dr. Poulain's remarks. He had, moreover, a certain belief in the doctor of the quarter. So on the threshold of the death-chamber he stopped and beckoned to Schmucke, but Schmucke could not bring himself to loosen the grasp of the hand that grew tighter and tighter. Pons seemed to think that he was slipping over the edge of a precipice and must catch at something to save himself. But, as many know, the dying are haunted by a hallucination that leads them to snatch at things about them, like men eager to save their most precious possessions from a fire. Presently Pons released Schmucke to clutch at the bed-clothes, dragging them and huddling them about himself with a hasty, covetous movement significant and painful to see.

"What will you do, left alone with your dead friend?" asked M. l'Abbé Duplanty when Schmucke came to the door. "You have not Madame Cibot now——"

"Ein monster dat haf killed Bons!"

"But you must have somebody with you," began Dr. Poulain. "Some one must sit up with the body to-night."

"I shall sit up; I shall say die prayers to Gott," the innocent German answered.

"But you must eat—and who is to cook for you now?" asked the doctor.

"Grief haf taken afay mein abbetite," Schmucke said, simply.

"And some one must give notice to the registrar," said Poulain, "and lay out the body, and order the funeral; and the person who sits up with the body and the priest will want meals. Can you do all this by yourself? A man cannot die like a dog in the capital of the civilized world."

Schmucke opened wide eyes of dismay. A brief fit of madness seized him.

"But Bons shall not tie!" he cried aloud. "I shall safe him!"

"You cannot go without sleep much longer, and who will

24

take your place? Some one must look after Monsieur Pons, and give him drink, and nurse him——"

"Ah! dat is drue."

"Very well," said the abbé, "I am thinking of sending you Madame Cantinet, a good and honest creature——"

The practical details of the care of the dead bewildered Schmucke, till he was fain to die with his friend.

"He is a child," said the doctor, turning to the Abbé Duplanty.

"Ein child," Schmucke repeated mechanically.

"There, then," said the curate; "I will speak to Madame Cantinet, and send her to you."

"Do not trouble yourself," said the doctor; "I am going home, and she lives in the next house."

The dying seem to struggle with Death as with an invisible assassin; in the agony at the last, as the final thrust is made, the act of dying seems to be a conflict, a hand-to-hand fight for life. Pons had reached the supreme moment. At the sound of his groans and cries, the three standing in the doorway hurried to the bedside. Then came the last blow, smiting asunder the bonds between soul and body, striking down to life's sources; and suddenly Pons regained for a few brief moments the perfect calm that follows the struggle. He came to himself, and with the serenity of death in his face he looked round almost smilingly at them.

"Ah, doctor, I have had a hard time of it; but you were right, I am doing better. Thank you, my good abbé; I was wondering what had become of Schmucke——"

"Schmucke has had nothing to eat since yesterday evening, and now it is four o'clock! You have no one with you now, and it would not be wise to send for Madame Cibot."

"She is capable of anything!" said Pons, without attempting to conceal all his abhorrence at the sound of her name. "It is true, Schmucke certainly ought to have some trustworthy person."

"Monsieur Duplanty and I have been thinking about you both——"

"Ah! thank you, I had not thought of that."

"—and Monsieur Duplanty suggests that you should have Madame Cantinet——"

"Oh! Madame Cantinet who lets the chairs!" exclaimed Pons. "Yes; she is an excellent creature."

"She has no liking for Madame Cibot," continued the doctor, "and she would take good care of Monsieur Schmucke who——"

"Send her to me, Monsieur Duplanty—— send her and her husband too. I shall be easy. Nothing will be stolen here."

Schmucke had taken Pons' hand again, and held it joyously in his own. Pons was almost well again, he thought.

"Let us go, Monsieur l'Abbé," said the doctor. "I will send Madame Cantinet round at once. I see how it is. She perhaps may not find Monsieur Pons alive."

While the Abbé Duplanty was persuading Pons to engage Madame Cantinet as his nurse, Fraisier had sent for her. He had plied the beadle's wife with sophistical reasoning and subtlety. It was difficult to resist his corrupting influence. As for Madame Cantinet—a lean, sallow woman, with large teeth and thin lips—her intelligence, as so often happens with women of the people, had been blunted by a hard life, till she had come to look upon the slenderest daily wage as prosperity. She soon consented to take Mme. Sauvage with her as general servant.

Mme. Sauvage had had her instructions already. She had undertaken to weave a web of iron-wire about the two musicians, and to watch them as a spider watches a fly caught in the toils; and her reward was to be a tobacconist's license. Fraisier had found a convenient opportunity of getting rid of his so-called foster-mother, while he posted her as a detective and policeman to supervise Madame Cantinet. As there was

a servant's bedroom and a little kitchen included in the apartments, La Sauvage could sleep on a truckle-bed and cook for
the German.   Dr. Poulain came with the two women just as
Pons drew his last breath.   Schmucke was sitting beside his
friend, all unconscious of the crisis, holding the hand that
slowly grew colder in his grasp.   He signed to Madame Cantinet to be silent; but Mme. Sauvage's soldierly figure surprised him so much that he started in spite of himself, a kind
of homage to which the virago was quite accustomed.

"Monsieur Duplanty answers for this lady," whispered
Mme. Cantinet by way of introduction.   "She once was cook
to a bishop; she is honesty itself; she will do the cooking."

"Oh! you may talk out loud," wheezed the stalwart dame.
"The poor gentleman is dead.   He has just gone."

A shrill cry broke from Schmucke.   He felt Pons' cold
hand stiffening in his, and sat staring into his friend's eyes;
the look in them would have driven him mad, if Mme.
Sauvage, doubtless accustomed to scenes of this sort, had not
come to the bedside with a mirror which she held over the
lips of the dead.   When she saw that there was no mist upon
the surface, she briskly snatched Schmucke's hand away.

"Just take away your hand, sir; you may not be able to do
it in a little while.   You do not know how the bones harden.
A corpse grows cold very quickly.   If you do not lay out a
body while it is warm, you very often have to break the joints
later on."

And so it was this terrible woman who closed the poor
dead musician's eyes.

With a business-like dexterity acquired in ten years of experience, she stripped and straightened the body, laid the
arms by the sides, and covered the face with the bedclothes,
exactly as a clerk wraps a parcel.

"A sheet will be wanted to lay him out.   Where is there
a sheet?" she demanded, turning on the terror-stricken
Schmucke.

He had watched the religious ritual with its deep reverence for the creature made for such high destinies in heaven ; and now he saw his dead friend treated simply as a thing in this packing process—saw with the sharp pain-that dissolves the very elements of thought.

" Do as you vill——" he answered mechanically. The innocent creature for the first time in his life had seen a man die, and that man was Pons, his only friend, the one human being who understood him and loved him.

" I will go and ask Madame Cibot where the sheets are kept," said La Sauvage.

" A truckle-bed will be wanted for the person to sleep upon," Mme. Cantinet came to tell Schmucke.

Schmucke nodded and broke out into weeping. Mme. Cantinet left the unhappy man in peace ; but an hour later she came back to say—

" Have you any money, sir, to pay for the things ? "

The look that Schmucke gave Mme. Cantinet would have disarmed the fiercest hate ; it was the white, blank, peaked face of death that he turned upon her, as an explanation that met everything.

" Dake it all and leaf me to mein prayers and tears," he said, and knelt.

Mme. Sauvage went to Fraisier with the news of Pons' death. Fraisier took a hack and went to the presidente. To-morrow she must give him the power of attorney to enable him to act for the heirs.

Another hour went by, and Mme. Cantinet came again to Schmucke.

" I have been to Madame Cibot, sir, who knows all about things here," she said. " I asked her to tell me where everything is kept. But she almost jawed me to death with her abuse. Sir, do listen to me."

Schmucke looked up at the woman, and she went on, innocent of any barbarous intention, for women of her class are accustomed to take the worst of moral suffering passively, as a matter of course.

"We must have linen for the shroud, sir; we must have money to buy a truckle-bed for the person to sleep upon, and some things for the kitchen—plates, and dishes, and glasses—for a priest will be coming to pass the night here, and the person says that there is absolutely nothing in the kitchen."

"And what is more, sir, I must have coal and firing if I am to get the dinner ready," echoed La Sauvage, "and not a thing can I find. Not that there is anything so very surprising in that, as La Cibot used to do everything for you——"

Schmucke lay at the feet of the dead; he heard nothing, knew nothing, saw nothing. Mme. Cantinet pointed to him. "My dear woman, you would not believe me," she said. "Whatever you say, he does not answer."

"Very well, child," said La Sauvage; "now I will show you what to do in a case of this kind."

She looked round the room as a thief looks in search of possible hiding-places for money; then she went straight to Pons' chest, opened the first drawer, saw the bag in which Schmucke had put the rest of the money after the sale of the pictures, and held it up before him. He nodded mechanically.

"Here is money, child," said La Sauvage, turning to Mme. Cantinet. "I will count it first and take enough to buy everything we want—wine, provisions, wax-candles, all sorts of things, in fact, for there is nothing in the house. Just look in the drawers for a sheet to bury him in. I certainly was told that the poor gentleman was simple, but I don't know what he is; he is worse. He is like a new-born child; we shall have to feed him with a funnel."

The women went about their work, and Schmucke looked on precisely as an idiot might have done. Broken down with sorrow, wholly absorbed, in a half-cataleptic state, he could not take his eyes from the face that seemed to fascinate him, Pons' face refined by the absolute repose of death. Schmucke hoped to die ; everything was alike indifferent. If the room had been on fire he would not have stirred.

"There are twelve hundred and fifty francs here," La Sauvage told him.

Schmucke shrugged his shoulders.

But when La Sauvage came near to measure the body by laying the sheet over it, before cutting out the shroud, a horrible struggle ensued between her and the poor German. Schmucke was furious. He behaved like a dog that watches by his dead master's body, and shows his teeth at all who try to touch it. La Sauvage grew impatient. She grasped him, set him in the armchair, and held him down with herculean strength.

"Go on, child ; sew him in his shroud," she said, turning to Mme. Cantinet.

As soon as this operation was completed, La Sauvage set Schmucke back in his place at the foot of the bed.

"Do you understand?" said she. "The poor dead man lying there must be done up, there is no help for it."

Schmucke began to cry. The women left him and took possession of the kitchen, whither they brought all the necessaries in a very short time. La Sauvage made out a preliminary statement accounting for three hundred and sixty francs, and then proceeded to prepare a dinner for four persons. And what a dinner ! A fat goose (the cobbler's pheasant) by way of a substantial roast, an omelette with preserves, a salad, and the inevitable soup—the quantities of the ingredients for this last being so excessive that the soup was more like a strong meat-jelly.

At nine o'clock the priest, sent by the curate to watch by the dead, came in with Cantinet, who brought four tall wax-candles and some tapers. In the death-chamber Schmucke was lying with his arms about the body of his friend, holding him in a tight clasp ; nothing but the authority of religion availed to separate him from his dead. Then the priest settled himself comfortably in the easy-chair and read his prayers; while Schmucke, kneeling beside the couch, besought God to work a miracle and unite him to Pons, so that they might be buried in the same grave; and Mme. Cantinet went on her way to the Temple to buy a pallet and complete bedding for Mme. Sauvage. The twelve hundred and fifty francs were regarded as plunder. At eleven o'clock Mme. Cantinet came in to ask if Schmucke would not eat a morsel, but with a gesture he signified that he wished to be left in peace.

"Your supper is ready, Monsieur Pastelot," she said, addressing the priest, and they went.

Schmucke, left alone in the room, smiled to himself like a madman free at last to gratify a desire like the longing of pregnancy. He flung himself down beside Pons, and yet again he held his friend in a long, close embrace. At midnight the priest came back and scolded him, and Schmucke returned to his prayers. At daybreak the priest went, and at seven o'clock in the morning the doctor came to see Schmucke, and spoke kindly and tried hard to persuade him to eat, but the German refused.

"If you do not eat now you will feel very hungry when you come back," the doctor told him, "for you must go to the mayor's office and take a witness with you, so that the registrar may issue a certificate of death."

"*I* must go!" cried Schmucke in frightened tones.

"Who else? You must go, for you were the one person who saw him die."

"Mein legs vill nicht carry me," pleaded Schmucke, imploring the doctor to come to the rescue.

"Take a coach," the hypocritical doctor blandly suggested. "I have given notice already. Ask some one in the house to go with you. The two women will look after the place while you are away."

No one imagines how the requirements of the law jar upon

a heartfelt sorrow. The thought of it is enough to make one turn from civilization and choose rather the customs of the savage. At nine o'clock that morning Mme. Sauvage half-carried Schmucke downstairs, and from the hack he was obliged to beg Rémonencq to come with him to the registrar as a second witness. Here in Paris, in this land of ours besotted with Equality, the inequality of conditions is glaringly apparent everywhere and in everything. The immutable tendency of things peeps out even in the practical aspects of death. In well-to-do families, a relative, a friend, or a man of business spares the mourners these painful details; but in this, as in the matter of taxation, the whole burden falls heaviest upon the shoulders of the poor.

"Ah! you have good reason to regret him," said Rémonencq in answer to the poor martyr's moan; "he was a very good, a very honest man, and he has left a fine collection behind him. But being a foreigner, sir, do you know that you are like to find yourself in a great predicament—for everybody says that Monsieur Pons left everything to you?"

Schmucke was not listening. He was sounding the dark depths of sorrow that border upon madness. There is such a thing as tetanus of the soul.

"And you would do well to find some one—some man of business—to advise you and act for you," pursued Rémonencq.

"Ein mann of pizness!" echoed Schmucke.

"You will find that you will want some one to act for you. If I were you, I should take an experienced man, somebody well known in the quarter, a man you can trust. I always go to Tabareau myself for my bits of affairs—he is the bailiff. If you give his clerk power to act for you, you need not trouble yourself any further."

Rémonencq and La Cibot, prompted by Fraisier, had agreed beforehand to make a suggestion which stuck in Schmucke's memory; for there are times in our lives when grief, as it were,

congeals the mind by arresting all its functions, and any
chance impression made at such moments is retained by a
frost-bound memory. Schmucke heard his companion with
such a fixed, mindless stare, that Rémonencq said no more.

"If he is always to be idiotic like this," thought Rémonencq, "I might easily buy the whole bag of tricks up yonder
for a hundred thousand francs; if it is really his. Here we
are at the mayor's office, sir."

Rémonencq was obliged to take Schmucke out of the coach
and to half-carry him to the registrar's department, where a
wedding-party was assembled. Here they had to wait for
their turn, for, by no very uncommon chance, the clerk had
five or six certificates to make out that morning; and here it
was appointed that poor Schmucke should suffer excruciating
anguish.

"Monsieur is Monsieur Schmucke?" remarked a person in
a suit of black, reducing Schmucke to stupefaction by the
mention of his name. He looked up with the same blank,
unseeing eyes that he had turned upon Rémonencq, who now
interposed.

"What do you want with him?" he said. "Just leave him
in peace; you can see plainly that he is in trouble."

"The gentleman has just lost his friend, and proposes, no
doubt, to do honor to his memory, being, as he is, the sole
heir. The gentleman, no doubt, will not haggle over it; he
will buy a piece of ground outright for a grave. And as Monsieur Pons was such a lover of the arts, it would be a great
pity not to put Music, Painting, and Sculpture on his tomb—
three handsome full-length figures, weeping——"

Rémonencq waved the speaker away, in Auvergnat fashion,
but the man replied with another gesture, which, being interpreted, means "Don't spoil sport;" a piece of commercial
freemasonry, as it were, which the dealer understood.

"I represent the firm of Sonet & Company, monumental
stonemasons; Sir Walter Scott would have dubbed me Young

Mortality," continued this person. "If you, sir, should decide to intrust your orders to us, we would spare you the
trouble of the journey to purchase the ground necessary for
the interment of a friend lost to the arts——"

At this Rémonencq nodded assent, and jogged Schmucke's
elbow.

"Every day we receive orders from families to arrange all
formalities," continued he of the black coat, thus encouraged
by Rémonencq. "In the first moment of bereavement, the
heir-at-law finds it very difficult to attend to such matters, and
we are accustomed to perform these little services for our clients. Our charges, sir, are on a fixed scale, so much per
foot, freestone or marble. Family vaults a specialty. We
undertake everything at the most moderate prices. Our firm
executed the magnificent monument erected to the fair Esther
Gobseck and Lucien de Rubempré, one of the finest ornaments of Père-Lachaise. We only employ the best workmen,
and I must warn you, sir, against small contractors—who turn
out nothing but trash," he added, seeing that another person
in a black suit was coming up to say a word for another firm
of marble-workers.

It is often said that "death is the end of a journey," but
the aptness of the simile is realized most fully in Paris. Any
arrival, especially of a person of condition, upon the "dark
brink," is hailed in much the same way as the traveler recently
landed is hailed by hotel touts and pestered with their recom-
mendations. With the exception of a few philosophically
minded persons, or here and there a family secure of handing
down a name to posterity, nobody thinks beforehand of the
practical aspects of death. Death always comes before he is
expected ; and, from a sentiment easy to understand, the heirs
usually act as if the event were impossible. For which reason,
almost every one that loses father or mother, wife or child, is
immediately beset by scouts that profit by the confusion caused
by grief to snare orders. In former days, agents for monu-

ments used to live round about the famous cemetery of Père-
Lachaise, and were gathered together in a single thoroughfare
which should by rights have been called the Street of Tombs;
issuing thence, they fell upon the relatives of the dead as they
came from the cemetery, or even at the grave-side. But competition and the spirit of speculation induced them to spread
themselves farther and farther afield, till descending into Paris
itself they reached the very precincts of the mayor's office.
Indeed, the stonemason's agent has often been known to
invade the house of mourning with a design for the sepulchre
in his hand.

"I am in treaty with this gentleman," said the representative of the firm of Sonet to another agent who came
up.

"Pons deceased !——" called the clerk at this moment.
"Where are the witnesses?"

"This way, sir," said the stonemason's agent, this time
addressing Rémonencq.

Schmucke stayed where he had been placed on the bench,
an inert mass. Rémonencq begged the agent to help him,
and together they pulled Schmucke toward the balustrade,
behind which the registrar shelters himself from the mourning public. Rémonencq, Schmucke's Providence, was assisted
by Dr. Poulain, who filled in the necessary information as to
Pons' age and birthplace; the German knew but one thing—
that Pons was his friend. So soon as the signatures were
affixed, Rémonencq and the doctor (followed by the stonemason's man), put Schmucke into a coach, the desperate agent
whisking in afterward, bent upon taking a definite order.

La Sauvage, on the lookout in the gateway, half-carried
Schmucke's almost unconscious form upstairs. Rémonencq
and the agent went up with her.

"He will be ill!" exclaimed the agent, anxious to make
an end of the piece of business which, according to him, was
in progress.

" I should think he will ! " returned Mme. Sauvage. " He has been crying for twenty-fours on end, and he would not take anything. There is nothing like grief for giving one a sinking in the stomach."

" My dear client," urged the representative of the firm of Sonet, " do take some broth. You have so much to do ; some one must go to the Hôtel de Ville to buy the ground in the cemetery on which you mean to erect a monument to perpetuate the memory of the friend of the arts, and bear record to your gratitude."

" Why, there is no sense in this ! " added Mme. Cantinet, coming in with broth and bread.

" If you are as weak as this, you ought to think of finding some one to act for you," added Rémonencq, " for you have a good deal on your hands, my dear sir. There is the funeral to order. You would not have your friend buried like a pauper ! "

" Come, come, my dear sir," put in La Sauvage, seizing a moment when Schmucke laid his head back in the great chair to pour a spoonful of soup into his mouth. She fed him as if he had been a child, and almost in spite of himself.

" Now, if you were wise, sir, since you are inclined to give yourself up quietly to grief, you would find some one to act for you——"

"As you are thinking of raising a magnificent monument to the memory of your friend, sir, you have only to leave it all to me ; I will undertake——"

" What is all this ? What is all this ? " asked La Sauvage. "Has Monsieur Schmucke ordered something ? Who may you be ? "

" I represent the firm of Sonet, my dear madame, the biggest monumental stonemasons in Paris," said the person in black, handing a business card to the stalwart Sauvage.

" Very well, that will do. Some one will go to you when the time comes ; but you must not take advantage of the gen-

tleman's condition now. You can quite see that he is not
himself——"

The agent led her out upon the landing.

"If you will undertake to get the order for us," he said
confidentially, "I am empowered to offer you forty francs."

Mme. Sauvage grew placable. "Very well, let me have
your address," said she.

Schmucke meantime being left to himself, and feeling the
stronger for the soup and bread that he had been forced to
swallow, returned at once to Pons' room, and to his prayers.
He had lost himself in the fathomless depths of sorrow, when
a voice sounding in his ears drew him back from the abyss of
grief, and a young man in a suit of black returned for the
eleventh time to the charge, pulling the poor, tortured victim's
coat-sleeve until he listened.

"Sir !" said he.

"Vat ees it now?"

"Sir! we owe a supreme discovery to Dr. Gannal: we do
not dispute his fame, he has worked the miracles of Egypt
afresh; but there have been improvements made upon his
system. We have obtained surprising results. So, if you
would like to see your friend again, as he was when he was
alive——"

"See him again!" cried Schmucke. "Shall he speak
to me?"

"Not exactly. Speech is the only thing wanting," continued the embalmer's agent. "But he will remain as he is
after embalming for all eternity. The operation is over in a
few seconds. Just an incision in the carotid artery and an
injection. But it is high time; if you wait one single quarter
of an hour, sir, you will not have the sweet satisfaction of
preserving the body——"

"Go to der teufel ! Bons is ein spirit—und dat spirit is in
hefn."

"That man has no gratitude in his composition," remarked

the youthful agent of one of the famous Gannal's rivals; "he will not embalm his friend."

The words were spoken under the archway, and addressed to La Cibot, who had just submitted her beloved to the process.

"What would you have, sir!" she said. "He is the heir, the universal legatee. As soon as they get what they want, the dead are nothing to them."

An hour later, Schmucke saw Mme. Sauvage come into the room, followed by another man in a suit of black, a workman to all appearance.

"Cantinet has been so obliging as to send this gentleman, sir," she said; "he is a coffin-maker to the parish."

The coffin-maker made his bow with a sympathetic and compassionate air, but none the less he had a business-like look, and seemed to know that he was indispensable. He turned an expert's eye upon the dead.

"How does the gentleman wish ' it ' to be made? Deal, plain oak, or oak lead-lined? Oak with a lead lining is the best style. The body is a stock size"—he felt for the feet and proceeded to take the measure—"one metre seventy!" he added. "You will be thinking of ordering the funeral service at the church, sir, no doubt?"

Schmucke looked at him as a dangerous madman might look before striking a blow. La Sauvage put in a word.

"You ought to find somebody to look after all these things," she said.

"Yes——" the victim murmured at length.

"Shall I fetch Monsieur Tabareau?—for you will have a good deal on your hands before long. Monsieur Tabareau is the most honest man in the quarter, you know."

"Yes. Mennesir Dapareau! Somepody vas speaking of him chust now——" said Schmucke, completely beaten.

"Very well. You can be quiet, sir, and give yourself up to grief, when you have seen your deputy."

It was nearly two o'clock when Monsieur Tabareau's head-clerk, a young man who aimed at a bailiff's career, modestly presented himself. Youth has wonderful privileges; no one is alarmed by youth. This young man, Villemot by name, sat down by Schmucke's side and waited his opportunity to speak. His diffidence touched Schmucke very much.

"I am Monsieur Tabareau's head-clerk, sir," he said; "he sent me here to take charge of your interests, and to superintend the funeral arrangements. Is this your wish?"

"You cannot safe my life, I haf not long to lif; but you vill leaf me in beace!"

"Oh! you shall not be disturbed," said Villemot.

"Ver' goot. Vat must I do for dat?"

"Sign this paper appointing Monsieur Tabareau to act for you in all matters relating to the settlement of the affairs of the deceased."

"Goot! gif it to me," said Schmucke, anxious only to sign it at once.

"No, I must read it over to you first."

"Read it ofer."

Schmucke paid not the slightest attention to the reading of the power of attorney, but he set his name to it. The young clerk took Schmucke's orders for the funeral, the interment, and the burial service; undertaking that he should not be troubled again in any way, nor asked for money.

"I vould gif all dat I haf to pe left in beace," said the unhappy man. And once more he knelt beside the dead body of his friend.

Fraisier had triumphed. Villemot and La Sauvage completed the circle which he had traced about Pons' heir.

There is no sorrow that sleep cannot overcome. Toward the end of the day La Sauvage, coming in, found Schmucke stretched asleep at the bed-foot. She carried him off, put him to bed, tucked him in maternally, and till the morning Schmucke slept.

When he awoke, or rather when the truce was over, and he again became conscious of his sorrows, Pons' coffin lay under the gateway in such state as a third-class funeral may claim, and Schmucke seeking vainly for his friend, wandered from room to room, across vast spaces, as it seemed to him, empty of everything save hideous memories. La Sauvage took him in hand, much as a nurse manages a child; she made him take his breakfast before starting for the church; and while the poor sufferer forced himself to eat, she discovered, with lamentations worthy of Jeremiah, that he had not a black coat in his possession. La Cibot took entire charge of his wardrobe; since Pons fell ill his apparel, like his dinner, had been reduced to the lowest terms—to a couple of coats and two pairs of trousers.

"And you are going just as you are to Monsieur Pons' funeral? It is an unheard-of thing; the whole quarter will cry shame upon us!"

"Und how vill you dat I go?"

"Why, in mourning——"

"Mourning?"

"It is the proper thing."

"Der bropper ding!—— confound all dis stupid nonsense!" cried poor Schmucke, driven to the last degree of exasperation which a childlike soul can reach under stress of sorrow.

"Why, the man is a monster of ingratitude!" said La Sauvage, turning to a person who just then appeared. At the sight of this functionary Schmucke shuddered. The new-comer wore a splendid suit of black, black knee-breeches, black silk stockings, a pair of white cuffs, an extremely correct white muslin tie, and white gloves. A silver chain with a coin attached ornamented his person. A typical official, stamped with the official expression of decorous gloom, an ebony wand in his hand by way of insignia of office, he stood waiting with a three-cornered hat adorned with the tricolor cockade under his arm.

25

"I am the master of the ceremonies," this person remarked in a subdued voice.

Accustomed daily to superintend funerals, to move among families plunged in one and the same kind of tribulation, real or feigned, this man, like the rest of his fraternity, spoke in hushed and soothing tones; he was decorous, polished, and formal, like an allegorical stone figure of Death.

Schmucke quivered through every nerve as if he were confronting his executioner.

"Is this gentleman the son, brother, or father of the deceased?" inquired the official.

"I am all dat und more pesides—I am his frient," said Schmucke through a torrent of weeping.

"Are you his heir?"

"Heir?——" repeated Schmucke. "Noding matters to me more in dis vorld," returning to his attitude of hopeless sorrow.

"Where are the relatives, the friends?" asked the master of the ceremonies.

"All here!" exclaimed the German, indicating the pictures and rarities. "Not von of dem haf efer gifn bain to mein boor Bons. Here ees everydings dot he lofed, after me."

"He is off his head, sir," put in La Sauvage. "It is useless to listen to him."

Schmucke had taken his seat again, and looked as vacant as before; he dried his eyes mechanically. Villemot came up at that moment; he had ordered the funeral, and the master of the ceremonies, recognizing him, made an appeal to the new-comer.

"Well, sir, it is time to start. The hearse is here; but I have not often seen such a funeral as this. Where are the relatives and friends?"

"We have been pressed for time," replied Villemot. "This gentleman was in such deep grief that he could think of nothing. And there is only one relative."

The master of the ceremonies lookeᵤ compassionately at Schmucke; this expert in sorrow knew real grief when he saw it.

He went across to him.

"Come, take heart, my dear sir. Think of paying honor to your friend's memory."

"We forgot to send out cards; but I took care to send a special message to Monsieur le President de Marville, the one relative that I mentioned to you. There are no friends. Monsieur Pons was conductor of an orchestra at a theatre, but I do not think that any one will come. This gentleman is the universal legatee, I believe."

"Then he ought to be chief mourner," said the master of the ceremonies. "Have you not a black coat?" he continued, noticing Schmucke's costume.

"I am all in plack insite!" poor Schmucke replied in heart-rending tones; "so plack it is dot I feel death in me. Gott in hefn is going to haf pity upon me; He vill send me to mein frient in der grafe, und I dank Him for it——"

He clasped his hands.

"I have told our management before now that we ought to have a wardrobe department and lend the proper mourning costumes on hire," said the master of the ceremonies, addressing Villemot; "it is a want that is more and more felt every day, and we have even now introduced improvements. But as this gentleman is chief mourner he ought to wear a cloak, and this one that I have brought with me will cover him from head to foot; no one need know that he is not in proper mourning costume. Will you be so kind as to rise?"

Schmucke rose, but he tottered on his feet.

"Support him," said the master of the ceremonies, turning to Villemot; "you are his legal representative."

Villemot held Schmucke's arm while the master of the ceremonies invested Schmucke with the ample, dismal-looking garment worn by heirs-at-law in the procession to and from

the house and the church. He tied the black silken cords
under the chin, and Schmucke as heir was in "full dress."

"And now comes a great difficulty," continued the master
of the ceremonies; "we want four bearers for the pall. If
nobody comes to the funeral, who is to fill the corners? It
is half-past ten already," he added, looking at his watch;
"they are waiting for us at the church."

"Oh! here comes Fraisier!" Villemot exclaimed, very
imprudently; but there was no one to hear the tacit confession of complicity.

"Who is this gentleman?" inquired the master of the
ceremonies.

"Oh! he comes on behalf of the family."

"Whose family?"

"The disinherited family. He is Monsieur Camusot de
Marville's representative."

"Good," said the master of the ceremonies, with a satisfied air. "We shall have two pall-bearers at any rate—you
and he."

And, happy to find two of the places filled up, he took out
some wonderful white buckskin gloves, and politely presented
Fraisier and Villemot with a pair apiece.

"If you two gentlemen will be so good as to act as pall-
bearers——" said he.

Fraisier, in black from head to foot, pretentiously dressed,
with his white tie and official air, was a sight to shudder at;
he embodied a hundred briefs.

"Willingly, sir," said he.

"If only two more persons will come, the four corners will
be filled up," said the master of the ceremonies.

At that very moment the indefatigable representative of the
firm of Sonet came up, and closely following him, the one
man who remembered Pons and thought of paying him a last
tribute of respect. This was a supernumerary at the theatre,
the man who put out the scores on the music-stands for the

orchestra. Pons had been wont to give him a five-franc piece once a month, knowing that he had a wife and family.

"Oh, Dobinard (Topinard)!" Schmucke cried out at the sight of him, "*you* love Bons!"

"Why, I have come to ask news of Monsieur Pons every morning, sir."

"Efery morning! boor Dobinard!" and Schmucke squeezed the man's hand.

"But they took me for a relation, no doubt, and did not like my visits at all. I told them that I belonged to the theatre and came to inquire after Maître Pons; but it was no good. They saw through that dodge, they said. I asked to see the poor dear man, but they never would let me come upstairs."

"Dat apominable Zipod!" said Schmucke, squeezing Topinard's horny hand to his heart.

"He was the best of men, that good Monsieur Pons. Every month he used to give me five francs. He knew that I had three children and a wife. My wife has gone to the church."

"I shall difide mein pread mit you," cried Schmucke, in his joy at finding at his side some one who loved Pons.

"If this gentleman will take a corner of the pall, we shall have all four filled up," said the master of the ceremonies.

There had been no difficulty over persuading the agent for monuments. He took a corner the more readily when he was shown the handsome pair of gloves which, according to custóm, was to be his property.

"A quarter to eleven! We absolutely must go down. They are waiting for us at the church."

The six persons thus assembled went two-and-two down the staircase.

The cold-blooded lawyer remained a moment to speak to the two women on the landing. "Stop here, and let nobody come in," he said, "especially if you wish to remain in charge, Madame Cantinet. Aha! two francs a day, you know!"

By a coincidence in nowise extraordinary in Paris, two hearses were waiting at the door and two coffins standing under the archway; Cibot's funeral was to take place at the same hour. Nobody came to pay any tribute of affection to the "deceased friend of the arts," lying in state among the lighted tapers, but every porter in the neighborhood sprinkled a drop of holy water upon the second bier. And this contrast between the crowd at Cibot's funeral and the solitary state in which Pons was lying was made even more striking in the street. Schmucke was the only mourner that followed Pons' coffin; Schmucke, supported by one of the undertaker's men, for he tottered at every step. From the Rue de Normandie to the Rue d'Orléans and the church of Saint-François the two funerals went between a double row of curious onlookers, for everything (as was said before) makes a sensation in the quarter. Every one remarked the splendor of the white funeral car, with a big embroidered P suspended on a hatchment, and the one solitary mourner behind it; while the cheap bier that came after it was followed by an immense crowd. Happily, Schmucke was so bewildered by the throng of idlers and the rows of heads in the windows that he heard no remarks and only saw the faces through a mist of tears.

"Oh, it is the nutcracker!" said one, "the musician you know——"

"Who can the pall-bearers be?"

"Pooh! play-actors."

"I say, just look at poor old Cibot's funeral. There is one worker the less. What a man! he could never get enough work!"

"He never went out."

"He never kept Saint Monday."

"How fond he was of his wife!"

"Ah! There is an unhappy woman!"

Rémonencq walked behind his victim's coffin. People condoled with him on the loss of his neighbor.

The two funerals reached the church. Cantinet and the doorkeeper saw that no beggars troubled Schmucke. Villemot had given his word that Pons' heir should be left in peace; he watched over his client, and gave the requisite sums; and Cibot's humble bier, escorted by sixty or eighty persons, drew all the crowd after it to the cemetery. At the church-door Pons' funeral procession mustered four mourning-coaches, one for the priest and three for the relations; but one only was required, for the representative of the firm of Sonet departed during mass to give notice to his principal that the funeral was on the way, so that the design for the monument might be ready for the survivor at the gates of the cemetery. A single coach sufficed for Fraisier, Villemot, Schmucke, and Topinard; but the remaining two, instead of returning to the undertaker, followed in the procession to Père-Lachaise—a useless procession, not infrequently seen; there are always too many coaches when the dead are unknown beyond their own circle and there is no crowd at the funeral. Dear, indeed, the dead must have been in their lifetime if relative or friend will go with them so far as the cemetery in this Paris, where every one would fain have twenty-five hours in the day. But with the coachmen it is different; they lose their tips if they do not make the journey; so, empty or full, the mourning-coaches go to church and cemetery and return to the house for gratuities. A death is a sort of drinking-fountain for an unimagined crowd of thirsty mortals. The attendants at the church, the poor, the undertaker's men, the drivers and sextons, are creatures like sponges that dip into a hearse and come out again saturated.

From the church-door, where he was beset with a swarm of beggars (promptly dispersed by the beadle), to Père-Lachaise, poor Schmucke went as criminals went in old times from the

Palais de Justice to the Place de Grève. It was his own
funeral that he followed, clinging to Topinard's hand, to the
one living creature beside himself who felt a pang of real regret
for Pons' death.

As for Topinard—greatly touched by the honor of the request to act as pall-bearer, content to drive in a carriage, the
possessor of a new pair of gloves—it began to dawn upon him
that this was to be one of the great days of his life. Schmucke
was driven passively along the road, as some unlucky calf is
driven in a butcher's cart to the slaughter-house. Fraisier and
Villemot sat with their backs to the horses. Now, as those
know whose sad fortune it has been to accompany many of
their friends to their last resting-place, all hypocrisy breaks
down in the coach during the journey (often a very long one)
from the church to the eastern cemetery, to that one of the
burying-grounds of Paris in which all vanities, all kinds of
display, are met, so rich is it in sumptuous monuments. On
these occasions those who feel least begin to talk soonest,
and in the end the saddest listen, and their thoughts are
diverted.

"Monsieur le President had already started for the Court,"
Fraisier told Villemot, "and I did not think it necessary to
tear him away from business; he would have come too late in
any case. He is the next-of-kin; but as he has been disinherited and Monsieur Schmucke gets everything, I thought
that if his legal representative were present it would be
enough."

Topinard lent an ear to this.

"Who was the queer customer that took the fourth corner?"
continued Fraisier.

"He is an agent for a firm of monumental stonemasons.
He would like an order for a tomb, on which he proposes to
put three sculptured marble figures—Music, Painting, and
Sculpture—shedding tears over the deceased."

"It is an idea," said Fraisier; "the old gentleman certainly deserved that much; but the monument would cost seven or eight hundred francs."

"Oh! quite that!"

"If Monsieur Schmucke gives the order, it cannot affect the estate. You might eat up a whole property with such expenses."

"There would be a lawsuit, but you would gain it——"

"Very well," said Fraisier, "then it will be his affair. It would be a nice practical joke to play upon the monument-makers," Fraisier added in Villemot's ear; "for if the will is upset (and I can answer for that), or if there is no will at all, who would pay them?"

Villemot grinned like a monkey, and the pair began to talk confidentially, lowering their voices; but the man from the theatre, with his wits and senses sharpened in the world behind the scenes, could guess at the nature of their discourse; in spite of the rumbling of the carriage and other hindrances, he began to understand that these representatives of justice were scheming to plunge poor Schmucke into difficulties; and when at last he heard the ominous word "Clichy,"* the honest and loyal servitor of the stage made up his mind to watch over Pons' friend.

At the cemetery, where three square yards of ground had been purchased through the good offices of the firm of Sonet (Villemot having announced Schmucke's intention of erecting a magnificent monument), the master of the ceremonies led Schmucke through a curious crowd to the grave into which Pons' coffin was about to be lowered; but here, at the sight of the square hole, the four men waiting with ropes to lower the bier, and the clergy saying the last prayer for the dead at the grave-side, something clutched tightly at the German's heart. He fainted away.

Sonet's agent and M. Sonet himself came to help Topinard to carry poor Schmucke into the marble-works hard by, where

* The old debtors' prison in the Rue de Clichy.

Mme. Sonet and Mme. Vitelot (Sonet's partner's wife) were eagerly prodigal of efforts to revive him. Topinard stayed. He had seen Fraisier in conversation with Sonet's agent, and Fraisier, in his opinion, had gallows-bird written on his malevolent face.

An hour later, toward half-past two o'clock, the poor, innocent German came to himself. Schmucke thought that he had been dreaming for the past two days; if he could only wake, he should find Pons still alive. So many wet towels had been laid on his forehead, he had been made to inhale salts and vinegar to such an extent, that he opened his eyes at last. Mme. Sonet made him take some meat-soup, for they had put the pot on the fire at the marble-works.

"Our clients do not often take things to heart like this; still, it happens once in a year or two——"

At last Schmucke talked of returning to the Rue de Normandie, and at this Sonet began at once.

"Here is the design, sir," he said; "Vitelot drew it expressly for you, and sat up last night to do it. And he has been happily inspired, it will look fine——"

"One of the finest in Père-Lachaise!" said little Mme. Sonet. "But you really ought to honor the memory of a friend who left you all his fortune."

The design, supposed to have been drawn on purpose, had as a matter of fact been prepared for de Marsay, the famous cabinet minister. His widow, however, had given the commission to Stidmann; people were disgusted with the tawdriness of the project, and it was refused. The three figures at that period represented the Three Days of July which brought the eminent minister to power. Subsequently, Sonet and Vitelot had turned the Three Glorious Days—"*les trois glorieuses*" —into the Army, Finance, and the Family, and sent in the design for the sepulchre of the late lamented Charles Keller; and here again Stidmann took the commission. In the eleven years that followed, the sketch had been modified to suit all kinds of requirements, and now in Vitelot's fresh tracing they reappeared as Music, Sculpture, and Painting.

"It is a mere trifle when you think of the details and cost of setting it·up; for it will take six months," said Vitelot. "Here is the estimate and the order-form—seven thousand francs, sketch in plaster not included."

"If Monsieur Schmucke would like marble," put in Sonet (marble being his special department), "it would cost twelve thousand francs, and monsieur would immortalize himself as well as his friend."

Topinard turned to Vitelot.

"I have just heard that they are going to dispute the will," he whispered, "and the relatives are likely to come by their property. Go and speak to Monsieur Camusot, for this poor, harmless creature has not a farthing."

"This is the kind of customer that you always bring us," said Mme. Vitelot, beginning a quarrel with the agent.

Topinard led Schmucke away, and they returned home on foot to the Rue de Normandie, for the mourning-coaches had been sent back.

"Do not leaf me," Schmucke said, when Topinard had seen him safe into Mme. Sauvage's hands, and wanted to go.

"It is four o'clock, dear Monsieur Schmucke. I must go home to dinner. My wife is a box-opener—she will not know what has become of me. The theatre opens at a quarter to six, you know."

"Yes, I know—but remember dat I am alone in die earth, dat I haf no frient. You dat haf shed a tear for Bons, enliden me; I am in teep tarkness, und Bons said dat I vas in der midst of shcoundrels."

"I have seen that plainly already; I have just prevented them from sending you to Clichy."

"*Gligy!*" repeated Schmucke; "I do not understand."

"Poor man! Well, never mind, I will come to you. Good-by."

"Goot-by; kom again soon," said Schmucke, dropping half-dead with weariness.

"Farewell, môsieu," said Mme. Sauvage, and there was something in her tone that struck Topinard.

"Oh, come, what is the matter now?" he asked banteringly. "You are attitudinizing like a traitor in a melodrama."

"Traitor yourself! Why have you come meddling here? Do you want to have a hand in the master's affairs, and swindle him, eh?"

"Swindle him! Your very humble servant!" Topinard answered with superb disdain. "I am only a poor super at a theatre, but I am something of an artist, and you may as well know that I never asked anything of anybody yet! Who asked anything of you? Who owes you anything? eh, old lady!"

"You are employed at a theatre, and your name is——?"

"Topinard, at your service."

"Kind regards to all at home," said La Sauvage, "and my compliments to your missus, if you are married, mister. That was all I wanted to know."

"Why, what is the matter, dear?" asked Mme. Cantinet, coming out.

"This, child—stop here and look after the dinner while I run round to speak to monsieur."

"He is down below, talking with poor Madame Cibot, that is crying her eyes out," said Mme. Cantinet.

La Sauvage dashed down in such headlong haste that the stairs trembled beneath her tread.

"Monsieur!" she called, and drew him aside a few paces to point out Topinard.

Topinard was just going away, proud at heart to have made some return already to the man who had done him so many a kindness. He had saved Pons' friend from a trap, by a stratagem from that world behind the scenes in which every one has more or less ready wit. And within himself he vowed to protect a musician in his orchestra from future snares set for his simple sincerity.

" Do you see that little wretch ? " said La Sauvage. " He is a kind of honest man that has a mind to poke his nose into Monsieur Schmucke's affairs."

" Who is he ? " asked Fraisier.

" Oh ! he is a nobody."

" In business there is no such thing as a nobody."

" Oh, he is employed at the theatre," said she ; " his name is Topinard."

" Good, Madame Sauvage !   Go on like this, and you shall have your tobacconist's store."

And Fraisier resumed his conversation with Mme. Cibot.

" So I say, my dear client, that you have not played openly and above-board with me, and that one is not bound in any way to a partner who cheats."

"And how have I cheated you ! " asked La Cibot, hands on hips.   " Do you think that you will frighten me with your sour looks and your frosty airs !   You look about for bad reasons for breaking your promises, and you call yourself an honest man !   Do you know what you are ?   You are a black-guard !   Yes ! yes ! scratch your arm ; but just pocket that, mister——"

" No words, and keep your temper, dearie.   Listen to me. You have been feathering your nest.   I found this catalogue this morning while we were getting ready for the funeral ; it is all in old Pons' handwriting, and made out in duplicate.   And as it chanced, my eyes fell on this——"

And opening the catalogue, he read—

" No. 7. *Magnificent portrait painted on marble, by Sebastian del Piombo, in* 1546.   *Sold by a family who had it removed from Terni cathedral.   The picture, which represents a Knight-Templar kneeling in prayer, used to hang above a tomb of the Rossi family with a companion portrait of a Bishop, afterward purchased by an Englishman.   The portrait might be attributed to Raphael, but for the date. This example is, to my mind, superior to the portrait of Baccio Bandinelli in the Musée; the latter is a little hard, while the Templar, being painted upon 'lavagna,' or slate, has preserved its freshness of coloring."*

"When I come to look for No. 7," continued Fraisier, "I find a portrait of a lady, signed 'Chardin,' without a number on it! I went through the pictures with the catalogue while the master of the ceremonies was making up the number of pall-bearers, and found that eight of those indicated as works of capital importance by Monsieur Pons had disappeared, and eight paintings of no special merit, and without numbers, were there instead. And, finally, one was missing altogether, a little panel-painting by Metzu, described in the catalogue as a masterpiece."

"And was *I* in charge of the pictures?" demanded La Cibot.

"No; but you were in a position of trust. You were Monsieur Pons' housekeeper, you looked after his affairs, and he has been robbed——"

"Robbed! Let me tell you this, sir: Monsieur Schmucke sold the pictures, by Monsieur Pons' orders, to meet expenses."

"And to whom?"

"To Messrs. Élie Magus and Rémonencq."

"For how much?"

"I am sure I do not remember."

"Look here, my dear madame; you have been feathering your nest, and very snugly. I shall keep an eye upon you; I have you safe. Help me, I will say nothing! In any case you know that since you judged it expedient to plunder Monsieur le President Camusot, you ought not to expect anything from *him*."

"I was sure that this would all end in smoke for me," said La Cibot, mollified by the words "I will say nothing."

Rémonencq chimed in at this point.

"Here are you finding fault with Madame Cibot; that is

not right!" he said. "The pictures were sold by private treaty between Monsieur Pons, Monsieur Magus, and me. We waited for three days before we came to terms with the deceased ; he slept on his pictures. We took receipts in proper form ; and if we gave Madame Cibot a few forty-franc pieces, it is the custom of the trade—we always do so in private houses when we conclude a bargain. Ah! my dear sir, if you think to cheat a defenseless woman, you will not make a good bargain! Do you understand, mister lawyer? É. Magus rules the market, and if you do not come down off the high horse, if you do not keep your word to Madame Cibot, I shall wait till the collection is sold, and you shall see what you will lose if you have Monsieur Magus and me against you; we can get the dealers in a ring. Instead of realizing seven or eight hundred thousand francs, you will not so much as make two hundred thousand."

"Good, good, we shall see. We are not going to sell ; or if we do, it will be in London."

"We know London," said Rémonencq. "Monsieur Magus is as powerful there as at Paris."

"Good-day, madame ; I shall sift these matters to the bottom," said Fraisier—"unless you continue to do as I tell you," he added.

"You little pickpocket !——"

"Take care! I shall be a justice of the peace before long." And with threats understood to the full upon either side, they separated.

"Thank you, Rémonencq !" said La Cibot ; "it is very pleasant to a poor widow to find a champion."

Toward ten o'clock that evening, Gaudissart sent for Topinard. The manager was standing with his back to the fire, in a Napoleonic attitude—a trick which he had learned since he began to command his army of actors, dancers, *figurants*, musicians, and stage-carpenters. He grasped his left-hand suspender with his right hand, always thrust into his vest; his head was flung far back, his eyes gazed out into space.

" Ah ! I say, Topinard, have you independent means ? "

" No, sir."

" Are you on the lookout to better yourself somewhere else ? "

" No, sir——" said Topinard, with a ghastly countenance.

" Why, hang it all, your wife takes the first row of boxes out of respect to my predecessor, who came to grief; I gave you the job of cleaning the lamps in the wings in the daytime, and you put out the scores. And that is not all, either. You get twenty sous for acting monsters and managing devils when a hell is required. There is not a super that does not covet your post, and there are those that are jealous of you, my friend ; you have enemies in the theatre."

" Enemies ! " repeated Topinard.

" And you have three children ; the oldest takes children's parts at fifty centimes——"

" Sir !——"

" Allow me to speak——" thundered Gaudissart. " And in your position, you want to leave——"

" Sir !——"

" You want to meddle in other people's business, and put your finger into a will case. Why, you wretched man, you would be crushed like an egg-shell ! My patron is his excellency, Monseigneur le Comte Popinot, a clever man and a man of high character, whom the King in his wisdom has summoned back to the privy council. This statesman, this great politician, has married his eldest son to a daughter of Monsieur le President de Marville, one of the foremost men among the high courts of justice ; one of the leading lights of the law-courts. Do you know the law-courts ? Very good. Well, he is cousin and heir to Monsieur Pons, to our old conductor whose funeral you attended this morning. I do not blame you for going to pay the last respects to him, poor man. But if you meddle in Monsieur Schmucke's affairs, you will lose your place. I wish very well to Monsieur Schmucke, but he is in a delicate position with regard to the heirs—and as the German is almost nothing to me, and the president and Count Popinot are a great deal, I recommend you to leave the worthy German to get out of his difficulties by himself. There is a special Providence that watches over Germans, and the part of deputy guardian-angel would not suit you at all. Do you see? Stay as you are—you cannot do better."

"Very good, Monsieur le Directeur," said Topinard, much distressed. And in this way Schmucke lost the protector sent to him by fate, the one creature that shed a tear for Pons, the poor super for whose return he looked on the morrow.

Next morning poor Schmucke awoke to a sense of his great and heavy loss. He looked round the empty rooms. Yesterday and the day before yesterday the preparations for the funeral had made a stir and bustle which distracted his eyes; but the silence which follows the day, when the friend, father, son, or loved wife has been laid in the grave—the dull, cold silence of the morrow—is terrible, is glacial. Some irresistible force drew him to Pons' chamber, but the sight of it was more than the poor man could bear; he shrank away and sat down in the dining-room, where Mme. Sauvage was busy making breakfast ready.

Schmucke drew his chair to the table, but he could eat nothing. A sudden, somewhat sharp ringing of the doorbell rang through the house, and Mme. Cantinet and Mme. Sauvage allowed three black-coated personages to pass. First came Vitel, the justice of the peace, with his highly respectable clerk; the third was Fraisier, neither sweeter nor milder for the disappointing discovery of a valid will canceling the formidable instrument so audaciously stolen by him.

"We have come to affix seals on the property," the justice of the peace said gently, addressing Schmucke. But the

26

remark was Greek to Schmucke; he gazed in dismay at his three visitors.

"We have come at the request of Monsieur Fraisier, legal representative of Monsieur Camusot de Marville, heir of the late Pons——" added the clerk.

"The collection is here in this great room and in the bedroom of the deceased," remarked Fraisier.

"Very well, let us go into the next room. Pardon us, sir; do not let us interrupt you with your breakfast."

The invasion struck an icy chill of terror into poor Schmucke. Fraisier's venomous glances seemed to possess some magnetic influence over his victims, like the power of a spider over a fly.

"Monsieur Schmucke understood how to turn a will, made in the presence of a notary, to his own advantage," he said, "and he surely must have expected some opposition from the family. A family does not allow itself to be plundered by a stranger without some protest; and we shall see, sir, which carries the day—fraud and corruption or the rightful heirs. We have a right as next-of-kin to affix seals, and seals shall be affixed. I mean to see that the precaution is taken with the utmost strictness."

"Ach, mein Gott! how haf I offended against hefn?" cried the innocent Schmucke.

"There is a good deal of talk about you in the house," said La Sauvage. "While you were asleep, a little whipper-snapper in a black suit came here, a puppy that said he was Monsieur Hannequin's head-clerk, and must see you at all costs; but as you were asleep and tired out with the funeral yesterday, I told him that Monsieur Villemot, Tabareau's head-clerk, was acting for you, and if it was a matter of business, I said, he might speak to Monsieur Villemot. 'Ah, so much the better!' the youngster said. 'I shall come to an understanding with him. We will deposit the will at the Tribunal, after showing it to the president.' So at that, I told him to ask Monsieur Villemot to come here as soon as he could. Be easy, my dear sir, there are those that will take care of you. They shall not shear the fleece off your back. You will have some one that has beak and claws. Monsieur Villemot will give them a piece of his mind. I have put myself in a passion once already with that abominable hussy, La Cibot, a porter's wife that sets up to judge her lodgers, forsooth, and insists that you have filched the money from the heirs; you locked Monsieur Pons up, she says, and worked upon him till he was stark, staring mad. She got as good as she gave, though, the wretched woman. 'You are a thief and a bad lot,' I told her; 'you will get into the police courts for all the things that you have stolen from the gentlemen,' and she shut up."

The clerk came out to speak to Schmucke.

"Would you wish to be present, sir, when the seals are affixed in the next room?"

"Go on, go on," said Schmucke; "I shall pe allowed to die in beace, I bresume?"

"Oh, under any circumstances a man has a right to die," the clerk answered laughing; "most of our business relates to wills. But, in my experience, the universal legatee very seldom follows the testator to the tomb."

"I am going," said Schmucke. Blow after blow had given him an intolerable pain at the heart.

"Oh! here comes Monsieur Villemot!" exclaimed La Sauvage.

"Mennesir Fillemod," said poor Schmucke, "rebresent me."

"I hurried here at once," said Villemot. "I have come to tell you that the will is completely in order; it will certainly be confirmed by the court, and you will be put in possession.

"You will have a fine fortune."

"*I?* Ein fein vordune?" cried Schmucke despairingly.

That he of all men should be suspected of caring for the money !

"And meantime, what is the justice of the peace doing here with his wax-candles and his bits of tape?" asked La Sauvage.

"Oh, he is affixing seals. Come, Monsieur Schmucke, you have a right to be present."

"No—go in yourself."

"But where is the use of the seals Monsieur Schmucke is in his own house and everything belongs to him?" asked La Sauvage, doing justice in feminine fashion, and interpreting the Code according to their fancy, like one and all of her sex.

"Monsieur Schmucke is not in possession, madame ; he is in Monsieur Pons' house. Everything will be his, no doubt ; but the legatee cannot take possession without an authorization —an order from the Tribunal. And if the next-of-kin set aside by the testator should dispute the order, a lawsuit is the result. And as nobody knows what may happen, everything is sealed up, and the notaries representing either side proceed to draw up an inventory during the delay prescribed by the law. And there you are !"

Schmucke, hearing such talk for the first time in his life, was completely bewildered by it ; his head sank down upon the back of his chair—he could not support it, it had grown so heavy.

Villemot meanwhile went off to chat with the justice of the peace and his clerk, assisting with professional coolness to affix the seals—a ceremony which always involves some buffoonery and plentiful comments on the objects thus secured, unless indeed one of the family happens to be present. At length the party sealed up the chamber and returned to the dining-room, whither the clerk betook himself. Schmucke watched the mechanical operation which consists in setting the justice's seal at either end of a bit of tape stretched across the opening of a folding door; or, in the case of a cupboard or ordinary door, from edge to edge above the door-handle.

"Now for this room," said Fraisier, pointing to Schmucke's bedroom, which opened into the dining-room.

"But that is Monsieur Schmucke's own room," remonstrated La Sauvage, springing in front of the door.

"We found the lease among the papers," Fraisier said ruthlessly; "there is no mention of Monsieur Schmucke in it; it is taken out in Monsieur Pons' name only. The whole place, and every room in it, is part of the estate. And beside "—flinging open the door—"look here, monsieur le juge de la paix, it is full of pictures."

"So it is," answered the justice of the peace, and Fraisier thereupon gained his point.

"Wait a bit, gentlemen," said Villemot. "Do you know that you are turning the universal legatee out of doors, and as yet his right has not been called in question."

"Yes, it has," said Fraisier; "we are opposing the transfer of the property."

"And upon what grounds?"

"You shall know that by-and-by, my boy," Fraisier replied banteringly. "At this moment, if the legatee withdraws everything that he declares to be his, we shall raise no objections, but the room itself will be sealed. And Monsieur Schmucke may lodge where he pleases."

"No," said Villemot; "Monsieur Schmucke is going to stay in his room."

"And how?"

"I shall demand an immediate special inquiry," continued Villemot, "and prove that we pay half the rent. You shall not turn us out. Take away the pictures, decide on the ownership of the various articles, but here my client stops—'my boy.'"

"I shall go out!" the old musician suddenly said. He had recovered energy during the odious dispute.

"You had better," said Fraisier. "Your course will save expense to you, for your contention would not be made good. The lease is evidence——"

"The lease! the lease!" cried Villemot, "it is a question of good faith——"

"That could only be proved as in a criminal case, by calling witnesses. Do you mean to plunge into experts' fees and verifications, and orders to show cause why judgment should not be given, and law proceedings generally?"

"No, no!" cried Schmucke in dismay. "I shall turn out; I am used to it——"

In practice Schmucke was a philosopher, an unconscious cynic, so greatly had he simplified his life. Two pairs of shoes, a pair of boots, a couple of suits of clothes, a dozen shirts, a dozen bandana handkerchiefs, four waistcoats, a superb pipe given to him by Pons, with an embroidered tobacco-pouch—these were all his belongings. Overwrought by a fever of indignation, he went into his room and piled his clothes upon a chair.

"All dese are mine," he said, with simplicity worthy of Cincinnatus. "Der biano is also mine."

Fraisier turned to La Sauvage. "Madame, get help," he said; "take that piano out and put it on the landing."

"You are too rough into the bargain," said Villemot, addressing Fraisier. "The justice of the peace gives orders here; he is supreme."

"There are valuables in the room," put in the clerk.

"And beside," added the justice of the peace, "Monsieur Schmucke is going out of his own free will."

"Did any one ever see such a client!" Villemot cried indignantly, turning upon Schmucke. "You are as limp as a rag——"

"Vat dos it matter vere von dies?" Schmucke said as he went out. "Dese men haf tigers' faces. I shall send sompody to vetch mein bits of dings."

"Where are you going, sir?"

"Vere it shall blease Gott," returned Pons' universal legatee with supreme indifference.

"Send me word," said Villemot.

Fraisier turned to the head-clerk. "Go after him," he whispered.

Mme. Cantinet was left in charge with a provision of fifty francs paid out of the money that they found. The justice of the peace looked out; there Schmucke stood in the courtyard looking up at the windows for the last time.

"You have found a man of butter," remarked the justice.

"Yes," said Fraisier, "yes. The thing is as good as done. You need not hesitate to marry your granddaughter to Poulain; he will be head-surgeon at the Quinze-Vingts."*

"We shall see. Good-day, Monsieur Fraisier," said the justice of the peace with a friendly air.

"There is a man with a head on his shoulders," remarked the justice's clerk. "That dog will go a long way."

By this time it was eleven o'clock. The old German went like an automaton down the road along which Pons and he had so often walked together. Wherever he went he saw Pons, he almost thought that Pons was by his side; and so he reached the theatre just as his friend Topinard was coming out of it after a morning spent in cleaning the lamps and meditating on the manager's tyranny.

"Oh, shoost der ding for me!" cried Schmucke, stopping his acquaintance. "Dopinart! you haf a lodging somveres, eh?"

"Yes, sir."

"A home off your own?"

"Yes, sir."

"Are you villing to take me for ein poarder? Oh! I shall bay ver' vell; I haf nine hundert vrancs of inkomm, und—I haf not ver' long to lif. I shall gif no drouble vatefer. I

---

* The Asylum founded by St. Louis for three hundred blind people.

can eat onydings—I only vant to shmoke mein bipe. Und—
you are der only von dat haf shed a tear for Bons, mit me ;
und so, I lof you."

" I should be very glad, sir ; but, to begin with, Monsieur
Gaudissart has given me a proper wigging

"*Vigging ?*"

" That is one way of saying that he combed my hair for
me."

"*Combed your hair ?*"

" He gave me a scolding for meddling in your affairs. So
we must be very careful if you come to me. But I doubt
whether you will stay when you have seen the place ; you do
not know how we poor devils live."

" I should rader der boor home of a goot-hearted man dot
haf mourned Bons, dan der Duileries mit men dot haf ein
tiger's face. I haf shoost left tigers in Bons' house ; dey vill
eat up everydings——"

" Come with me, sir, and you shall see. But—well, anyhow, there is a garret. Let us see what Madame Topinard
says."

Schmucke followed like a sheep, while Topinard led the
way into one of the squalid districts which might be called
the cancers of Paris—a spot known as the Cité Bordin. It is
a slum out of the Rue de Bondy, a double row of houses run
up by the speculative builder, under the shadow of the huge
mass of the Porte Saint-Martin theatre. The pavement at the
higher end lies below the level of the Rue de Bondy ; at the
lower it falls away toward the Rue des Mathurins du Temple.
Follow its course and you find that it terminates in another
slum running at right angles to the first—the Cité Bordin is,
in fact, a T-shaped blind alley. Its two streets thus arranged
contain some thirty houses, six or seven stories high ; and
every story, and every room in every story, is a workshop and
a warehouse for goods of every sort and description, for this
wart upon the face of Paris is a miniature Faubourg Saint-

Antoine. Cabinet-work and brass-work, theatrical costumes, blown glass, painted porcelain—all the various fancy goods known as *l'article Paris* are made here. Dirty and productive like commerce, always full of traffic—foot-passengers, vans, and wagons—the Cité Bordin is an unsavory-looking neighborhood, with a seething population in keeping with the squalid surroundings. It is a not unintelligent artisan population, though the whole power of the intellect is absorbed by the day's manual labor. Topinard, like every other inhabitant of the Cité Bordin, lived in it for the sake of the comparatively low rent, the cause of its existence and prosperity. His sixth-floor lodging, in the second house to the left, looked out upon the belt of green garden, still in existence, at the back of three or four large mansions in the Rue de Bondy.

Topinard's apartment consisted of a kitchen and two bedrooms. The first was a nursery with two little deal bedsteads and a cradle in it, the second was the bedroom, and the kitchen did duty as a dining-room. Above, reached by a short ladder, known among builders as a "trap-ladder," there was a kind of garret, six feet high, with a sash-window let into the roof. This room, given as a servant's bed-room, raised the Topinards' establishment from mere "rooms" to the dignity of a tenement, and the rent to a corresponding sum of four hundred francs. An arched lobby, lighted from the kitchen by a small round window, did duty as an antechamber, and filled the space between the bedroom, the kitchen, and house doors—three doors in all. The rooms were paved with bricks, and hung with a hideous wall-paper at six sous a piece ; the chimneypieces that adorned them were of the kind called *capucines*—a shelf set on a couple of brackets painted to resemble wood. Here in these three rooms dwelt five human beings, three of them children. Any one, therefore, can imagine how the walls were covered with scores and scratches so far as an infant arm can reach.

Rich people can scarcely realize the extreme simplicity of

a poor man's kitchen. A Dutch-oven, a kettle, a gridiron, a saucepan, two or three dumpy cooking-pots, and a frying-pan —that was all. All the crockery in the place, white and brown earthenware together, was not worth more than twelve francs. Dinner was served on the kitchen table, which with a couple of chairs and a couple of stools completed the furniture. The stock of fuel was kept under the stove with a funnel-shaped chimney, and in a corner stood the wash-tub in which the family linen lay, often steeping over-night in soapsuds. The nursery ceiling was covered with clothes-lines, the walls were variegated with theatrical placards and woodcuts from newspapers or advertisements. Evidently the eldest boy, the owner of the school-books stacked in a corner, was left in charge while his parents were absent at the theatre. In many a French workingman's family, so soon as a child reaches the age of six or seven, it plays the part of mother to younger sisters and brothers.

From this bare outline, it may be imagined that the Topinards, to use the hackneyed formula, were " poor but honest." Topinard himself was verging on forty; Mme. Topinard, once leader of a chorus—mistress too, it was said, of Gaudissart's predecessor—was certainly thirty years old. Lolotte had been a fine woman in her day; but the misfortunes of the previous management had told upon her to such an extent that it had seemed to her to be both advisable and necessary to contract a stage-marriage with Topinard. She did not doubt but that, as soon as they could muster the sum of a hundred and fifty francs, her Topinard would perform his vows agreeably to the civil law, were it only to legitimize the three children, whom he worshiped. Meantime, Mme. Topinard sewed for the theatre wardrobe in the morning; and with prodigious effort, the brave couple made nine hundred francs per annum between them.

" One more flight ! " Topinard had twice repeated since they reached the third floor. Schmucke, engulfed in his sorrow, did not so much as know whether he was going up or coming down.

In another minute Topinard had opened the door; but before he appeared in his white workman's blouse Mme. Topinard's voice rang from the kitchen—

"There, there! children, be quiet! here comes papa!"

But the children, no doubt, did as they pleased with papa, for the oldest member of the little family, sitting astride a broomstick, continued to command a charge of cavalry (a reminiscence of the Cirque-Olympique), the second blew a tin trumpet, while the third did its best to keep up with the main body of the army. Their mother was at work on a theatrical costume.

"Be quiet! or I shall slap you!" shouted Topinard in a formidable voice; then in an aside for Schmucke's benefit— "Always have to say that! Here, little one," he continued, addressing his Lolotte, "this is Monsieur Schmucke, poor Monsieur Pons' friend. He does not know where to go, and he would like to live with us. I told him that we were not very spick and span up here, that we lived on the sixth floor, and had only the garret to offer him; but it was no use, he would come——"

Schmucke had taken the chair which the woman brought him, and the children, stricken with sudden shyness, had gathered together to give the stranger that mute, earnest, so soon-finished scrutiny characteristic of childhood. For a child, like a dog, is wont to judge by instinct rather than reason. Schmucke looked up; his eyes rested on that charming little picture; he saw the performer on the tin trumpet, a little five-year-old maiden with wonderful golden hair.

"She looks like ein liddle German girl," said Schmucke, holding out his arms to the child.

"Monsieur will not be very comfortable here," said Mme. Topinard. "I would propose that he should have our room, at once, but I am obliged to have the children near me."

She opened the door as she spoke, and bade Schmucke come in. Such splendor as their abode possessed was all concentrated here. Blue calico curtains with a white fringe hung from the mahogany bedstead and adorned the window; the chest of drawers, bureau, and chairs, though all made of mahogany, were neatly kept. The clock and candlesticks on the mantel were evidently the gift of the bankrupt manager, whose portrait, a truly frightful performance of Pierre Grassou's, looked down upon the chest of drawers. The children tried to peep in at the forbidden glories.

"Monsieur might be comfortable in here," said their mother.

"No, no," Schmucke replied. "Eh! I haf not ver' long to lif, I only vant a corner to die in."

The door was closed, and the three went up to the garret. "Dis is der ding for me," Schmucke cried at once. "Pefore I lifd mit Bons, I vas nefer better lodged."

"Very well. A truckle-bed, a couple of mattresses, a bolster, a pillow, a couple of chairs, and a table—that is all that you need to buy. That will not ruin you—it may cost a hundred and fifty francs, with the crockeryware and strip of carpet for the bedside."

Everything was settled—save the money, which was not forthcoming. Schmucke saw that his new friends were very poor, and, recollecting that the theatre was only a few steps away, it naturally occurred to him to apply to the manager for his salary. He went at once, and found Gaudissart in his office. Gaudissart received him with the somewhat stiffly polite manner which he reserved for professionals. Schmucke's demand for a month's salary took him by surprise, but on inquiry he found that it was due.

"Oh, confound it, my good man, a German can always count, even if he has tears in his eyes. I thought that you would have taken the thousand francs that I sent you into account, as a final year's salary, and that we were quits."

" We haf receifed nodings," said Schmucke ; " und gif I
kom to you, it ees because I am in der shtreet, und haf not
ein benny. How did you send us der ponus ? "

" By your portress."

" By Montame Zipod !" exclaimed Schmucke. " She
killed Bons, she robbed him, she sold him—she tried to purn
his vill—she is a pad creature, a monster ? "

" But, my good man, how come you to be out in the street
without a roof over your head or a penny in your pocket,
when you are the sole heir ? That does not necessarily follow,
as the saying is."

" They haf put me out at der door. I am a voreigner, I
know nodings of die laws."

" Poor man !" thought Gaudissart, foreseeing the probable
end of the unequal contest. "Listen," he began, " do you
know what you ought to do in this business? "

" I haf ein man of pizness !"

" Very good, come to terms at once with the next-of-kin :
make them pay you a lump sum of money down and an annuity,
and you can live in peace——"

" I ask noding more."

" Very well. Let me arrange it for you," said Gaudissart.
Fraisier had told him the whole story only yesterday, and he
thought that he saw his way to making interest out of the case
with the young Vicomtesse Popinot and her mother. He
would finish a dirty piece of work, and some day he would be
a privy councilor at least ; or so he told himself.

" I gif you full powers."

" Well. Let us see. Now, to begin with," said Gaudissart, Napoleon of the boulevard theatres, " to begin with,
here are a hundred crowns——" (he took fifteen louis from
his purse and handed them to Schmucke).

" That is yours, on account of six months' salary. If you
leave the theatre, you can repay me the money. Now for
your budget. What are your yearly expenses? How much

do you want to be comfortable? Come, now, scheme out a life for a Sardanapalus——"

"I only need two suits of clothes, von for der vinter, von for der sommer."

"Three hundred francs," said Gaudissart.

"Shoes. Vour bairs."

"Sixty francs."

"Shtockings——"

"A dozen pairs—thirty-six francs."

"Half a tozzen shirts."

"Six calico shirts, twenty-four francs; as many linen shirts, forty-eight francs; let us say seventy-two. That makes four hundred and sixty-eight francs altogether. Say five hundred including cravats and pocket-handkerchiefs; a hundred francs for the laundress—six hundred. And now, how much for your board—three francs a day?"

"No, it ees too much."

"After all, you want hats; that brings it to fifteen hundred. Five hundred more for rent; that makes two thousand. If I can get two thousand francs per annum for you, are you willing?—— Good securities."

"Und mein tobacco."

"Two thousand four hundred, then. Oh! Papa Schmucke, do you call that tobacco? Very well, the tobacco shall be given in. So that is two thousand four hundred francs per annum."

"Dat ees not all! I should like some monny."

"Pin-money! Just so! Oh, these Germans! And calls himself an innocent, the old Robert Macaire!" thought Gaudissart. Aloud he said, "How much do you want? But this must be the last."

"It ees to bay a zacred debt."

"A debt!" said Gaudissart to himself. "What a shark it is! He is worse than an eldest son. He will invent a bill or two next! We must cut him short. This Fraisier cannot take large views. What debt is this, my good man? Speak out. '

"Dere vas but von man dot haf mourned Bons mit me. He haf a tear liddle girl mit wunderschönes haar; it vas as if I saw mine boor Deutschland dot I should nefer haf left. Baris is no blace for die Germans; dey laugh at dem" (with a little nod as he spoke, and the air of a man who knows something of life in this world below).

"He is off his head," Gaudissart said to himself. And a sudden pang of pity for this poor innocent before him brought a tear to the manager's eyes.

"Ah! you understand, Mennesir le Directeur! Ver' goot. Dat man mit die liddle taughter is Dobinard, vat tidies der orchestra und lights die lamps. Bons vas fery fond of him, und helped him. He vas der only von dat accombanied mein only frient to die church und to die grafe. I vant dree tausend vrancs for him, und dree tausend for die liddle von dat——"

"Poor fellow!" said Gaudissart to himself.

Rough, self-made man though he was, he felt touched by this nobleness of nature, by a gratitude for a mere trifle, as the world views it; though for the eyes of this divine innocence the trifle, like Bossuet's cup of water, was worth more than the victories of great captains. Beneath all Gaudissart's vanity, beneath the fierce desire to succeed in life at all costs, to rise to the social level of his old friend Popinot, there lay a warm heart and a kindly nature. Wherefore he canceled his too hasty judgments and went over to Schmucke's side.

"You shall have it all! But I will do better still, my dear Schmucke. Topinard is a good sort——"

"Yes. I haf chust peen to see him in his boor home, vere he ees happy mit his children——"

"I will give him the cashier's place. Old Baudrand is going to leave."

"Ah! Gott pless you!" cried Schmucke.

" Very well, my good, kind fellow, meet me at Berthier's office about four o'clock this afternoon. Everything shall be ready, and you shall be secured from want for the rest of your days. You shall draw your six thousand francs, and you shall have the same salary with Garangeot that you used to have with Pons."

" No," Schmucke answered. " I shall not lif. I have no heart for anydings; I feel that I am attacked——"

" Poor lamb !" Gaudissart muttered to himself as the German took his leave. " But, after all, one lives on mutton ; and, as the sublime Béranger says : ' Poor sheep ! you were made to be shorn ; ' " and he hummed the political squib by way of giving vent to his feelings. Then he rang for the office-boy.

" Call my carriage," he said.

" Rue de Hanovre," he told the coachman.

The man of ambitions by this time had reappeared ; he saw the way to the Council of State lying straight before him.

And Schmucke? He was busy buying flowers and cakes for Topinard's children, and went home almost joyously.

" I am gifing die bresents——" he said, and he smiled. It was the first smile for three months, but any one who had seen Schmucke's face would have shuddered to see it there.

" But dere is ein condition——"

" It is too kind of you, sir," said the mother.

" De liddle girl shall gif me a kiss and put die flowers in her hair, like die liddle German maidens——"

" Olga, child, do just as the gentleman wishes," said the mother, assuming an air of discipline.

" Do not scold mein liddle German girl," implored Schmucke. It seemed to him that the little one was his dear Germany. Topinard came in.

" Three porters are bringing up the whole bag of tricks," he said.

"Oh! here are two hundred vrancs to bay for eferydings," said Schmucke. "But, mein frient, your Montame Dobinard is ver' nice; you shall marry her, is it not so? I shall gif you tausend crowns, and die liddle von shall haf tausend crowns for her toury, and you shall infest it in her name. Und you are not to pe ein zuper any more—you are to pe de cashier at de teatre——"

"*I?* instead of old Baudrand?"

"Yes."

"Who told you so?"

"Mennesir Gautissart!'

"Oh! it is enough to send one wild with joy! Eh! I say, Rosalie, what a rumpus there will be at the theatre! But it is not possible——"

"Our benefactor must not live in a garret——"

"Pshaw! for die few tays dat I haf to live, it ees fery komfortable," said Schmucke. "Goot-py; I am going to der zemetery, to see vat dey haf don mit Bons, und to order som flowers for his grafe."

Mme. Camusot de Marville was consumed by the liveliest apprehensions. At a council held with Fraisier, Berthier, and Godeschal, the two last-named authorities gave it as their opinion that it was hopeless to dispute a will drawn up by two notaries in the presence of two witnesses, so precisely was the instrument worded by Léopold Hannequin. Honest Godeschal said that even if Schmucke's own legal adviser should succeed in deceiving him, he would find out the truth at last, if it were only from some officious barrister, the gentlemen of the robe being wont to perform such acts of generosity and disinterestedness by way of self-advertisement. And the two officials took their leave of the presidente with a parting caution against Fraisier, concerning whom they had naturally made inquiries.

At that very moment Fraisier, straight from the affixing of

the seals in the Rue de Normandie, was waiting for an interview with Mme. de Marville. Berthier and Godeschal had suggested that he should be shown into the study; the whole affair was too dirty for the president to look into (to use their own expression), and they wished to give Mme. de Marville their opinion in Fraisier's absence.

"Well, madame, where are these gentlemen?" asked Fraisier, admitted to audience.

"They are gone. They advise me to give up," said Mme. de Marville.

"Give up!" repeated Fraisier, suppressed fury in his voice. "Give up! Listen to this, madame:

"'At the request of '—— and so forth (I will omit the formalities)—— 'Whereas, there has been deposited in the hands of M. le President of the Court of First Instance, a will drawn up by Maîtres Léopold Hannequin and Alexandre Crottat, notaries of Paris, and in the presence of two witnesses, the Sieurs Brunner and Schwab, aliens domiciled at Paris, and by the said will the Sieur Pons, deceased, has bequeathed his property to one Sieur Schmucke, a German, to the prejudice of his natural heirs:

"'Whereas, the applicant undertakes to prove that the said will was obtained under undue influence and by unlawful means; and persons of credit are prepared to show that it was the testator's intention to leave his fortune to Mlle. Cécile, daughter of the aforesaid Sieur de Marville, and the applicant can show that the said will was extorted from the testator's weakness, he being unaccountable for his actions at the time.

"'Whereas as the Sieur Schmucke, to obtain a will in his favor, sequestrated the testator, and prevented the family from approaching the deceased during his last illness; and his subsequent notorious ingratitude was of a nature to scandalize the house and residents in the quarter who chanced to witness it when attending the funeral of the porter at the testator's place of abode:

" Whereas as still more serious charges, of which applicant is collecting proofs, will be formally made before their worships the judges :

" ' I, the undersigned Registrar of the Court, *et al.*, on behalf of the aforesaid, etc., have summoned the Sieur Schmucke, pleading, etc., to appear before their worships the judges of the first chamber of the Tribunal, and to be present when application is made that the will received by Maîtres Hannequin and Crottat, being evidently obtained by undue influence, shall be regarded as null and void in law; and I, the undersigned, on behalf of the aforesaid, etc., have likewise given notice of protest, should the Sieur Schmucke as universal legatee make application for an order to be put into possession of the estate, seeing that the applicant opposes such order, and makes objection by his application bearing date of to-day, of which a copy has been duly deposited with the Sieur Schmucke, costs being charged to—— etc., etc.'

"I know the man, Madame la Presidente. He will come to terms as soon as he reads this little love-letter. He will consult Tabareau, and Tabareau will advise him to take our terms. Are you going to give the thousand crowns per annum ? "

"Certainly. I only wish I were paying the first installment now."

"It will be done in three days. The summons will come down upon him while he is stupefied with grief, for the poor soul regrets Pons and is taking the death to heart."

"Can the application be withdrawn ? " inquired the lady.

"Certainly, madame. You can withdraw at any time you may please."

"Very well, monsieur, let it be so—go on ! Yes, the purchase of land that you have arranged for me is worth the trouble ; and, beside, I have managed Vitel's business—he is to retire, and you must pay Vitel's sixty thousand francs out of Pons' property. So, you see, you must succeed "

"Have you Vitel's resignation ?"

"Yes, monsieur. Monsieur Vitel has put himself in Monsieur de Marville's hands."

"Very good, madame. I have already saved you sixty thousand francs which I expected to give to that vile creature Madame Cibot. But I still require the tobacconist's license for the woman Sauvage, and an appointment to the vacant place of head-physician at the Quinze-Vingts for my friend Poulain."

"Agreed—it is all arranged."

"Very well. There is no more to be said. Every one is for you in this business, even Gaudissart, the manager of the theatre. I went to look him up yesterday, and he undertook to crush the workman who seemed likely to give us trouble."

"Oh, I know Monsieur Gaudissart is devoted to the Popinots."

Fraisier went out. Unluckily, he missed Gaudissart, and the fatal summons was served forthwith.

If all covetous minds will sympathize with the presidente, all honest folk will turn in abhorrence from her joy when Gaudissart came twenty minutes later to report his conversation with poor Schmucke. She gave her full approval; she was obliged beyond all expression for the thoughtful way in which the manager relieved her of any remaining scruples by observations which seemed to her to be very sensible and just.

"I thought as I came, Madame la Presidente, that the poor devil would not know what to do with the money. 'Tis a patriarchally simple nature. He is a child, he is a German, he ought to be stuffed and put in a glass case like a waxen image. Which is to say that, in my opinion, he is quite puzzled enough already with his income of two thousand five hundred francs, and here you are provoking him into extravagance——"

"It is very generous of him to wish to enrich the poor fellow who regrets the loss of our cousin," pronounced the presidente. "For my own part, I am sorry for the little squabble that estranged Monsieur Pons and me. If he had come back again, all would have been forgiven. If you only knew how my husband misses him! Monsieur de Marville received no notice of the death, and was in despair; family claims are sacred for him, he would have gone to the service and the interment, and I myself should have been at the mass———"

"Very well, fair lady," said Gaudissart. "Be so good as to have the documents drawn up, and at four o'clock I will bring this German to you. Please remember me to your charming daughter the vicomtesse, and ask her to tell my illustrious friend the great statesman, her good and excellent father-in-law, how deeply I am devoted to him and his, and ask him to continue his valued favors. I owe my life to his uncle the judge, and my success in life to him; and I should wish to be bound to both you and your daughter by the high esteem which links us with persons of rank and influence. I wish to leave the theatre and become a serious person."

"As you are already, monsieur!" said the presidente.

"Adorable!" returned Gaudissart, kissing the lady's shriveled fingers.

At four o'clock that afternoon several people were gathered together at Berthier's office: Fraisier, arch-concocter of the whole scheme, Tabareau, appearing on behalf of Schmucke, and Schmucke himself. Gaudissart had come with him. Fraisier had been careful to spread out the money on Berthier's desk, and so dazzled was Schmucke by the sight of the six thousand-franc bank-notes for which he had asked, and six hundred francs for the first quarter's allowance, that he paid no heed whatsoever to the reading of the document. Poor man, he was scarcely in full possession of his faculties, shaken as they had already been by so many shocks. Gaudissart had snatched him up on his return from the cemetery, where he had been talking with Pons, promising to join him soon—very soon. So Schmucke did not listen to the preamble in which it was set forth that Maître Tabaraeau, bailiff, was acting as his proxy, and that the presidente, in the interests of her daughter, was taking legal proceedings against him. Altogether, in that preamble the German played a sorry part, but he put his name to the document, and thereby admitted the truth of Fraisier's abominable allegations; and so joyous was he over receiving the money for the Topinards, so glad to bestow wealth according to his little ideas upon the one creature who loved Pons, that he heard not a word of lawsuit nor compromise.

But in the middle of the reading a clerk came into the private office to speak to his employer. "There is a man here, sir, who wishes to speak to Monsieur Schmucke," said he.

The notary looked at Fraisier, and, taking his cue from him, shrugged his shoulders.

"Never disturb us when we are signing documents. Just ask his name—is it a man or a gentleman? Is he a creditor?"

The clerk went and returned. "He insists that he must speak to Monsieur Schmucke."

"His name?"

"His name is Topinard, he says."

"I will go out to him. Sign without disturbing yourself," said Gaudissart, addressing Schmucke. "Make an end of it; I will find out what he wants with us."

Gaudissart understood Fraisier; both scented danger.

"Why are you here?" Gaudissart began. "So you have no mind to be cashier at the theatre? Discretion is a cashier's first recommendation."

"Sir——"

"Just mind your own business; you will never be anything if you meddle in other people's affairs."

"Sir, I cannot eat bread if every mouthful of it is to stick in my throat. Monsieur Schmucke! Oh, Schmucke!" he shouted aloud.

Schmucke came out at the sound of Topinard's voice. He had just signed. He held the money in his hand.

"Thees ees for die liddle German maiden und for you," he said.

"Oh! my dear Monsieur Schmucke, you have given away your wealth to inhuman wretches, to people who are trying to take away your good name. I took this paper to a good man, an attorney who knows this Fraisier, and he says that you ought to punish such wickedness; you ought to let them summon you and leave them to get out of it. Read this," and Schmucke's imprudent friend held out the summons delivered in the Cité Bordin.

Standing in the notary's gateway, Schmucke read the document, saw the imputations made against him, and, all ignorant as he was of the amenities of the law, the blow was deadly. The little grain of sand stopped his heart's beating. Topinard caught him in his arms, hailed a passing cab, and put the poor German into it. He was suffering from congestion of the brain; his eyes were dim, his head was throbbing, but he had enough strength left to put the money into Topinard's hands.

Schmucke rallied from the first attack, but he never recovered consciousness, and refused to eat. Ten days afterward he died without a complaint; to the last he had not spoken a word. Mme. Topinard nursed him, and Topinard laid him by Pons' side. It was an obscure funeral; Topinard was the only mourner who followed the son of Germany to his last resting-place.

Fraisier, now a justice of the peace, is very intimate with the president's family, and much valued by the presidente. She could not think of allowing him to marry " that girl of Tabareau's," and promises infinitely better things for the

clever man to whom she considers that she owes not merely
the pasture-land and the English cottage at Marville, but also
the president's seat in the Chamber of Deputies, for M. le
President was returned at the general election in 1846.

Every one, no doubt, wishes to know what became of the
heroine of a story only too veracious in its details; a chronicle
which, taken with its twin sister the preceding volume, proves
that Character is the great social force. You, O amateurs,
connoisseurs, and dealers, will guess at once that Pons' collection is now in question. Wherefore it will suffice if we are
present during a conversation that took place only a few days
ago in Count Popinot's house. He was showing his splendid
collection to some visitors.

"Monsieur le Comte, you possess treasures indeed," remarked a distinguished foreigner.

"Oh! as to pictures, nobody can hope to rival an obscure
collector, one Élie Magus, a Jew, an old monomaniac, the
prince of picture-lovers," the count replied modestly. "And
when I say nobody, I do not speak of Paris only, but of all
Europe. When the old Crœsus dies, France ought to spare
seven or eight millions of francs to buy the gallery. For curiosities, my collection is good enough to be talked about——"

"But how, busy as you are, and with a fortune so honestly
earned in the first instance in business——"

"In the drug business," broke in Popinot; "you ask how
I can continue to interest myself in things that are a drug in
the market——"

"No," returned the foreign visitor, "no, but how do you
find time to collect? The curiosities do not come to find
you."

"My father-in-law owned the nucleus of the collection,"
said the young Vicomtesse; "he loved the arts and beautiful
work, but most of his treasures came to him through me."

"Through you, madame? So young! and yet have you
such vices as this?" asked a Russian prince.

Russians are by nature imitative; imitative indeed to such an extent that the diseases of civilization break out among them in epidemics. The bric-à-brac mania had appeared in an acute form in St. Peterburg, and the Russians caused such a rise of prices in the "art line," as Rémonencq would say, that collections became impossible. The prince who spoke had come to Paris solely to buy bric-à-brac.

"The treasures came to me, prince, on the death of a cousin. He was very fond of me," added the Vicomtesse Popinot, "and he had spent some forty-odd years since 1805 in picking up these masterpieces everywhere, but more especially in Italy——"

"And what was his name?" inquired the English lord.

"Pons," said President Camusot.

"A charming man he was," piped the presidente in her thin, flute tones, "very clever, very eccentric, and yet very good-hearted. This fan that you admire once belonged to Madame de Pompadour; he gave it to me one morning with a pretty speech which you must permit me not to repeat," and she glanced at her daughter.

"Madame la Vicomtesse, tell us the pretty speech," begged the Russian prince.

"The speech was as pretty as the fan," returned the vicomtesse, who brought out the stereotyped remark on all occasions. "He told my mother that it was quite time that it should pass from the hands of vice into those of virtue."

The English lord looked at Mme. de Marville with an air of doubt not a little gratifying to so withered a woman.

"He used to dine at our house two or three times a week," she said; "he was so fond of us! We could appreciate him, and artists like the society of those who relish their wit. My husband was, beside, his one surviving relative. So when, quite unexpectedly, Monsieur de Marville came into the property, Monsieur le Comte preferred to take over the whole collection to save it from a sale by auction; and we ourselves much preferred to dispose of it in that way, for it would have been so painful to us to see the beautiful things, in which our dear cousin was so much interested, all scattered abroad. Élie Magus valued them, and in that way I became possessed of the cottage that your uncle built, and I hope you will do us the honor of coming to see us there."

Gaudissart's theatre passed into other hands a year ago, but M. Topinard is still the cashier. M. Topinard, however, has grown gloomy and misanthropic; he says little. People think that he has something on his conscience. Wags at the theatre suggest that his gloom dates from his marriage with Lolotte. Honest Topinard starts whenever he hears Fraisier's name mentioned. Some people may think it strange that the one nature worthy of Pons and Schmucke should be found on the third floor beneath the stage of a boulevard theatre.

Mme. Rémonencq, much impressed with Mme. Fontaine's prediction, declines to retire to the country. She is still living in her splendid store on the Boulevard de la Madeleine, but she is a widow now for the second time. Rémonencq, in fact, by the terms of the marriage-contract, settled the property upon the survivor, and left a little glass of vitriol about for his wife to drink by mistake; but his wife, with the very best intentions, put the glass elsewhere, and Rémonencq swallowed the draught himself. The rascal's appropriate end vindicates Providence, as well as the chronicler of manners, who is sometimes accused of neglect on this head, perhaps, because Providence has been so overworked by playwrights of late.

Pardon the transcriber's errors.

FINIS.

www.ingramcontent.com/pod-product-compliance
Lightning Source LLC
Chambersburg PA
CBHW022024110726
47901CB00006B/1654